Virginia Poole

Born in the heart of the Black Country, amongst its factories, furnaces and canals, Victoria Poole fell in love with writing during her time at Dudley Girls' High School. A career in teaching followed her three years at Liverpool University, first in Staffordshire and Derbyshire and then, after her marriage to Martin, back in the Black Country: she retired recently as senior teacher at her old school (now Castle High), where she was responsible for pastoral care.

Determined to have an active retirement, Virginia still teaches part-time at Summerhill School in Kingswinford, as well as embarking on a second career as an author. Martin is doing the same, as an artist. They have three very special children, Nat, Kathryn and Holly.

Song of the Nightingales

by

Virginia Poole

HEATHCOTES
Publishing

A Heathcotes Book

Published by Heathcotes 2004

Copyright © Virginia Poole 2004

The right of Virginia Poole to be identified as the author of this work has been asserted by her in accordance with the copyright, Designs and Patents Act 1988

All Rights Reserved
No reproduction, copy or transmission of this publication may be made without written permission.
No paragraph of this publication may be reproduced, copied or transmitted save with the written permission or in accordance with the provisions of the Copyright Act 1956 (as amended).
Any person who does any unauthorised act in relation to this publication may be liable to criminal prosecution and civil claims for damage.

First published in 2003.

A CIP catalogue record for this title is available from the British Library

Cover from an original water colour by Martin W T Poole

ISBN 0 9549099 0 9

HEATHCOTES

Publishing

6 Sunbeam Studios
Sunbeam Street
Wolverhampton
WV2 4PF

Dedication

*For my family -
past, present and future*

Acknowledgements

My thanks to Martin for his encouragement and support, Without which the story would never have been told, and to Mike Richardson, whose patient editing encouraged an ugly duckling to turn into a swan.

My appreciation too, goes to Miss Hilary Edwards, my dedicated and innovative English teacher, and my friend Anthea Davies, for her generous help with the Black Country dialect.

Chapter One

Viciously, the boy worked the squeaking pump handle up and down watching the spout expectantly. "Stuck-up, bloody, blonde bitch, looking down 'er noose at me. I'll gie 'er what for one day," he muttered, glancing towards the object of his bitterness.

Instead of water a spider issued from the pipe, crawling rapidly around its edge, anxious to scramble away to some dark crevice.

The boy pumped harder but to no avail. Water had been piped into the school and the playground pump was dry.

A look of dissatisfaction clouded the determined face, its features distorted with frustration. The lad's eyes focused on the spider and with a swift swipe he swept it into the empty trough. Then he raised his boot and placed it firmly on top of his scuttling victim, screwing the sole round and round inside the ancient stone vessel.

Satisfied, the boy leapt from the trough and ran across the playground to disturb a hopscotch game where, thirst forgotten, he was soon balanced, stork like, in one of the squares marked out in the dust.

The younger children stood back and watched the scowling newcomer display his expertise, only one brave boy daring to mouth quietly, "Yow podged, Billy Nightingale. It warn't yower tern."

A washing line rope beat the earth in time to the sing-song chants of a group of girls. Gritty dust rose in a cloud, dirtying the hems of petticoats and sidling its way into boots.

Knots of older children chatted and teased, gossiped and tormented each other, enjoying the short afternoon break. They had been reciting tables forwards and backwards and would soon be copying their teacher's minute copper plate handwriting exercise.

Two girls, almost young women, one of them that blonde and detested cousin of the young bully, huddled in the shelter of the cinder wall, deep in conversation. The pretty fair girl seemed to be imparting some information of great importance for her companion listened most attentively, nodding her head in understanding and encouragement.

"That's a really good start, Gertie, and you've got a gift you know," the listener broke her pattern of silence. "I can't understand why you're so shy still when you can talk like you can. You sort of live the parts! Listenin' to you is almost like a play."

Gertie smiled, her face reddening with the pleasure of the compliment for she loved reading and retelling the stories to her friend. Reading had been Gertie's escape from a world of dim shapes and vague outlines, a world in which sounds often alerted her to activities she could not clearly see, an environment inhabited by outspoken individuals whose expressions were always hidden from her. Gertie's shyness had masked her active mind and to supplement her rare moments of sociability she escaped into her world of books. She read by daylight, gaslight, lamplight and candlelight and had even been caught bending over the glowing coals squinting at a printed page by firelight.

The family berated Gertie for risking her poor sight still further but she continued to read avidly, identifying with the heroines and living her life through their joys and disappointments.

Books were her companions and, on days when her friend Clara could not attend classes, Gertie could be found huddled in some sheltered spot at playtime reading. Whilst the playground hummed and roared, skidded and skipped Gertie wrapped herself in her shawl and lost herself in dark scudding clouds, tempest tossed seas and mysterious turreted castles.

Gertie's best friend and neighbour was Clara Watkins, a good reader and equally fond of books but with little time to indulge herself. Clara's mother was an invalid, a very sick lady who spent much of her time lying weakly on her bed in one corner of their kitchen. This meant that Clara had become housekeeper and nurse as well as confidante and disciplinarian to her two younger sisters.

Her education was frequently interrupted by her responsibilities and her escapism limited to joining Gertie in her flights of fancy.

"I'll read the rest tonight," promised Gertie. "I'm sure I can finish it. Then I can tell you the end tomorrow. You are coming to school tomorrow, Clara?"

"I'll try. I know I've missed a lot of days lately but Mother's so poorly and Father daren't not work because of 'is pay. But, Gertie, if I don't come could you run round for a bit tomorrow night? Would your father let you? I don't really want to leave our 'ouse."

"He might, Clara. But," Gertie shrugged her shoulders in resignation, "you know I can't promise. Mother says he's mercurial in temperament and that's supposed to excuse his moods."

"To be honest he scares me, Gertie. I can't make him out. He's such a God fearing man. Always at Church, reading his Bible. It doesn't make sense that such a religious person can be so harsh to his family. You'd expect 'im to love you most." Sympathy suffused Clara's homely face. " 'E does look so very fearsome but, Gertie, 'e must surely be a good man at 'eart."

"You couldn't be more wrong, Clara. My father is a hard, unfeeling man. He's very difficult to live with. He's never satisfied with anything we do and he's especially down on Abel. Poor Mother's spirit seems to disappear when he's at home. I know she hates him. And I think she is actually frightened of him. I know I am."

"How does your mother stand it, Gertie? Has 'e always been the same? Why did she marry 'im in the first place?"

"Well, Abel says that Mother told him that she had to marry Father."

"No!"

"Not had like that, Clara! Mother wouldn't. Had to because her family owed him money. Something about a debt of honour. I don't really know. She only talked to Abel about it and he said she sort of muttered and didn't explain things properly. Apparently she seemed guilty because she was talking about it at all. I'm really not sure but there must have been quite a drama, Mother being a sort of sacrifice!"

A pinafored monitor strode officiously into the middle of the playground, great handbell held close to her chest, clapper gripped in her closed fist. She raised the bell and then, loosing the clapper and holding the handle with both hands, she swung it vigorously.

At the first clang bodies froze and then, to the continued frenzied pealing of the bell, pupils moved in an orderly fashion to form their class lines, ready to be admitted to the last lesson of the day.

This was the hour that Gertie hated. Her short-sightedness resulted in a genuine difficulty for her in deciphering Miss Smith's copperplate hand. Normally they worked on slates but for this lesson they had to use pens and precious paper.

During break two monitors had filled the inkwells with fresh ink from the long spouted ink cans, distributed the fine-nibbed pens and put sheets of unlined white paper onto each desk.

As the class filed into the room Gertie's throat tightened in apprehension. Miss Smith had filled the board with her tiny, beautiful writing, each line of pothooks a master of uniformity and grace.

Clara moved to her seat near to the window. As she slid along the bench she accidentally caught Gertie's paper which fluttered innocently to the floor to lie snow white and virginal in the gangway, right in the path of scuffling boots. Gertie bent quickly to retrieve it, trying to save it before any oafish footprint blighted its perfection.

"Clumsy girl!" Miss Smith fixed Gertie with her piercing stare.

A bad start! Gertie lifted the paper gently, shook it slightly and returned it to her desk. Anxiety made her over cautious. She held it in place and blew gently to remove any minute particles of dust.

"A young lady does not blow through her teeth," came Miss Smith's critical rasp. "Gertrude, give out the handsheets".

Gertie stood to take the proffered paper then she walked up and down the rows distributing the paper squares on which the pupils' hands were to rest whilst writing. The class was busy, pens dipping experimentally into overflowing inkwells.

Gertie returned to her place, already concerned that she was beginning after the rest of the class. She squinted at the board. The title remained tantalisingly indistinct. Was it 'Daffodils' or 'Differences'?

Clara, alert to her friend's distress, whispered the title. Gertie sighed and proceeded to write.

Supported by the whispered promptings, Gertie managed to copy her first few lines, unaware that Miss Smith had fixed her attention on the two of them.

"Clara!" That one word split the atmosphere like a thunderclap. "You, my lady, are whispering. One stroke of the ruler for you, if you please. Come here!"

Nervously Clara stood. "I'm sorry Miss Smith. I was only....."

"Don't only me, young lady. Get yourself here and hold out your hand".

Gertie stood reluctantly and moved to let Clara pass.

"Palm up, if you please," Miss Smith was holding her ruler purposefully, menacingly.

Clara stood, eyes down, hand outstretched. The whole class was hushed. No nibs scratched. No one breathed.

Gertie was still standing in the gangway. The ruler was poised to fall. "Miss Smith. It wasn't Clara's fault. I...... I can't......."

"Silence! How dare you take your friend's part against me! Sit down, Gertrude Nightingale. Pick up your pen and get......." the ruler cracked down, ".......on with your work. Speak when you are spoken to."

Gertie hesitated long enough for Clara to resume her place, tears of injustice clouding her already misty vision. Such humiliation. Such unfair humiliation for girls of their age. She dug her pen sharply into the inkwell and withdrew it, aiming the pointed nib almost viciously at her paper. At that moment Gertie saw that her nib trailed a kite tail of fluff and cotton, small but significant enough to have dropped an unsightly blot onto her work.

Miss Smith, attracted by Gertie's horrified intake of breath, glanced across at her desk, "Gertrude. A blot! A careless blot on good, clean, expensive paper. Wastrel! Waste not, want not! I prophesy you will be one to want before you are done. Perhaps a dose of this will cure your lapse of concentration". She had put down the ruler and was reaching across her desk to a length of garden cane propped against the wall. At some time it must have lain in a pen tray on which red ink had been spilt. Now an ominous red stain had spread along part of its quivering length, a colour that gave foundation to the rumour that Miss Smith drew blood.

Gertie rose and with a pounding heart, she advanced towards her tormentor.

As she passed the front desk of the parallel row a brave whisper reached her ears. "Spit on yer 'ond. It dow 'ert so much." Carrots Carter, a poor mathematician and experienced recipient of Miss Smith's doses, was risking his very soul to help her.

Automatically Gertie raised her palm and licked its length, leaving a shiny trail of saliva visible and horrifyingly obvious to Miss Smith's sharp eyes. Hand extended, Gertie stood, waiting for her punishment, her countenance averted from the indistinct sea of faces that were to be witness to her shame. The hushed room had the bloodthirsty expectancy of a crowd assembled to witness an execution. They were at once excited and horrified, anxious to see whether the stinging stick would indeed draw blood.

"Hmph!" Miss Smith took the wet hand in her own icy grasp, dragged it into the folds of her skirt, wiped it, thrust it back into position and brought the cane down sharply. Before Gertie could withdraw her trembling palm a second lightning stroke whipped her already stinging skin. "Never do that again! Gertrude Nightingale!

I shall make it my business to tell your father what a Miss you are developing into! Spitting in public - and onto your own hand. Disgusting madam!"

How Gertie regained her seat she never knew. That she finished her writing was a miracle. It was handed in, complete with blot and smudged with tears. She had finished last, after the rest of the pupils had been dismissed and had the further disgrace of seeing Miss Smith's opinion of her efforts.

The sharp nosed spinster glanced at the paper, looked into Gertie's reddened eyes and, without lowering her gaze, crumpled the paper into a ball, raised it above the wastepaper basket and dropped it theatrically into the rubbish. "You are dismissed, Miss", she hissed.

Gertie stumbled out into the coat- pegged entrance and hurried into the late afternoon gloom. A pair of arms was thrust out towards her and she found herself weeping onto Clara's shoulder. "Never mind, Gertie, love. It's all over. Let's go home. Your mother will know what to do." Clara gently thrust Gertie away from her and, taking her arm, guided her down the darkening streets towards home.

★ ★ ★ ★ ★ ★ ★ ★ ★

Gertie's mother did indeed know what to do. An hour later Gertie sniffed into her hot tea, holding the comforting warmth of the big white mug between both hands. She was hunched into her father's large wooden chair - the only one in the house with arms – her feet on the fender, watching the coals settling comfortably in the grate. Her mother was angrily detailing what she would like to do to that "officious, vicious Miss Smith." Clara had gone home to get her family's evening meal but not before describing the injustices of the afternoon and drawing attention to the swollen, reddened state of her friend's fingers.

Mrs. Nightingale, a mouse whenever her husband was present, was a tigress in his absence if the well being of her children was concerned. She was a neat woman, tidy in her person, usually calm and economical with her movements so that she exuded an unexpected grace peculiarly incongruous in this kitchen. She had the air of being a parlour lady.

This evening her animated face had lost its accustomed serenity and strands of her once golden hair had worked loose from her bun. She ceased her furious patrol of the room's outer limits and came to a standstill, her open palms slapping decisively onto the scrubbed table top. "You're not going back, Gertie. I appreciate how you are about learning. You're like your grandmother in that but enough is enough. That crabby old woman is out to make your life a misery. She gives you no encouragement, just criticism and now – punishment! Unreasonable chastisement! And she knows about your eyes. I went down to the school. I told her myself at the beginning of the year – that's why you're always by the board. She knows alright and the likes of her doesn't forget. She's an embittered old spinster – couldn't marry for fear of losing her precious job – turned herself sour she has. Her problem isn't blots and whispers. It's jealousy. She can't stand the sight of a pretty young girl with her life before her, and I'm not letting you fall into her clutches again! This caning is one too many. Let the school board ask her why she's lost two able pupils – for Em won't want Clara to go back without you."

Mrs. Nightingale ceased her tirade long enough to take in her daughter's beautiful face, puffy now with weeping, and her dejected body slumped in her father's chair.

"Now look, love. It's not the end of the world. This road doesn't have to lead to the factory floor. Mr. Leadbetter, in Bridge Street, he's wanting a girl in his shop. Nellie's not up to much these days and is only hanging on till he finds a replacement to his liking. She's anxious to go to her sister's in the country. He's a decent man and his shop has some higher class trade than most round here. I'll go and speak to him tomorrow. No! Why not now? Strike while the iron's hot. You sit there. I won't be long. Watch the meat and don't let the potatoes boil dry."

Gertie's mother reached her shawl, drew it up over her head and, clasping it tightly beneath her chin with one hand, lifted the latch with the other and stepped out into the darkness of Twenty Four Court.

By the time Mrs. Nightingale's returning steps could be heard in the 'entry'- that dank, arched tunnel giving access to the yard around which six houses huddled - Gertie was no longer a scholar but a working girl. Mr. Leadbetter had been pleased to start a quiet young lady, literate, numerate and of a pleasant, well brought up disposition. He had also been of no mind to refuse Nightingale's daughter.

"Now don't go into a panic, love. You'll be fine. You can see close to, so bills will be no problem and you'll soon learn where everything is on the shelves. Nellie is staying on 'till they see how you do. Come on, dear, try to look on the bright side. There's lots who'd be pleased to leave old sour puss and be working. And you're not in any dirty, noisy work place either. If you can work hard, and I know you will, you'll have a nice little job there and be a credit to us - and you'll be earning. You'll still have time to read and improve your mind. You can even join the new free library when it opens."

Gertie nodded her acceptance of her mother's wisdom but privately she regretted the manner of her leaving school and the loss of her dream to become a pupil teacher. Shop work was not what she had wanted for herself nor, she feared, was it what her father had envisaged. He had a son working in a stiff collar and suit in an office and he wanted to be seen to have a daughter doing similarly well. Gertie knew quite clearly that his children's success was intended to reflect Ben Nightingale's effectiveness as a father - not that he had ever been one! No, she felt that her father would not be pleased.

When Abel came home he voiced the very same misgivings. By the time their father's metal shod steps were heard sharply clipping the silence of the entry the three of them were nervous and apprehensive.

"Not a word, remember, until after he's eaten," whispered their mother, biting her underlip. "Let him eat and then leave it to me. Gertie, quick, out of his chair!"

The latch lifted and the door swung open to admit a heavily built, swarthy man who lurched into the kitchen, famished and fatigued. He lowered himself onto the vacated chair, put his great feet onto the fender and unlaced the offending, ill-fitting boots. His released toes wriggled as life returned to them and then, with no more than a grunt of acknowledgement to his family, Ben Nightingale walked over to the stone sink where a metal bowl of steaming water stood ready for him.

Nightingale stripped off his coat and passed it behind him to his wife, standing ready at his elbow. His waistcoat and neckerchief followed. He raised his chin. Sarah Nightingale stepped forward and undid his collar button then, as the chin was lowered, the rest of the shirt buttons. He shrugged out of his shirt and let it hang loosely from the waistband of his trousers.

The room was silent except for the sluicing of water as the man washed the grime of the furnaces from his great, bull neck and morose features.

Satisfied, at least with his cleanliness, their father moved to the scrubbed table, now decently covered with its white cloth. He took his seat, undressed as he was, his wooden chair now in the warmest position with its back to the fire.

Abel and Gertie sat in silence whilst their mother carried a black pot from the hob on the range to stand on a low metal trivet on the table. Sarah then lifted the Dutch oven from beside the fire and rested it on the range. A very small piece of meat sizzled on the hook and dripped its fat into the pan. She unhooked the mutton and sliced it into two, placing the larger piece on one plate which she put in front of her husband, the smaller one on a second for Abel. Gertie heaped potatoes from the black pot onto both plates. Meanwhile Sarah dipped a piece of bread into the meat fat and added that to

Gertie's plate of potatoes. Her own meal consisted of the vegetable only.

Abel's hand moved towards his fork and hesitated. His father looked at him directly, almost menacingly. Then, without closing his eyes or dropping his head he began grace as if it were some threat or evil incantation.

"For what we are about to receive let Our Lord make us truly thankful."

Abel's hand twitched. His father noticed and continued spitefully," Bless this home and all who dwell within its sheltering walls."

No one moved.

The "Amen" was quiet.

Everyone waited for Nightingale to begin to eat and when he did they too began their meal. But still no one spoke.

Sarah Nightingale seemed to have lost stature since her husband's homecoming. She had shrivelled like a candle too suddenly thrust into a flame, had become distorted, her aspect limp and frightened, her spirit a brittle miniature of the capable afternoon lady.

When Nightingale had finished eating she cleared the plates, put out dishes and reached a custard baked in pastry from the slow oven. As she crossed the rag rug her toe caught in a ripple and she pitched forward, steadying herself just in time, her hand on her husband's shoulder. He turned his head, looked at the hand, appeared to wait until it was removed and then he stroked his skin as if to brush away the offending contact.

Abel caught Gertie's eye and both young people looked away to reduce their mother's embarrassment. Pudding consumed, Gertie and her mother cleared the table and washed the pots. Abel sat beside the fire, silent and thoughtful, occasionally glancing at his father who slumped, uncommunicatively, in his chair.

No one spoke.

No one dared to break the oppressive silence.

In the end it was Nightingale who roused himself from the depths of his despondency to address his family. "Ten laid off today. Rest of us expecting short time." No one commented. No one commiserated.

"A good thing," Nightingale continued," you're doin' so very well, my lad, or your mother would have a hard time to keep food on the table." There was a sneer in his voice as he expressed what a stranger might have taken as a compliment to his son. "I've been thinkin' what else there is to be done. I'll not 'ave yer mother workin'. She's not been born to it and it'd delight too many to see 'er brought so low. It'll 'ave to be you, my girl. You've 'ad a good fair run o'schoolin'. More un most. Now it's time for you to be looking for employment."

Nightingale's eyes were resting on his daughter. He looked almost benevolent for a moment. "I'd a good job in mind for you, Gertie, - respectable. Copy clerk in the office. Nice an'light, warm. But Sawyer's girl turned up this afternoon, bold as brass. It's not what yer know but who!"

Abel and Gertie looked towards their mother expectantly. This was an opportunity made in Heaven. She opened her mouth to speak, closed it, opened it again then wiped her hands on her pinafore and resumed her silence.

Abel glanced at Gertie. He wasn't sure what game his mother was playing. She nodded towards him encouragingly and so it was Abel after all, who plunged into the frightening abyss of space and forked lightening. He surfaced, "Father, Gertie - I'…er….. believe that Leadbetter is looking for a girl for his shop. Clean work. Respectable."

Nightingale put his hands onto the arm of his chair, half rose with, "I'll not….." then sank back as if defeated. "Then go, Gertie. Go tomorrow. Go to see him."

"Yes, father." Her words came out as a sob of relief but Nightingale took it to be one of distress.

"Never mind, my girl. You have a duty to your family, which I trust you will not shirk. No, I know you will not avoid. It may not be work to your liking but go, tomorrow, early. Tell Leadbetter that your father will see it as a personal favour if he'll see you right."

Then Nightingale stood, reached up onto the line strung across the kitchen on which a freshly ironed shirt hung. He pulled down the garment, tugged his soiled one out of his trouser waistband and shrugged himself into the clean one. He fastened his button and then stood, head erect, whilst Sarah put the studs into his clean loose collar. Waistcoat and coat in place, Mr. Nightingale ostentatiously checked and wound his fob watch that he had reached down from the mantelpiece and fixed Abel with his flinty glare. "Now then, Abel. I know you think yourself a big man nowadays – own set of office keys and all that – but don't get locking up 'ere until I'm 'ome; d'you 'ear? I'll be at the vicarage for an hour and then maybe in the kitchen of The Shoulder of Mutton". His voice hardened, "No, I'll not be drinking. Raising money for the Sunday school roof as you well know. Now remember, Abel, don't shoot that bolt – or there'll be trouble. I won't be knocking to be let in to me own 'ouse."

No one said a word as Nightingale left. Three pairs of ears strained to listen to his heavy footfall as he clumped down the entry. Then, as the sounds of the father receded into the night, the family heaved sighs of relief and exchanged conspiratorial smiles.

"All's well that ends well," Gertie quoted.

"It hasn't ended yet," added her mother.

Abel caught the weary tone in her voice and knew that she was thinking of her husband's return and the hasty, unloving coupling that he would undoubtedly force beneath the sheets in the pious name of marital duty. She would close her eyes, pretend to sleep and know that it would make no difference. She would lie limp like a rag doll and hope that he would satiate himself quickly. She would endure what she could not avoid. Nightingale would not be drunk. He would be literally stone-cold sober – and all the more hateful for that.

His arm circled his mother's shoulders as Abel tried to will his own strength into her. She bent her greying head sideways so that it rested against her son's dark thatch.

"Have an early night, Mother. Gertie and I will sit and read a while beside the fire. I'll stay up until Father gets in."

"And after?"

"And a while after," added Abel aware that his mother hated the thought of him just feet away from where she lay with his father. The partition was thin and did no more to deaden noise than a thick fustian curtain might have done.

Gertie raised her face for her mother's kiss, "Well then goodnight, love. Don't be reading too long. You've a big day ahead of you. Abel, don't let your sister strain her eyes in bad light. Keep the lamp trimmed."

"No, Mother. Yes, Mother. We're fine Mother. Up to bed with you! Get some sleep.....while you can." He could have bitten off his tongue as he watched his mother's face blush with shame as she turned, opened the stair door and began to climb wearily up the narrow, triangular treads which led to the two bedrooms above their kitchen.

Abel and Gertie listened to their mother's movements until at last the silence told them that she was at rest, if only temporarily. Then brother and sister settled into companionable peacefulness. Gertie was deep into her novel in her favourite position, hunched over the book, feet on the fender. Abel stirred the coals with the long poker and watched them settle into a landscape of fiery caves and gorges.

Through the thin chimney breast he could hear next door's fire being raked and damped down for the night. He could imagine Clara securing the door and lights before leaving her mother to cough her way through another interminable night. Mr. Watkins was on permanent night shift. It paid better and he preferred to be away from home when other men sought the comforts of theirs. His was a bachelor's bed or as good as and had been these seven years or more. He had been a careful husband, a good provider. An affectionate man by nature, he had loved his Em too much to sit by and watch her die little by little. He liked to be out of the house or asleep upstairs – just passing through, dropping a kiss on Em's hot forehead and either being off to work or just back. Occasionally he sat beside her, held her hand, told her what a good girl Clara was, gossiped a little about the families in Twenty Four Court up the next entry. Theirs was not a house in a court but one in a row, with its own tiny strip of back garden and its own outside lavatory. It adjoined the Nightingale Court house and he was glad of their proximity for Sarah Nightingale and Em had been friends for years, acquaintances even before marriage had brought joy to the one and so much sorrow to the other. And now sorrow was reaching its long fingers into his life and there was no escape!

Abel thought of Clara climbing the twisting stairs and hoisting herself into the big bed that she shared with her two younger sisters. She was a good girl, a steady friend for his shy young sister and already a marvellous little housewife. She was five years younger than he was but recently he had realised how swiftly that gap was closing. She had become a young woman and he had become increasingly aware of how often his thoughts had begun to turn towards her. Clara was not the beauty that Gertie was but she had a quality, a warmth, an earthy, comfortable feeling about her that Abel found attractive.

Abel was not aware, however, that as Clara lay amongst the tangled limbs of her sisters she was reciprocating his interest, creating her own web of fantasies around the brother of her best friend.

Chapter Two

Long before it was light Sarah Nightingale had the draught tin over the fire and was coaxing the embers into a glow with the long snouted bellows. A kettle sat optimistically on the hob and on the table was the heel of a loaf and some cheese.

It was a cold morning and she was keen to see a bright fire burning but the cheap coal was full of brickbats and it was slow to catch.

Sarah had slipped out of the dead embrace of her husband an hour earlier, anxious to scurry outside to the privy to relieve herself of the burden of the night. She was thankful that she no longer needed to worry about fruitfulness for her womb was surely a barren thing – a relief in one way but an added concern in another, for her monthly courses had offered some respite from the unwelcome attentions of her husband.

Sarah had swilled herself in cold water, packed Nightingale's tucker box and by now had expected her husband to have followed her down into the kitchen. Pride made her want to look clean and unperturbed, her housewifery skills beyond reproach.

When a thin spire of smoke heralded the fire's new life, Sarah stood up, automatically straightening her pinafore and tucking loose strands of hair into her bun as she heard the creaks of floor boards above. Em's regular muffled coughing penetrated the wall and, for a moment, Sarah almost envied her sick friend, waking to a house full of affection and a husband so solicitous for her comfort. With distaste Sarah recalled her own husband's animal use of her only a few hours earlier.

With her thoughts focused on the man who, even now, was coming down the stairs, Sarah looked at the slice of bread out ready for him. The corners of her mouth turned down as the expression on her face hardened. Then she slowly and deliberately lifted the butter knife to her mouth. She allowed a small bubble of saliva to settle on the blade and then she rapidly spread the frothing spittle onto the dry bread. Sarah exhaled her satisfaction, cut several chunks of cheese and laid them, almost reverently, on top of the bread.

By the time Nightingale lumbered into the kitchen a mug of steaming tea stood beside the bread and cheese. He neither looked at his wife nor spoke to her but sat, morosely, breaking his fast.

Food eaten, Nightingale pulled on the work clothes warming over the fire guard, laced up his boots, took his tin tucker box from his wife's outstretched hand and was gone, his cloud of resentment billowing around him, almost tangible evidence of his self righteous dissatisfaction.

Other doors were opening and slamming in the court. Other boots were clumping and slithering down the yard. Funnelled into the entry, the men of Twenty Four Court moved together into the darkness of the morning destined for the mines and the furnaces, to hew coal and form metal, to stave off poverty for themselves and to turn their employers into rich men.

Sarah savoured her peace and relived her satisfaction at seeing Nightingale breakfasting on her spittle. She had passed behind him to busy herself at the range and had held the steaming kettle aloft. For one brief second she had recalled her stumble of the night before and had wondered whether she dared to repeat her unsteadiness with the scalding water. But no, she had too much sense. He was a powerful man and, as yet, his strength had only threatened and cowed her. She preferred to maintain that situation.

The kettle had been replaced on the hob to sing the time away until Abel and Gertie should appear. This was the moment that Sarah Nightingale loved best – when the day stretched ahead of her with twelve hours of her husband's absence. It would be filled with all the usual chores but there would be the precious moments to share with her children and with Em next door. She laid the table ready for Abel and Gertie and, for once, felt that she had some things to be thankful for.

In fact life had not been all bad for Mrs. Nightingale. There had been a time when she had not even borne that name, when she had been Sarah Williams of 320 Duddington Port, the only child of a loving family.

In an age when families were large, both by design and accident, Sarah's had been an oddity. Her mother had conceived only once and the resulting child had become the focus of family life, the proof of past love and an investment for a future.

The Williams' home was a huge double fronted house with its two bay windows separated by a front door that opened directly into the street. Each window belonged, in fact, to a shop, one a pawn broking business run by her father and grandfather, the other a draper`s shop - the result of her mother's natural business acumen.

Behind the shops were a number of rooms, some small and cosy, others large and imposing. The heart of the house was the outer kitchen, a simple stone flagged room dominated by its huge black cooking range and furnished with wooden chairs and scrubbed deal table - all more practical than fashionable. It was in this room that Sarah's grandparents lived out their twilight years, scraping their new potatoes to an incredible whiteness, singing hymns passionately and eating apple sandwiches in the afternoons. Such were her isolated memories of two cheerful people who had loved her. In this room Sarah had been taught to read, to waltz, to play dominoes and tiddly-winks, to knock down a tower of cards and to listen to stories - really listen. It had been her grandmother's hands that had held the hot bags of salt against her aching tooth, her grandmother's fingers that had been warmed by the fire before even trying to fasten that impossible liberty-bodice button. She had been the old couple`s future as well as the repository for their memories of the past.

In the evenings, after eating together as a family, Sarah had gone with her parents to the little sitting room, a cosy chintz affair where her father busied himself with ledgers and her mother usually read or sewed. If she were sewing then she would tell Sarah stories, tales that she had originally read herself. Sarah's favourites were Shakespeare's and her mother made the characters come alive, altering her voice to suit each one and often quoting the glorious words that made pictures in Sarah's head.

Sarah's mother had had a Sunday School group and on summer evenings after the shop shutters were up it was not unusual for some of that class of youngsters to congregate on the front steps begging for one of Mrs William's stories. Invariably they were invited inside, only scurrying home when dusk reminded them of their darkness curfew.

As that little group of children grew older it had become a weekly Friday night habit to gather in the parlour for a story and lemonade. Sarah enjoyed these nights of flickering firelight and low lamplight, sitting on a footstool leaning against her mother's skirts and listening to Shakespeare told and retold. She liked the company of young visitors, feeling safe to associate with these poorer, rougher neighbours in the secure haven of her own home.

One of these young people had been Em, another a Nightingale; Ben Nightingale – a dark lad, swarthy and gypsy-looking, like the rest of his family. His father was a carter who supported his numerous offspring by driving his horses to an early grave and winning his prize fights by fair means or foul. He was a bad tempered fighter, only popular because of his size and the certainty of those who backed him of doubling their stakes.

Young Ben looked like his father and had surely inherited his cruel streak for stories were told of him pulling wings from flies and it was certain that he was always over- eager to assist with killing fowls or Autumn pig sticking. Nevertheless, Ben enjoyed stories and listened from his usual seat in the corner, half hidden amongst the shadows, never varying his position and rarely joining in any conversation. He would fix his eyes on the storyteller with such an intensity that it looked as if he were reluctant to even blink in case he wasted one moment of the precious sight of her. He drank in the tales, enjoying the drama and the escapism. Like Sarah he saw Romeo's passion for Juliet, witnessed the agony of Shylock as he lost both jewels and daughter and shared the terrible indecision of Brutus as he weighed the arguments concerning Caesar's assassination.

As the years went by the little group grew smaller as courting and marriages took their toll but no matter who else was missing Ben Nightingale was not. Every Friday Ben was there in his shadowy corner, silent and staring, listening and watching.

Sarah's father did not like Nightingale. He never had.

"He's a rum young bugger. Can't tell what goes on inside him. I'm afraid he's got the same streak as his father."

"No, dear. Don't be so judgmental. Just because his looks are like the man who fathered him, it doesn't follow that his insides are the same." Sarah's mother was typically generous in her assessment of the young man.

"I didn't trust him as a boy and I haven't changed my opinion. He makes me want to count the spoons after he's gone," Mr Williams complained.

Sarah's mother had laughed and after that she always laid the table with her knives, forks and 'nightingales' which, to some extent, defused her husband's antipathy.

Sarah's uneasiness about their visitor was not so easily dispelled. She only knew that Ben Nightingale made her feel uncomfortable. As a child she had felt jealous of the way he had looked at her mother so covetously. She wasn't sure when the object of his attention had altered, only that suddenly it seemed that those eyes which had swallowed her mother now threatened to draw her into their dark depths. He always seemed to be there in the shadows, in their fireside corner, at her elbow at the vicarage garden party, beside her at the fair. Weddings, funerals, church services – whatever the occasion – Ben Nightingale would materialise from the edges of the crowd, peel himself away from a knot of young men , walk towards her from the trees, the tents, the yawning grave itself. He would proffer an arm, produce a much needed umbrella, simply walk beside her as if he were the official escort. There was never any attempt at conversation just a nod, a gesture, – but even that was too much and too often for Sarah.

Ben was actually doing rather well for himself. As a lad he had accidentally taken up with a bargee, a lonely old chap who had been glad of Ben's muscle and his company. When the old man had died he had left Ben his boat – or, at least, Ben had claimed it and nobody had questioned his ownership.

Work had come easy to Ben. He was young and strong so he could load and unload his cargo quickly. He worked all the hours of light and never needed to stop off to share a drink and a laugh with any mates. He was a natural loner quite content with his horse and a full hold.

It wasn't long before he'd a second barge, a couple of horses and a string of lads who watched out for his boats at the locks and worked them through. Very soon he was making a good living and always he was careful of his horses and his men. His profits grew and were ploughed back into his business until by the time he was twenty four Ben Nightingale's six green barges, decorated with their castles, flowers and the characteristic bird in the gilded cage were well known along his home stretch of waterway.

Meanwhile the William's family had been less fortunate. Old Mr Williams and his wife had died within weeks of each other leaving Sarah and her parents grief-stricken. Then young Mr Williams, Sarah's father, had become ill. At first her mother had talked of exhaustion, running the shop single-handedly whilst still distressed by the death of both parents. When the prescribed rest did no good Dr. Wilson was called to diagnose what was, in fact, a death sentence – the wasting sickness, 'lung fever'.

The draper's shop was shut up and Sarah's mother tried to run the more lucrative business – the pawn shop. She failed. She did not have the expertise to recognise value and she could not concentrate on business when her heart was upstairs with her dying husband.

Sarah was distraught.

One Friday night Sarah sat with her mother in the parlour whilst her father slept fitfully upstairs. Ben Nightingale stared out, as usual, from his shadowy corner. He came late now, after his horses had been tethered or stabled and only when his captains had secured their barges for the night. He looked tired but was obviously trying to wear his most sympathetic face.

It was not a night for story telling.

Sarah recalled every detail of that night with amazing clarity even the weather and what they had eaten for supper earlier. Her mother had been weeping again, talking of selling up, worrying about how to move such a sick man. There had been a movement in the bedroom upstairs and Sarah had gone racing up to see to her father. She had plumped his pillows, moistened his lips, tried to warm those cold fingers plucking at the eiderdown.

Eventually Sarah had gone back down the stairs, quietly, to avoid disturbing her father, so quietly in fact that no stair creaked, no footstep echoed, no hall quarry clinked on its uneven bed. She knew the house so well that she could avoid every potential sound. When she returned to the parlour she had opened the door gently, not intending to be secretive but still anxious to keep the house quiet. Someone had drawn the thick door curtain, made of wine- red velvet, in her absence and so her return went unnoticed. She had halted, sensing something unusual about the conversation inside the room; perhaps it was the tone, the almost secretive murmurings. Sarah was not an eavesdropper but she suddenly had the distinct urge to adjust a shoe strap, unavoidably hesitating so that the voices of Ben and her mother could be heard, although still not distinctly.

"It's too kind, Ben. Repayment...... not easy....... terms. God send ...." Her mother's words were muffled, followed by Ben's laughter. Laughter! With her father dying upstairs!

"Usurer.......... not a Shylock!"

"But, Ben. You have to think of yourself. Something - interest. If not money..........only right."

"No.......necessary....insist....my pound of flesh....Sarah....." Her own name leapt at her from behind the curtain.

Sarah recoiled, her face flaming with indignation. Her mother's laughter was clear now, a shrill, false trilling, unrecognisable as her own. With a dramatic sweep, Sarah pulled back the curtain and stood, framed in the doorway looking at what – to her – seemed to be an almost adulterous scene. Her mother was seated on the end of the chaise longue, where she had left her, but Ben Nightingale was no longer in his corner. He was lounging beside Mrs Williams, one of his work callused hands resting familiarly on her shoulder, the other in her lap covering her clasped hands.

At Sarah's rather theatrical entrance Ben, obviously startled, moved swiftly away from her mother. Embarrassed, Sarah took refuge in busying herself with closing the door, tugging the curtain back into place and kicking the draught excluder into position. When she turned to face the room once more her mother seemed composed and anxious to know how her father was. Ben was in his corner again, his features hidden from her view, his shadowy familiars seeming to hang about him.

Sarah would never have forgotten her eavesdropping or the parlour scene but she might have pushed it from the forefront of her mind in the distress of her father's worsening condition. As it was, Ben Nightingale's behaviour kept the memory of his Shakespearean bargain with her mother uppermost. Considering he had a business to run he seemed to find an excessive amount of time to be at the house. He still treated Sarah with some deference but he had a proprietorial air about him. He began to pass comments that she considered personal such as her looking heavy-eyed and needing more sleep or if she did not eat properly she would develop salt cellars and he abhorred women with bony shoulders. Only politeness had stopped her from asking why his preferences should be of any concern to her. Sarah felt that Mr Nightingale was encroaching on her personal space, that his shadow fell across hers too frequently, that she preferred his silence to this new loquaciousness.

It was clear that Mrs Williams was turning to Ben more and more when decisions had to be made, when tradesmen needed to be spoken to, when arrangements were too unpleasant for her to handle. In consequence it was not surprising that at the end it was he who organised Mr William's funeral and supported her mother at her father's graveside. Sarah found herself walking in Mr Nightingale's footsteps, following him when he took the weight of her mother's grief whilst she bore her own alone.

Sarah was confused. Ben had shown interest in her and yet was becoming her mother's companion. In the nightmare weeks that followed her father's death they were frequently closeted together in the small sitting room, the door shut firmly and Sarah clearly excluded. Strangers arrived at the house: black clad men who came in ones and twos and left envelopes, apologetically, for Mrs William's 'perusal' and 'at her convenience'. Sarah discovered that this was the way in which more and more unpaid bills were arriving, long-standing debts delivered.

Ben Nightingale, however, did not desert them and at times Sarah found herself questioning her critical judgement of him. Had it really been coloured by her father's obvious dislike of the young man? Had she become jealous of the reliance her mother placed upon him? Mr Nightingale's loyalty to his two lady friends extended to settling accounts, even to disposing of some of his own assets in order to see them comfortable again. He was the epitome of discreet generosity, seeming content to be rewarded by Mrs William's graciousness and his entree to their home.

The months of covered mirrors and black mourning merged with the distressing hours of weeping and sadness but, as spring arrived and Sarah found herself dressing in mauves and able to look at her reflection again, the optimism of youth returned. She tried hard to steer her mother from the doldrums but it was difficult. The great house seemed too large and there were too many empty spaces where previously quite valuable art or porcelain had been. Mrs Williams felt that she had lost both her past and her future. She seemed blind to the fact that she still had Sarah to live with and for. Only Ben seemed able to rouse her from depression.

One Sunday morning Sarah winkled her mother from the shell of the house and persuaded her to set foot in the church, which she had vowed never to visit again after the sadness of the funeral. For once, Sarah was glad of Ben's company for three enlivened the homeward conversation a little and he seemed to raise her mother's spirits somewhat.

As they were reaching the main road a rather smart horse and trap pulled alongside them. Mr. Massey and his daughter were intent on offering them a lift home. He assured them that he had room for three.

"Why thank you, Mr. Massey. That's good of you for, though the sun is spring-like, the wind still thinks that it is winter." Mrs.Williams was bright enough to sparkle again in company.

Mr. Massey had jumped down and was busy at the rear door, reaching inside the trap for the mounting box.

"Here you are, ma'am," Mr. Massey smiled good-naturedly," Up you go. Soon 'ave you 'ome and out of this blustery weather. Now you, sir, if you please."

Ben had his foot on the box and was about to spring into the trap when he hesitated; Sarah was speaking behind him.

"I've a beastly headache, Mr. Massey. If you don't mind I'll walk. The fresh air will do me good. There are several acquaintances ahead of me who are going my way. I'll not be alone." Sarah had foreseen the seating arrangement in the trap and could not endure the physical proximity of Ben Nightingale.

"If you're sure, Miss Williams," Mr. Massey did not seem perturbed by Sarah's independence.

Mrs. Williams smiled down from the trap, "Walk briskly, dear.

Don't get cold. We shall no doubt be home before you and have the fire blazing."

"I'll walk with you, Miss Williams," Ben had turned and was moving away from the trap towards her.

" No indeed, Mr. Nightingale – that is not necessary." Sarah's voice was firm.

"Not necessary but my pleasure, Miss Sarah."

When the trap finally moved off Mrs Williams was comfortably conversing with Miss Massey whilst Miss Williams was intent on no conversation at all. In fact she was so put out by her plan being thwarted that she fully intended to walk home in total silence.

The couple began to walk, Sarah setting such a pace that soon their breathing was audible in the Sunday silence. As they crossed the main road Ben supported her elbow and then moved around her very properly so that once on the pavement again he was walking on the kerb side. Uncharitably Sarah felt critical of Ben's attempts to ape a gentleman's behaviour. She was breathing heavily now, the unaccustomed exertion taking its toll.

"Miss Sarah, I've been waiting for such a moment," Ben was speaking, his head turned sideways, his eyes scanning her face," a convenient time…. like, when we could speak – privately."

Startled, Sarah slowed and looked directly at her escort. "Mr. Nightingale?"

"It's been a long time, a long time since I've been coming to your house and lately……. Well, I mean. It was alright when I was a nipper but now we've growed an' there's talk."

"Talk! Talk of what?" Sarah couldn't believe what she was hearing.

"I've a mind to protect your reputation, Miss Sarah".

"My reputation! The best way you can protect my reputation," Sarah snapped, "is to keep well away from me!" She increased her pace.

"I had your father's blessing afore he died," Ben blustered.

That stopped Sarah. "You did not. You could not!"

"Oh yes I did, Miss. You see 'e knew 'ow much I was assisting your ma. He was beholden to me. He said as he felt he could trust me at last."

"Maybe with money but... not... with ...me."

"Oh yes, Miss. I knew exactly what 'e meant. Your mother too. She's laughed with me. She knows my interest – knows it is you. Called you my little pound of flesh we 'ave – joking acourse – joking."

"Don't be so ridiculous!" Sarah stiffened her back and marched off so fast that Ben had to scurry to keep up with her.

"I'd be good to you, I would. I've allus loved you. I'd care for you, Sarah, and your mother."

How clearly Sarah recalled those words that came to her on the wind as she hastened away from Ben Nightingale. It was the "and your mother" that proved to be her undoing. It was these words that were to twist her heart and shape her future.

Ben's declaration was not repeated. Summer came and went without any happening of moment. Autumn brought an unusually beautiful fall, slow and colourful and then quite suddenly it was winter again. All through those passing seasons the two women had rattled around in that great house trying to recreate the old atmospheres and failing miserably. Ben arrived almost nightly and continued to see to whatever was needed. The trouble was that as time went on they needed more and more.

Sarah's mother became notably listless during the summer, passing off her tiredness as the effect of the heat. By autumn, as the nights drew in, she was excusing herself to retire early, often even before Ben left. Then, at the beginning of December the doctor was fetched for a feverish cold that went onto her chest. Sarah had to bind a sheet around her mother's ribs to ease the pain from her coughing. Though she recovered temporarily it was only weeks before she was ill again, the cough becoming more hollow and, to Sarah's ears, more reminiscent of her father's.

On Christmas Day Mrs. Williams sat downstairs to make a show of eating dinner with Sarah. Ben arrived uninvited but expected. Sarah noticed an unnatural brightness in her mother's eyes and a pretty flush on her cheeks disguising the pallor of the skin beneath. It was quite obvious that Mrs. Williams was dying from consumption.

Ben had never spoken to Sarah again of his intentions but behaved as he had always done, providing what was necessary, inveigling himself into the warp and weft of their lives. Sarah, in her role of nurse, never questioned what he was doing. She only recognised that nutritious food was in the kitchen, that the serving women were paid, that regular loads of coal kept the house warm and that Mrs. Williams never had to worry about bills. In spite of all the care and attention Mrs. Williams faded rapidly. She did not love life and showed no tenacity in trying to keep hold of it. On a cold February night when she burned with fever and even sleep was a fitful and terrifying kaleidoscope of dreams, Mrs. Williams simply opened her eyes very wide and was gone.

It was Sarah whom Ben supported at the next funeral and after it she had been too exhausted to argue when he had communicated his intention of staying at the house that night. He was very proper, sleeping downstairs in his clothes, lying on the chaise longue covered only by an old garden blanket. Nor had Sarah argued at breakfast when he ladled fresh porridge into a bowl and bid her eat up so that he could have his say.

This time Ben gave Sarah no option. He simply made a statement of fact. "Sarah," sharply, "there's some men who'd not 'ang about when there's precious little to gain but I'm not one of 'em. I'll not desert you when you've a reputation to consider."

"And you've your pound of flesh to collect," Sarah murmured bitterly.

"What was that you said?" Ben looked puzzled – then as his brain supplied the missing pieces, angry. He bit back what he might have said and left the house with," I'll 'ave the banns read."

And so it came about that Miss Sarah Williams was married quietly, very quietly, to Mr Ben Nightingale, shockingly close to her mother's funeral, still wearing her mourning clothes. Her neighbour, Emily Baker, attended her. Mrs. Nightingale, Ben's mother, came to see her eldest son wed to a young lady. The rest of his family had been told to keep away. Sarah had no relatives to invite.

Ben took and enjoyed Sarah's flesh that afternoon. He had waited a long time and his passion produced a fervour that Sarah regarded as rape. That it was done in daylight, with curtains open, emphasised its shame. Sarah had submitted, lying on her back staring at the ceiling above her parents' great bed. Tears of self- pity ran down her cheeks, tears that her husband mistook for the emotion of a young and inexperienced lady unused to doing her duty.

At first Ben had been delighted with his good fortune. His business was flourishing and he was managing to maintain the Williams's big house which - of course - was now his. He had an educated lady for a wife and enjoyed the effect that his new address and status had on his family, who were very impressed by Ben's meteoric rise into the middle class. Mr Nightingale found the time to attend Church, which he did with new clothes on his back and his new wife on his arm. He had gained what he had always coveted - respectability. At the end of the year the church elders invited Mr Nightingale to become more active - asked him in fact to join the committee responsible for the restoration and alteration of the church. He accepted with pleasure. Mr Ben Nightingale was a pillar of the community, a solid citizen.

Ben went through life like a coiled spring. He had an incredible energy which was effectively disguised by an outward mask of calmness. In reality Ben had a determination to outplay and out do his opponents and even the rest of his own team. This pent-up vivacity, this controlled aggression went unnoticed by many - but not by his wife. Sarah had long recognised Ben Nightingale's dark ambition and knew that his pride in her was one of ownership. Her home and her body had been his prize and he had won them both by default, in the same manner as his first barge – there had been no other contenders.

Sarah knew that there could be no happiness for her in this union but she tried to make herself content and to keep up appearances. She joined the Vicar's Bible Class for Ladies held on Thursday afternoons, helped with the Band of Hope every other Tuesday evening and became a loyal member of the Dorcas Society. She did her housekeeping thoroughly, embroidered their linen attractively and bore her husband's too regular attentions without complaining. He was not ungentle with her, simply coarse, pleased that his wife took no pleasure in the union but behaved as a 'lady' should. He was not cruel. He bought her presents, complimented her on her looks, on her activities, and enjoyed being seen out with her but he did not love her. Ben Nightingale loved only himself.

For her part, Sarah felt demeaned. She had married beneath herself. This man had grown up in the same street but in a different world. Her home had been a commercial property with coach house and stables. There had been daily maids and drivers, stable boys and shop assistants. Her family had been educated, literate. Ben had lived in a 'two up and one down' house in a neighbouring court, shared a bed with three other brothers and been ashamed of his illiterate boor of a father. With such disparate backgrounds it would have been hard for even a love match to continue to flame. As it was, Sarah had no wish to cross into her husband's one-time-world and he was destined to remain awkward in hers. Their marriage bed was cold.

This mismatch, these poorly synchronised social mechanics of their union, were eventually adjusted but in a totally expected way.

It was Christmas time two years into the marriage. Sarah had been heavily pregnant with Abel but even so had felt it appropriate to go to midnight mass with her husband. Her clothes, well cut with no need to skimp material, had allowed her to feel thoroughly concealed, and in any case, she argued, what better service was there for a mother-to-be than this one. And so they had gone and were returning in an almost convivial mood, their boots crunching on a thickening white frost and the welcoming lamp in their bay window calling them home through the darkness.

Sarah had gone up swiftly to bed leaving Ben to see to the lamps and secure the door. By the time he came upstairs she was standing beside the window brushing her hair. Ben had come to stand behind her, his stubbled chin nuzzling into the hollow of her neck, his thickset fingers caressing her hair.

"God, how I do love thee Sarah Nightingale." He held her close and she felt his male hardness grow against her. Surely he wasn't contemplating....? " I aught to be down at the cut. I aught to have a quick look at the barges. There's no one on board tonight - just the lad who watches the 'osses. I aught, I aught, I aught - but I just want to..........."

Sarah sought to distract him. "Ben, the sky over the station - it's pink, a pretty deep pink - it's uncommon, almost a glow…..! Ben – look!"

But Ben was of no mind to look through windows or anywhere for that matter except at his wife. Her pregnancy had softened her skin, enhanced the lustre of her hair. Her swollen body was all the more desirable for it bore his stamp, his proof of ownership.

Sarah remembered only too vividly her protests as he snatched the curtain across the panes to obscure her view and led her firmly to the high double bed. "No, Ben! No! The baby! You can't. We can't!"

"I'll be careful. Don't fret. It's my child. I'll not harm him but I need you, Sarah - now."

Ben had stood behind her, pushing her forward onto the bed, then, seeing it was too high for his purpose led her, now none too gently towards the ottoman at its foot. There, he had pressed her firmly onto her knees, her arms and head resting on the cold luxury of the sateen cover, her stomach touching her thighs and her child kicking at her ribs.

"No! Not like this! Even the Bible......."

Ben's hand had clamped over her mouth, "Shut up, woman. I'm no sodomite. I know what I'm about!" And somehow he had entered her from behind, whilst images of dogs at their bestial procreation had filled her mind and she had sobbed both with fear for her child and with humiliation.

After he had left her, Sarah remained on her knees in an attitude of prayer but the words that filled her mind were neither mild nor humble. They were incantations of smouldering intent that one day she would reverse their roles and that he would lie at her feet.

Sarah felt Ben moving about the room but she didn't raise her head. She sensed him go over to the window, heard the curtains rasp as he pulled them open and then the exclamation of horror as he looked out into the darkness of Christmas Day. His shout coincided with the clatter of running boots in the street and a pounding on their door below. Nightingale threw up the sash window and shouted down into the horse-road. "Hey! Up here! What's up? What the bloody hell is gooin' on?"

"Mr Nightingale! Sir! Oh sir," a child's thin voice wailed, "Come quick. The station's afire and it's spread to the cut. Even yer boats are blazin'. They'm savin' yer 'osses, mister, but you better cum to yer barges."

For one split second Sarah felt that God was in his heaven after all, that Ben Nightingale was indeed a bird without a song to sing. The picture of her husband with his mouth open and nothing to say struck Sarah as amusing and it was to his wife's bitter laughter that Ben ran from the room and out into the street, stuffing shirt into trousers as he dashed to save his livelihood.

The fire, which had begun in the waiting room of the little wooden station had spread with amazing swiftness, setting alight buildings, platform and the narrow covered bridge which spanned the line. Even the fields of sparse grass that grew on the spoil heaps of the old open cast mines around the station were ablaze. The very ground burned and smoked – a fair replica of hell itself. The canal towpath was inhabited by smouldering ropes snaking towards the already blazing barges. Open boats packed with coal burned with an unimaginable ferocity. How the fire had reached its peak so quickly and without being discovered was incredible. By the time Nightingale got to the flames men were already toiling with buckets and brooms trying to stop the fire from spreading. Simply to contain it would be a victory.

Christmas morning dawned upon charred ruins and blackened, sinking hulls that steamed in the frosty air. Women, their faces white and drawn with fatigue, stood at their doors waiting for their exhausted men folk.

It was not his wife who stood at Ben's door. Em, Sarah's friend, waited for his return and when he did she hardly recognised the grimy spectre of a broken man. She was half afraid to heap another trouble on his head, but whispered that his mother was upstairs with his wife, whose labour was already dramatic in its intensity.

Ben hauled himself up the stairs and, hearing Sarah's groans of pain, opened the bedroom door and pushed his protesting mother aside.

Sarah was aware of his arrival and, through her haze of agony, the words, "You laughed, you bitch. You laughed whilst my boats burned. God sent birth pains to humble women and I'm prayin' that yourn are good'uns. Suffer little children to come unto me! You do the sufferin' ma wench and the boy'll come unto me alright. He'll be mine. D'you 'ear? Mine!"

Abel, conceived in loneliness and shame was born into the smoking ruins of a relationship that had never even begun.

Nightingale never forgave his wife for laughing that Christmas morning and he never forgave himself for satiating his lust when he might have listened to her warning and saved his barges. His bitterness overwhelmed them both.

★ ★ ★ ★ ★ ★ ★ ★ ★ ★ ★ ★

It took almost a year to rebuild the station – this time in brick – and it took the same length of time to sell the Williams' property and move into a tiny house next to the head of the entry in a neighbouring court.

Nightingale was back where he started, working for other men's profit. His only consolation was that he had pulled Sarah down with him.

Mrs. Sarah Nightingale, however, set out to astonish the gossips. She was well aware that no one expected her to be able to adjust to the severity of her new life. She hated the poky little house, its lack of light and running water but worse was the shared closet, the queuing at the stand pipe, the washhouse with its camaraderie from which she felt excluded. Even so Sarah had embarked upon her own private war. Never did she intend to let Nightingale see her fail.

The women of Twenty-Four Court witnessed Sarah's amazing adaptability as she developed unexpected skills and brought new richness into the court. She was always the outsider but they grew to respect a woman who could read and who didn't object to turning her hand to unpleasant jobs. Her kitchen was as damp and dreary to begin with as theirs but whitewash, soap and a mop did wonders and a gleaming range with its cheerful fire did the rest.

Most of her belongings had had to be sold and in any case would have been out of place but Sarah had kept her books and some of her mother's tableware. The books lined one wall of the room on shelves that Nightingale had deigned to erect and meals were always set on a spotless tablecloth set with napkins in their rings, polished cutlery and flowers culled from hedgerow and cobble cracks. Sarah Nightingale, nee Williams, would remain true to her origins – if she could.

Sarah's indomitable spirit might have prevailed except that she remained a woman. In the marriage bed Nightingale was master.

Out of it his muscle power and latent ferocity created an aura of male authority in a world of masculine domination. He hated her. He daily witnessed her loss of status and this symbolised for him his own failure. Only through his children could he now be seen to succeed and being seen to rise up that ladder again remained all- important to Ben Nightingale- seen by the inhabitants of Twenty-Four Court, seen by the congregation at the church which he still frequented and seen by his alienated family who had watched his downfall from a distance and relished it.

Chapter Three

Gertie was woken by the bang of the kitchen door followed by the muffled sounds of her father in the entry. She heard him emerge into the roadway coughing and clearing his throat noisily beneath her window. There was a moment's hesitation and then the sound of his heavy boots on the cobbles trudging away into the darkness.

Now fully awake, Gertie turned over and pushed one hand under the curtain that divided her bed from Abel's. She tugged at his bed covers. "Abel", she whispered, "he's gone. It's time to get up."

"Huh?" Abel stirred and stretched, "You too working girl. What's sauce for the gander is sauce for the goose."

"Who are you calling a goose? Anyway I'm up." Gertie was standing at the window looking down into the street below, where indistinct forms, bent slightly against the gradient, were already hurrying to their employment. In a short while she would be one of them, a schoolgirl no longer.

Fifteen minutes later Sarah was putting bread and tea in front of her young people whilst the flat iron heated to smarten up the flounces on Gertie's clean, white pinafore. She spread the garment on a folded sheet already covering half of the scrubbed table top.

Abel was teasing his sister good naturedly about the size of her expected wage packet and Sarah felt the warm glow of satisfaction as she looked at her offspring. How she had managed to produce two such open, uncomplicated, young people she found it hard to imagine. It was as if they had selected all their qualities from their Williams' roots – gentle, scholarly traits that their mother had nurtured and their father seemed to despise. Only in Abel's looks had the Nightingale influence shown and there the thick set, muscular body had been drawn out into a taller athletic build whilst the dark swarthiness had mellowed into an attractively olive skin which complimented his dark hair.

Both children had been reading long before school had claimed them from her, and Sarah was satisfied that they were now using their education to avoid the long hours and awful conditions of the local factories.

Sarah reached the heavy iron off the hob, holding its handle carefully with the pot cloth. She upturned it and spat accurately onto its flat bottom. The globule of spit sizzled like hot fat signifying that the iron was ready for use. She recalled her husband's breakfast and smiled.

By half past seven Abel was on his way to the Detheridge office whilst Gertie was nervously arriving at Leadbetter's shop. She was concerned about which door she would be expected to use – the shop or the house but she need not have worried for Nellie came scurrying round the corner, sharp on the half hour. They were just in time to be standing together in the shop doorway as the 'Closed' sign on the inside of the glass swung round to 'Open' and a pair of bespectacled eyes peered out over the top of it. Seeing his employees standing outside, stamping their feet to keep warm, Mr. Leadbetter, 'grocer extraordinary', nodded approvingly and pulled back the door bolts.

Gertie was ushered inside by Nellie, only to stand uselessly amidst a frenzy of activity as shutters were lifted down and stacked in the passage behind the shop, blinds were rolled up and gas jets turned higher. Then there were sacks to be opened, scoops put ready, tea weighed and butter cut and patted.

By half past eight the shop was functioning and Gertie was receiving advice from Mr. Leadbetter. "Familiarise yourself with the whereabouts of stock, my dear. All goods are priced. We'll show you the cash register..."

"After breakfast," chorused Nellie cheerfully.

"Thank you, Nellie,... later," Her employer allowed a ghost of a smile to hover around his mouth and then disappeared into the living quarters for his breakfast.

"On the dot, 'e goes. Daren't be late for his vittels or the old dragon'll 'ave 'im. Best keep out of 'er way. Now luv, let's show you this register."

By the end of the day Gertie felt that she knew what she needed to know about shop practices. She'd made herself useful sweeping the yard, decanted vinegar from the big barrel, and ruled out some new pages in the order book ready for use. Nellie had been glad of her help in bolting up the shutters and when they were let out of the back door into the entry the old lady puffed out her relief that Mr. Leadbetter had taken Gertie on.

"'Ee's a decent bloke, Gertie. Not unreasonable at all but 'es not one for changes. E knows as I've wanted to finish these six months or more but 'e wouldn't 'ave it – kept on asking me to do another stint and like a fool I 'ave. Mi sister needed me when 'er 'usband took sick. I should 'ave gone but I didn't and she managed. Now she's by erself and, well, I'd like to go to 'er – prune the roses, mek some jam together, mek up with 'er really, I suppose."

Gertie nodded her understanding. "It's worked out alright then for both of us, Nellie. I needed a job and this one's fine. Just another couple of days and I'm sure I'll be useful."

Three days later Gertie was useful and Mr. Leadbetter was delighted. The change that he had dreaded had been accomplished very smoothly. Nellie had taken herself off to her widowed sister and his new assistant was providing a competent and cheerful service to the very regular clientele who patronised Leadbetter's Grocery Emporium.

Perhaps one of the most valued customers was a widow of very comfortable means who swept into the shop towards the end of Gertie's first week.

Mrs. Peake was a large lady with a full bosom of which she was immensely proud. She blew into the shop like a full rigged galleon, sails billowing and all hands on deck. She had an impressive presence that commanded immediate attention.

Whatever else she wore Mrs. Peake decked that splendid chest with her spoils of war – her frothy, expensive Flemish lace jabots held in place by one of her many magnificent cameo brooches. She similarly adorned her fingers with gold and diamonds that would have made any pirate's eyes sparkle.

Mrs. Peake enjoyed her widowed status immensely, living very well on the proceeds of her dead marriage and sharing her ample resources with a small close circle of similarly placed lady friends. They travelled, enjoyed music and the theatre, discussed their avid reading in tea shops and parlours, and, of course, became social benefactors of numerous good works. In fact Mrs. Peake appeared to be, like the rest of her set, a lady very much in control of a busy and satisfying life.

The truth of the matter was that although the good lady did enjoy this rather self- indulgent existence there was an emptiness in her heart.

Mrs. Peake felt that she had earned her pleasures by thirty-five years of marriage to a dry stick of a man rather older than herself. He had been distant and pompous. Behaving civilly towards him had been a trial only made bearable by his increasing wealth. She now felt that her freedom was a much-valued commodity and, of course, she had sufficient funds to enjoy it but she had to admit to a secret loneliness.

Mrs. Peake had produced two children from her cold marriage bed. The first had very nearly killed her. Its overlarge head had refused to be born and she had held onto the towel slung across the bars of the bed head for two days whilst the doctor tried to save the baby at the mother's expense. The medical man's directions had been quite clear. The child had not been baptised. It must be saved physically so that it was at least long enough in this world to be prepared for the next. Mrs. Peake had received her last rites. Her husband had been and gone with no show of emotion.

The doctor failed. The dead infant was pulled in pieces from the womb and the mutilated mother lived.

From then on Alice did her very best to avoid her husband, a situation that did not appear to concern him over much so long as the social niceties were preserved. Then he reached his half-century. This high water mark appeared to affect the prematurely ageing gentleman who saw death staring him in the face. His business was thriving, his house respectable, his bank account wealthy - and yet he had no heir. In consequence he set about begetting one. He coldly disregarded his wife's genuine fear of a repeat performance of her previous labour and eventually succeeded in rooting his seed.

Isobel was a disappointment to her father and a joy to her mother. Mr.Peake had wanted a son and so he was not pleased. Mrs. Peake loved this tiny little girl child who had slipped so easily into this world without sending her mother into the next.

No further pregnancies ensued. Mr. Peake contented himself in scheming for an advantageous marriage and pinning his hopes on a malleable son-in-law to inherit the business. A carriage accident that claimed the life of his daughter and her governess put an end to his plans.

At seventy Mr. Peake felt too old and too dispirited to do anything but accept life's afflictions, and so he simply died: dying as quietly and tidily as he had lived, little colder in death than he had been in life.

The deceased's widow - twenty years younger - felt quite unwilling to be buried with her husband and was certainly of no mind to replace him and risk childbirth again. In consequence she made the most of her freedom, but missed her daughter sadly.

Alice Peake had never been an empty headed, feather brained woman. She had always taken an active interest in her home, overseeing the work of her servants, planning and costing, evaluating efficiency. She maintained a collection of receipts and when she wasn't socialising then she was adding to it or reading voraciously, escaping as she had always done into other women's lives. Her husband's demise might have altered some of her habits but she retained her love of reading and her meticulous supervision of her housekeeping.

It had long been Mrs. Peake's practice to check shop prices regularly and to buy in certain luxury items like good tea and candied fruits herself. In consequence she was a regular personal customer at Mr. Leadbetter's and instructed her servants to shop there too. Her household was small but its constant diary of entertaining made her orders worth having.

On this particular Friday morning Mrs. Peake was very anxious to organise her purchases wisely.

"Good morning Mr. Leadbetter." Mrs Peake spoke loudly, disregarding the presence of other customers, assuming precedence over everyone.

"Mrs. Peake, ma'am," Leadbetter stood back from the cheese he was cutting and gently directed Gertie to complete serving his current customer who showed no surprise at his desertion.

In her periphery vision Gertie could see her employer dancing attendance on his best customer, assuming a servile stoop as he approached Mrs. Peake, rubbing his hands together as if to warm them. "Uriah Heep," Gertie thought attaching the name of one of her favourite author's characters to Mr Leadbetter. Totally on cue she heard Mrs Peake's strident tones.

"Why, Mr Leadbetter, you should go into music hall – dramatise some literary characters – I do declare you are a regular Uriah this morning."

The grocer missed both the critical edge on Mrs. Peake's voice and the point of her sarcasm directed at his sycophantic servility. Gertie, appreciating the literary allusion, grimaced at the cheese.

Mrs. Peakes' sharp eyes missed nothing. She noticed the slight bob of the young assistant's head and her tightly compressed mouth. Gertie felt the older woman's glance and momentarily looked up. Their eyes met and in that brief second both their mutual understanding and complicity were affirmed.

The next half hour was spent in attending to a steady queue of customers, but by the time Mrs. Peake had finished noting her list of prices and checking on delivery dates for her specific varieties, Gertie was free. She stood beside the shop door, hands clasped neatly in front of her as she had been taught. Mrs. Peake's voice carried across to her.

"And now Mr. Leadbetter, I need to think about dishes for a very particular dinner. The son of a business acquaintance and two of his young friends are coming up from Oxford - walking along Hadrian's Wall for a holiday - mean to stop over with me for one night. French boy. Here learning English. Father's in wine. Met him through my late husband. Business association. Glass. I'd like to have an appropriate menu but I feel quite out of touch with young people these days and so is cook. Have you anything new, perhaps in your tinned range of products or even bottled that are a favourite amongst young men? But. Oh! Mr. Leadbetter, how foolish we are! You have a young person on your staff. Would you mind? I'd appreciate discussing options with your young lady."

"But of course, ma'am," Mr. Leadbetter retreated, shuffling backwards as if from royalty and gesturing to Gertie to take his place.

Gertie was nervous about assisting this larger – than - life lady who appeared to be such a strong, forceful character but she did not need to be anxious for Mrs Peake's sharp wit was not to be directed against her. She genuinely wanted to discuss dishes and commodities and hear what the young assistant had to say. Gertie had, of course, absolutely no experience of high class cookery, her own home having always been too poor to indulge in any food other than staple sustenance. Nevertheless, she entered into the spirit of the discussion, describing the size of Abel's appetite and his preference for meat and cheese to sweet puddings. Mrs. Peake took this for confirmation that she should advise cook to emphasise the savoury courses and omit the soufflés and creams in favour of a good cheese board and fresh fruit.

Content with the conclusion of their discourse, the two ladies drew apart and Mrs. Peake prepared to leave. As she turned to bid the proprietor goodbye she found him leaning over the counter sorting the contents of his money drawer. He had made several piles of coins and was in the act of straightening each column into regular, neat little metal pillars.

"Mr. Leadbetter, I'm off now. No - don't disturb yourself. Your girl will see me out. Far be it for me, dear man, to interrupt Silas Marner at his labours."

Once again Mr. Leadbetter failed to comprehend the literary reference, this time to a solitary miser and smiled ingratiatingly at the retreating form of his best customer. "A very good day to you ma'am - a very good day indeed!"

As Gertie held open the door for Mrs. Peake to sweep through she uncharacteristically forgot her lowly status enough to venture a comment that almost cost her her job.

"You are well read, Mrs. Peake," she said, admiration lighting her face, " Do you love books as I do?"

Mr. Leadbetter almost jumped over his polished counter in his desperate anxiety to separate Mrs. Peake from the unacceptable conversation of his new assistant. He all but flew over the stone flags of his shop floor in his desperation to stop the attempt at familiarity and equality that he was witnessing. He scurried across the intervening space and then applied his brakes frantically as he heard the impossible response.

"Indeed I do, my dear. I have a vast number of novels that sit dustily upon my shelves at present. If you would care to call, with the small packet of special tea Mr. Leadbetter has promised, I shall be very pleased to show them to you - even lend you a volume should you find one to your fancy. I shall look forward to seeing you...Miss....?"

"Nightingale ma'am."

"Nightingale. It suits you - the name. I shall look forward to your call, Miss Nightingale." Without waiting for a reply Mrs. Peake swept from the room, leaving her invitation crackling in the air. If she had amazed Mr. Leadbetter Mrs. Peake had also surprised herself. She was not in the habit of inviting shop assistants home but.....well, this little Nightingale..... she seemed rather uncommon.

Mr. Leadbetter, deciding that discretion was the better part of valour, turned on his heel and strode back to his treasure, confident that the world in which servants mixed with their masters was indeed a topsy-turvy one.

Chapter Four

At the end of the day Gertie hurried home through the chill darkness with a light step. She felt that she had met a kindred spirit in Mrs. Peake and was genuinely excited by the prospect of access to more reading material.

Sarah Nightingale recognised the approaching footfalls of her family and could even tell their respective moods from the weight of their step and the speed of their walking. Even before Gertie hurtled into the kitchen, her hair awry and her words tumbling over each other, Sarah knew that something of moment had happened. She took the clammy shawl from her daughter's shoulders, hung it on a peg on the wall and pressed Gertie onto Mr. Nightingale's chair beside the fire.

"Warm yourself, Gertie love, while I brew some tea. Then tell me, slowly, what has got you all aflutter."

Gertie described her meeting with Mrs. Peake, her caustic wit, her grandeur and lastly her invitation. Mrs. Nightingale was duly impressed. It would do her daughter no harm to mix a little with people who were more suited to her than the likes of these in Twenty-Four Court.

The story of Mrs. Peake grew in its telling. For Abel, Mr. Leadbetter had been impressed by her striking such a chord of conviviality with their best customer. By the third repetition later that night in Clara's kitchen the incident contained a certainty of like minds in communion, with no possibility of the invitation being merely a casual pleasantry.

Clara listened wide eyed to the description of Mrs. Peake's almost cruel humour and laughed at the picture of pompous Mr. Leadbetter preening himself amidst misunderstood sarcasm which he had taken for compliments.

The two girls sat beside the embers of the fire talking in whispers whilst Clara's mother, Em, dozed fitfully in her corner bed.

Clara had not returned to school after the caning incident and had settled resignedly into her role of housekeeper, nurse and surrogate mother to her sisters.

Em was a wonderful patient. She knew that her life could not be long and so she basked in the warmth of her daughter's care, savouring each precious day that brought her contact with those she loved so deeply. Em's homespun philosophy was a system of checks and balances. . Death brought loss but also Heaven. Her sad illness brought the recompense of a closeness denied to many healthy mothers and daughters. Clara never ceased to be amazed at her mother's stoic acceptance of the manner of the end of her life. She had never heard her complain and her only regret seemed to be the unselfish despair at being unable to help her family. Clara respected as well as loved her dying mother and in her turn Em was proud of her eldest daughter's gentle capability.

Tonight Em slept. She had had a bad day with bouts of painful coughing and fever. Exhausted by her illness, she had drifted off into a restless doze and so was only dimly aware of the two girls who continued to exchange news of their respective days.

Suddenly a muffled knock sounded twice on the wall.

"Oh Clara! That's for me. Mother said she'd warn me when she was sending Abel round for me."

At the mention of her friend's brother Clara was aware of her colour rising. Clara had known him all her life and felt as though she had loved him forever. She longed to see Abel, to speak to him, but she always shied away, conscious of her unworthiness. She appreciated that she was plain and insignificant yet all the common sense in the world could not control her quickening heartbeats.

Clara knew everything about Abel. She had listened to Gertie's innocent references to her brother, watched him whenever she dared and spoken to him occasionally when he had initiated any brief conversation. Now her love actually hurt her as his nearness threw her into a panic of anticipation and awkwardness.

Gertie was totally unaware of her friend's secret, completely oblivious to Clara's discomposure. Usually so sensitive to emotions, so ready to empathise and sympathise, in this matter Gertie was quite blind. She was not, however, incapable of noticing the sounds in the yard.

Two sets of footsteps were approaching the back door, masculine boots on the bricks. The girls were confused, concerned. Who could this be so late at night? Thank goodness Abel was on his way. The back door was open before the raised hand outside could knock and Clara could see that one of the shapes was Abel's, the other was the looming black-caped shape of the doctor.

The two men entered. Their quiet movements reflecting a respectful awareness that this was a sickroom as well as a home. Their bulk and masculinity seemed overpowering and yet each man individually was intent upon gentleness and reassurance. Doctor Wilson was the first to speak, raising his eyes to the two girls' faces in turn, "Gertie, Clara," he acknowledged them both. "I do apologise for calling so very late but I was on my way home from Mrs.Potts's confinement- another girl bless her- and I bumped into young Abel here. When I asked after you all, Abel said that he thought he'd heard Em coughing badly tonight so I decided to just drop in for a moment to see how you are doing."

"That is good of you doctor," Clara had moved to stand beside her mother's bed, "She's not so well." Abel and Gertie had withdrawn to stand close together before the fire, not wanting to intrude and yet unwilling to leave Clara alone.

Em had woken but was clearly mithered, her head moving slowly from side to side, looking first at her daughter who held her hot hand on one side of the bed and then at the doctor who held her wrist professionally on the other.

"Good Evening, Em. You're in the best place. Nice and warm in here. A horrible night outside. Even the stray dogs have gone and sought shelter. Well, well, well, now what have we here? You're a bit warm, young lady. We'd better try and get you cooler. How are you feeling? A bit poorly?"

Em looked at the Doctor, suddenly lucid and clear. "Doctor. I feel......it's time. I really feel ready. I want to sleep - proper sleep. I want....to.....die."

Em didn't see the Doctor nod his head understandingly. She didn't see the horror in the exchanged glances of her young neighbours. Instead her head had turned towards her daughter whose breath had caught in her throat, "No, luv. No, I don't. I'm not ready yet. Don't tek any notice of me. I'm just being foolish."

Clara's eyes had filled with tears. Her lip trembled. As usual she sought solace in being practical and reached for the cool barley water on the stone shelf near the bed. The dangling beads of the linen cover clicked against the rim of the jug as she took it off and poured the misty liquid into a heavy bottomed glass.

Doctor Wilson helped Em to raise her head and take a few sips.

"Keep her cool, Clara. Keep your mother comfortable. Take no notice of the women in the court. They'd have you shut your windows and bank up your fire 'till it's a fair replica of Hell in here. Just keep the good lady comfortable. You can do no more. Now expect her breathing to become disjointed. She'll start to take rests sometimes. You'll begin to think she'll not breathe again but she will. I'll leave you something to help her sleep. She's tired Clara. She needs to sleep. We'll help her."

A bout of Em's coughing stopped the Doctor's advice and poor Em was almost lifeless when it ceased and she was laid down. The doctor looked at the piece of clean linen that he had held to Em's mouth. They all saw the blood before he folded it inside and threw the rag onto the back of the fire. As he pulled away from the flames he steadied himself, his hand on Gertie's shoulder. "She'll be needing you – Clara, I mean. Friends are going to be needed very soon."

Clara, busying herself at her mother's bed heard the Doctor's whisper and Abel saw her jaw clench and her expression stiffen as she fought the tears.

"A hot drink, Doctor?" Abel assumed control of the situation.

"Come next door. My mother will be pleased to see you. We'll not disturb Mrs. Watkins if we go to our house."

Clara looked at Abel gratefully. She wanted to show proper concern for the doctor but she would be glad to have the room quiet again, less claustrophobic. Doctor Wilson nodded his acceptance, took a small bottle from his bag and offered it to Clara, "Be careful with this, my dear. Keep it away from your sisters. A spoonful when she needs to sleep. As often as you like. It won't alter anything you understand – just make your mother comfortable."

Clara's eyes sought Gertie's and locked into her friend's unspoken message of understanding. Then Gertie smiled, opened the door and led the doctor out into the cold drizzle of the November night. Abel began to follow, hesitated and turned to Clara. He stretched out his arm and placed a hand very gently over her tightly clasped ones. He let it rest there for a moment, its soft pressure burning into the young woman's skin whilst she stood trembling inwardly and staring down at the rag run beneath their feet. Clara longed to look up, to meet Abel's gaze with her own but just as she gained the courage to do so Abel lifted his hand and turned to leave. "Remember Clara, we're only next door if you need us. Just knock. Anytime." And he was gone, leaving just the echo of his footfall and the tingling warmth of his hand on Clara's skin.

Em lingered for another week, half awake, half asleep.

The doctor's poppy potion sedated her and his visits reassured Clara that keeping her mother asleep was the kindest thing to do. If the medicine hastened death a little, only the compassionate medical man was to know.

The laboured breathing took on the anticipated pattern and Clara found herself, not dreading the end as she had expected but wanting it to come. She felt no guilt in wishing for her mother's demise for she had come to recognise Death, not as some gaunt spectre stealing her mother's life away but as a gentle visitor come to escort a weary soul to a better place. Clara's heart sank each time when, after a quiet interval, her mother breathed again. She longed for her mother to be at peace and in her weariness she thought- guiltily- of the uninterrupted sleep that had so long been denied her.

When the end finally came Doctor Wilson was actually present. By some good fortune he had stopped by and was easing Clara's fatigue a little by turning Em's pitifully thin body in order to relieve the pressure on her cracked heels and sore back. He had given her a dose of medicine and was purposefully lingering whilst warming his hands.

Both doctor and Clara heard the chain breathing become increasingly laboured and the room was suddenly silenced save for the ticking of the clock as they held their own breaths and waited for Em to breath again. This time she did not. "She's gone, Clara," whispered the Doctor," At last, my dear, she's gone."

Doctor Wilson closed Em's eyes and gentled the grimace of death into a more peaceful repose. As he straightened what was left of the poor emaciated body he asked, "Clara, do you want your mother's jewellery? If so we need to remove it now."

Clara heard her voice say, "Yes", and felt like a thief as into her hand were passed the plain gold wedding ring and the little gold brooch which had clasped her mother's bed shawl - the treasures of a lifetime. The gold was still warm with her mother's life and as she slipped the ring onto her finger Clara made a silent, solemn vow to fulfil her mother's obligations to care for the family. She looked down at the brooch resting now in the palm of her hand - two entwined hearts bearing the inscription – 'The Lord be between me and thee, when we are apart one from another.' The hearts were her sisters, the words lay like a bridge between her mother and herself.

By the time the girls returned from school and her father came down stairs from his restless, guilt-ridden sleep Em lay clean and at rest in her bed, ready for her loved ones to grieve over.

Whilst the house was wracked with shuddering, terrible sobs, Clara moved like an automaton. She neither wept nor spoke but reaffirmed her love for her father and sisters in the thousand practical things that needed to be done and in doing these she felt closer to her mother.

Sarah and Gertie were Clara's stalwart companions, taking her and the two girls into their own beds in Twenty-Four Court for the night. Clara was too exhausted to object. Meanwhile it was Ben Nightingale and Abel who kept watch over Em through the dark hours, with her distraught husband, missing his shift and being left alone upstairs to have, at least, some privacy in his grief.

Although Abel bore little affection for his father he had to grudgingly admit that Ben Nightingale was a good man to have around in difficulties. It was Ben who organised Em's final journey with the precision of a military operation. It was his authority that kept the distraught little girls and their father sufficiently under control to make some show of respectability out of doors and it was his arm that steadied Clara at the graveside.

Throughout the sorrow of the next two days both of Nightingale's children wondered at a side of their father that they had never seen. They could have been forgiven for mistaking his behaviour for altruistic concern - not so their mother. Sarah recognised her husband's "helpfulness" for what it was. She saw through his opportunistic sympathy and knew that throughout the whole tragic episode Ben Nightingale was acting out a role. He was fulfilling a carefully considered plan, enhancing his standing in the community, impressing the church-folk.

When Sarah saw how truly Em's husband grieved she found herself gripped by the sin of envy and envy of a dead woman surely had to be the most grievous sin of all.

"What have I become," wondered Sarah," envying my dead friend, begrudging my only friend, love?" She nursed her bitterness and let it mingle with her grief and sadness, sitting hunched over her sorrows, rocking back and forth as if she held a dead child in her arms.

Abel was alarmed at the intensity of his mother's grief. His father preferred not to notice.

Chapter Five

The brown tomb of winter earth cracked apart. White snowdrop drifts bloomed in sheltered spots. Snow laden clouds scudded across a cold, leaden sky without dropping their load. The twisted, grief stricken winter profiles of stark trees softened as leaves budded and began to unfurl. Despite the sorrow that still hid in the dark corners of Twenty- Four Court, springtime was coming and its invigorating message of optimism could not be denied.

Gertie crawled from beneath the covers of her bed and scrambled over to the windowpane, wincing as her bare feet came in contact with the cold floor. Her short- sighted eyes focused on the frost patterns on the inside of the glass whilst her fingers traced the grain of each shape.

"Just think, Abel, the magic of it all. These ice creatures and castles were our breath last night. Our goodnights froze into these wonderful grottoes and goblins. Oh look, Abel, do come and look, oh quickly do. This one's got a sharp little face.... and pointy ears and....."

"Gertie, you never grow up," Abel's voice, still gruff from sleep came from behind the curtain. "Look at you, lost in your magic world when it's time to rush around and get to work." He was moving now, groping for undergarments, shivering. " I bet Clara's been up making fire and breakfast this last hour or more!"

"Abel! That's unfair and you know it is. Clara does work hard but at least she's in a warm kitchen all day and not gritting her teeth in an ice cold shop!"

They bantered on, Abel emphasising Clara's positive qualities and Gertie accepting each paean of praise for her friend as a criticism of herself. What had begun as teasing became serious and sour until at last Gertie hissed, "Abel, stop it! You're making me quite jealous with such open admiration for Clara. I know you mean to josh but it seems to me that you are noticing my friend quite a lot. Indeed

I'm beginning to think that there is more to this than meets the eye. I'm going down - perhaps Mother will still appreciate me!"

Half an hour later brother and sister were striding down the road together, sliding unsteadily over the sparkling frost and stopping to crack the thin ice in the frozen wheel ruts like children, their sharp words forgotten.

A cab passed, its horses breathing steam and their metal shod hooves striking sharply on the frozen ground. Brother and sister halted to let it pass before crossing the road and taking the narrow alley that skirted the lock keeper's cottage. This neat little house was a delight, for its gardens were extensive and cultivated most professionally. Passers by could see easily over the green metal fence that surrounded the plot and often stopped to admire the geometrical fascination of its paths and beds. During three seasons of the year there was colour and fruitfulness to wonder at but at this time it was mostly drab, brown earth and similarly lifeless looking vegetation. This morning, however, canes, rustic fencing, bushes and the very ground itself was dressed in a silver tracery of frost, whose myriad crystals were reflecting light like the facets of a treasury of precious stones. Along the border of the garden clusters of early daffodils had forced their way through the hard ground and now neat, little, yellow buds sheltered amongst sharp green lances.

Gertie's vague sight beautified the little garden still further, seeing only the whiteness and sparkle against the earthy, brown background of the soil. She stopped beside the fence drinking in the sight of the early daffodils, dangerously coming into bloom in such proximity to the frost. "Daffodils are encapsulated sunshine," Gertie smiled up at Abel, proud of her choice of vocabulary.

"And so are you," her brother replied, the fondness in his voice palpable. He looked down at his sister's face and, not for the first time, wondered how such a beautiful girl with such a quicksilver mind could have issued from the ugliness of his parents' union. He let his gloved fingers trace the outline of her upturned cheek, "Be careful, little sister, how you cross these roads. Watch out for 'uggin's 'osses." And, leaving Gertie giggling at their childhood joke, Abel hurried away to his own employment.

Gertie dropped her head and began to walk swiftly. Without Abel beside her the old shyness had returned. Unable to see clearly and so identify passers-by, she was desperately nervous of nodding to a complete stranger or, worse still, ignoring an acquaintance. If she looked at the ground, as if picking her way carefully, she could avoid both pitfalls. In consequence, with her heavy shawl pulled up over her golden hair, its folds falling shapelessly about her shoulders and with her lovely eyes watching only where she put her feet, Gertie looked like any one of the other girls bundled up against the coldness, scurrying to their shops and factories.

When Gertie reached the vicinity of Leadbetter's Grocery Emporium she slowed her speed slightly so that she rounded the corner with some show of decorum. She could make out a tall, thin shape ahead, manhandling the shutters into the side entry where they would lean until needed again at night. Mr. Leadbetter sensed his assistant's approach and turned his balding head, smiling genially over his shoulder. He was well pleased with his new employee.

Gertie had proved to be an excellent addition to his small staff. She obviously enjoyed the military precision and order of his well-stocked shelves and overflowing baskets. At first he had been concerned that her natural reticence would produce a mouse like servitude, a scurrying, squeaking, frightened service not in keeping with his high-class establishment. He had expected more spirit, more strength from a Nightingale. But the beautiful young girl had quickly become comfortable with his customers, obviously delighting in being of service and swiftly developing a familiarity with his regular clientele which enabled her to remind them of forgotten items and even make tentative suggestions to add to their lists. Gertrude Nightingale was a natural saleswoman yet there was no aggression or pushiness about her.

Yes, Mr. Leadbetter was very pleased with Gertie. Whilst his sales rose agreeably he could even forgive her for forgetting her place with Mrs. Peake. In fact he was beginning to see a value in her growing habit of chatting companionably in quiet moments with certain customers. Several ladies, the older, reticent maiden ladies had begun to choose to shop at the less busy times, obviously lingering in the hope of conversation and often making one last extra purchase as if in gratitude for a few moments of Gertie's time – or perhaps to ensure her good offices for their next visit. He had noticed how often talk was of reading – periodicals, novels, the building of the new public library and its imminent opening. Indeed he had begun to wonder whether the little passageway which led through to the rest of the house might not profitably be cleared of its sacks and bundles, lined with slim shelves and filled with novels. His thoughts hadn't yet crystallised as to whether they ought to be there for sale or for borrowing, whether they would be there as a profitable venture or simply as a customer service – a sprat to catch a mackerel so to speak. Whatever the outcome of his deliberations, of one thing Mr. Leadbetter was perfectly sure. As he had repeatedly told his wife, "Gertrude Nightingale is an asset, Mrs. Leadbetter, a very definite asset. I don't know how we ever did without her."

"Good morning, my dear," the endearment sounded awkward as if the speaker was unused to such expressions of fondness.

"Mr. Leadbetter, sir." Gertie bobbed her head in acknowledgement of her employer's greeting, her hands already unclasping her shawl as she headed for the hook on which hung her pinafore. It was maintained to a snowdrift whiteness and as stiff and starched as the good lady who had been required by her husband to launder his employee's uniform. It had been sensible that Gertie did not carry her pinafore for, no matter how carefully it was ironed at home, it would, of necessity, arrive folded and creased. Mr. Leadbetter had simply seen the importance of smartness. Mrs. Maude Leadbetter's silent acquiescence and stiffened back told a different tale.

"Eggs first, my dear, then start to weigh out the tea- quarter pound packets, please."

By eight o'clock the shop was ready and Gertie was standing beneath one of the gas lights, warming her hands on a big mug of weak but welcome tea. Mrs. Leadbetter was a careful housekeeper.

Gertie's Tuesday had begun well, for her employer was on time for his breakfast and the Ceylon had arrived. This was the special tea that Mrs. Peake had requested. Mr. Leadbetter had not forgotten the arrangement and so, instead of the packet being labelled and added to the delivery boy's basket, it was sitting under the counter for Gertie to drop off on her way home. Gertie was excited.

The day continued in the same positive vein until by seven o'clock the shop was shuttered for the night, its front door bolted securely and Mr. Leadbetter counting up the takings with a gratified expression on his satisfied face. Only one gas light popped and flared now above Mr. Leadbetter and it shone on his polished forehead accentuating the retreat of his receding hairline. His long, thin fingers patted each pile of coins at the sides. He liked to see each column neat with no overlapping edges. He didn't raise his head as Gertie reached for her shawl with a "Goodnight, sir," but mumbled his response absentmindedly.

"I've got Mrs. Peake's tea, sir," she said.

Gertie went through the shadowy passage and tapped on the house door to be let through the kitchen into the entry. When there was no response she turned the knob experimentally and pushed gently.

Mrs. Leadbetter was bent over the range, lifting a saucepan. She straightened up as Gertie walked shyly into the kitchen.

"Oh, I'm sorry Mrs. ………" Gertie was embarrassed. She had thought the room was empty when no one had responded to her knock.

Mrs. Leadbetter's pinched face glared at Gertie through the yellow gas light. Her skin looked taut, stretched like old parchment across bones that were too big, "Is'e still in there then?"

"Yes, ma'am."

"Is 'e coming through?"

"I don't know, Mrs. Leadbetter."

"Well! There's a turn up for the book. You don't know! I was hunder the himpression that YOU knew everything, everything from the stock to the customers' needs. In fact, my girl, I was beginning to think you might be himagining that you knew your employer's needs too," the woman was staring at Gertie with unveiled hostility, her hands on her hips, obviously seeking confrontation.

Gertie felt exceedingly uncomfortable, totally at a loss to understand the woman's enmity, "Yes, Mrs. Leadbetter, ma'am. I hope I do. I try to do whatever Mr. Leadbetter needs me to do."

This was the wrong answer. It was not what the jealous wife wanted to hear. The angry woman turned on her heel, spinning round to face the range where she banged the pots down onto the metal hobs muttering furiously.

Gertie, confused and distressed, slipped behind her employer's wife, gained the back door, lifted its latch and hurried over its uneven step out into the entry. The day had been soured and Gertie didn't understand why.

Clutching the packet of tea, Gertie scurried away from the scene of her embarrassment, passing from the pools of light beneath each street lamp into the sporadic anonymity of the intermittent darkness. She was upset and wanted to talk to Abel. He would know why Mrs. Leadbetter was behaving so oddly. He always understood things. At this moment Gertie no longer cared about going to Mrs. Peake's. All that she wanted was her own home and her mother. But Gertie was trapped by her own good character, her innate reliability fuelled her sense of obligation to complete her delivery. So, shawl about her head and shoulders, eyes characteristically downcast, she continued into the cold night.

Gertie knew the street in which Mrs. Peake lived but was so lost in her analysis of her ordinary daily behaviour at Mr. Leadbetter's that she passed the address without realising it. She was startled from her reverie by a team of carriage horses being pulled to a halt just behind her.

Recognising that she had walked beyond the house that she sought, Gertie turned and retraced her steps to stand before the door of The Gables, hesitating whilst she pondered whether to knock, ring or try to find a tradesman's entrance. In the meantime a person was alighting from the now stationary coach and had followed her to the door. Whilst Gertie considered the propriety of the situation, the door before her swung open and simultaneously a familiar voice behind her urged, "Go in then, young lady. I'm glad that you have come."

The next hour did much to eradicate the earlier upset. The housekeeper, a Mrs. Horton, alerted by the arrival of the carriage, had been at the door ready to take Gertie's shawl and Mrs. Peake's travelling cape before moving ahead of them along a dim hallway into a cosy sitting room. There, she removed the fire guard, tickled the coals into a blaze and accepted a tray from a maid who appeared, bobbing and smiling, in the doorway. Then buxom, comfortable Mrs. Horton exchanged pleasantries with Mrs. Peake, commented on the sharpness of the weather, poured two cups of tea and, with a glance of benevolent curiosity directed towards her employer's young visitor, left the two ladies together.

Mrs. Peake had taken a chair on the opposite side of the fire, one identical to that which Gertie now occupied, a soft, padded, upholstered chair like nothing Gertie had ever experienced before. The nervous girl sat stiffly, her back ramrod straight, her mouth dry and all thoughts of conversation banished.

Her hostess reached for a long- handled toasting fork that hung incongruously on a hook beside the fire place and proceeded to push half rounds of buttered bread onto its prongs. "Nothing like tea and beggar's toast on a cold night, " she said, holding the bread near to the bars of the firegrate, "And I like to make it myself."

Gertie might have marvelled at an astonishing lack of formality or she might have experienced awkwardness at the breakdown of a formidable class barrier. In fact she did neither. She was affected only by the apparent normality of Mrs. Peake's actions. Suddenly it seemed absolutely right that she should be here in this delightful room with this approachable lady who was as welcoming now as she had been intimidating when she had first swept into the shop.

Conversation immediately focused on their shared interest in reading, novels at first and then Shakespeare. Mrs. Peake was full of regret that Miss Nightingale, who knew the substance of the works so well, had never actually seen a play performed.

"We should remedy that situation forthwith, my dear," stated the elder lady, giving Gertie the distinct impression that she had just been invited to the theatre. "But come along, Miss Nightingale, I wanted you particularly to see my collection of books. Now, be prepared. It is not, not, a library. My late husband always referred to this room," she was rising, leading the way out into the cold hallway, "as the study. Sounds so male and stuffy don't you think? I simply call it the...... here we are," she threw open a door, "the bookroom." She stood aside to give Gertie a first uninterrupted view of her little sanctuary, her much loved retreat, a room which had, in fact, always been hers despite her husband's nominal claim to it.

It was not a large room but it was lit by the glow of a welcoming fire and a table lamp spilling its light onto a desk littered with scissors and cuttings and pots of paste, all the paraphernalia of a recipe collector. Amongst the shadows at the edges of the room Gertie could see the walls lined with shelves and each shelf supporting its rank of books, impressive leather- bound volumes, a veritable treasury of tales. A comfortable chair stood at ease beside the fire, a footstool conveniently near it and a carriage rug draped across its arm. The atmosphere was at once studious and yet cosy.

"So many volumes," whispered Gertie entering the room reverently, "and so beautifully bound. May I?" She reached for a small book already lying to hand on the desk, caressed its binding, raised it and inhaled the wonderful leather, paper, bookish smell she so loved. Gertie turned the volume and stroked the uneven edges of its hand-cut pages. Mesmerised, she replaced the book and moved to the shelves, letting her fingers run along the leather spines as a musician might touch the keys of a new piano.

Mrs. Peake followed her guest into the room and very quietly closed the door. A big house is full of unwelcome draughts and her housewifely sense reminded her to conserve warmth. She felt very pleased to be in a position to give this young lady an opportunity to explore literature. It was a modern sentiment, this widening of opportunity, and one to which she was happy to subscribe.

"You may borrow….." and there the mistress of the house faltered, for she found herself looking, not at an impressed little shop girl but at a young lady whose face was alight with intelligence and enthusiasm. Gertie's myopic blue eyes were wide open, her quite beautiful face framed by strands of gold that had escaped the confines of her severe bun. Mrs. Peake steadied herself against the desk. This girl was almost the same age as her daughter would have been, her dead child, the lost companion of her widowhood and old age. "You will enjoy these books, my dear Isobel, and I? Well, I shall enjoy your enjoyment"

If Gertie even noticed the use of a wrong forename she was far too polite to correct her most mature hostess whose smile was so generous and whose laugh was now tinkling like that of a younger woman.

Gertie remained for a further hour leafing through volumes, expressing her delight at meeting old favourites and her excitement at reviewing new titles. Meanwhile Mrs. Peake sat contentedly beside the fire and saw in its depths the two of them in Birmingham, London, Paris, exploring galleries, enjoying the theatre, discussing a menu in an exciting restaurant. She spared no thought for Gertie's family, seeing only her own generosity. There was no inkling that in all this giving there might be some aspect of theft. She simply saw Gertie in frills and flounces, her face alight with appreciation and gratefulness. Alice Peake was imagining herself in the role of benefactress but she was not acknowledging that the giving that she envisaged was simply a route to receiving what she needed most.

By the time that evening was concluded the unlikely friendship was sealed. Gertie all but ran home, having protested that she did not need a carriage or an escort, either of which would have startled her family to say nothing of her neighbours. Her steps were as light as her heart and three novels were clutched beneath her shawl. Mrs. Peake watched from her window as Gertie's slim figure sped away into the darkness, leaving her with a sense of excitement that she had not experienced for a long while. Hope, that was it, hope and the joy of looking forward again.

★ ★ ★ ★ ★ ★ ★ ★ ★

Spring was evident only in Nature that year. Trees bore their leaves, buds burst and blossom tossed amidst the verdant foliage as usual. Amongst Englishmen, well versed in the topic of the weather, there was plenty to discuss for the March winds swept in like hurricanes and the April showers combined in a ceaseless deluge. Petals whirled in the air like confetti until the streets were knee-deep in discoloured blossom. By May the year had been written off as the coldest, wettest, most unpleasant in living memory and then came.... June.

During this inclement period Mrs. Peake had progressed gently with Gertie, making sure that the foundations of their relationship were truly firm. She did not want to frighten her away. This friendship mattered too much. Gertie was made welcome at The Gables, book changing usually coinciding with tea and an analysis of recent reading. If the young lady called and the mistress happened to be out, then Mrs. Horton, obeying instructions, let Gertie into the bookroom and brought her refreshments. If she wished to stay and read then the fire was lit and the lamp turned up. If she wanted to stay late then Mrs. Peake insisted that the stable lad escort her home. There was no need for Abel to become nervous and come seeking his sister.

Gertie was happy. She read voraciously, enjoying not only the new books available to her but also the opportunity to sit in that wonderful room, absorbing its atmosphere. In fact she loved Mrs.Peake's home, its smells of lavender and beeswax, its carpeted and polished floors, its fresh flowers and its pictures but the bookroom was her favourite place. It was so quiet. No street sounds reached the back of the house and Gertie valued the absence of noise. No slamming doors. No raised voices. No rattling buckets or privy latch. Gertie loved to curl up beside the fire, disturbed only by the coals settling or the sound of teacups trembling on the approaching tray.

By June Gertie was a relaxed and comfortable visitor. Mrs. Peake judged that the time was right to be more generous.

The skies were all rained out, only their blueness remained. The days were long and hot, evenings bound to be dry and pleasant, perfect for open-air theatre. 'Romeo and Juliet' was to be performed in the courtyard of the castle ruins before an invited audience and Mrs. Peake had two tickets.

She broached the subject of the entertainment and was delighted with her young friend's excited response. The Nightingale family did not object and saw reason in Gertie staying overnight with Mrs. Peake so that any post-performance celebrations could be enjoyed.

That evening was the first of many such pleasures for Gertie. She behaved with decorum and was such a delightful companion that her benefactress was quite charmed, although not at all surprised. Gertie would never be educated in society's sense of the word for she could only appreciate music not play or sing and her talents at drawing or needlework would always be corrupted by her short-sightedness. But she was well read and had a freshness about her criticism which made conversation lively

Gertie loved being Mrs. Peake's companion but she was under no illusions. She knew her own limitations. In consequence she retained her self- effacement and shyness, allowing her conversational skills to show only when Mrs. Peake encouraged them to do so.

Such moments appeared with increasing regularity as Gertie began to accompany her older friend to convivial little dinners and musical evenings more frequently.

Of course her wardrobe had needed attention but Mrs. Peake had seen to that and so delicately, suggesting that her family might be offended to see their daughter rigged out without their expenditure. It had seemed wise to keep her clothes hanging in the bedroom next to Mrs. Peake's. It would not be used. Gertie could regard it as her own. And so it came about that Gertrude Nightingale had a second home, richer, offering more opportunities and, it appeared, cushioned with genuine and growing affection.

Some of Mrs. Peake's friends although superficially charmed by this fresh young lady declared themselves, privately, to be rather concerned that a shop girl should be so at ease amongst them. Although they were careful not to offend, Mrs. Peake could not help but be aware of a certain 'atmosphere', an almost imperceptible cooling- off of camaraderie. Benevolence, it seemed, was only valued when recipients were anonymous and distant. Dear Mrs. P. was taking her 'good works' a little too far.

Meanwhile attitudes were changing in Twenty-Four Court. Mrs. Nightingale, who had always stressed her gentle origins and had been proud of her bookishness along with the literary interests of her children, seemed to have become angular and full of prickles where culture was concerned. She, who had decried the common crudity of her husband and had been pleased to see her daughter mixing with decent folk, appeared suddenly critical of Mrs. Peake.

"Drop you, she will. Give you the taste for the fine life then leave you high and dry, our Gertie. Stands to reason. You can't accompany her like she wants. She'll find another little pet. Just you wait and see."

"Mother, she's not like that." Gertie was not blind to the hurt in her mother's eyes. "I understand what you're saying, that you're trying to protect me – that maybe you even miss me....."

"Gertie! Of course I miss you. Don't you think I'd like to be with you at the theatre and all, but I've done it, love. I don't feel jealous of you doing it. It's how and who with that worries me. I know how you're going to feel when that door doesn't open for you. I've got to remind you that you're a shop worker, love. You work in a grocery."

"I know, Mother, but I live here, with you. I come home and I can always come home – can't I?"

Sarah wagged her head sagely, "Home's home, love. Forever. Just be careful, that's all."

Abel, too, worried about Gertie. He shared his concerns with Clara on many an occasion when he delivered a message from his sister, excusing her absence yet again because of an unexpected commitment to Mrs. Peake. Clara missed her friend's regular company although she delighted in the second hand experiences that they still shared occasionally. She and Abel had smiled as they recalled Gertie's discovery of the power of opera glasses and her prancing and posing as she relived a theatre performance for them. But they remained afraid for Gertie in her new existence, leapfrogging between classes, a shop girl in a parlour. They were desperately concerned that she was going to get hurt.

Mrs Peake was not unaware of the unconventionality of the situation. She saw the difficulties that late nights brought to Gertie's early mornings although, secretly, she was rather proud of the way her young friend coped with the social gymnastics involved. Nevertheless, she had grown protective of Gertie and did not want to expose her to even the slightest ostracism. She knew how some of the young ladies raised their eyebrows when expected to take tea or a seat next to a shop girl.

A woman of the world, Mrs. Peake recognised that it was time for change. Gertie was blossoming, becoming more astute with her fashions, developing an alluring beauty that put other young ladies on their guard. They would be looking for reasons to exclude her – to avoid her competition. Something had to be done.

It would have been easy for Mrs. Peake to have suggested that Gertie left her grocery employment, that she become her paid companion but that smacked of manipulation – and, whilst Mrs. Peake turned over this possibility in her mind she also sought another alternative route to respectability.

The answer eventually came in the form of Mrs. Peake's younger brother, Samuel. Samuel Lees was a cultured and educated gentleman but one who liked being gainfully employed and appreciated the extra independent income. Since his university days he had enjoyed association with books, working first as a scientific proof- reader and more recently with a publishing firm. Suddenly a change of opportunity had occurred. The new town library, a grand affair, was to open in September and sought a librarian – a chief librarian, to nurse the council's status symbol through its birth pangs. They needed a gentleman of breeding, education and stature. Mr. Lees was their man.

The new Free Library as it was locally called did not, as yet, house an enormous number of books but Mr. Lees was to be granted an assistant, so long as it was one who did not command an exorbitant salary.

One evening Samuel was pondering on the working of an advertisement which he intended to post and which he hoped would attract applicants with the attributes he required. He was seated at one end of his sister's rather long and splendid dining table, enjoying one of her appetising dinners. He had just finished elaborating the traits that he would be looking for in his assistant when his hitherto silent sister suddenly put down her claret, looked at him forcefully and stopped his musings with, "Samuel….. I've got it! You don't need to advertise. You can avoid tedious interviews, speed up the whole process. No need for references. I know the very person."

Samuel stopped chewing and looked at Alice, waiting with interest for her suggestion.

"Gertrude, Samuel. Gertrude Nightingale."

Samuel resumed his mastication, picked up his glass and dismissed the idea with, "Oh, your little companion! Really, Alice! What next?"

"Talk to her, Samuel. This isn't a stupid suggestion. Talk to her properly, my dear. You never have. Please, for my sake, talk to her about books."

Neither Alice nor her brother told Gertie what had passed between them. Alice was adamant that Gertie would be perfect for such employment, which she saw, quite rightly, as an entrée into a different social class. Mr. Samuel Lees was equally as certain that the whole idea was nonsense and that he would prefer a man in any case. Nevertheless, to please his determined sister, he engaged the young lady in question in a conversation on the very next available opportunity.

Once the subject of literature had been broached it quickly developed into a deep discussion that moved from favourite authors to detested works, from unfair and unenlightened criticism, to bindings and illustrators. Samuel even found himself inviting Gertie to offer her ideas on the function of a public library and the relative size of the fiction section. In her interest Gertie forgot to be shy. In her enthusiasm for poor people having free access to books she sparkled. She left Mr. Lees, Chief Librarian, in no doubt at all and as convinced as his sister that he had found a reliable assistant – and after all a female would not expect to be paid such a great salary. The committee would appreciate the economics of his choice.

Mr. Lees was, however, a cautious man. An interview in a

drawing room was still not quite enough. He needed to support his professional judgement, perhaps see Gertie in her place of work, yes that would do.

In consequence Mr Lees went so far as to accompany Mrs. Peake to Leadbetter's Emporium where he was agreeably affected by its order and by Gertrude's professional manner. She was not servile at all but efficient and smart. Even so, it was an unusual leap from shop to library and, had it not been for his sister's forceful encouragement, Mr. Lees may very well have developed cold feet about the whole business.

As it was he found himself talking quietly to Mr. Leadbetter about his intentions and exploring how soon Gertie could reasonably be released from this employ, — should she wish to leave, of course. Mr. Leadbetter was not a happy man and showed great tenacity in trying to keep his 'golden girl'. The grocer's reluctance to part with his assistant served to increase Samuel's keenness to have her and so the two men repaired to the house to discuss the matter in relative privacy.

"I depend on her a great deal." Mr. Leadbetter was firm. "I really can't do without her."

"With due respect, Mr. Leadbetter. She is not your property. I don't believe she has signed any articles with you. She is not bound at all."

"Not the point. Not the point, sir," argued the worried grocer.

"Indeed it is, the very point. I shall, I fully intend to offer Miss Nightingale this position. I feel sure that she will wish to accept. The whole point of my conversing with you is to establish a fair term of notice – a week, sir, a fortnight?"

"A month!" spat out Mr. Leadbetter, recognising that he had lost.

"Excuse me, gentlemen," Mrs. Leadbetter sidled across to them from the fringes of the discourse. "I wonder if I might make a suggestion." Her husband shot her a suspicious glance. "If I were to take Miss Nightingale's place in the shop for a period then we could free her almost at once." Her suggestion was rewarded by a withering look from her husband and a beaming smile from the librarian. The matter had been settled but, as yet, Gertie knew nothing.

It was actually Mrs. Leadbetter who broke the news to Gertie, a crowing wife, confidently assuming her position once more as her husband's partner and glad to see the last of a too pretty young assistant. She bustled imperiously into the shop ahead of the gentlemen, interrupted Gertie's quiet conversation with Mrs. Peake and announced the arrangements for Gertie's change of position, if she so wished. She managed to make the alteration sound like a definite demotion but Mr. Leadbetter's sad face confirmed the truth of the situation. "I don't want to lose you, my dear. Indeed I do not. But we won't stand in your way if that is what you want." – And of course it was.

Chapter Six

As Sarah walked back down the yard from the privy, comfortable household sounds reached her as she passed the homes of other court residents. She recognised ashes being raked, the squeak of fire bellows and the brief morning exchanges of families still emerging from sleep. She never ceased to wonder at the use of the word 'court' to describe this collection of poor homes crowded together around the dark little yard. It was a far cry from the splendour of the Queen's Court, she felt sure.

It was early, not yet seven o'clock. An autumnal mist was shrouding the rooftops, the ground and windowsills damp as if with rain. A door opened and Matthew, still shrugging into his coat that was barely large enough for his lanky frame, came out into the courtyard. Mrs. Baker followed him, billycan and tuck box in her hand. She was a small, spry, bird-like little woman who never ate enough because she was too busy feeding the cuckoos in her nest. Her husband had played away from home with amazing regularity when he was younger and, being a soft hearted, affectionate fellow, had usually brought his dirty linen home to be washed. In consequence his longsuffering little wife had brought up a tumble of tousled heads, her own and other women's with an unexpected warmth and compassion. The result was one of the happiest families in the court and a father on a short leash now that his offspring were old enough to keep him under control.

"Forget your 'ead our Matthew, if it were loose." The busy woman thrust the supplies into her son's arms, nodded at Sarah in acknowledgement and hastened back inside her house, shutting the door forcefully – almost a slam.

It was the sharpness of the sound that hurt Sarah. She felt it like a slap in the face. Matthew had hastened off ahead of her and she followed his retreating form as he hurried towards the entry and was gone.

She stood for a moment on her own threshold, the weight of her sorrows heavier than usual this morning. She tried to tell herself that Mrs. Baker had not intended any slight, that a capricious wind on this still morning had snatched the door from her neighbour's hand but it was of no avail. Sarah knew herself to be ever the outsider. Even after a quarter of a century of sharing their lavatory, their washhouse, their births, their sickness and their deaths she was still on the edge, still only tolerated, the lady living amongst the gypsies. Only in Em's little house had she felt wanted and now that there was a widower there her visits had been curtailed. The demands of propriety were strict. When people lived on top of each other and personal space was negligible, social rules were clear and unrelenting.

Sarah felt so alone. She wished there were another woman of her own age that she could talk to, someone who would understand her concern. She had gone over a year without any sign of her monthly visitation then, suddenly, the covered rag bucket was full of her soaking cloths. The metallic smell of blood had flooded her nostrils and she had realised that once again she must face the fear of unwanted pregnancy....... or worse. The latter, nameless fear niggled perpetually at the back of her mind for weeks, even more so since after the bleeding there had been this terrible, utter exhaustion.

With the tiredness and dreadful depression had come the awareness of having lost, and perhaps that was worst of all. Throughout the greater part of her marriage Sarah had supported herself with one determination: not to lose. She had vowed to herself over and over again that one day she would be the victor in this power struggle with Ben Nightingale, even if the only way was to out live him. She had wanted to be in the position to belittle that possessive, aggressive man who called himself her husband. Now she was beginning to fear that she never would. She was worn out, no different from the other women in the court, flinching from a man's muscle unable to balance the relationship by flaunting any sexual attraction. None remained. Nightingale hated her as vehemently as she loathed him. Yet still he used her, demanded his right to demean the woman that once upon a time he had wanted as much as life itself.

Sarah let out a long drawn out sigh and bestirred herself to enter her own kitchen. Gertie was kneeling in front of the fire drying her hair. The luxurious curtain of silk fell around her face and shoulders reminding her mother of fairy story princesses. Sarah smiled and felt her burden lighten a little.

Abel had finished breakfast and was fastening his coat, "I'll be late, Mother. Now don't forget and go worrying when I don't come home. You know that Mr. Detheridge is off work again and that I'll not come home till all is finished and I can lock up. 'Late' could mean very late. And good luck little sister. Enjoy your first day at the library. What time did you say you had to be there? Wasn't it ten o'clock?"

"A quarter to nine," responded Gertie, "and yes, it is a proper job and yes, I do get paid and yes, it does demand a few skills – unlike your post which only expects you to sit with your feet on a desk all day, drinking tea."

"Now then you two," interrupted Sarah, "That's enough leg pulling. You'll be late, Abel."

Abel bent to hug his sister, genuinely wished her well and left, kissing the air in his mother's direction.

A sour smell lingered in the entry. Abel was relieved to walk out into the street even though a mist still clung to the rooftops and its dampness threatened to creep into his bones. He peered up into the whiteness and found the sun, a glimmering ghost trying to penetrate the gloom.

One day, Abel promised himself, he would have a house with a sweet-smelling garden in which the sun could shine. He would save Gertie from the court and his mother from his father. This dream was an old one and, as Abel increased his pace walking briskly towards his office, he had to admit a new dimension had entered his fantasy. A shadowy female figure had hovered in the background for some time – it was now distinct enough to be recognisable as Clara. He couldn't go and leave Clara behind.

Immersed in these thoughts Abel arrived at the office more quickly than he had anticipated and he felt a sense of disappointment as he glanced up at the lightening sky for he knew that the mist would clear and that the day would be a fine one. Once inside the office today he expected to stay there. Resignedly, Abel drew a chain from his inside pocket and proceeded to employ two of the keys attached to it to unlock his firm's premises.

Mr. Detheridge was involved in several business interests, this particular one being the property office. Here, Abel had begun five years previously as a copy clerk but he had swiftly impressed Old Man Detheridge with his accuracy, industry and reliability. He had soon been entrusted with counting and accounts. Then he had been allowed to go out rent collecting, and so he had gone on, enlarging his experience and his responsibilities until now he had oversight of all aspects of this particular business, even to interviewing prospective tenants and maintenance of properties.

Rent collectors were not generally popular men but Mr. Detheridge was a humane proprietor who allowed Abel to indulge both sympathy and practical kindness. The Old Man had soon recognised that Abel possessed both integrity and originality. He was capable of independence and that was what Mr. Detheridge valued most – a manager who could be trusted to act upon initiative in a logical manner and make the decisions he himself might have made. He saw himself young again in Abel and felt a satisfaction in advancing a worthy employee's career.

Abel was exceedingly fortunate for when most rent collectors were unwelcome visitors he was received with smiles and invitations to 'warm himself' or 'take a drop'. He earned this appreciation by just being himself and it was entirely due to his employer that he had the freedom to be that. If times were hard then Mr. Nightingale had been reasonable about waiting for rent or even taking it in instalments. If an old lady felt it too embarrassing to visit the pawn shop then Abel had been known to save her feelings by passing under the three balls himself and getting her a better price than she might have otherwise obtained. Whilst other houses fell into dilapidation and there was overcrowding and squalor, Detheridge properties were damp free and generally housed only the more responsible tenants. It was enjoyable work. In fact Abel felt that, although his first concern was to ensure a profitable return for his employer's investment, his second was to provide decent, habitable houses for his tenants – and this he liked.

Old Man Detheridge appreciated the fine balance required to ensure profitability and respectability. He trusted Abel to maintain this. Of late this trust had been well tested for ill health had increasingly dogged the ageing gentleman, who had only been able to work in fits and starts.

Of course there was his son, Young Mr. Detheridge, but although he occasionally put in an appearance he was soon off to some appointment at the other establishment. This second, and perhaps more lucrative firm bearing the family name, was a solicitors' office which gave employment to eight legal brains and an army of office workers who supported their superiors' endeavours. Young Mr. Detheridge had received appropriate training and surprised both himself and his father by qualifying.

A potentially wealthy man, Arthur Detheridge enjoyed life. He was a horse man – racing, hunting, breeding, gambling or just plain talking horses was much more to his taste than working. He preferred to spend money rather than bothering to make it. Mr. Arthur still officially lived at home with his father and sister but, unofficially, he maintained another discreet residence, which was run by a housekeeper of uncertain years and questionable morals. That she had 'trodden the boards' in her youth was certain. That she had graduated to become a close friend of Lord Rothersby was a fact. That the now voluptuous lady had an infant who looked incredibly like Arthur Detheridge was a rumour not without foundation.

The Detheridge family was respectable. Had the Old Man learned of his son's predilections he would have responded severely and so a veil of secrecy hung over the leisure time of his son, who made a show of visiting the offices and putting his name to partnerships dealing with certain high profile cases, though acting only in the capacity of oversight, of course.

Arthur's sister, Agnes, knew very well how her brother spent his time, but, aware of her likely dependence upon him in the future, kept her knowledge to herself and maintained an aloof, if outwardly respectful, distance from him.

Abel had seen Miss Agnes on several occasions. She had swept into the office and out again with a rustle of silk petticoats and a suggestion of a smile on her very plain face but he had never exchanged more than politeness demanded. In consequence he could not know that she had wit and sympathy behind her heavy features and that whilst a stalwart heart beat within her ample breast, a keen intelligence nestled beneath her neat little hats.

Abel completed his unlocking and shepherded in the waiting clerks who had appeared at his elbow and were anxious to get out of the morning's chill. Soon there was a bustle in the office, a rolling up of blinds, a perusal of post, a lighting of fires and a filling of inkwells – everyone about his business and business being the only item on the agenda.

Soon the fires were burning cheerfully and the high, vaulted rooms began to loose some of their clamminess. Even in summer these rooms remained cool and so Mr. Detheridge liked to see each grate with its smoke spiralling upwards on every day of the working year. On a morning like this one the crackle and brightness of the hungry flames brought a homely feel to the premises.

Abel prided himself on doing everything as if his employer might arrive at any moment and so he was not concerned when at half past ten iron shod hooves and carriage wheels slowing and turning into the yard announced the arrival of Mr. Detheridge Senior himself. The old man entered the office with a joviality and sprightliness that his employees were delighted to see.

The clerks greeted their employer with genuine regard and were rewarded by his acknowledging each by name and in some cases his making reference to their families. Abel stood to one side, waiting to be noticed, a feeling akin to what he might have wanted to feel towards a father welling up inside him. He was glad to see Mr. Detheridge back on his feet again.

"Abel, my boy. Not caught you napping have I?" The venerable gentleman stretched forward a hand to grasp Abel's. It felt light and cold, its skin paper-thin.

"Yes indeed, sir. I'm afraid so. Just had my feet on the desk and my head back. You know me, sir! Just a quick snore mid-morning. Lucky I heard your carriage!"

"Come into the office, lad," Mr. Detheridge caught Abel's elbow and began to steer him between the standing clerks towards a room at the back, separated by a glass-paned door from the activity of the main offices. " I want to chat with you. Parton!" He looked around for a young lad scarcely in his teens, "Ah George! There you are. Bring tea will you please. And run out for a couple of crumpets. Toast them by the fire. Good lad! Glad to see they're lit properly. Best butter!" he raised one finger in mock authority.

The rest of the morning was spent companionably, Abel reporting to Mr. Detheridge, obtaining his agreement to a variety of larger expenditures and explaining a deficit here and a profit elsewhere.

The tea and crumpets had not long been digested when lunch was suggested and the two men repaired to the The Red Lion.

Once out of the office, conversation became less official. They ate amongst the red plush and polished brass of the pub's back room and talked of South Africa, married women's rights, the concept of model villages and the price of candles. Abel spoke of his pleasure at his sister's recent good fortune and his anticipation on her behalf as today was her first day at the library.

"Then she'll no doubt meet Agnes," Mr. Detheridge put down his fork and leaned forward confidentially. "Lives and dies for her books, my daughter. I know she plans to become a member of the New Free though I've told her she doesn't need any second hand books. She could have them new. She knows that! Should have been a boy, you know. She'd have done well in the legal profession. Shows more interest in business than that rapscallion son of mine."

"Young Mr. Detheridge, sir?" Abel responded with polite interest, aware that perhaps this was not a topic in which he should share.

"Yes, but no longer so young! Approaching middle age and showing no sign of marriage and settling down. I want grandsons, ye know. I keep telling Arthur, he's a duty to do. I'll not live for ever".

"You are looking better, sir. I'd not expected to see you back at work so soon. You quite took me by surprise this morning."

"Meant to, mi lad, meant to. Know you're trustworthy but it's the rest of the buggers. They might respect you but when all's said and done you're not me. Need to keep 'em on their toes. Now after lunch I'll be off down to t'other office. Jumped up little gentlemen we have down there. Oh yes, 'ighly h'educated, "he deliberately misused his aitches. "and very sure of themselves but quite capable of underhandedness. Need to know I'm checking receipts of fees, time spent on various suits. Quite capable of using my premises and my time – and the stationary come to think of it – to conduct a bit of private business. They tend to forget that I was a young lawyer once upon a time."

Abel allowed a sympathetic look of disapproval to show. It warmed the old man to his subject.

"And would my son check on them? To be honest, Abel, he's more likely to join in, making a bit on the side – a bit that doesn't go through the books or me."

Abel opened his mouth to disagree, to support the idea of a reliable 'and son' but his innate honesty destroyed his good intention and he remained silent. He suspected that however critical Mr. Detheridge was of Arthur there was still much more that he didn't know.

"Look lad." The old man had finished eating and had pushed his plate aside. One elbow was resting on the table, a pale chin cupped in an even whiter hand. "I've been pleased with what I've seen this morning. Not that I didn't expect to be – I did. You'll be supposing that now I'm back in harness you'll hand me back the keys and all will go on as before. Now it's not going to. Agnes has been talking 'sense' to me. I've promised her that I'll not overdo things, so I want you to keep your set of keys – carry on in charge – just report to me regularly and no doubt I'll poke my nose where it's not wanted."

"Well thank you, s......."

"Don't stop me yet lad. I'm just getting to the best bit. It's a responsible thing to carry keys. Responsibility equals pay. I'll be upping yours in accordance."

Abel let his delight show. He grinned at his employer, a wide, boyish grin of sheer happiness.

The old man laid a fatherly hand, gnarled and very slightly trembling on top of the strong, capable fingers at rest on the tablecloth, "My pleasure, my boy; my pleasure." he said.

Chapter Seven

Whilst Abel was busy at his ledgers in the early morning Gertie, in her new brown outfit and hair scraped back into as severe a style as she felt suited her new position, was walking with some trepidation towards the library.

It was an impressive building mainly of yellow stone but decorated with so many arches and buttresses, leaded windows and tiles that it was almost a fantasy. It was impossible to put a period to its style for the windows were Tudor, the tiles had a Roman aura and the arches were distinctly Norman. However, no one seemed to be at all concerned as to its authenticity so long as it was luxurious, a monument to benevolence, a source of gratification to those men listed on the board as donating incredible sums for the benefit of the working classes.

The caretaker had already opened the black, metal gates that swung across the outer edge of the porch at night to dissuade vagrants from taking shelter. In consequence Gertie walked through the echoing shadows of the porch past the notice boards, unreadable in the gloom and arrived punctually at the library entrance. She put a nervous hand onto the polished brass handle of the heavy mahogany door and pushed. It swung open on its newly lubricated hinges, allowing Gertie to move forward into a dream.

The library was one great room, vaulted like a church, with huge, arching windows which began at head height and reached almost to its ceiling. Below the high windows the walls were lined with shelves, many already full of books. More volumes filled enormous bookcases standing back to back to form a maze of little alleyways. Glass paned doors with their gleaming brass handles stood open, revealing an alcove furnished with tables and chairs, the former strewn with neatly arranged fans of news-sheets and periodicals.

Near to the doorway where Gertie stood entranced was the issue desk – a counter filled with an army of neat little rectangular trays in which numbered cardboard tickets stood to attention, awaiting the slips from borrowed books.

As Gertie entered, Mr. Samuel Lees looked up from sorting the morning's newspapers. Recognising her, he moved from beside the reading desk with one hand outstretched, the other adjusting the spectacles that rested precariously on the end of his nose. He took Gertie's small hand, pressed it within his own and let his eyes twinkle at her over his glasses, "Miss Nightingale. Welcome. Good morning to you and, again – welcome."

"Sir," Gertie smiled, " I am pleased to be here, Mr. Samuel, truly I am." She could see her new employer quite clearly now. He had lost the approachability of the parlour, seemed to be crisper, smarter, more alert. Suddenly Gertie's little confidence deserted her. She was untrained. She didn't know what to do – not even how to address Mr. Samuel Lees.

As if recognising his new employee's growing panic, Mr. Lees moved towards the issue desk and, in a kindly manner, indicated a door that led to a small convenience in which there were pegs for her coat, a washbasin and water closet. By the time Gertie emerged she was calmer and able to stand, gazing at the array of shelves, ready to admit that she felt as though she had died in the night and had just arrived in heaven.

Mr. Lees smiled when Gertie articulated that feeling, "Well, my dear Gertrude, I doubt if that sensation will last. There's a deal to do here – just the two of us. Now, in a way it's a bad day for you to start. Though the official opening was a month ago – and I'm sorry that you didn't manage to join us then – today is the first occasion that we are open to the public. No doubt we shall have gawpers and sightseeing riff-raff bringing dirt and cold draughts into our library but I hope, after a while, things will settle down so that we can concentrate on those with a genuine interest in reading.

Let me show you around, explain the systems to you, show you the ropes and then you'll soon be in a position to be of some assistance to me. Of course I've been buying and shelving for months on my own. It's rather nice to have company." The librarian smiled again, adjusting his glasses. He was beginning to feel more at ease himself. It had felt odd to receive a lady, whom he had conversed with in a parlour, as a new employee. He wanted to get it right – that balance between authority and approachability. "No need for you to deal with the public yet, not until you're sure of the layout. I'll deal with queries and issues. You just concentrate on becoming familiar with arrangements. Keep books in the right places – that sort of thing."

The morning passed swiftly. Gertie, handling the volumes as if each one were precious, didn't even notice the midday striking of the library clock. At this time the library closed for one hour. It was a temporary arrangement, just until the new assistant could be left to cope alone. Samuel had wondered whether he should invite Miss Nightingale to lunch but, deciding against it, went for sustenance leaving Gertie - locked in - to eat her bread and cheese alone. She didn't mind at all but predictably read while she ate. Then she carefully dusted the crumbs into the palm of her hand and deposited them in the waste- paper basket.

Mr. Lees, returning early from his lunch, was in time to glance through the glass in the library door and glimpse his new assistant pirouetting on the parquet, her skirts billowing around her like a skater's. "She's on thin ice," he thought." She'd better not be flighty".

During the afternoon Mr. Lees taught Gertie the issue system and permitted her to use the stamp. Her first duty of each day was to be to change its date accordingly.

The library was busy that afternoon but mostly with people who drifted in and out, heads on a swivel and eyes like saucers. Gertie wondered how many of them could actually read. A few people stayed to explore the newspapers and by 7:00p.m. it was necessary for the librarian to clear his throat dramatically and point to the sign displaying the opening and closing times. Then, jangling his keys officiously and turning out the lights one by one, Mr. Lees managed to persuade the last few readers that he was in earnest about closing the building. He shepherded out the remaining member of the public, left on the last gas light and locked the inner door.

"The caretaker will be along presently," he said, more to reassure himself than Gertie, "He'll check the gas and lock up safely. Now, Miss Nightingale – I confess I hardly know how I should address you – may I escort you through these ruffians who are playing hopscotch on our pavement?"

The gallant librarian offered his arm to his assistant and the two left the building in harmony, each with their own private reasons for satisfaction.

Gertie and Abel arrived home at exactly the same time, both bubbling with excitement and news. For once their father did nothing to spoil their pleasure and actually basked in their reflected glory. Meanwhile Sarah said little and sat in her straight-backed chair, her face uncharacteristically long and sour as if pained by happiness. Only when Clara appeared, anxious to hear how Gertie's first day had been, did Sarah's mood lighten for a moment as she made tea for her dead friend's child. Then she sat, a spectator, not participating in the high-spirited chatter that filled her kitchen for the rest of that evening.

When Abel came down stairs the next morning he was startled by his mother's pale face and closed expression. It confirmed what he had feared the previous evening – something was wrong – more wrong than usual. He ate breakfast and left with little conversation, worried by the obvious deterioration in his mother's health. When he had come in from the privy she had been wiping the back of her hand across her mouth and tipping water into the sink as if to swill something away. He hadn't asked and so she hadn't told him that not only had the bleeding stopped and the exhaustion followed but that the sickness had now begun.

Having seen Gertie off to work, Sarah tried to blacklead the grate, tried to peel potatoes, tried to scrub the table. Each task left her retching into a bucket and feeling absolutely ghastly.

Clara's home did not look out into the same court as that of the Nightingales'. It was one of a row of houses with long, thin backyards and it just happened to be the end one, and the end adjacent to Twenty Four Court. This meant that it shared a wall and a chimney. Just as Em's coughing had penetrated that thin back wall of the hearth so did the sound of Sarah's sickness.

At midday a worried Clara was knocking on the door, a concerned expression creasing her young face. She heard Sarah's weak response and hurried into the kitchen to find her friend's mother prostrate. Clara was no stranger to sickness and quickly assumed control, making Sarah comfortable so that at least she could feel ill in peace knowing that the scrubbing was being done and a stew soon bubbling on the hob. Only when all was spotless and organised did Clara stop to brew some weak tea and try to talk to Mrs. Nightingale. The roles should have been reversed but the older lady badly needed to share her troubles with someone.

"I've not eaten anything bad, Clara."

"Well then what can it be, Mrs. Nightingale? 'Ave you 'ad it before?"

"I was the same with Abel and with Gertie".

Clara was aghast. She knew what Sarah was suggesting and she knew of other older women who had been 'caught' in the change but for it to happen to Mrs. Nightingale and to know that Mr. Nightingale must be responsible seemed dreadful. Clara had allowed her original misconception of her friend's father to be corrected long since. "Oh Mrs. Nightingale. I'm so sorry!" It wasn't the most tactful of responses. Perhaps she ought to have seemed pleased, offered congratulations.

"So am I, love, so am I." Tears were running down Sarah's face unchecked. "How can I tell Abel? What shall I say to Gertie? What will people think? How can I go out?"

Clara supplied no answers. None had been expected. The silence swirled about the two women whilst the younger one, so used to giving, did what came naturally and put her arms around the older one who buried her face in the young girl's chest and cried for her shame.

When Sarah was able to speak again it was to utter her final fear, "Deformed," she gasped, "children born to old women are weak in the head or deformed! Poor mite, what will become of it with a grandmother for a mother? And what a weight for our Gertie when anything happens to me! Oh Clara, the sins of the parents...... What shall I do?"

Sarah dried her eyes on her pinafore and, as composure slowly returned, she recognised the wisdom of patience. May be she wouldn't carry this child. Yes, she could hope for its death – a gentle death in her womb where its flesh could sleep and rot into contamination, poisoning her own. Sarah's depression found solace in imagining her own end.

Clara, misjudging the calmness and believing its root lay in optimism, promised to remain silent. She returned to her own home, her thoughts already focusing on ways to help her friend's mother.

Chapter Eight

Miss Gertrude Nightingale lived a charmed life. Every morning as she waited for the librarian to unlock the library door Gertrude felt a flutter of excited anticipation. Familiarity did nothing to diminish her pleasure.

Gertie had no sensation of going to work, of reporting to do a job. This wonderful experience was nothing like paid employment. It was a privilege, sheer self-indulgence. Had she been a lady of leisure then Gertie felt that the library was where she would have chosen to spend her day.

Whatever Gertie's feelings about the nature of her post, Ben Nightingale appreciated both his daughter's new status and her raise in salary. He liked to think of her leaving home smartly dressed in the daylight hours, not scurrying out into murky dawns like a factory girl. Gertie did not have to report until a quarter to nine and finished at seven on most nights, five o'clock on Wednesdays. Her mother had been gratified to hear that she had proper breaks and that a woman was employed to come in to make a pot of tea every day at four o'clock.

Appreciation of the new situation was not one sided. Mr. Lees, too, had a distinct sense of gratification seeping through his ink filled veins. He had very quickly recognised what a treasure he had in Miss Nightingale and understood at last why his sister had singled the young lady out for so much attention.

Although Samuel retained his position at the issue desk in charge of the card index and jealously maintained his power to date stamp books, he had swiftly felt able to extend his assistant's activities. She was efficient at shelving, could capably review new acquisitions and posted details of recommended authors along with her synopses of novels which, he felt, were successfully designed to whet any jaded appetite. Had Gertie profited from a university education, Mr. Lees felt that she could have done no better job. He could trust her to rotate notices on the board. He was aware of her patient helpfulness with enquiries. He could relax and allow her to find her own direction, seeing what needed to be done almost as quickly as he did. Above all, Miss Nightingale was quiet. She moved between the book stacks like a drifting wraith and, above all things, the librarian loved silence.

Of course, the library needed Mr. Lees. It was his presence that maintained the whispered hush, stilled the bouts of coughing with a glance and kept the vagabonds from seeking out the warmth of the reading alcove during inclement weather. Without the librarian's formidable eye there would have been a stream of late returns or refusals to pay fines. Without him there would have been a lack of male authority. Without Gertie, though, Mr. Lees felt that the spirit of the building would have been …..well….. lost. Under her light hand spines were level, book numbers visible and in line, shelves labelled, a place for everything and everything in its place. In her own private heaven Gertie glided past her bookshelves revelling in their order, excited by their content.

Mrs. Peake had become a regular caller, not only to have words with both her brother and friend but also to abuse her position of sister and have access to the new arrivals. She would breeze into the library and annoy Samuel by the loudness of her whisper and her assumption that it was perfectly in order to pocket a novel without it being issued in the proper way.

Gertie had to smile at the familiar battle of wills that she witnessed as elder sister sought to dominate the younger brother - and always did.

Mrs. Peake continued to enjoy Gertie's company and felt more comfortable with her young friend's newly acquired status in the library. In fact she felt rather proud that she had initiated this improvement in Gertie's situation and enjoyed accepting the credit for having acted as fairy godmother to a transformed Cinderella.

Samuel watched his sister closely. He was very fond of his only surviving sibling and had felt her misfortunes deeply, especially the death of his niece. He had been pleased to see Alice rising above her sadness and enjoying the latter part of her life in comfort and comparative freedom. The fifteen year gap between them had always given the elder the advantage, providing her with an almost motherly role towards Samuel. But he was a sensitive man and he had not been so busy asserting his independence that he had failed to recognise his sister's loneliness even when it was well disguised. In consequence Samuel recognised the thread that bound Alice to Gertie. He saw it swelling into a lifeline which pulled his sister from the sea of self indulgence onto a shore where she dared care and love again, plan wardrobes and experiences – in short – enjoy bringing a 'daughter' out into society.

Between her new occupation as assistant librarian and her developing social life with Mrs. Peake, Gertie was - simply – happy. She loved her working days and enjoyed her cosy fireside evenings with Mrs. Peake as much as the exciting new experiences that her friend organised for her.

Since her school days Gertie's life had indeed changed dramatically. So had her appearance. She now dressed very smartly. Out were the heavy boots and shawl, in were the neat, buttoned, soft leather shoes, the trim dresses and coats that skimmed her hour glass figure. Gertie's sheer joy in being alive lent her a glow and sparkle that had begun to attract attention.

Several young men had noticed Mrs. Peake's companion and were engaged in persuading their mothers and grandmothers to become better acquainted with the good lady. In consequence Mrs. Peake was gratified by the increased number of calling cards and invitations that were left in her vestibule. She was under no misapprehension and recognised that it was her young friend's budding social life that was about to burst into bloom.

Of course Gertie still had her eyesight problem that even a visit to Mrs. Peake's practitioner had failed to eradicate. There seemed to be no lens that removed the haze from her vision and pulled the distortion of distant shapes into focus. In consequence Gertie remained at a disadvantage in social situations which left faces and their expressions an indistinct blur. Her resultant shyness and obvious nervousness was seen by the grander members of local society as a very appropriate reticence to push herself forward. It was accepted by her peers as a gentleness that invited others to be concerned for her – a vulnerability which aroused masculine protective instincts.

Once Gertie was involved with a small group or seated at a dinner table, secure in the proximity of her identifiable neighbours, she became an interested and interesting companion. Her wit had sharpened, her reading of newspapers ensured that she remained abreast of current affairs and her natural interest in the lives and characters of other people meant that she was both an invigorating conversationalist and an attentive, sympathetic listener. She also had a beauty that was fast becoming breathtaking. Despite this, she did not possess any arrogant self-confidence which meant that Gertie remained acceptable to young women who might otherwise have resented the way in which gentlemen's glances settled on Gertie rather than on themselves.

Mrs. Peake was very satisfied to see Gertie so animated and so obviously successful. Occasionally she allowed herself to wonder how the Nightingale family viewed the little butterfly that had emerged from the colourless cocoon of their inadequacy. That the fullness of her evenings depended directly upon the emptiness of theirs was not a thought which intruded upon her conscience often.

★ ★ ★ ★ ★ ★ ★ ★ ★

One Wednesday just before Advent, Mrs.Peake was settled before her fire and looking forward to sharing dinner with her brother and his young assistant. Christmas was fast approaching and she needed to discuss plans with them both. A fog was rapidly thickening out of doors and she listened as footfalls on the cobbled pavement began to display a familiar hollow echo. Sounds were becoming increasingly muffled and she wished it were six o'clock and both her dear ones ensconced with their sherry beside her. There had been some very nasty accidents in the fog of last winter, carriages colliding, horses run through with shafts, pedestrians trampled underfoot. Mrs. Peake was apprehensive.

The thick yellow fog swirled around the town, a suffocating blanket playing havoc with men's conception of distance as well as with their lungs.

It was from this sulphurous soup that a damp and dishevelled figure emerged to cough and splutter in the entrance hall of the library. The covered entrance, though sheltered, was still full of the drifting fog and, genuinely anxious to breathe, the young man staggered into the library itself.

Mr. Lees looked up from his place at the issue desk, annoyed at the disturbance that the young man's entrance had created. His eyebrows arched into two little tents of disapproval and his chin tilted down so that the librarian could look over the half moons of his spectacles. He looked directly at the intruder and, when the coughing did not subside, he cleared his own throat dramatically, trying to draw attention to his presence. Still the young man persisted in his interruption. Mr. Lees officiously date stamped a piece of blotting paper, the ominous thud lost amidst that racking cough. The librarian seemed powerless to elicit the desired response.

Gertie was by now alerted to the embarrassing situation and scurried towards the young man to enquire if he might like a glass of water.

"Very kind….. Fog……outside…….thick…..short of breath….." the young man managed to gasp out between splutters as he tried to control his cough.

Gertie ministered to him gently, even to the point of daring to adjust the young gentleman's muffler in a motherly manner as Clara might have done. When the young man's cough subsided the public began to reluctantly file past, none eager to leave the clean, warm library to venture into the 'peasouper' outside. Mr.Lees locked drawers brought Gertie her coat and stood tapping his foot beside the open library door.

Gertie shrugged into her coat and, forgetting to be shy in her concern for the young man, took his arm to encourage him to attempt to walk out of the library. He managed to mutter that he was to meet his brother at the corner and so Gertie supported him as he quite weakly left the premises and made his way towards the meeting place. The fog swirled and whirled around them, footsteps echoed in an eerie unnatural way and shapes loomed up at them alarmingly out of the dirty greyness that had enveloped and smothered the world. A tall, top-hatted figure already paced the pavement looking anxiously in all directions. As Gertie and the young man approached the figure recognised her patient and turned towards them.

"Richard, my dear fellow. I told mother you shouldn't be out in this. What were you thinking of? The carriage – too dangerous to bring it into a narrow street in this fog. Seen too many accidents. It's around the corner in the square. Come along old chap." As the tall stranger proceeded to offer his support to the young man, Gertie relinquished her role and stepped slightly away. Her presence was suddenly acknowledged, "Oh, Miss…err…!. Thank you. My anxiety for my brother has made me forget my manners. Thank you so much for your help…."

He might have said more but Gertie muttered something about her dinner engagement and, suddenly alarmed by the physical proximity in which she had held a stranger, she turned on her heel and walked rapidly away, the curtain of fog falling between them.

She regained the library. Samuel exited, pocketing his keys. He drew Gertie's arm into the crook of his elbow," Come along, Miss Nightingale. Stick close. We could lose each other in this peasouper. Soon be at Alice's. Shan't want to venture out again after a fine dinner. Think I'll invite myself to stay over with you two ladies". And together they glided into the eerie streets, a tall thin figure leaning almost imperceptibly to offer shelter to the slim form that moved beside him.

The fog hung around the town for two more unpleasant days and nights. It drifted around buildings like greedy ghosts insinuating themselves through any open entrance and into any orifice. Even the patient horses snorted their discomfort as their eyes reddened and their loads weighed on them more than usual. Only those who had no alternative ventured out and found even the time of day confusing for at midday the street lamps still glimmered and a hazy sun that tried to burn its way into the heart of the fog only penetrated sufficiently to produce a watery moon-like haze.

On the third day the sun pierced the suffocating blanket with shining metal lances and, as if by magic, the fog became a mist and the mist raised itself to a low cloud as the earth steamed and sweated below.

Whilst the rest of the population murmured about the peculiarity of the climate, shopkeepers heaved sighs of relief and ushered in December with their usual optimism. The cloud lifted. Skies were clear. England had returned to its crisp, sharp winter. People were freed from the heavy burden of oppressive weather and began to anticipate Christmas.

In her haven Gertie was oblivious of everything save her books. Mr. Samuel, from his station at the issue desk, watched his young assistant with satisfaction. His fingers flicked mechanically up and down his alphabetically arranged card index. His mind was checking and rechecking its accuracy but his eyes feasted on the order and serenity of his library and the arresting beauty of his young assistant.

Gertie, sorting notices, was marvelling yet again at the power of this building, its almost ecclesiastical atmosphere. People entered with a subdued reverence and handled the books with an almost religious respect. Conversations were whispered, movements controlled and gentle. The only sounds were the occasional muffled cough and the wonderful rustle of pages being carefully turned. It was a sound that reminded Gertie of autumn leaves, crisp and curled – another luxury of sensation.

Just as her mind was full of the richness and colours of fallen leaves, Gertie's attention was attracted to the library door which had opened slowly, allowing a huge bunch of chrysanthemums to venture into the room, followed by a body hidden by the immensity of the golden and auburn blooms.

Gertie watched intrigued as the bouquet arrived at the issue desk and a whispered conversation between the bearer and Mr. Samuel ensued.

"Highly irregular! Council employees...... not accept gratuities."

Gertie caught snatches of Mr. Samuel's professional gruffness. She couldn't hear anything said in reply but she watched as the flowers were laid down on the counter and her superior, clearly annoyed, snatched them away before they could contaminate his efficient order. The flowers disappeared behind the issue desk. Mr. Samuel resumed his aggressive scowl.

Deprived of his camouflage the purveyor of these unacceptable blossoms was revealed as the young gentleman patient of a few days earlier. It was quite obvious that he had come in the hope of seeing the young lady who had helped him. It was even more apparent that Mr. Samuel had no intention of his employee receiving callers during working hours, no matter how well spoken or well intentioned.

The young man turned, catching a glimpse of Gertie staring worriedly from between the book stacks. He hesitated and moved slightly towards her, the expression on his face as determined as if he were a knight about to storm a castle. Then his gaze encompassed the dragon breathing fire behind the issue desk and her champion's shoulders drooped. With a last anguished glance in her direction he turned dejectedly and left, slowly, his blooms captured by the dragon and his princess a prisoner in the tower.

Order restored, the librarian busied himself with some invoices, already checked and paid and tried to make sense of his somersaulting emotions.

It was Wednesday, shops shut at lunch- time and the Free Library at five o'clock. At five to five Mr. Samuel was already caressing the brass keys in his pocket and thinking of the good meal and warm fire awaiting him at his sister's house. They were to spend the evening discussing shares, investments and general family business and so Gertie had for once been excluded from their conviviality. It was an unusual pattern for midweek but Gertie did not mind for she was anxious to swoop upon her flowers - the first she had ever received - and take them home, a trophy to put on display. In consequence Gertie came out of the library a little ahead of her superior who had been waylaid at the door by an anxious caretaker. She stood at the top of the library steps clutching her flowers to her bosom enjoying the feel of the cold evening air stinging her skin. After days of fog and working indoors Gertie felt exhilarated by the clear air and her sense of freedom. As another gust of wind buffeted the petals of her flowers and snatched at the tendrils of hair escaping from her bun, Gertie reached up and withdrew the pins that held the rest in place.

And so it was that Richard's first real view of his gentle nurse was of a trim little figure clutching his blossoms, standing for a moment like a statuesque mascot and then loosening out a cape of gold that flowed about her shoulders like silken veils. He watched her as she smiled in sheer delight at some secret thought and then hastened down the steps.

Richard stepped forward. His polite, "Good evening, Miss......," suddenly became a panicky clutching of an arm as the elusive fairy almost slipped past him. Then ensued what was almost a struggle as Gertie, alarmed by an unknown man stepping into her line of vision and accosting her, tried to wriggle away from him and escape. The whole episode was quite ridiculous and as Gertie flailed her arms nervously and Richard attempted to calm her, the precious flowers slipped to the floor to lie in a bedraggled heap between them.

"I do apologise. I didn't mean to startle you!"

"No. I'm sorry. It's my fault. I didn't see you until you were upon me. I was alarmed – most unnecessarily. Oh my flowers!"

Richard retrieved the blooms and stood holding them, a bemused expression settling onto his face. "Let me carry them. I'll see you home. May I?"

Not for one moment did Gertie hesitate. Not one fleeting flood of shame affected her. For all Gertie's newly acquired knowledge of what homes could and should be like and awareness of the drab poverty of her own by comparison, she did not falter. Gertie was filled with the supreme confidence that this young man was not going to be deterred by bricks and mortar or the lack of them!

In consequence the two young people headed for Twenty Four Court, soon talking easily like old friends and quickly discovering shared interests. Richard was floating in a cloud of incredulity. This beautiful creature was as literary minded as he, had seen the same plays recently, read the same revues, disagreed similarly with the critics. As they walked, both happy in their mutual discoveries, Richard assumed that he was heading for some neat town house – not a wealthy home for she was a working girl. Their journey took them, however, out of the more respectable neighbourhoods and, as they entered the dark streets of tall factories and narrow court entries, Richard began to feel less at ease. He was out of his depth, walking into a world that he had only heard about around the port decanter, passing places that one didn't mention in front of the ladies unless it was to embark upon some enlightened political discussion. To learn that Gertie came from this land of darkness and degradation did not alarm Richard although it did surprised him. In fact, he marvelled at her tenacity in climbing out of this slough, and determined to admire her all the more.

Gertie, with a confidence she had never known before, led her beau right to the archway of her entry where she halted, her face turned up to his. Had Richard been even slightly concerned or reticent about continuing their friendship, any doubts that he might have harboured disappeared at that moment. Her blue eyes sparkled up at him, her mouth smiled its gentle smile and Richard Grant was utterly and irretrievably lost.

Clara, bustling down the street, her apron gathered up to ensure the safety of half a dozen newly laid eggs, stopped and stared at her friend gazing into the countenance of the most beautiful man she had ever seen. Gertie, too, was noticing that thin, intelligent face, with its sharply chiselled features, absolutely symmetrical and pleasingly proportioned. She was drowning in the warm depths of soft brown eyes that promised so much kindness and friendship. Dark hair curled at his temples and fell onto his collar. "He looks like a poet", thought Gertie, "a writer – a dream."

Clara slowed her approach, giving the couple a respectable time to part. The young man held out the flowers, gave a mock salute and turned, leaving Gertie, a fairy-tale silhouette in the shadowed arch of the entry.

For the second time that evening, Gertie was startled by someone's approach. When Clara appeared out of the darkness and spoke her name, Gertie's eyes flew open as if she had been disturbed from sleep.

"Gertie?"

"Clara! Oh it's you! Look at my flowers, my lovely, lovely flowers."

"They're beautiful – like the ones we had when Mother …..died." Clara could have bitten off her tongue but her comment seemed to have gone unnoticed.

"Did you see him?"

"Gertie! Yes, of course I did, but it's late. Today's your early – you'd better go in. Your father! Tell me later," urged Clara as the two girls moved down the length of the damp, drab entry.

Clara was right. It was getting late and her father would be sitting at the table waiting for her – knowing that tonight she was expected home for tea. She lifted the latch of her door, "I'll come round," she stage whispered, "about eight."

A sour smell of sickness hit her as Gertie entered the little kitchen. Her mother was kneeling on the rug in front of the fire, retching into a bowl. Her father was sitting at the table, drinking a mug of tea with apparent composure.

"Mother!" Gertie laid the flowers on the table and hurried to the woman, doubled up in her pain. Gertie dropped to her knees and put her hand on the forehead over the basin, using the other hand to scoop the loose hair away from her mother's face. Gertie was horrified by the whiteness of Sarah's skin and the shameful lack of privacy.

"Flowers," Nightingale spat out. "You bringing flowers for 'er when we could do with bread and meat!" He got to his feet, reached for his coat and slammed out of the back door.

By the time Abel arrived, Sarah was lying on an eiderdown on the hearth, the bowl still beside her head but smelling now of lavender. She was less nauseous and the pains in her back were less violent. The flowers, the cause of her father's hasty exit, stood in a bucket near the pantry door.

"What's wrong with her, Abel?" Gertie begged her brother as soon as he entered. "Why is she so sick all the time?"

Abel knelt down beside his mother. "Go round and ask Clara. She'll explain better than I can. I know she's been with Mother when we've been at work."

But Gertie never did hear Clara's explanation for suddenly Sarah was pulling up her knees and writhing again in agony. Moaning and vomiting her mother threw the blankets from her contorted body, revealing a deep red stain spreading from beneath her.

Clara didn't need to be summoned. She'd heard enough through the wall and was rattling the latch before Abel had even begun to run for the doctor.

Chapter Nine

Ben Nightingale knew before he entered his kitchen that something untoward had occurred in his absence. As he had meandered unsteadily down the uneven road that tilted and swayed beneath him, he'd smelt the smoke issuing from his chimney. At a time when fires were damped down with slack for the night his was alive and blazing.

When the door opened, the last bundle of bloody newsheets was already burning, flames leaping intermittently as a new surface uncurled. Somewhere amongst that debris of his wife's womb a tiny scrap of unidentifiable life burned. Son or daughter, he was never to know what it might have been, – only that it was the fruit of his loins and not of his heart. That minute little soul had loosened its tentative hold on life amidst the paroxysms of pain with which he had cursed his wife so long ago. It had drowned in the red current of its mother's blood whilst its father had been drowning his sorrows in gin, silently and secretly beneath the damp, dripping roof of a canal bridge.

He had left the house that night in the darkest yet of his deep depressions. He never drank. He was a temperance man, familiar with what gin and ale could do and yet tonight he had walked into a dilapidated gin palace, elbowing his way through the urchins at the door and the bawds inside until he'd stood at the counter, money in his outstretched hand.

He'd had no jug for his medicine, no container for the remedy he required but the barmaid had been obliging and he'd left with a borrowed bottle secreted inside his jacket. It had been a short walk down to the canal; its crude towpath had been dark and safe. He'd walked the stretch he knew so well until he reached the bridge, all cold brick and even colder ironwork. There in the darkness, his back against the damp wall he had sat, knees hunched up to his stomach and tried to drink himself into oblivion, tried to forget for once the pain of his frustrated ambition. When the gin had gone Nightingale had been heartily disappointed for his head felt clear and the shroud of depression was still wrapped around him. He had stood and turned in the direction of home and it was only then that his vision had blurred and his jelly legs had bent and buckled like those of a newborn foal.

It had been a slow journey home, sitting on walls, resting on the towpath capstans and fumbling his way around factory railings. And all that time Sarah had been writhing in agony until her body lay torn and spent, exhausted by the days of sickness. Nightingale had missed his perfect opportunity to gloat.

Eventually the doctor had declared the ordeal over and Sarah safe, so long as she was kept clean and no bad air reached her womb. He didn't fully understand the source of potential infection but he knew enough of post- partum death to fear it and warn against it. At least these two young women knew what cleanliness was. Sarah was in good hands.

It was just before midnight, when Abel had gone with the lamp to walk Clara to her own doorstep, that Nightingale had lurched up the entry to stand, swaying, on his threshold. Only Gertie occupied the kitchen. At first her father didn't see her, then a sudden shifting of the coals and a spurt of flame cast enough light into the darkness of the stairway for Nightingale to make out the humped shape of his daughter sitting on the bottom step.

"Out of my way, girl. I'm to bed." His breath, stinking of spirits, wafted around his slurred words like a foetid vapour.

"That you won't, Father." The last word was firm and bitter.

He stood, unsteady, fixed by the hard diamonds that glinted at him from a stranger's face wavering in the gloom. His meek, fragile daughter had become a tigress. When next she spoke it was through clenched teeth and from behind a mask, a distortion of her features, unrecognisable as his gentle Gertie. Nightingale could only think that a strange court woman blocked his way. Her clothes were soiled and sticky with sweat, her hair greasy and knotted. She had aged ten years in three hours. "If you try to reach my mother, you will have to go through me, for I will not move."

Gertie saw her father raise his hand, pause – and then, with a theatrical yawn, he moved backwards, away from her and lowered himself unsteadily onto the rag rug before the fire. With uncharacteristic mildness, Ben Nightingale blessed his daughter, gave her into God's keeping, curled up and slipped immediately into sleep. She was not to know that her father dreamed of a young girl whom he had watched from the shadows and thought that he had wanted.

When Abel returned he ushered Gertie to bed and settled himself in the fireside chair not so much to watch over his father but to keep watch for his mother. She should not be disturbed tonight.

For a long while Abel could not sleep. His brain was a cauldron of disconnected thoughts that bubbled and seethed, surfaced and dived. Occasionally he dozed but woke with a start as his elbow jolted over the edge of the slim arm of the wooden chair. Then he'd sleep again, his restless mind overactive with its dreams.

The night was quiet save for Nightingale's snores and one burst of voices from deep in the Court, the sound of a quarrel, pans landing on the dirt yard with muffled thuds followed by a woman's voice, a scream and a slammed door. No doubt Millie Hooper would hide her face until Monday and then appear in the wash-house with eyes still banged up and yellowing bruises jaundicing her face.

The row disturbed Abel but Gertie slept on, trapped by insensibility in a cat and mouse game which stretched her emotions taut and near to breaking point. She tossed amid blood soaked rags, grasping outstretched hands that clawed the air and twisted bed rails into grotesque shapes of giant chrysanthemums. A stranger's eyes looked at her through a sanguine fog, which swirled around brown curls and suffocated an open, screaming, bloody mouth. The silent scream woke Gertie. Immediately alert she sat up, listening. Was that her father on the stairs? Had he escaped from Abel's watch? She threw back the covers and put her feet onto the bare floor. Then, avoiding any creaking boards, she padded silently to the head of the stairs. The stairwell was empty.

Through the open bedroom door Gertie could see the still form of her mother. Reassured, she descended into the kitchen and sought her brother's shape in the chair.

There was still a little warmth from the fire and so Gertie curled up near to the comforting glow, leaning her weight against Abel's knees and in a while she slipped into a dreamless and comfortable rest, undisturbed by her father's restlessness.

The stirrings of the court woke the three Nightingales at dawn. Ben struggled up from the rug, grunting and cursing, trying to work the stiffness from his limbs. He stumbled out into the yard and soon the creaking of the pump handle accompanied the gush and gasp as cold water sluiced some reality into the muzziness of his brain.

Abel and Gertie feigned sleep as their father completed his clumsy ablutions and left with no breakfast or tucker box. He had made no attempt to go near the stairs.

Once their father had gone Gertie busied herself with her mother's tasks whilst Abel prepared himself for work. Having reassured himself that his mother was no worse he left his sister with what he felt were comforting words.

"Don't worry Gertie. I'll have to go to unlock but I'll pop back during the day and I know Clara will be in and out."

In fact Clara was only waiting respectfully for Abel to leave. Once the men had gone she felt she could run next door to offer her support. Gertie could go to the library. Clara was totally dependable – and utterly unprepared for her friend's brittle attitude.

Gertie was dressed for the library, smart and smooth. Her face was expressionless, a window with its shutters closed. Clara was immediately all concern, her soul open and defenceless, ready to give, unready to repel words that felt like sharp tipped arrows piercing her flesh.

"You knew, Clara. You knew."

Clara's heart quickened. She was hurt by the sudden attack. "But it wasn't my place to tell you, Gertie. It was your mom's secret – not mine to share."

"You might have known she wouldn't. You could have."

"I'm sorry. But Gertie, I thought she would tell you – eventually – when it was the right time or… ."

"Or?"

"Well I thought you'd just know – guess I suppose."

"And I didn't, did I?"

"Perhaps it was because you weren't home much – you being so busy, I mean." Even in her distress Clara was offering her friend a lifeline – an excuse for not knowing, a bolthole for her conscience. Once again Gertie took her by surprise.

"Oh – so that's it Clara – you're jealous. I never would've thought it of you. Not you, Clara. Never!" Gertie's head moved from side to side disbelievingly, her overwrought state causing her to misread her friend's concern. "Well, as you and mother are so close I've no doubt you'll look after her today and probably discuss my life while you're about it." Gertie picked up her hat, rammed it down on top of her head and stuck a hatpin viciously through its crown and into her own hair. Then she turned, her eyes misted with self-righteous tears and hurried blindly out into the yard and into the entry. She hesitated once; covering her quivering lips with a trembling hand, then walked on swiftly in the direction of her employment.

Clara could hardly believe what had happened. It had all been so quick, so unfair and so disastrously dreadful.

"Gertie? Clara, is that you?" Sarah's voice quavered from upstairs.

"Coming, Mrs. Nightingale." Clara swallowed hard and mounted the stairs.

When Clara bustled into the bedroom she was trying to look cheerful. Her friend's mother was sitting up, or at least she was propped up on one elbow, a little less white but her face puckered with anxiety and worry. Every word of the brief and heated exchange had floated up through the uncarpeted floorboards. She lay back on her pillows, her face all concern and held out her arms. Em's daughter fell to her knees, pressing herself into the motherly embrace, neither woman knowing where giving and taking began or ended. It was mutual solace, whilst tears spilled down both cheeks. Though they shared one emotion, one wept for a lost life and the other for a broken friendship.

"It was for the best," sobbed Sarah, " It likely would've been sickly or backward. I'm too old."

"Yes," sighed Clara, "and I feel old too. I'm worn out, Mrs Nightingale – worn out with giving and grieving and with loss."

During the rest of that long day Clara ran back and forth between the houses, taking care of Sarah's body and home, whilst from the four corners of her soul Sarah dredged the strength to give sustenance to a young girl who had been forced to be a woman too soon.

Abel took his lunch break very early that day and hurried home half way through the morning. He walked quietly and tried to lift he latch without making a sound but it rattled as it settled back into place, just enough to startle Clara bent over the range. She turned, the black lead cloth in her hand, her eyes wide open. For a second her plain and homely face was taut, her rounded cheeks sharper, more defined, eyes larger. "Why," thought Abel, "Clara seems different, or have I never looked at her properly before?"

Clara smoothed her pinafore, allowed her features to return to their natural passivity and tried to assume a respectable humility, eyes downcast, not meeting Abel's.

"How is she?" he asked.

"Better. Resting."

"And you…, Clara, are you alright? Not doing too much? We are grateful." Abel moved towards, Clara.

"I'm fine, Abel, but Gertie…. She's…..."

"I know – overwrought. This has shaken her badly. Made her think of your loss. Frightened her."

Clara bit her lip. She longed to unburden herself to Abel but didn't dare – his sympathies would be bound to lie with Gertie. He was close to her now. She could feel his eyes, his breath, his warmth. "Abel……the flowers. I've put them in a jug."

"Yes. Gertie must have brought them. Mother would like them. I'll take them up to her." The spell was broken. He moved away, picked up the jug of chrysanthemums and mounted the stairs.

Chapter Ten

There was a noise in the court: men's voices raised, firm and annoyed, a single woman's shrewish and sharp.

Clara, just going into the Nightingale house paused to look down the yard, criss-crossed with washing lines and billowing garments. She could make out men's boots and rough trousers, coal-black, – miners, but not from this court. The men and boys in Twenty- Four worked in the furnace and metal shops.

"We bay out to mek no trubble, missis," - one man's conciliatory tones reached Clara - "but we'm tryin' to tell ya...."

"Tell me? Who d'yow think yow am – tellin' me, tellin' me?"

"Now look 'ere missis; be fair. If it wuz yower mon's livin' what'd bin spilte yow'd want ter dew summat."

"Oh ar! I would but it wouldn't be ter goo ter a woman's dooer wi' a gang o' bloody chaps the back on me."

The wind lifted the washing momentarily and Clara caught sight of Mrs. Hooper standing on her doorstep, arms akimbo, clearly angry and distressed.

Other doors were open now. Women were moving into the yard, checking washing, re-pegging it, stopping ostensibly to talk but in reality offering support to a neighbour.

Clara moved down the yard, put her hand to a sagging prop. She could see more clearly now.

Four men, their faces bright, morning - clean oases in their coal-dust covered working clothes, were gathered round the Hooper door. The spokesman, the eldest by the look of his sagging features and frost- rimed hair had half turned away, seemingly exasperated. He rubbed his fingers over his frowning forehead and then, appearing to think better of leaving, returned his attention to Mrs Hooper.

"Look 'ere, missis," he tried again, his voice gentling her as he might a horse, "we'm all family blokes. We bay 'ere to be 'ard. It's just as we want t' goo t' werk. It's our shift but allus on a Monday when we'm agooin' past yower entry, a little wench, a little curly-'aired wench, is sittin' in the gutter, by the 'oss road."

"Er bay 'ertin yer, is er?"

"No missis but mi mates and me, we 'ave ter tern round and goo wum. Now, yow understand. Yow dew, missis."

"Oh yes," Milli almost spat out her words now." Oh yes; I know yow'm a superstitious lot o' buggers, yow miners. Yow wow goo down the pit even if a whistlin' woman crosses yower path. 'A whistlin' woman an' a crowin' 'en", she crooned rudely.

"Is neither good to God nor men", one of the other miners finished off the old rhyme.

Mrs. Hooper seemed calmer, suddenly less aggressive. She held out her hands, palms up helplessly, "Well mi little wench wor whistlin', an' 'er bay gonna suck through her teeth.... Yow jus' tek a look at 'er." Millie Hooper reached behind her and scooped from amongst her skirt folds a tiny little girl whom she pushed forward into the gaze of the miners.

Beatrice Victoria Hooper, a rotund cuddle of dimples and tousled blond curls, took her thumb out of her mouth and, clearly born to grace the stage, dropped into a deep theatrical curtsy. Then, raising her face to the sun's watery rays, eyes closed, she smiled - a mischievous open-mouthed grin that displayed her gums, rosy and bursting with her new and as yet uncut teeth.

Mrs. Hooper pursed her lips in satisfaction, confident that she had made her point. Beatrice, who couldn't whistle could certainly not suck through non- existent teeth.

The men looked down at the little doll, still collapsed into its tumble of skirts, its face still raised to the sunshine, its spiky eyelashes still splayed seductively out from closed lids onto smooth-skinned baby cheeks.

"But missis," the men mumbled and paused, none of them wanting to utter the hurtful words. They looked towards their spokesman.

"I'm really sorry, ma wench," the older man began, "but it's 'er een – 'er's cross-eyed."

The child, still enjoying the spotlight attention, opened her lids and looked directly at her accusers, at least her countenance faced them but her poor eyes, unfocused and wild, roamed independently in opposite directions. She was indeed cross-eyed.

"And that's the trouble missis. 'Er's in our path and we'm bound to goo wum. All we'm askin' is for 'er to stay in the court till we'm passed."

The men didn't wait for an answer but turned and walked away with heads bent, whilst the women hurried to lift the washing, making a tunnel for them to pass through without the laundry being dirtied.

No one spoke as the drama ended. The women stood silently until the echoes of the miners' boots had died away and then Mrs. Hooper enfolded Beatrice in her arms. She held the little girl close for a moment and then, in a flurry of flounces and mutterings, mother and daughter disappeared into their house and slammed the door. The court women dropped their poses and turned to each other, sisterly concern etched on all of their careworn faces.

"Poor little mite," murmured Clara, feeling the embarrassment of the Hoopers. "Poor little girl,; as if the affliction weren't enough, superstition makes her an outcast."

The whistle of a train sounded along the track startling the yard into a bustle of activity. The women scurried amongst the lines feeling the washing, bringing dry garments in before the train thundered past the bottom of the yard, blowing its black smuts onto their labours.

Clara went into Mrs. Nightingale, her arms full of Abel's white shirts. "Dry enough to iron, Mrs N.," she called, "they won't need damping down if we're quick."

Clara spent more and more time with Sarah. Bound together by their experience of loss and pain, they nevertheless struggled independently to be optimistic, each for the sake of the other.

Sarah had begun to realise that Clara was fond of Abel and so cheered her with anecdotes of his childhood and teased her with suggestions that he would chop wood or mend a shelf if invited. The older woman was openly matchmaking and enjoying the delight that she found she could engender in her young friend.

Clara's mother had been very dear to Sarah and it would have been tidy and comforting to see a union between their children. If the two young people were not exactly fairly matched in looks, what Clara lacked in attractive physical attributes she more than made up for in her affectionate and practical nature. She would make a good wife and mother.

A shared interest in housewifery also bound the two women together and Clara found that she had much to learn from Mrs. Nightingale whose earlier years had brought her broader experiences. She knew how to make a table look attractive and how to combine the most basic ingredients into recipes beyond the experience of most court women. Sarah had an artistic touch and showed Clara how to cut white paper into doilies and to turn a worn-out skirt into a flounced pinafore that cheered the dullest dress.

Clara was not the only person who profited from Mrs. Nightingale's talents, for a certain Miss Beatrice Hooper was also enamoured of Sarah's skills.

Since the day that the miners came calling little Miss Hooper had been forbidden to go down the entry onto the street. The court had become her prison.

As the Nightingale house was the one nearest the head of the entry it was also the demarcation of her freedom. Since she could stray no further, Beatrice often ended her travels sitting on Sarah's worn step or inside the house on the fender beside the fire.

Beatrice didn't have much of a home life. Her mother loved her little cross-eyed daughter but her father had no time for her. He drank and when gin was his mistress life in their little one up one down became unbearable. Mrs. Hooper - beaten, often senseless, and used abominably - had rarely any energy to attend to Beatrice. The little girl was growing up in spite of her parents, certainly not because of them. Mr. Hooper, ashamed of his misbegotten whelp, taunted his wife with descriptions of his tall, strong, straight-eyed sons who lived with their various mothers in neighbouring streets. The fact that none of the identified young Adonises were, in fact, his, did not lessen his wife's distress or, for that matter, his daughter's.

Beatrice was ashamed: ashamed of not being a boy, ashamed of being a 'bad luck wench', ashamed that she was not loved by anyone, (for she discounted her mother as a person). Life was hardly a happy experience for little Bea, and so, with the resilience of childhood, she created her own joy. She escaped into a song and dance world of humming and clapping, singing and dancing, a world of bows and curtsies to an appreciating audience, a world of make believe.

There was one place in which Beatrice didn't need to avoid reality. If she could sit with Mrs. Nightingale then she thought herself in heaven. Here were the hands that cut her strings of paper dollies, here were the warmth and the cooking smells of a real home. If a story flew her way from Sarah whilst she ironed or baked then little Bea knew joy beyond all bounds. If Clara had the time to sit and cuddle her on her lap for half an hour then this was indeed bliss. Beatrice Hooper, with her quaint theatrical ways, was increasingly becoming an integral part of the two women's lives.

Twenty-Four Court was rarely a peaceful place, being more like a rabbit warren than a residence - overcrowded and inhabited by some of the rowdy, coarser elements of society. It did, however, have its quieter times and mid- morning was usually one of these. The men had long since gone, followed by scurrying young women and the sleepy eyed children who worked illegally. Even the scholars had gone, dragging their feet, reluctant to take advantage of what, being free, seemed of little value.

The court was clean, newly swilled down and swept. The gutter, which ran down the centre of the yard, had been cleared out and - for once - the yard was sweet and habitable. The women had filled their buckets at the pump and had hung out the little washing that would not wait until Monday. They were mostly now gathered around their ranges in their little groups of two and three, enjoying a few moments' respite from their daily tasks.

Clara, up since before six and well ahead with her chores, was coming up the entry to spend an hour with Sarah. She smiled at the sight of Mrs. Stevenson banging bad temperedly on the closet door and demanding her rights to be admitted before she had 'an accident'.

The Nightingale door was unlatched and swung open at Clara's touch. Its creak announced her arrival.

"Come in then Clara, love. Kettle's boiling. Tea?"

Clara nodded her assent and stood at the sink gazing through the upper half of the window where the panes were unobscured by the half nets. "Little Bea not about yet? Their door's closed. Funny, though; she's usually running about earlier than this. He's not been at 'em again 'as 'e, Mrs.Nightingale?"

Whilst Clara was feeling uneasy about the absence of their regular little visitor, a man, youngish but bearing a strong resemblance to the older miner who had acted as spokesman some weeks earlier, was racing up the road which led from the pit to Twenty-Four Court.

He had been sprinting but now his pace had slowed to an exhausted lope. Having gained the opening to the entry the man, clearly in a distressed and anxious state, wheeled round and leaned the inside of one arm against the wall. He buried his face in the comforting crook of his bent limb and shuddered - long bitter shivers that shook his frame. The man appeared to collect himself and then ventured further into the court.

The first house was the Nightingale home and, their door still being ajar, the occupants could not help but be aware of the miner's arrival. They looked towards his shadow expectantly.

The man's black face with his two white, doleful eyes peered into the kitchen. Sweat was running in clean little rivulets down his begrimed features and his eyes were red rimmed, glistening with unshed tears.

Clara was first to the door, opening it wider, ushering him in. Coal dust was no stranger there.

"Whatever's the matter? Is there trouble?" asked Sarah worriedly.

"An accident at the pit?" Clara volunteered, horrified already by the unshared news.

The man's putty face squeezed itself into furrows of concern. His gestures were those of distress and anguish, "Oh, missus", he said, almost beside himself in his trouble, "summat dreadful 'as 'appened down at the pit! That little lass, the cross-eyed one mi brothers wuz 'ere abaht….."

"Beatrice?" two voices spoke as one.

"Yes. That'd be 'er. 'Er mother's chucked 'er down the shaft. I 'eard 'er scream – just like a stuck pig it wuz. And then…."

"Oh no!" Clara was already untying her pinafore, grabbing for her shawl, ready to run.

"Then what?" demanded Sarah, realising that the man's tale was not yet done. "What else?"

"Well, missis. I 'erd this scream - terrified, terrifying - and then the mother shouted, 'No!' An agony it was – like the cry a woman meks when 'ers 'avin' a babby. 'No!' 'er screamed, and then, afower anybody could shift ter stop 'er, 'er jumped over the edge of the shaft. Two broken dollies they am; two poor, broken little dollies."

The man was shaken, clearly desperately distressed. Sarah led him to a chair and motioned Clara towards the kettle. If anyone needed their help now it was the living.

"My God! Mrs. Nightingale," Clara was looking towards her friend as though she might have some understanding of this terrible event - "whatever made 'er do it?"

Whilst Sarah shook her head sadly the miner, having gained a little strength from being seated, was prepared to end his tale. "Some on'm as sayin' as 'ow 'er 'usband 'it 'er on account of mi brothers comin' round. Said it wuz 'er fault that 'is mates 'ad to tern round and goo wum. 'E 'it 'er 'cuz 'e wouldn't tek it out on the babby. One bloke as knows, 'Eesays 'e 'eard 'er 'usband say as 'ed ram the washing dolly down 'is missus's wazzin if 'er day keep the child out of the 'oss road."

"Poor, poor Beatrice. Poor little girl", Clara wept.

"And poor Mrs. Hooper," added Sarah wiping her eyes, "Abel said that he'd heard them quarrelling again."

The Hooper's door remained shut. Mr. Hooper never dared to show his face again — or if he did it was only under cover of darkness. Without a wife to hoard his wages it seemed likely that he was drinking himself to death in some harlot's hovel. No one in Twenty-Four Court cared enough to seek him out.

The 'shaft suicide', as it became known, was the natural topic of sympathetic conversation for weeks. The court only ceased to argue the relative culpability of the Hoopers when another momentous incident claimed precedence. The Hugginses, complete with 'osses', did a 'moonlight flit'. They took to their heels in the middle of the night, carting their few meagre possessions away on wheelbarrow and trap, scarpering from their debts and making enough hullaballoo to wake the corpses in the graveyard. Only one of the family looked back with regret - young Howie Huggins.

To Sarah it was as if no one cared about living according to what was right and honourable any more. A sort of desperation grew inside her, accompanied by a very real anxiety to see both her children comfortably settled, secure against the turmoil of life.

Chapter Eleven

Mr. Lees could hardly take exception to a respectable member of the public using his library, and Richard Grant was decidedly respectable. The cut of his clothes, his bearing and his diction all proclaimed him a gentleman.

The snatches of conversation overheard between his assistant librarian and the young man all pointed to a genuine interest and knowledge of literature. When Mr. Grant had applied for his library ticket and Mr. Lees had taken his address and names of guarantors, the latter had not been able to avoid being affected. Mr. Grant had a socially impressive background.

Why, then, couldn't the librarian feel warmer towards this young fellow? There was no doubt that Mr. Lees harboured most uncomfortable feelings. No matter how genuine Mr. Grant appeared to be, the librarian just did not trust him. When he tried to isolate the origins of his dislike Mr. Lees could focus on two. The first was health. Mr. Grant coughed. In fact he coughed a great deal, some days more than others. And he often looked pale or at the other extreme artificially healthy – but it was the cough that was most disturbing. The second reason was the young man's obvious awareness of Miss Nightingale.

Mr. Lees took to pretending to be busy at his desk and then unexpectedly bobbing up his head to try to catch Mr. Grant at it - and he often did. Mr. Grant, gazing quite openly at the assistant librarian, watching her as she went about her duties, turning quite blatantly in his chair so as to view her better.

The librarian's exasperation reached its height one day after he had carried the steps so that his assistant could work on a rather high and relatively inaccessible shelf where over-large reference books were stored, obscure volumes donated to the library and rarely required. He had returned to the issue desk and, having dealt with one of his regular borrowers, prepared to return to assist Miss

Nightingale. He had to cover quite a distance and to negotiate various obstacles. His approach was not swift; time enough to see Mr. Grant staring at the hem of Miss Nightingale's skirt, very possibly glimpsing her ankles. Annoyed beyond measure that young Grant should assume such liberties, Mr. Lees barged forward only to find the young man had risen and was blocking his approach, passing books from the table up to Gertie.

Mr. Samuel Lees harrumphed. He could do no more. Then settling his spectacles firmly on the bridge of his nose, he interrupted the proceeding in his coldest and most professional tone, "Thank you, sir, but we would not wish to disturb your studies – or your leisure. This is a task which we are both employed to do."

Richard could not miss the frostiness of the tone nor the hostility in the older man's eye. He returned to his table and for the rest of the morning kept his gaze on his book and his mind ostentatiously on his task.

Mr. Lees, however, was not satisfied and took the opportunity to raise the subject of Mr. Grant with his sister when next they were together. She was not sympathetic.

"My dear sister, maids are not allowed followers and neither are assistant librarians!"

"No, brother dear – but you have to admit that Gertie is very pretty so it's hardly her fault that she has an admirer and you said he was a gentleman."

"You all over, Alice. One rule for others – another for yourself! But I still want to know what are we to do?"

"We, my dear? You, perhaps. I don't propose to do a thing – except maybe to invite him to tea."

Samuel Lees might conceivably have died of apoplexy there and then. His jaw hardened as he clenched his teeth to bite back a sharp retort, giving time for his sister to continue, "If Gertie has a respectable beau my only concern is to get to know him better."

"Your problem is ….," Samuel stood up, paced to the fire and turned his back to the welcome heat, "Your problem is," he repeated, "you've forgotten her station. You think of her as a daughter. You're trying to....."

"I know very well what I'm trying to do," Mrs. Peake's ample bosom heaved. "I haven't lived all these years without learning a little about myself. And yes, you're right. Gertie is dear to me – as dear, almost, as a daughter. I know I can't replace Isobel but that doesn't mean I can't try and enjoy the trying. Who does it hurt? Not Gertie!"

"No, not Gertie. At least not yet. But what happens when she gets ideas above her station? What if she expects to receive treatment like a ....."

"Lady," interrupted his sister. "Well, Samuel, well. She is one. Perhaps not born and bred but she is quite definitely a lady."

"No she is not, Alice. I admit that I, too, see her as you do. She's genteel, charming. Why, I feel almost fatherly....."

"Fatherly?"

"Fatherly, towards her. But we mustn't forget where she lives – not here, my dear, no matter if she does have a room here and a wardrobe. Her address – her legal abode - is Twenty- Four Court! Her father ruined himself by letting fire burn his barges. Life's work lost through carelessness. And I know of her father's father. Why, he was a common carter and a prize fighter, a pugilist, in his spare time."

"You have done your homework, Samuel! Now stop it. You've said enough – too much in fact. There are things that you don't know and I do."

"Which are?"

"The young people are friends – nothing more, so don't raise your eyebrows at me. And if there were a little something brewing then there would be no harm. He has escorted Gertie home. He knows where she lives."

"Met her family I suppose – which is more than we have!"

"Not exactly, Samuel, but he is aware of Gertie's background. He knows her origins and has not decried them."

"Introduced her to his own family then, Alice? Has he? Has he?"

"No, not yet."

"Yet! There's the magic word – not yet! He won't, Alice, he won't! And if this young girl gets her heart broken it won't be my fault. It will be yours."

"Samuel, I think you are overestimating my influence and underestimating this young gentleman. He is from, not just a respectable family, but an exceedingly well-off one. His father has a factory in Yorkshire, properties in Scotland, business interests here. His elder brother is articled to solicitors, Merridews, and.."

"And?"

"Well, his mother plays whist with Ada."

"And shouldn't! I don't approve of women playing cards!"

"Stuff and nonsense, Samuel. Let the matter rest."

The conversation was drawn to a close by a knock on the door and the arrival of post along with the news that Uncle Harry's coachman was in the kitchen awaiting a reply to an invitation that he had delivered for some Christmas festivity.

Samuel was forced to let matters drop but his blue eyes remained steely and his jawline was unnaturally tense. In fact Alice felt quite concerned about her younger brother. The library was a big undertaking. She resolved to persuade him to take a short holiday. He was after all the wrong side of middle age.

Whilst Gertie's new friendship was causing comment from her friends it was Richard's family who were, in fact, the most concerned. They were quite ignorant of Gertie's existence but they were aware of Richard's departure from routine and of a change in his demeanour.

The Grants were a close-knit family who valued mutual affection and were conscious of their responsibilities towards each other.

Richard was the younger son and the youngest child. He had

at first been cossetted by his older siblings simply because of their genuine delight in his birth, but later because of his susceptibility to illness.

Whilst his brother, Ralph, had developed into a sturdy young man, able to ride and fence, a keen tennis player and a superb dancer, Richard had been the pale face looking on, cheering, supporting and wishing like hell that he could participate. Breathlessness, coughing, bouts of feverishness and general tiredness left Richard the perpetual onlooker, a blanket on his knees and being encouraged to move in and out of the house according to the warmth of the sun.

His sisters were wonderful. They played chess, shared his delight in reading, kept him company in their box at the theatre and protected him from absolutely anything that might hurt him or shorten his life.

Doctors in different shapes and sizes and of varying degrees of experience had been consulted about Richard's 'condition'. Though they differed in their choice of words and in the acceptability of their bedside manner, all eventually gave the same verdict. Richard was consumptive and would never make old bones. Nevertheless, the Grants were optimistic – or, at least, refused to appear otherwise. They were of tough Highland stock, well able to face up to whatever ill fortunes came their way and they refused to accept Richard's death sentence without a fight. Determined to believe in miracles and to make one happen with or without God's help, they put aside any thought of an end and concentrated all of their efforts into making Richard's life a celebration of the present. He was denied nothing and was cosseted like a rare bloom.

It might have been expected, with all this affection and pandering to his whims, that Richard would have become selfish and self-willed. He did not. A generous, sympathetic young man, he delighted in his family's attention and determined not to die. Life, on good days, was not to be missed.

Richard could have gone to Italy or Switzerland – warm

climates, thin air. He might have cruised balmy waters. He had the opportunity to spend summers in the clean Speyside air of Scotland with relatives, and winters in mild, temperate Cornwall, but none of these alternatives was remotely tempting to Richard. He loved his family and would remain with them. When he was poorly he needed to be nursed and he liked to be read to. When he was well - well he wished for goodness sake that they would leave him alone, occasionally. After all, he was a man and he needed to have some independence.

Richard had been having a good spell and that certain November day had dawned fine and clear. He had decided to do some early Christmas shopping. The habit of being always ahead of the calendar had developed in response to never being quite sure when an attack would arrive. He'd completed his purchases and determined on lengthening his afternoon - a sort of show of being able to be alone. He called into Merridew's office for a quick conversation with his brother, nonchalantly arranging to meet at the corner near the library just after five o'clock. They could travel home together in the carriage, which would call to meet Ralph as usual.

Subsequently he had drifted into an artist's gallery followed by a bookshop at which he could not resist another purchase and then, feeling a little tired, he had made for the teashop used by his family quite regularly. The afternoon was closing in. A mist was making the streets wet and the air thick. The tea-shop bell had announced his arrival and at once he had been recognised and directed to a good table beside an open fire. The Green Room Café had a delightful atmosphere, being decorated with theatrical momentoes; programmes, pictures and even wall-sized scenes of dancers in costume. Around the fire were shining brasses and little lanterns flickering with lit candles. Wall brackets held globed gaslights that popped conspiratorially and cast a honeyed light into the cosy room. Chintz curtains, tablecloths decorously covering too shapely table legs and padded seats produced a comfortable atmosphere. Richard had felt at home in the familiar room, cocooned by the hum of conversation, comforted by the hot tea and muffins dripping with butter. He had sat reading the novel he had just purchased and only when he became aware of the silence enveloping him did he realise how late it had become. The proprietress had allowed the fire to dwindle to a mere glow, and was quite noisily making a show of turning the pendulous "OPEN" sign on the door window to "CLOSED."

Richard, full of apologies for overstaying his welcome and keeping the good lady later than he ought, paid his bill and unsteadily regained the pavement. Once on his feet again he had to admit to feeling less than well. To make matters worse the mistiness that Richard had noticed earlier had turned into a fog - a thick white cloud, damp and clinging. As he made his way across town towards the library Richard had begun to cough and by the time he reached the new Free Library he was desperate for shelter. He had pulled his muffler round his mouth and tried to breathe only the warm air but the effort was a dismal failure. He saw the entrance to the library as a haven, coughed his way up the steps into the porch and then stumbled inside to hang onto the edge of the issue desk, coughing as if his lungs were about to burst.

Richard was used to the ministrations of women, the comfort of cool, gentle fingers on a hot forehead, the soft tones of female voices radiating care and concern. So it was not Gertie's gentle sympathy that made such an impact on the sick young man. He was only dimly aware of her help and support and totally oblivious of the embarrassment his disturbance had created inside the library. Richard's fevers contaminated real life with a dream-like quality- a fantasy of unreality. Distances, sizes, shapes became distorted - sometimes grotesque and occasionally beautiful. Ceilings crushed him, chandeliers swung low until he ducked before their onslaught, streets became enveloped in yellow, swirling mists whatever the weather.

Amongst these mists had been a young woman. Her face he did not see, her figure he could not describe but she had an aura of such attractiveness and seemed so familiar that she floated with him into his carriage and lay with him in his tangled, sweated sheets.

When Richard emerged, as he always did, from the distress of his torment, the memory of the young woman, hazy and incomplete as it was, remained with him and he had determined to see her again.

Armed with his bouquet, Richard had retraced his steps to the library not at first being certain whether the young woman he sought was an employee or simply a customer. He had seen Gertie as soon as he had entered and had known that access to her must be via her superior. He had been unprepared for the librarian's strict attitude. He had been dismissed like a naughty child. Nevertheless, he had left his flowers and settled to wait outside. His reward for his patience had been the sight of the most beautiful young woman who he had ever seen, hesitating on the library steps, clutching his flowers.

Once Richard had seen Gertie, really seen her, he loved her. He supposed that he fell in love, for the feeling was akin to falling, the pit of his stomach going down forever leaving a space where it used to be. His heart beat more strongly and his muscles felt powerful and taut. He loved the sight of her, the sound of her voice, the softness of her skin, the silkiness of her hair. He couldn't get enough of her conversation, her opinions, her experiences. Gertie became the pivot of his existence, his raison-d'etre. Gertie was his, his own, his secret.

Not for one moment would Richard have experienced any problem in introducing Gertie to his family. Admittedly she worked for a living, but in a library. Certainly her home was in a court but she was such a lady, refined and well read. She had a respectable friend, Mrs Peake, who was known in quality circles and with whom she visited the theatre, concerts, dinner parties. Had Richard known it, his family would not have cared one jot for Gertie's original background. It would have been sufficient for them to see that she made their beloved Richard happy, that for the rest of his life, however long that may be, he could experience what it meant to be a man.

But Richard was so wrapped up in his own experience, this new and overpowering emotion that he wanted to savour it, exploit it, keep it for himself like the jealous lover that he was. He would tell the family when he was ready. For a while he would escape, be an independent individual with this own life.

The Grants worried about Richard at first, this going off alone was so unusual. Yet he seemed much brighter, stronger. Whatever his new interest was they resolved to let him alone so long as he remained well. In consequence Richard appeared in the library regularly, walked Gertie home to the head of her entry, was introduced to Mrs. Peake, escorted them both to plays and enjoyed countless evenings by the fireside chatting about authors, about books and about life.

Christmas was magical, a fairytale for Gertie as her dear Mrs. P. renewed her wardrobe and allowed Richard to join their festivities whenever possible. Gertie, desperately afraid that her bubble of happiness might burst, said little at home. Sarah and Abel assumed that her friendship with Richard Grant was just one of the many new experiences designed by her benefactress to bring the glow to her cheeks and the sparkle to her eyes. Clara, however had seen Gertie with Richard, recognised him for a gentleman and suspected how wrapped up in this young man her friend really was. She was very much afraid that Gertie was going to be hurt.

Gertie spent little time with Clara now. It was not that she harboured any grudge against her friend for having become so close to her mother, for having known of Sarah's pregnancy. It was simply that Gertie's life was a whirl of work and wonderland. She only had time to talk to Abel and her mother whilst she dried her hair at the fire or stood on a stool to have a drooping hem re-stitched.

Clara's misgivings were echoed by another person - Mr. Samuel Lees. He still queried the propriety of a young man being so obviously enamoured of a young lady without introducing her to his family.

"The whole business smacks to me of intended rape and pillage," he muttered as he fingered the stem of his port glass experimentally.

"You do talk such nonsense, bachelor brother mine," scoffed Mrs. Peake. " They are just getting acquainted under my eye. I'm a very efficient chaperone, far better than the Nightingales would be."

"And what's more the lad's not well. That cough, that hollow cough. And some days his cheek is bright and his eye is, well, far away. I don't know, Alice. I don't know but I'm not content. In fact I am most discontented."

"Is Gertie doing her job properly, Samuel? Are you trying to tell me she's failing you?"

"No! No. It's not that. She's a good girl. Couldn't be better. In fact it would not surprise me if she couldn't manage a library on her own."

It was that last sentence that echoed in Gertie's ears as she entered the drawing room that night, for no other reason than the pleasure of Mrs. Peake's company and the possibility of talking about Richard.

It was that sentence which Gertie remembered and repeated at home, full of pride and a sense of achievement. Of course Sarah and Abel were pleased to hear such praise, however indirectly it had been given, but it was her father who crowed with delight.

Nightingale had been odd since Sarah's miscarriage. He had missed church on several occasions. He had returned home, walking carefully and smelling of spirits quite regularly. He never spoke now except on matters of business or to be critical. He criticised the lack of heat from the range, the quality of food on the table, Abel's high-handed attitude and Sarah. His wife could do or say nothing that escaped his censure. Even her silence was 'dumb insolence', her inactivity 'error'. Only Gertie escaped his displeasure. She was to be her father's reincarnation. Gertie was going up in the world, back to where he belonged.

Gertie and Richard were only alone in very public places, walking in the street, sitting in an alcove in a drawing room, conversing in galleries or for a brief moment in the library. Their love affair blossomed under the watchful, bespectacled gaze of Mr. Samuel and the motherly acquiescence of Mrs. Peake. Their mutual respect and admiration had to be channelled through a look, the brief pressure of a hand on an arm or a publicly expressed compliment.

By April the two young people were head over heels in love and at last Richard was ready to share his Gertie. It was after all, the only way that he could have more of her. His parents were away in Paris and so he and Gertie planned what he would say on their return in May. Gertie, too, felt sufficiently confident to tell her family about her feelings for Richard. She began to consider how best to break the news and whether Richard should dare to ask for her hand formally, confronting her father in his lair.

The spring warmth gave the two young people a new opportunity to enjoy each other's company. They walked. At first it was the park with its benches where two bodies could sit close, very close together. Then it was the castle walls with their ancient arrow slits at which two people had to stand so near in order to both look at the view at once and then it was the river bank with its meanders and woodland reaching right to its edge.

On one never-to-be-forgotten May day, when the sun was unbelievably warm, Gertie and Richard strolled very slowly out of the town and down to the river. Richard became increasingly hot. He was aware of the old tell-tale signs of fever, the recognisable feeling of distance and unreality. He had tried to ignore his lassitude and fatigue but as they walked on he had to admit to feeling totally exhausted. His cough was unusually painful, like a knife blade driven in between his ribs. As they followed the profile of the river Gertie became more and more concerned.

"Should we turn back, Richard, get you home, my dear?"

"No, love. Just a rest. I need to rest…. try to sleep a little, in the sunshine."

They found a dell, a sunny dip with trees on three sides and the bulrushes of the river on the fourth. The May blossom was like a white curtain drawn around them. Gertie spread her coat for Richard to lie on. He lay curled up until another bout of coughing made him straighten and arch in pain. Then, exhausted, he lay back on the slope with his eyes closed.

Gertie lay down beside him, spread the material of her skirts over his body to keep him warm and pulled his head onto the cushions of her breasts. He dozed, his arms under her skirts, his cold hands together as if in prayer, flat and still between her warm thighs. The sun moved but the lovers did not. Richard slept fitfully, waking in a half dream, confused in his fantasy world. Gertie lay still, loving him, willing him to feel better. Richard's hands moved between her legs, gently at first stroking the soft bare skin above her stockings. She should have been shocked, stood, shaken out her skirts and moved on. She did none of these things but lay whilst the sick man awakened her womanhood and buried his hot face in the coolness of her skin. It was Gertie who sought to give comfort and relief, Gertie who recognised in some instinctive way that she could guide this man to a peaceful harbour within her. It was her nature to be generous, to give all she had and Richard in the irresponsibility of sickness, accepted what she offered.

Richard's climax was not cataclysmic. There was no volcanic eruption, no earth shaking shudder – just a stiffening, a rigidity; and then, on a sigh he slipped into sleep. He lay, joined to her physically, her soul an innocent cloud drifting protectively around him.

When Richard awoke Gertie moved, knelt beside him, straightened his clothes and encouraged him to rise. He was obviously very poorly.

Anxiety lent her strength and, in a repetition of their first meeting, Gertie supported Richard's frail form as they retraced their way along the bank towards the town.

It was necessary to rest frequently, leaning against trees, sitting on the footrest of the stile, collapsing momentarily on the jutting stone of a wall, but eventually they reached a street on the outskirts of town where Richard lived. A few more steps and they were at the great ornamental gates that yawned their welcome at the foot of the drive.

Gertie was overcome with shyness. She looked down the length of the gravel drive, narrowing her eyes to squint at the vague looming shape of the Grant house amidst its long lawns and laurels. She felt so terribly insignificant. Without Mrs. Peake beside her the confidence of her new identity slipped away. Gertie was a Twenty-Four Court girl out of place. The words 'interloper,' and 'social climber' insinuated themselves into her mind.

"Richard, we're here."

The sick young man raised his head, recognised home and momentarily roused himself. "Gertie. My dear. Come in with me. Now. We'll tell them. Talk about our marriage. Let Mother get things organised. Date. Important to me."

His temporary lucidity was slipping again but his intentions were quite clear. Gertie could have gone into the house then, Richard leaning on her, needing her. The family were all there, home at last. They would have welcomed her.

"No, Richard. Not today. Wait. Wait until you are well. Can you manage the last little way alone?"

"Oh, my dear, my very, very dear." Richard's head was swimming again, a cough welling up. He began to splutter.

"Go in. Go in. Richard, do, please. Don't try to talk. Perhaps I should come with you."

But Fate stepped in and solved Gertie's dilemma. A young gardener had halted in his digging to examine a thrush's egg lying on the ground underneath the trees. The rasp and thud of his spade at work had ceased as he crushed and ground the shell underfoot and so the sound of anxious voices alerted him to their presence.

Hearing his young master's cough and recognising Richard's drooping form, Billy Nightingale risked approaching with an offer of help. Richard all but fell into those strong arms so anxious to bear his sagging weight whilst Gertie, in her preoccupation with her lover, failed to recognise her own estranged cousin or the look of malevolence that he directed towards her.

And so Gertie stood, watching Richard lurch away from her, supported by one who had always wished her ill, their indistinct shapes quickly enveloped by the falling shadows of evening and lost, too soon, to her own poor sight.

Chapter Twelve

Gertie was not surprised that Richard did not come to the library nor meet her after closing time. He had had bouts of illness before which had kept them apart. This time, however, Gertie found separation harder to bear. She wished that she had accompanied him home. Perhaps now she could have been visiting him, nursing him, raising his spirits. She was able to share her concern with Mrs. Peake, of course, but at home Gertie still spoke little of Richard. Being in Twenty-Four Court reminded her of the seemingly impossible gulf between them. It was easier to remain silent.

Sarah had derived so very much pleasure from seeing her daughter successful and involved with the kind of society that she had enjoyed as a young girl. When Gertie was at home the little kitchen had been full of marvel and excitement, satisfaction and hope. In consequence Sarah was immediately sensitive to the lapse in her daughter's high spirits and the old fear of Gertie's ultimate rejection had surfaced. She had never actually met Mrs. Peake and so she had nothing but her imagination to fuel her distrust.

It was late on the Thursday afternoon when this lack of contact was remedied. Sarah and Clara were enjoying a moment's respite together when the unusual but unmistakable jingle of carriage horses slowing at the head of the entry caused them to cease their conversation. The sound of footfalls, slow and feminine, and the murmur of a voice, its low pitch unlike the local strident tones, sent Sarah's heart fluttering with anticipation.

By the time she reached the already open door its space was filled with Gertie, white faced and anguished. Sarah took one look at her daughter's drowning countenance and enfolded her in a protective embrace. Gertie clung to her mother, allowing herself to be led towards the hearth and her father's chair, leaving the doorway open for a large but fashionable lady to hesitate on its well-worn, downtrodden step.

There was no need for introductions. Each knew the other. Each harboured her own jealous reasons for discord and each appreciated the reason why it must never show. Their shared concern passed from her mother's arms into Clara's. The months of animosity shrank away. Clara wrapped Gertie in the warmth of their old friendship and led her away to the stairs.

Sarah stepped backwards and opened her hands, her palms gesturing to the centre of the room, an unspoken invitation for Mrs. Peake to enter, but the lady remained where she was. The room looked to her too small for the two of them. " Won't you come in?" Sarah's tone was cold and precise, polite and surprisingly refined.

For a second Mrs. Peake almost accepted but then she heard her horses stirring, her coachman gentling them as a cart rumbled and clinked its way laboriously past in the narrow street. " No, Mrs. Nightingale, thank you. I believe that I may be causing some blockage outside....er...Mrs. Nightingale...er......

Gertie has had a shock. A dear friend, you understand. I heard of his demise. Took the liberty of collecting your daughter from the library. Obviously taken it hard. She would come home, to you. I would have kept her- but she wanted to come home!" Mrs. Peake's normal resilience, her ebullient self-confidence had quite deserted her. She had been so sure of her place in Gertie's life and then this afternoon, when she had wanted so very much to comfort her dear young friend a metaphorical door had been slammed in her face.

"Take her home," Samuel had said.

"Yes, of course. Put the dear child to bed. I'll send a note to her mother and..."

"No, Alice, take her to her mother. This is no time for playing games. I'll get her coat."

The tone of the chief librarian's voice had brooked no argument even though Mrs. Peake had wished to remonstrate that Gertie would be far more comfortable with her. "To her mother, Alice," he had repeated, while Gertie had nodded her acquiescence and Mrs.Peake had suddenly felt the outsider, lonely again.

During the short journey home Mrs. Peake had cradled Gertie in her arms, murmuring comforting words into the softness of her hair but for the first time in their friendship there had been no response. It had been like holding a corpse. She had clasped Gertie's body to her but it was as if its soul had fled and gone wandering in the mists calling, weeping, whilst its home was as stiff and cold a temple as ever Death could have wished.

Alice left Twenty-Four Court feeling dreadfully depressed. It was as if she had lost Gertie. In contrast Sarah felt strangely comforted. Whatever had happened she still had a place in her daughter's life. So it was with a vague sense of satisfaction that she heard Mrs. Peake's steps retreat down the entry, the slam of her carriage door followed by the rattle and stirring of horse and harness as her adversary and benefactress retired from the scene.

It was a white faced, lack lustre Gertie who appeared at her post three days later. Gertie behaved as if she too was waiting for Death to claim her.

Mr. Samuel Lees was more affected by Gertie's sadness than he would ever have thought possible. He tried in little ways to lighten her load but she was like a doll on a musical box, a graceful, mechanical miniature. Gertie had shrunk into herself, lost her spirit. Mr. Samuel could not reach her. Death seemed to have her in his grasp.

Mrs. Peake's own sense of distress was lessened somewhat by the recognition of her brother's shared, sincere concern. She reassured him that time would heal but as the days became weeks there was no sign of any change in their young friend. There was no indication of any healing, no awareness that a Christian death was ultimately salvation. In fact, Samuel confided to Alice that he feared Gertie was genuinely ill. Could she, he wondered, have caught the consumptive disease?

Mr. Samuel had noticed that Gertie's face had become thinner, that she went all day without eating, pushing food away as if the very sight of it was sickening. At times he heard her being physically sick.

Gertie blamed her symptoms on grief but the nausea became so intense and relentless that she was driven to search the medical manuals on the library shelves. It was there, between the book stacks, that Gertie died a second time. She put a name to her symptoms and knew that she was with child – unmarried and with child.

Gertie looked so appallingly ill, so dreadfully distraught that Mr. Samuel could do nothing by five o'clock but suggest that she leave early. He would manage alone until the library closed. It was Friday and a busy two hours were envisaged as borrowers organised their weekend reading but he would manage. Gertie went through the motions of refusing his offer but they both knew that it was only the strings of politeness that tied her.

In consequence, shortly after five Gertie stood at the top of the library steps and tried to breath slowly. It was a very different young woman who stood there to the innocent girl Richard had seen and loved. Gertie's face was so thin that her eyes had become large, pitiful pools of sorrow but not of regret. She was frightened. To be a fallen woman was a terrible thing, bastardy a significant social handicap. Nevertheless, despite her fear, Gertie knew that she could have withheld nothing from Richard and that there was some comfort to be found in the part of him left within her. Her emotions leapt from despair to a kind of joy, from fear to elation.

As Gertie steadied herself she tried to think logically and decided not to go rushing off into the heat of the late afternoon but to sit quietly and to review her options. Any onlooker would have been moved to see that tragic figure bent as though carrying the burdens of the world. So obvious was her pain that the young man hastening from his office to meet his family's carriage on the corner near the library could not help but notice her. He stopped his headlong rush, hesitated, half recognised Gertie tragically poised on the steps, raised his hat and then moved on, clarity dawning upon him at the last moment. Richard's brother had recognised the girl of the fog. Simultaneously Gertie had looked at the young man, been momentarily startled by Richard's eyes in a stranger's face and then recognised this hesitating young man as her lover's brother.

There are so many forks and crossroads in life, so many times when we hover between one choice and another, only to reminisce in later life and daydream about what might have been. This was one of those moments. As Ralph moved on he very nearly turned back to speak. Gertie almost caught his arm. Had she done so, told her story, acknowledged her fall from grace she would have received –contrary to her expectations -only respect and gratitude. Instead, Gertie chose to let the moment pass and so could not be told that the Grants had been grateful because Richard's last illness had been so short, that they had appreciated the secret joy that had carried him through those final months of his life with a vigour and determination decrying all medical prognosis.

Eventually when sickness had claimed him they had taken their turns by his bed sharing his final fevered nightmares but it had been Ralph who had shared his dream. It had been hard to tell if Richard were lucid at first or whether he had been lost in his phantom world but as dawn had streaked the lightening sky Richard had breathed slowly, speaking each word as he exhaled, using his last painful breaths to speak. " I would have married her. I wanted to marry her. Now…..too late. Find her. Love her for me. Buy her …… books."

Ralph had known his brother's final secret but not the identity of his loved one.

It had been a sensitive issue, but Ralph eventually had felt able to share the substance of his brother's last joy with his family, "He had been in love, Richard had fallen in love." His sisters wanted to find out the girl's identity, ask around for people who might have seen them together. Mrs. Grant urged caution. "There must have been a reason why Richard, dear Richard, did not bring her home – did not invite us to meet her family."

"Normal thing," his father spoke gruffly, trying to contain his emotion. "You ladies don't appreciate. Normal. Sown a few wild oats. Nothing to be ashamed about."

"Perhaps best left," agreed Ralph, "Unless she comes looking for us." An almost ominous tone tinged his words.

"Leave that to me. I'll settle accounts," his father had blown his nose and walked to look out at the long shadows of the May evening, sharing his emotion with the windowpane. " I'm grateful to the lassie, whoever she is. My boy knew ...... happiness, it seems."

"But Father," Muriel, Richard's youngest sister had not lost her faith in her brother. The beauty of his character still shone like a light in her head, "Richard wouldn't. Not a lady of the night."

"Muriel," her mother gasped, "There is no need for you to use such words."

Muriel was not abashed. She stood, holding her small round embroidery frame like a shield before her, chin up, eyes hard and bright with unshed tears. "Have you forgotten so quickly what Richard was like? Ralph said, he did, that Richard would have married her. Somewhere out there is a respectable girl – breaking her heart – and we ought to find her."

Had Ralph stopped that night and looked into Gertie's eyes he would have known beyond a shadow of a doubt that her grief mirrored his own, that the slipper fitted! But he didn't stop. He didn't look back and Gertie didn't reach out. Her ghost walked away from the steps, slipped through the iron gates of the park and sat on a bench, blind eyes turned towards the ducks squabbling unconcerned on the lake.

It seemed incredible to Gertie that normal existence could be going on. She could hear birds chirping in the trees above her, the sound of water playing on parched earth as a gardener attended to his particular responsibility for life and the pat and bat of ball as a child walked past concentrating proudly. Gertie looked at life through her veil of tears and committed the sin of wanting to die.

For a fleeting moment the memory came back to her of Em turning from doctor to daughter with her contradictory desire to die and to live. She understood. It would have been easy to die, to reach out to Richard but she knew she had no real option but to live.

From beneath a laurel bush a skittering sound brought Gertie back to reality. A tiny black kitten crept then darted from the shadows into the sun. It walked mincingly down a sun-baked storm furrow and out into the path to stop in front of her. A winter leaf, brown and curled, lay where it had been wafted from its grave beneath the bench. The kitten patted it with velvet paws. The leaf moved. The kitten pounced and reduced the leaf to dust. Only the memory of it remained. Gertie bent to the little bundle of fur. It allowed her to pick it up and cradle it on her lap, luxuriating in the sun that still held some heat. Its black, button eyes looked up at her trustingly while she stroked and petted it. Suddenly Gertie felt the connection. The kitten was the symbol of the new life within her. She dabbed at her tears and tried to think. Stroking the soft creature seemed to have calmed her, quelled the rising panic. Decision time!

Gertie felt that she had three alternatives. Doing nothing was not one, for the problem was not going to go away. She stiffened as she thought of the bloody sheets and her mother's pain – no not that way. The viable alternatives all hinged on whom to go to for help.

The obvious person was her mother. Sarah would be strong and brave, brazen out the shame, love her and the child but she would suffer for it. Father would see it all as her mother's fault, his princess brought to bed of a bastard. She could hear him ranting, raving, see her mother reduced to a frail shadow. No, that would not do.

Mrs. Peake. She would help – broad-minded, practical, relatively wealthy. Gertie was sure that their mutual affection was strong enough to withstand this present distress but how would her mother feel to see her beloved daughter scurrying to a stranger in her time of need? No, that would not do.

Since Gertie, failed to consider the Grants as an option that left only Abel. Abel would know what to do.

A bed of blue cornflowers nodded their fringed heads as a passing breeze disturbed their composure. The kitten, attracted by the movement, rolled to the bench, sat transfixed and then leapt towards the flowers like a tiny panther. An elderly gentleman walking purposefully past had to disturb the rhythm of his step to avoid the little creature.

"Thought black cats were lucky. Lucky black cat," he muttered as he went on his way, "mischievous little bastard!"

The last word pierced Gertie like a sword. She stood, squared her shoulders and walked in the direction of Abel's office. There was more at stake than her reputation. She had a child to consider.

Detheridge and Son, at half past six, was closing up for the night. One of the junior clerks was bolting the shutters into place and whistling. He didn't hear Gertie's approach and as the bolt went home he unselfconsciously twirled into a dance step stopping suddenly in a characture of a triumphant cricketer, arms outstretched and a cry of, "Howzat!" To find his superior's beautiful sister bearing down upon him with her face frozen into a mask of distress filled Howard Huggins with horror. He could only imagine that it was his unprofessional conduct outside these respectable premises that was the cause of her concern. He stood aside, allowed Gertie to walk into the outer office ahead of him, and then stumbled in to announce her arrival to Abel.

Abel needed only to glance at his sister's face to understand that something was again dreadfully wrong. He nodded at Huggins. "Off home, Howie. Go see to your Dad's 'osses". It was the same every night, a sort of joke between them for Howard, thanks to Abel, had hoisted himself above his father's "osses' and kept his hands clean. In fact, he lodged with a respectable widow and spent his evenings perfecting his copywriting, as far away from horses and family as he could get. He didn't wait to be told twice. With his face flaming and every spot three feet high, he pulled off his shirt armbands, fastened his cuffs, grabbed his waistcoat and fled into the deepening shadows of early evening.

Abel had risen at this sister's approach and gently led her to a chair beside the fire that smoked, ready as always, for Mr. Detheridge.

He bent and poked the embers into a glow. The inner office was cool even today. He pulled his own chair round to sit near to her, bent forward and covered one of her icy hands with his own.

When Gertie spoke she was surprised by the normality of her tone. "You're working late, Abel. Still at your desk and the shutters up. You don't alter do you?"

Able sensed refuge in the familiar topic, "You know the situation, Gertie. Old Man Detheridge relies on me. Never lets me forget I'm his right hand. He's getting on now, takes more time off than ever when he's under the weather. Last week he told me that I was not only his right hand but his left as well. Spent half an hour on a diatribe against his son. He seems to have got the message at last that our Arthur is not much good. Apparently, he swans in and out of the other office, all matey with his fellow solicitors, turning a blind eye to their foreigners and taking only the odd case himself and that only a will or a marriage settlement. Nothing too onerous. Nothing that might tie him down to a court date."

"It's no surprise to you, "Gertie spoke automatically trying desperately to show a polite interest in her brother's conversation.

"No. Of course not. Trouble is, Gertie, that this time the Old Man is really bad. Coachman told me there's to be straw put down in the street outside the house and towels looped round the doors from knob to knob to stop them slamming. He's got to be kept quiet and peaceful. That means I'll have Arthur showing his face here. And I can do without that!"

Abel, judging that his sister had calmed a little, became quiet, gave her the opportunity to choose the topic of conversation.

"Abel..... I ..... Abel, there's much I haven't told you."

"I guessed, love. Is it time to tell now?"

It was. And Abel teased out the full story of his sister's meeting with Richard Grant, their friendship and their love. As he listened he couldn't help but feel some anger towards Alice Peake who had usurped his mother's role in observing tasteful etiquette. He resented on his mother's behalf that a young man had been allowed and even encouraged to pursue his sister without parental blessing or even knowledge. His better sense told him to understand, to appreciate the social gulf that Gertie had been bridging but his emotional response was bitterness and anger. His reactions mirrored Mr. Samuel's.

"And he hasn't told his family about you, Gertie? He's met you, he's courted you, he's proposed marriage to you and never asked permission of your father nor spoken of you at home! He's nothing but a bastard, Gertie. He's not to be trusted! Let me get my hands on him, causing you this distress," Abel had stopped listening and jumped to the understandable conclusion that his sister was in a state because she had been ill used, led on and dropped! "Just give me a chance to talk to him the ….."

"He's dead, Abel. He is the one who died. He's the friend I've been weeping for. You can't. I can't …. talk to him ever again", and Gertie's composure slipped, her memories of the joy and laughter, the shared interests, the pleasure had faded and left only a void - an aching, endless void.

Gertie could not bring herself to tell the rest of her story and so it was Abel, suddenly old and very worldly who, by gentle question, nods and gestures, laid bare his sister's shame.

His fury flared momentarily only to be doused by Gertie's sobs that it had been her fault. It was she who had initiated the closeness and, between her agonies of despair, she painted the picture for her brother of the sunlight and the dappled privacy of the little dell where two innocent creatures had loved for the first and last time.

Abel could not remain angry. Faced with such love, such hopeless tenderness, in the light of what Gertie had unconsciously recognised as Richard's certain death, how could he condemn her? For her sake he excused the dead man's sin.

Brother and sister clung to each other long after the lamp lighter had passed by and the street was criss-crossed with theatregoers in their finery. Abel dried Gertie's tears and reassured her of his affection.

"I'll not desert you Gertie, love. You did right to come to me. I can clearly see what has to be done. Now look, let's be off home. Mother won't be worried for she'll think you to be with Mrs. Peake but go home you must, nowhere else, and not a word. Say you're not yourself. She knows of your grief for a dead friend. She'll not ask questions. Plead sickness. You look ill. Go to bed. Pull the curtain close and don't sob. Mother will surely hear your tears and prise the story out of you. For her sake and your own, Gertie, be silent. I'll see you to the entry and be home later to tell you what must be done."

Clara, pulling her upstairs curtains, left sufficient gap to allow the light from the street gas lamp to fall in a pool on the floorboards of the bedroom. She had turned down the bed ready for her two sisters to come upstairs and lingered for a moment at the panes, marvelling at the silence of a street that had so many different faces.

By day its cobbles had been traversed by horses and carts, men striding along in their hobnailed boots, women in pinafores and pattens, children running with hot dinners and swinging billycans. Its evening face had been full of swaggering young men who walked up and down past giggling girls gathered in little knots round front door steps. Younger lads had bowled hoops and little girls swung their ropes, trying to look efficient and busy. Women had collected at the entries, shawls over their heads, arms crossed, gossiping and watching for their men folk. Now darkness had fallen the street was deserted. Only occasional footfalls echoed and rare shadowy shapes flitted between the pools of light.

Watching now, Clara saw the silhouettes of a man and woman, locked together making their way slowly towards her home. She recognised Gertie almost at once, her slight and delicate frame, the fashionable swing of her clothes. She supposed she should have withdrawn as the couple stopped beneath her window but it was such a relief to see Gertie taking an interest in life again after weeks of grieving for a dead friend. Clara felt almost a maternal satisfaction well up inside her.

"This gutter smells." The unromantic words drifted up in Abel's voice. "Go in now, love. Be silent." Clara was confused. Never had she seen Abel bring Gertie home with his arm around her shoulders. Why had he sent Gertie in and gone out again himself? It was past nine. She watched Abel's beloved shape until once again it was swallowed up by the darkness. She heard the metal click as Gertie lifted up her door latch at the end of the entry. Clara felt uneasy but she knew that it was better to remain invisible. If Gertie needed her she would ask.

Abel's direction was to the fashionable house occupied by the Detheridge family. It was one of many similar houses, imposing dwellings, situated around a square. The central square had railings around it and had been developed like a small park with its swathes of manicured turf, cool walkways and gazeboes beneath a canopy of green, swaying foliage. Only one gate led into this miniature Garden of Eden. Each house had its own key and so the creation was reserved for residents only, with one exception. An ancient, gnarled, old man pottered around paradise, maintaining its glory and periodically disturbing its peace by racing at the railings and shouting abuse at boys with sticks who ran their length hitting each one methodically. Where the old man lived no one seemed to know for he was there at daylight and, if a maid stole the key for a secret assignation, you could be sure that his shadow would loom up from the darkness. His body was twisted like a branch of some old tree and Abel wondered, not for the first time, if the old man had actually been planted there in the garden and could only move so far as his roots would allow.

Tonight, as Abel walked the length of two sides of the railings, he was aware of a shuffling shadow on the inside dogging his footsteps. It was late but here in the square lights still shone from windows, uncurtained and open to the balmy air. The chink of glasses and gusts of laughter wafted from the ground- floor rooms and as Abel walked past the steps to basements the occasional shrieks of servants and clatter of crockery reached his ears.

On the short side of the rectangular, misnamed, square Abel could see the evidence of his employer's ill heath. Straw had been soaked and laid to deaden the sound of passing traffic - iron horse shoes and carriage wheels. For a moment he stood, hesitating. Was it too late to call? He decided it wasn't. He would go to the basement tradesman's entrance, ask to speak to Mr. Detheridge's manservant, enquire after his employer's health and beg an appointment for the morning.

His arrival at the steps coincided with the front door opening and a smartly dressed male figure issuing from the silent depths of the house. The door was closed quietly behind him by unseen hands. The gentleman put on his hat jauntily and, taking a silver-headed cane from beneath his arm, beat a smart tattoo on the stone hand rail as he tiptoed light-heartedly down the steps. Brought face to face, Abel and Arthur recognised one another immediately.

"Sir, I ….."

"Don't Sir, me. Damn you! What are you doing hanging around here at this time of night?" Arthur was on the attack, slightly embarrassed that his bearing had been less than the serious attitude that might have been expected under the circumstances.

"Sir, I…."

"If you need to see, my father, don't even think about it. Far too unwell. Cope, man; cope. That's what you're paid to do. Talk to my father when, IF, he's better." He pulled on white gloves, ostentatiously adjusted their wrinkles and, without any attempt at civility, was gone with a light step and a wry smile. The "if" had been a sweet word.

Abel was non-plussed. His plans turned on their head. Without access to his employer quickly he was in trouble. He needed money

– more than his salary. He needed a considerable advance to supply his sister. His idea was for her to move. She would pretend to her parents that she had promotion, a bigger library in the city. He would arrange lodgings for her, respectable rooms for a smart young widow to have her baby in peace. His plans had even envisaged him seeking employment near to her so that eventually he could move to make a sort of family for the baby, try to dispel the shadow over its birth. It had occurred to Abel that he was sacrificing his own life, his prospects of continuing a good career and even his own marriage, but he was driven by his profound sense of responsibility and could see no alternative. Without money none of this salvation would be possible. The resulting shame and distress could not be born.

Abel dug his hands into his pockets and walked back along the railings of the square, conscious of the old man's eyes watching him from he darkness. "Good night," he thrust the words through the railings.

"Good night, sir," rasped a polite reply.

"Don't sir me," Abel replied under his breath, mimicking young Detheridge's rudeness and trusting the remark was low enough to have gone unheard.

Abel's frustration had allowed him to give vent to an uncharacteristic churlishness that he immediately regretted. He grimaced at the memory of Clara's comment to one of her younger petulant sisters, "Monkey on your shoulder? Careful it don't bite your ear." The origin of that peculiar statement was lost on him but the idea of a malevolent little figure sitting like an evil spirit, presiding over one's life was appealing just at that moment. He strode on into the darkness and tried to think.

He reached the centre of town where carriages waited outside a restaurant and groups of men and women were laughing and calling their goodnights. He paused on the paved square, listening to the fall of the fountain, leaning on its parapet. His fingers worked deep in his pockets, mechanically fingering matches, handkerchief, pocket-knife, keys. Keys! Of course – he had the keys!

Abel walked fast, turning and twisting down alleyways and short cuts until he reached the Detheridge premises. Feeling more like a thief than the master, Abel used the several keys to unlock and let himself into the office. Moonlight lit the outer office through one unshuttered window, high up over the door. The inner office was like hell – pitch black. Abel was so familiar with its shape and furniture that he could feel his way over to the safe. The metal was cold beneath his fingers. He felt for the safe key and inserted it in the lock. The heavy door swung open. This was stupid. He had every right to be here. Why move about in the dark like an intruder? Abel reached into his pocket. He took out matches, struck one and used it to locate the gas tap on the wall bracket. He turned on the gas. Its hiss sounded loud, like the warning of some slimy serpent that had followed him from the garden. He struck a second match, held it near to the mantle and the jet flared into light.

That was better. Abel sat at his desk. Now it was more like working late. He looked at the open safe door. Inside he knew was a lot of money, rents waiting to be banked, wages waiting to be paid, money to settle accounts.

Abel picked up his pen, lifted the lid of his inkstand, dipped his pen, cleaned it on the side of the well and wrote.

Mr. Detheridge, Sir – In your absence I have taken £150 from the safe. It is for a personal matter of which you would approve. I have no doubt of your approval. I shall repay the money to you by arrangement of salary deductions.

Abel signed and dated the paper, slipped it into an envelope and heated the sealing wax with his third match. The hot, red wax fell on the point of the flap and sealed Abel's action and his fate.

Fifteen minutes later the envelope was in the safe, propped up conspicuously where it could not be missed. £150 was in Abel's pocket. The light was off. The door was locked. The young man, convinced of the rightness and acceptability of his action, was on his way home. Humane Mr. Detheridge would have approved if Abel could have reached him.

Hours later, Clara, still watching from her window for Abel's return saw him come down the street and heard his weary footfall in the entry below.

Chapter Thirteen

A web of lies and deceit accompanied Gertie's eventual departure and left her feeling sullied and exhausted. Both Mrs. Peake and Mr. Lees had been bewildered by her determination to leave them and her beloved library. The sudden appearance of a wealthy relative who needed her was just too convenient, especially when there was a transparent reluctance to offer an address and a distinctly cool response to their suggestions of visits.

Clara, too, was convinced of a mystery. Gertie had told the family that she was moving for promotion but she displayed no excitement and had seemed preoccupied, only confiding whatever was on her mind to Abel. Sarah blamed Mrs. Peake for engineering the move, convinced it was another ploy to break the family ties. Ben Nightingale, however, was not critical. He basked in his daughter's 'achievement' until Gertie felt revolted by the extreme proprietorial pride which he exhibited, embarrassed by both the assumption of their closeness and the false foundation on which her father glorified.

There was another reason for Clara's discomfort too. Abel had changed. Overnight it seemed he had stopped meeting her eyes, become careful that the casual contact that had been so regular did not occur. He avoided her as if her nearness burnt him. What had been nontheless real for being unspoken between them was as if it had never been. Clara didn't know why. She only suspected that it had something to do with Gertie's distress at the death of her friend and her removal from home.

For Abel the weeks prior to Gertie's leaving had been a strain. He had been busy with enquiries concerning lodgings, overburdened at the office by Mr. Arthur's time-wasting, superficial visits on his father's behalf and distressed that, as yet, he had been unable to set the record straight with Mr.Detheridge. The letter remained propped up, visible and obvious in the safe which no one opened save himself.

On the day of Gertie's departure she was accompanied to the

station by both parents and Clara, as well as Abel who was travelling with her. Gertie was relieved that neither Mr. Lees nor Mrs.Peake appeared but paradoxically hurt by their absence. Ben Nightingale professed that he was surprised to find Gertie preferring her brother's company to his own, especially when he had so much more experience of travelling and 'foreign' places. Gertie marvelled at the impervious, thick skin of her father, to whom she gave no encouragement and who, nevertheless, felt that they had this special bond. It had surprised her how easily he was letting her go – a daughter leaving the family and not to wed – ah, but of course, she had belatedly realised that her 'success' bathed him in reflected glory.

Leaving her mother was different. She longed to cling to that comfortable body, to pour out her heartbreak and her fear,-so much fear of the unknown- but for her child's sake and her mother's she had to be strong. She had to remain silent. Gertie allowed Able to steer her out of her old life and onto the train, settling her in a compartment, thankfully almost empty and the departure time imminent.

Sarah stood, back pressed against the closed door of the little waiting room, her face white and anxious, watching the hurried activity of porters and passengers. The stationmaster raised his flag, blew his whistle once and glanced along the run of carriages. A cacophony of slamming doors and a hiss of steam preceded his second double blast, which heralded the dropping of his flag and the slow, laborious churning of the great wheels. The iron horse was on its way and, like its wooden Trojan counterpart, its belly held deception. Gertie's fixed goodbye smile didn't reach her eyes.

Both Clara and Sarah were nervous of the hiss and shudder of the train but, despite their natural instinct to move together for their mutual support, they maintained a discreet distance. Gertie's last view of their proximity should not hurt her. They stood apart, silent and uncomfortable, eyes fixed on that pale, beautiful face which was so dear to both of them, its vacant, lost expression pulling at their heart strings. Why was Gertie making herself take this promotion? She clearly did not want to leave them.

It took only seconds for the train to gather speed and, as the last carriage disappeared, Sarah's arm went out to Clara, who caught the elder woman's sleeve and moved closer to support her. Then, ignoring her husband, Sarah made her way back to the court voicing her misgivings to an equally concerned Clara. Nightingale did not follow them.

"It's all very well, our Gertie coping round here, locally, but how will she get on in a strange place? She almost forgets that she can't see well. I do so worry about her, Clara."

"She'll manage, Mrs. Nightingale. She looks slight and frail but she's a game' un. You know that."

"Oh, I know she's got spirit but I still can't comprehend her leaving us. It's not right. Young women don't do that kind of thing – lads, yes, but not girls. It's most irregular, out of order. I'm sure that Mrs. Peake is at the bottom of it – probably got tired of her, wanted her out of the way – engineered this promotion. You notice she's not on the platform."

Clara privately believed that there was every likelihood of Mrs. Nightingale being absolutely correct but saw the need to reassure her, "You're right, Mrs. Nightingale, girls of our sort don't travel away except if they go into service –but ladies do; they go to finishing schools and travel abroad. Don't forget Gertie 'as been a lady or mixing with them at least, so it's likely that some of their ideas have rubbed off on 'er."

The conversation continued as they made their way along Saturday streets, both women concerned for Gertie's pallor and her oddly withdrawn determination and both drawing some comfort from Abel being with her for her first night in a strange place.

Meanwhile, the train had left the town and was puffing its way laboriously through the countryside and on towards the city, past rows of houses, over bridges, alongside lanes and canals. Sometimes the track ran with a road and for a while a trotting smart carriage horse, head up on its bearing-reign, kept pace with them but eventually the steam train pulled ahead and the horse was left behind in the past. Gertie imagined that the train was racing away from her past too and for a while felt hope and a little excitement welling within her. Then she recalled how much she owed to Abel, wondered how on earth they would ever repay the Detheridge loan, felt fearful of the dangers of her pregnancy and once more fell back into despondency.

Brother and sister rarely spoke. Both were lost in past and future. For a while the present had no need of them. The other passenger in their carriage, an elderly gentleman, inhibited conversation and to some extent eased their journey for there could be no show of emotion in front of a stranger.

The train screeched to a halt at one o'clock and, laden with baggage and feeling hungry, Abel decided to take a cab to their lodging. They had no difficulty in climbing aboard one of the several waiting patiently outside the station. It was a pleasant ride at a sedate pace to the street where Gertie was to lodge - a respectable boarding house recommended by one of Abel's new tenants who had recently moved from this area. Abel had received confirmation of his booking two days earlier and had been relieved that they were to have somewhere to lay their heads that night. He had said that he was sure the accommodation would be good but privately he was wary of lodging houses and wished he could have afforded to rent a whole house for Gertie. She had professed herself very satisfied with arrangements, preferring to have company to being alone.

The cab stopped outside an establishment at the corner of Holland Street. It was a peculiar building with a variety of sloping roofs, which made it look as if it were a conglomerate rather than one building. Tacked onto its corner, overhanging the thin strip of garden which ran round its front and side, was a circular turret with a little pointed roof, a fairy tale room amidst ordinary urbanism. Gertie and Abel glanced at each other and hoped.

Abel helped Gertie down from the cab, lifted out their baggage and, having paid the fare, heaved their belongings up the steps preparing to ring the bell. There was no bell. Neither was there a knocker. Abel flipped the letterbox open, allowing it to shut. Over and over again he repeated the action so that the metallic clap echoed through the building.

"No one at home," said Gertie.

"There has to be. I specifically said in the letter – Saturday, half past one." He opened the flap again and this time bent over to peer through it. When he let go it didn't fall back. Instead it remained propped open and a pair of eyes stared back out at him.

"Whatcha want?" hissed a disembodied voice.

"Mrs. Mac – if you please," said Abel. "We're expected." He straightened up, looked at Gertie and shrugged.

It took another five minutes, several shrieks and growls and a great number of bolts pulled back before the door was opened and they were greeted by the eyes. They belonged to the smallest man that Gertie had ever seen. His head was normal and so was his torso but his legs were stumpy and his arms equally short. He laughed up at their surprised faces, uttered one word, "Circus!" and disappeared down the length of the hallway shrieking with laughter.

They stood there, the door still ajar behind them. Another door must have been opened at the end of the passage for a sudden draught pulled the front door to with a bang. They swivelled towards the noise and when they turned back a lady stood before them. That she was a lady there was no doubt for her skirts billowed around her almost as wide as if supported by an old-fashioned farthingale and her face was painted and patched as if she were about to walk onto a spotlit stage. Her theatrical gestures confirmed their first impressions —she curtsied, raised a ring encrusted hand to her mouth, splayed its fingers like a fan and from behind them uttered one word "Theatre!", but that one word was enough for Abel – it was a man's voice which spoke.

Abel had no second thoughts. He caught Gertie by the arm,

picked up her portmanteaux and, struggling with her boxes managed to open the door and exit into the garden. He uttered three words, "Circus! Theatre! No!" then, despite all their misfortune, brother and sister dissolved into laughter.

Turning down the corner house did not prove to be such a tragedy as might be imagined for the street was full of boarding houses and small private hotels. Many had 'Accommodation Full' signs but several exhibited vacancy notices and it took little time to settle on one that looked clean and inviting.

A shy, diminutive lady showed them to the vacant rooms. She said little but nodded and smiled and scurried around them, drawing their attention, with her quaint shrugs and gestures, to all the homely details which were likely to interest them. She had led them to two second floor rooms, one a delightful living room which looked out over the tree lined street and boasted a fireplace with a small hob and chimney hook, the two sufficient to hold a saucepan and kettle. There were gaslights on the walls and a sweet little arched doorway, curtained neatly, through which a small bedroom could be reached. In here was space for luggage, a bed and chest of drawers, a small marble topped wash stand and - luxury itself, a commode to 'augment the facilities out back' The latter had been thoughtfully draped with a length of material to match the counterpane and curtains. The window looked out over the outhouse roofs and yard at the back of the house.

The landlady drew the door curtain back still further, secured it with a neat chain which hung from a convenient hook and with a fluttering of hands and smiles showed how the little bedroom could receive light and warmth from the sitting room as it had no fire and only candles.

To Abel's practised eye, used to appraising accommodation, the rooms were quite comfortable, no apparent damp and obviously clean. Gertie cast him a reassuring look. She was more than satisfied.

Able took the lady of the house towards the sitting room

window and there, leaving Gertie to explore the nooks of the bedroom, he explained in undertones the sad situation of his 'widowed' sister-in-law. He tried to hand over money - extra for coals, water brought to the room, ashes and chamber pot to be emptied. He pursued his hope to be allowed to stay whenever he could visit but all his requests were met with a head shaking and negativity that quite confused him.

Eventually the little lady raised her bright, button eyes to his and managed to utter a few squeaky whispers that reminded Abel of a door that needed oiling. "Oh, sir, I be that sorry for the poor young lady but I daresn't do any special arranging or take any money off you. It's Mr. Littlejohn, my husband, as does all that sort of thing."

"And may I meet, Mr. Littlejohn?" asked Abel assuming a normal tone.

"Oh certainly," the lady maintained her whisper" but yous'll 'ave to come downstairs. I'm afeard 'e's crippled, you see. Doesn't come upstairs. 'E's in our basement kitchen."

"Then we'll go down?" suggested Abel, gesturing to Gertie to stay in the rooms. "You look around, dear; leave the business to me."

And so the decision was made. Gertie had a new home and Abel was as content about it as he could be under the circumstances. They spent the night eating food brought with them and, whilst Gertie tested the comfort of the bed, Abel confirmed the delights of the little rocking chair beside the fire.

There had been discrete noises during the evening, an awareness of other tenants moving around the house but the night had been quiet and Abel was reassured about the safety and respectability of the neighbourhood.

By the time Abel left on the Sunday morning Gertie was well provided with a store of sovereigns, secure in the knowledge that her brother had paid in advance for twelve months rent and services along with 'extra to cover any necessary medical attention.' Abel felt that he had planned for any eventuality as well as he could.

Mr. Littlejohn, in the shadows of his basement, had cracked his knuckles, flexed his powerful arms and impressed upon Abel that, though he could not mount the stairs, he had a wife who was kindness itself. She would befriend young Mrs. Nightingale – his sister-in-law .The significance of the slight emphasis on that word 'sister', the almost indecent narrowing of eyes was not lost upon Abel though the sentiments that the landlord uttered cocooned his attitude in propriety. Mr. Nightingale was not to concern himself. "No indeed, sir. Not concern at all. I quite appreciate the delicacy of your....err ..... situation. We shall be ..... ahem..... ah......discreet and kindness itself. And of course you will be welcome, sir, in our premises, whenever your ....err ......other.......err... responsibilities allow."

Abel's colour had heightened. He had known what the odious man had been suggesting. He was doubtful of Abel's relationship to Gertie, suspicious of his motives, made doubly so by a reluctance to leave any other than an employment address. Why, if Littlejohn had not been a cripple Abel would have been very tempted to knock him down. As it was, he had contented himself with the satisfaction that, cooped up in his basement, there was small likelihood of Mr. Littlejohn ever even speaking to his sister.

Abel had left Gertie with a heavy heart. Her brightness was as brittle as thin ice. He knew that once she was alone that ice would crack and beneath it was a lake of tears. Yet he had joined her in the charade of cheerfulness and promised to return whenever funds allowed. He had left her a supply of plain postcards and advised her to use these rather than letters to all but Clara and her mother. Addresses were not expected on cards. She needed to maintain her cloak of secrecy. At the back of his mind was the germ of the idea of allowing Clara to share their secret. What a comfort for Gertie if he could bring her! What a relief if she could stay awhile when Gertie's real trial arrived! In the mean time he would encourage her to write.

The journey home was without incident. Abel returned to his

mother's anxiety and a barrage of questions. He described Gertie's rooms close to the library, mentioned her genial and thoughtful superior and then urged his mother next door to put Clara's mind at rest. He did not accompany her but sat with Nightingale at the fireside, the two of them staring morosely into the depths of the coals, each one alone with his thoughts. Abel's recalled a childhood shared, Gertie's trusting companionship and her eyes when he left her, wide like those of a frightened deer above that tightly smiling, brave, little mouth. Nightingale's dark mood brooded on what might have been: his lost boats, his failed aspirations and how his fortunes had turned on just one fateful night.

Had they been able to share their thoughts these two men just might have found some philosophical satisfaction in the recognition of how a moment's passion could load the dice in Fate's vengeful favour and alter the whole course of her victim's life.

Chapter Fourteen

Monday morning was wet. The washhouse was already bustling with activity as the women of the court splashed through the puddles in their high-soled pattens, glowering at the lowering skies. Abel walked quickly to work, unlocked and had the shutters down before the rest of the office workers arrived. Howard was soon busy with the scuttle making sure Old Man Detheridge's fires were lit just in case, and a kettle was quickly steaming on the hob over the fire. The homely atmosphere of the office was spoiled by the direction of the wind. Whenever it blew from the east the fire smoked and soon the office was not a pleasant place to be as, periodically, billows of black smoke issued into the room and set them coughing.

At lunchtime, desperate for some fresh air, Abel left the office determined to walk over to see if he could obtain news of Mr. Detheridge's health. It took him twenty minutes of brisk walking to reach the house, striding over steaming pavements and sidestepping puddles. The road with its wet straw was a quagmire despite its cobbles and Abel was slow to pick his way around the square towards the Detheridge house.

As he was almost completing his slow traverse of the carriageway, Old Mr. Detheridge's manservant appeared on the front steps of the house. He had come up from the basement servants' quarters and was tacking a notice onto the front door, hammering in small nails with what looked like a toffee hammer. Then, wiping his eyes on his sleeve, he quickly returned to the bowels of the earth. Able knew without approaching any closer what the notice was. It was a white card edged in black. Unseen hands were closing curtains until the very face of the house itself was dead. As if awaiting this signal, other houses in the square began to draw their blinds. No horses, no vehicles, no people moved in the square. Even the birds fell silent as if out of respect for a passing soul..

Abel's heart dropped into the pit of his stomach. For a moment grief welled up almost unbearably. Then, recalling his place and his duty, he turned and crossed back into the centre of the square following the railings round the garden, head bent, unseeing eyes glazed with tears. Suddenly Abel was aware of a presence. It was strange, almost – for a moment, unnerving, but it was the old gardener again, walking with him, keeping pace on the inside of the garden, appearing and disappearing with the pattern of the vegetation. He was muttering, head down like Abel's, clearly distressed and almost incoherent.

As Abel neared Eden's gate, it swung open and the old man stood there acknowledging his presence with a stare. "It's a bad day," he said, "The young bugger's no cop!" Then he clanged the gate shut and shuffled away. Abel was never sure whether the old man's eyes were rheumy with age, or whether perhaps he was crying.

The office too pulled its metaphorical blinds. They let the fires go out and took the kettle off the hob. It was business, but not as usual. Voices were subdued and eyes downcast. Every single employee genuinely mourned an old man with a sharp tongue and the biggest heart in the world. Tomorrow they might be concerned for their own futures. Today they only considered the past and the hole left in their personal worlds.

Abel was a hard working employee but his dinner break was his own although he frequently chose to work through it. However, on the Thursday, two days before Mr. Dethridge's funeral as he sat eating his bread and cheese he felt no awkwardness about writing a letter to Gertie. He was so deep into his description of how affected so many people had been by Old Man Detheridge's death, including the old gardener, that he didn't notice a quiet step move into the outer office. Nor was he aware of a body standing over him until a hand fell, fingers outstretched, on his paper smudging the wet ink.

"Don't tell me this is business, Nightingale." Looks like a private letter to me!"

Abel stood, facing his new employer.

"It's my dinner break, sir. I'd not do it otherwise!"

Mr. Detheridge, no longer Junior, moved around the desk and manoeuvred himself into Abel's vacated chair. "Ledgers, if you please." He made a show of checking what he couldn't be bothered to understand and then he asked for the key to the safe. Abel wondered why he didn't use his father's but since his was attached to his person he opened it.

As the heavy door swung back Abel could see his letter, propped up significantly. For a moment he wished he had never written it. This fop wouldn't have realised the safe was £150 short but it wasn't in his nature to prevaricate and all he said as the grasping finger closed over the envelope was, "It was meant for your father, sir."

What followed was a nightmare. Mr. Detheridge, sir, was affronted. He used words like, 'untrustworthy', 'theft', 'embezzlement'. When Abel protested that the letter explained things and, moreover, that he had been promised a raise in salary that he had not received, the irate young solicitor became even more bellicose and shouted, "Huggins – the police, boy – fetch the Runners!" – and he did.

It was half past six by the time that Howard Huggins was free to run again, this time to Sarah Nightingale to tell her that her only son was detained in the police station.

It was to Clara that Sarah went at once, shaking and trembling in her disbelief, whilst Nightingale self- importantly set out for the police station.

When he returned from his jaunt he declared himself to be not one wit surprised as "blood would out and Abel had always been Sarah's!" He ordered, quite clearly, that Sarah was not to write to Gertie. She must not be told, not worried in her new position. Then leaving the two women distressed and weeping he mounted the wooden stairs to sleep soundly in his own bed.

The case of Detheridge versus Nightingale arrived in court very speedily, the charge: embezzlement. Abel's only defence was that he had not been paid his promised raise in salary during his employer's illness and that he had explained his action in a letter. He added nothing else to his explanation and the prosecuting council enjoyed himself at Abel's expense.

"Are we to excuse a murderer because he writes us a letter to give us reasons before he chops off his daughter's head with an axe?"

"Can we believe a fellow who takes money from a sick old man?"

"Before you took the money you visited your employer's house to make sure that he was too ill to check on the safe. You did, didn't you?"

"If Mr. Detheridge Junior hadn't taken you unawares, and you were unawares because he caught you writing love letters in the firm's time! I repeat, if he hadn't caught you before you could act you would have removed that letter after your employer's death and kept your theft a secret – wouldn't you?"

The allegations, suggestions, loaded questions tied Abel in knots and his refusal to answer concerning the purpose for which the money was destined added more insult to injury. He was a betting man. Perhaps he had a whore to keep. He had committed some other terrible crime and needed to pay off a blackmailer. Suggestions rained down upon him until his refusal to answer made the jury certain that he had committed one, if not all, of the imagined crimes.

Abel heard his character derided and criticised and yet failed, repeatedly, to defend himself for fear he would be led into revealing Gertie's shame. The proceedings took on a dream-like quality, fingers pointing, hands grasping, mouths questioning, questioning, questioning. He was in a tunnel of panic, running away from the light. He had wanted to move faster but his limbs were paralysed. He tried to speak and his mouth had opened to silence. The reality was that he dared not explain! In the jury's eyes he was a Nightingale and blood would out!

When metal had grated on metal and clanged shut on his life, Abel had woken to the realisation that everything was over and it was too late to redeem himself. He was locked into a cell and out of his life.

That feeling of having left everything too late did not, however, last long. When the initial panic and fear had subsided Abel knew that he had made the right choice at every turn. He really had had no option. His actions and silence had ruined his reputation but had preserved his sister's honour.

Abel withdrew into himself. He spoke little, replying only to warders' practical questions about laundry or slopping out. He tried to live mechanically, without thinking.

Each day he sat beneath the hissing, popping gaslights and squinted through the heavy, yellow light at the coarse mail cloth that he was required to sew. Somehow the prison staff discovered he was literate and set him to copy endless lists and numbers and then to sit beside fellow prisoners and take down their dictated letters. He had contact with others but kept himself separate, apart, an automaton whose life had gone into cold storage.

Nights were long and invariably cold. During hours of light Abel read and tried to lose himself in the pages of printed words but too often he needed to reread a page because his mind had wandered off elsewhere. In the darkness he either paced his cell or lay awake listening to the night noises of the prison. He rarely slept and when he did he dreamed, waking to tears spilling down his cheeks and his breath coming in great rasping sobs. Like a drowning man, he had seen his life suspended in one terrible picture - past, present and the future he might have had. All was clear, comprehensible and out of reach. He would stuff the thin prison blanket into his mouth, bite on it hard to stifle the sobs and then, exhausted by distress, drift off into a restless doze again.

These pictures sometimes insinuated themselves into Abel's waking consciousness. There was his mother, tall, strong, sleeves pushed up above her elbows working at the scrubbed kitchen table, working, working - always working - feet planted firmly on that familiar rag rug. There, before her shining, hissing range, her hands ever scraping, baking, darning, scrubbing, she was a capable, decisive figure, dependable, warm – a real mother, his mother.

Then suddenly the light would change becoming a gloomy, yellow, gaslight. Like melting wax she seemed to shrink and shrivel to a mere presence overpowered by the aura of his father.

Ben Nightingale never appeared in Abel's pictures. He didn't see the rough, bristling bulk of the man, the pale, bony knuckles or the heavy brute boots. There was no actual sight of the narrowed eyes with their tiny points of cold steel. He was simply aware of his father as a force, a power which dominated and changed whatever or whoever came into contact with him.

Nightingale's looks had always confused people outside the family. They expected a hard and violent man and instead found him to be the epitome of the unexpected. They discovered him to be a pillar of the community, upright and virtuous in the extreme. He brooked no slipshod ways, no watered down standards. In public he never allowed himself to appear irritated, never betrayed any emotion other than apparent patience. He was never seen to be violent or even abusive. He was the first to volunteer to dig a pauper grave, the first to offer his nightly vigil beside a new corpse and had, despite his own sad business loss, managed to bring up his small family effectively. Yet onlookers remained confused for Nightingale radiated a disturbing power – a power that lay not so much in what was but in what might have been. He seemed to hold himself in check so tightly as if he knew how easily he could have snapped, reverted to type. Oh yes, Nightingale did work hard and he did pray hard but then he was a hard man, though only his family knew how hard.

And that was why Gertie could not have born her father knowing of her shame. She had, Abel knew, been genuinely afraid that Father might have killed her, or, more likely, that the power of his anger would have made her try to kill herself. Even to think of suicide, self-killing, murder by another name was a sin and sin was now a commodity in which Abel was well versed. In hiding his sister's fall from grace he had allowed a cloak of wickedness to be dropped around his shoulders, a heavy mantle which swept the ground in great muddy, all- enveloping folds.

Abel recollected how the sharp, pointing fingers had wagged at him, informing him of his sin of treachery, to rob a dying old gentleman – nay worse, to steal from the business of a good employer while he lay dead upon his bed, as yet unburied. In one unguarded moment Abel had muttered ferociously that he wished he had told someone else at the office what he'd done, called another employee to witness his action. That had provoked another storm of condemnation and accusation of trying to shift blame, of embroiling others in his own perfidy. The prosecuting lawyer's forked tongue had skilfully shifted the argument and Abel had recognised his total inability to protect himself whilst still defending his sister's honour and he had resumed his silence which had inhibited the defence, a silence which had led him to prison and left Gertie alone. What price honour? What would be the ultimate cost?

Chapter Fifteen

The light had gone out of her life. Each day and night seemed to stretch interminably forward, a flat plain with no relief. Until now, Alice Peake had enjoyed her widowhood, at first its exciting freedom and lately the opportunity to play fairy godmother. Gertie had been perfectly cast for her rags to riches Cinderella role. Alice had so enjoyed herself rediscovering all the cultural pleasures of life and initiating Gertie, ever so gently, into what had seemed to be her natural place in society. It had been refreshing to see things through Gertie's eyes - like being young again or like having a daughter to share things with.

Samuel had warned her to remember her place, not to forget that Gertie had parents and owed a duty to them. Alice had listened and honestly tried to avoid developing an unattractive, possessive trait but Gertie was such a love that it had been hard. There had never been any self-seeking greed about Gertie. She had only wanted companionship and the opportunity to talk about her reading. Anything else was an unlooked for bonus. She had appeared genuinely fond of Mrs. P. The less Gertie wanted the more Alice had given - opportunities, experiences, clothes. If she had been concerned for Gertie's family it was only fleetingly and then only when Samuel reminded her of them. In fact she had developed a self-protecting screen of resentment against both Gertie's parents for allowing such a gem to go unpolished and to remain raw for so long. She felt that they could – no - ought to have done better.

The discovery that Gertie had an aunt, a wealthy lady, had been a surprise. It appeared that Aunt Muriel was actually an aunt of Gertie's mother, who had distanced herself from the family years before when her sister, Gertie's grandmother, had 'gone into trade', opening the drapery and helping in the pawn shop. This Aunt had behaved in a very highhanded fashion and had eventually reaped her just rewards by the early death of husband and tragic demise of her children from cholera. She now faced a lonely old age and had written to offer to make Abel her beneficiary if he would move to live with her.

It appeared that Gertie's mother had resented Aunt Muriel's intrusion and had refused but her father, his eye to prosperity, had suggested that Gertie become the sacrificial lamb.

Alice recalled the unshed tears in poor Gertie's eyes as she had explained to both her and to Samuel how she had to go and must exchange her wonderful work at the library for that of companion to an ancient dowager whom she had never even met. Brother and sister had been furious to see their Gertrude being used as a pawn in the family game and Alice had risen agitated, distressed beyond measure, offering to talk to both parents or aunt.

Gertie, flushed and looking exceedingly frail, had refused to contemplate any intervention on her part. She was convinced that she had to do her duty. Samuel had offered to hold her job at the library open for a few weeks in case the old lady, already ill and into her eighties, should die but – no - Gertie would not hear of any special consideration. In fact she had hurried from the room that night and rushed out into the street in a most unusual fashion, declaring that her brother would be waiting and she would, of course, work her notice. Samuel had lifted the curtain after the front door had slammed and there had been the brother, a tall shape emerging from the shadow, a respectable, upright looking fellow who offered his arm to his sister and drew her close, protectively, as they had disappeared into the night.

After she had gone Samuel and Alice had shared their concerns. This upheaval following on so quickly after young Richard's death was enough to turn a gentle girl's mind – but what was to be done? Neither had any right to interfere.

Alice had concluded in her usual determined fashion that what could not be changed must be borne, that this was to be only a temporary loss. In the days that followed she tried hard to penetrate the veil that Gertie seemed to have dropped about herself, to talk of what they would be able to do in the not too distant future but the distressed young girl was impossible to reach.

One lunchtime, Mrs. Peake had persuaded Gertie to take her break and meet her in Shaw's Tea Shop. The room had been a buzz of feminine conversation and she had already been seated at a corner table when Gertie had arrived and had stood pale and breathless, peering amongst the sea of tilting hats for her friend.

Alice had half risen, waved and been rewarded with an obvious expression of relief as Gertie moved towards her, "I'm sorry Mrs. P., am I so very late?"

"Not at all, my dear. I know you've only an hour so I have taken the liberty of ordering for you. I know what you like."

The hot onion soup and fresh warm rolls had arrived immediately and so conversation could focus upon punctuality, tastiness and quality of ingredients.

By the time the pressed tongue and salads arrived, conviviality demanded more personal observations.

"How are your plans for removal going, my dear?"

"Well, thank you, Mrs. P. Abel is to go with me next weekend, see me settled at Aunt's." Alice noticed the rising colour again. "He won't need to miss work but will return on the Sunday."

"You'll go by carriage, of course. So much more convenient when you have a lot of boxes and luggage. Door to door, so to speak."

"No. By train. I shall take only a little, just a small trunk of clothes- nothing more."

"And the address, Gertie? You must leave your address. I want us to write. Regularly. And I can visit you."

"But I don't....."

"I know you wouldn't want to impose on your Aunt. You don't know the circumstances yet. But don't be alarmed. I can put up at a hotel perfectly respectably and enjoy your company for dinner at least. The old dragon can't shut up my princess in her dungeons for ever!" Mrs Peake had smiled, tried to lighten the mood.

"Yes", agreed Gertie, eyes exploring the weave of the linen tablecloth. "of course."

But the veil had dropped again and this time it had become an impermeable steel shutter. Conversation had been steered onto safe subjects, hats and the horror of the Miss Banner's bicycle bloomers. The hour dissipated and Gertie rushed back to the library.

The days sped by with Gertie becoming paler and quite sick with apprehension. Then she had gone, whisked away by her, oh – so reliable, brother. Alice had pushed down the bile of bitterness, the horrible selfish sense of loss and stared ahead into an empty abyss.

★ ★ ★ ★ ★ ★ ★ ★ ★

Several weeks went by. Alice was perturbed, not by Gertie's silence, but by the quality of her contact. Cards; no letters – just plain, white cards with no space for anything but a brief greeting and still no address to facilitate a reply. Alice had passed through her loneliness and now felt a very genuine concern. Something was wrong. She discussed the situation with Samuel who had been the recipient of two similarly brief greetings. They agreed that something needed to be done. Alice was all for going to Twenty-Four Court and visiting that mother. Samuel was afraid for his sister, anxious that she was not exposed to the licentious, drunken choler of such an environment. He preferred to contact Abel and to do so within the formality of the Detheridge office. It was agreed that he should go when the library closed early on Wednesday and then dine with his sister to impart his news.

So, on the Wednesday evening Alice was listening impatiently for her brother's arrival, waiting anxiously for his own peculiar doorbell ring. At just after seven o'clock Tweeny pattered down the hall in response to the typically impatient Samuel-type jangle.

Brother and sister entered the hallway together – one cold, wet and very confused the other warm, dry but equally worried.

Rain cape and galoshes removed, Samuel sat before his sister's roaring fire and shook his head.

"Incredible!" he said, "Bloody incredible."

"Samuel!"

"Well, Alice, I'm sorry but it is! We know Gertie's brother worked for Detheridge, held a responsible position. It was a fact."

"Yes, of course."

"They'd not heard of an Abel Nightingale. A young clerk, putting up shutters, wanting to be off home, said categorically that there was no Mr. Nightingale who worked there. I tried to go into the office. Met a middle-aged man, blustering his way out. I stopped him, though he was obviously in no mood to be stopped!"

"Tut - and you might have been a client, Samuel."

"Yes indeed. I very well might. But he did stop and I asked him. 'Abel Nightingale' I said, very precisely, quite distinctly. He gave me a strange look, piercing, as if he would have liked to know who I was. Then he thought better of it and rushed out into the night with a grunt and a, "No Nightingale here nor ever will be!" A youngish gentleman came hurrying out then, so anxious to reach my rude companion that he almost knocked into me. Gave 'young Mr. Detheridge' a forgotten brolly and was left, empty-handed and apologetic, as his uncooperative employer - for that is who it obviously was - took to his heels and ran into the rain."

"Well I never!"

"That's not quite the end, Alice, for the young chap was clearly awkward about my treatment. He'd almost collided with me, a gentleman, whom he must have seen treated in an exceedingly cavalier manner by the Detheridge fellow. So he hesitated there, in the doorway, to pass a remark about the inclemency of the weather"

"And, Samuel? Hurry up! Get to the point. Did you ask him?"

"I certainly did, whilst rummaging in my pocket quite obviously looking for a half-sovereign".

"Did it work?"

"Well, in a way. I mentioned Abel again and as he took the offered coin he said, 'Mr. Nightingale? Who would have ever thought it? But I'm sorry, sir, I'm instructed - we all are - to forget that name. As far as the company is concerned he has never been an employee of ours. We don't know any man by that name – if you understand me, sir, though very sorry I am indeed to have to say it.' And he went inside and shut the door!"

"I knew it, Samuel. There is a mystery. Gertie is in some kind of trouble or her brother is. I'm going to Twenty-Four Court……. tonight."

"Don't be hasty, Alice. Go tomorrow. See the mother when the father isn't there. You're more likely to find out something from another woman. At least tomorrow it may be dry!"

By ten o'clock the next morning Mrs. Peake was picking her way delicately along the entry that led into the court, her coachman having been instructed to return in an hour. Her heart was thudding nervously as she stepped into the yard for a second time.

Mrs. Peake's memory of her first visit had led her to expect the worst but what she saw in day light was like a miniature village - the dirt floor neatly swept and the gutter down the middle of the court clean and sweet. Six doors opened onto the belly of the court, each one with an identical sash window beside it. Two other houses looked out onto the washhouse and lavatory opposite them. At the bottom of the yard was a midden pit, its surrounding wall sufficiently high to contain the daily vegetable refuse and ashes thrown into it. Next to the pit was a pigsty leaning drunkenly against a high cinder wall and a lean-to shed from which ensued the comfortable sound of hens.

A door opened and a young woman came out with a bucket, which she carried over to the pump outside the washhouse. She glanced curiously at Mrs Peake.

Alice, recollecting the Nightingale door, knocked hesitantly. When there was no response she screwed up her courage and knocked again more firmly, aware of eyes looking through windows and doors opening, just a crack.

The Nightingale door swung open almost immediately and Alice was confronted by Sarah, black skirt and white blouse all covered by a voluminous white pinafore. She stared almost rudely at Mrs Peake, jealously taking in the quality of material and style, which stood upon her doorstep. That this was their second meeting did not lessen its awkwardness. Alice opened her mouth to speak.

"You'll be Mrs Peake, then?" a lady's voice enquired, hostility prickling its tones.

That modulated, composed, almost cultured voice had issued from this raw-boned creature, this pale ghost-woman with her greying hair scraped back into the nape of her neck and her face lined with the ravages of a whole life time of cares. The woman, Gertie's mother, stepped back into her hovel.

"Come inside," she said.

Alice Peake gulped the clean air of the court and stepped into an Aladdin's cave that almost took her breath away. A watery sunbeam had found its way into the court and squeezed through the top pane of the Nightingale window. It teased Alice by twinkling on the burnished range, the copper knob of the polished black kettle, the gold of the shining brass fender. It drew her eyes to the whiteness of the scrubbed wooden table and the redness of the clean quarry tiles. She knew that she was staring, rudely taking in the order and homeliness of this poor abode. Then, as her eyes rested on the shelves at the end of the kitchen, bent with the weight of Shakespeare, Marlow, Dickens, her mouth dropped open and she uttered just a single sigh. How wrong she had been! This woman had not failed Gertie. The child had been her success. No wonder she had been so easy to train, to turn into a young lady. Why! She had always been one.

It pleased Sarah to see Alice Peake discomfited for she had harboured a jealousy of this woman who had 'adopted' her child.

Gertie had never suggested that she loved her mother less because she loved Mrs. Peake more but, with a finite number of hours in a day, Sarah had seen less of her daughter than she had liked and had shared in her successes only at second hand.

Now they were face to face each woman, each lady, needed to settle her own feelings before she could even speak to the other.

The silence was broken eventually by Sarah, Mrs. Nightingale, the hostess.

"Will you take tea?"

"Yes. Please. It would be welcome."

busied herself filling the kettle from the water ewer, put it directly onto the coals. She reached into a cupboard for a tin. She sliced seed cake delicately, placed it on a plate and put it onto the table, a corner of which was covered by a small incongruous lace-edged tray cloth.

Tea made, the two sat facing each other. Sarah felt at home on her own ground, strangely possessing the upper hand even though she was aware of her lack of style and fashion.

"Well, Mrs. Peake, what can I do to help you?"

"Alice, please," a small voice said of its own accord.

"Alice, then – thank you. I'm Sarah."

"Sarah." Alice nodded appreciatively. "Yes, of course. Gertie is Gertrude Sarah is she not?"

"Indeed."

"Well, Sarah. It's Gertie – Gertrude - I have come about. I need……. I would like…… to write to her."

"That's no problem. I have her lodgings here." Sarah stood and reached behind a can of spills on the mantelpiece. A card, white and business-like, identical to those sent to Samuel and Alice, was removed. In one corner was an address.

Immediately Alice was alerted. She was sharp enough to know that a young woman who goes to stay with an aunt at the request of her family does not need to send an address. They already know it.

"I'll copy it out for you," murmured Sarah. "So good of the chief librarian to arrange such suitable rooms for Gertie. And, to think she has your brother to thank for the promotion, Gertie being in sole charge of the reference section."

Alice pursed her lips. Gertie's address was transferred onto a scrap of torn paper, the edge of a news-sheet. She would leave without making any errors. Then her voice spoke again seemingly of its own accord: "So fortunate that Gertie has her relative in er......, Aunt Muriel, I think."

Mrs. Nightingale stepped back, looked at Mrs. Peake somewhat curiously, "Why no! We have no relatives. Both my mother and I were only daughters. We don't see Mr. Nightingale's family at all."

"Ah, my mistake. I'm sorry. The ageing process has its disadvantages."

"And I suppose you are missing my daughter, Mrs Peake........ Alice?"

Alice was not unaware of the emphasis on the possessive pronoun.

"I am. I must be honest - I am."

Suddenly eyes met and they were on first-name terms again, sitting together, comparing their loss, their different loneliness: and then Alice made her second mistake. "And your son, Abel, — he is not still living at home with you?"

Sarah stood, suddenly tense, mouth pulled into a straight line.

"We don't speak that name! Mr. Nightingale has forbidden it. But, no," - she was trembling visibly- "he's not living at home."

"I'm sorry. I didn't mean to ..... upset you. I didn't know. I only knew that he wasn't at his place of work. I assumed that he'd gone to be near his sister, on hand in case of..."

"What? In case of what?"

"In case of ....." Alice was floundering.

"In case of?"

"In case Aunt Muriel..... died!"

It was all too much for Sarah Nightingale. Her stiff, starchy pride crumbled. She collapsed onto a chair, put her arms down onto the table and, burying her head in the dark cave of loneliness, she sobbed very quietly. Mrs. Peake, feeling uncomfortably awkward and incapable of stooping to offer any consolation, wanted only to walk away from what she didn't understand.

Suddenly the latch on the door clicked and the empty doorframe filled with sunlight. A young woman stood there, strong, big-boned, defiant. She swung into the room, put down two covered pails of water and hurried to stand over Gertie's mother.

"It's alright. I'll look after 'er. You came for something. Have you done it? Have you got it?"

"Yes. Her daughter's address. Thank you. I'll leave then?"

"Alright, Mrs. Peake, it would be for the best."

How did this girl know her name? Questions crowded in on Alice but she was incapable of pressing any of them. She stood, shook out her skirts and, holding the copied address tightly, she walked out into the yard and down the dark entry to her waiting carriage.

Chapter Sixteen

A hot little wind stirred the tendrils of creeper that overhung the window. They whirled and quivered and then hung again in artistic stillness, draped from the red brickwork as if arranged by unseen hands. Nothing else moved, not a cloud, not a person, not even a bird.

Gertie sat at her window feeling feverish and swollen, uncomfortable in the Indian summer evening. She no longer felt lonely. She had learned to cope with being alone.

Since Abel had deposited her with her trunk of clothes and books she had developed an enviable self- sufficiency. At first she had been afraid. Night noises, the creaks of floorboards, shutting of doors, muffled voices had seemed threatening. Her imagination had allowed her to invent terrifying scenarios that haunted the hours of darkness. Light had brought some relief and then its own particular public terrors: possible recognition, fear of being labelled with as-yet-unwhispered words such as 'scarlet woman', ' whore', 'mistress'- words that echoed down the corridors of her mind.

Gertie had fought back, unwilling to let her unborn child be crippled by fear. She had developed an existence, a life focused on her child.

There were many days at first when sickness and depression had suffocated appetite and tempted her to lie down ready for distress to engulf her. Then common sense had won and she had tried to eat, to nourish Richard's baby.

Gertie did not rest well at night and only relaxed into a deep sleep when daylight fringed the sky. Then her fancies fled away and the comforting sounds of dogs and horses, wheels and footfalls finally allowed her to slip into real sleep. By nine o'clock she was normally refreshed, up and washing her face in the cool water left the night before, ready in her bowl. It took but a few minutes to twist paper and build a tent of wood, balance coals precariously, use a match to light a spill and then the spill to coax a small comforting flame out of the heart of her edifice.

Once the fire was alight she would make a nourishing porridge with oatmeal and water, eat it sweetened with a spoonful of treacle and then quickly don her outdoor clothes to go for her 'constitutional'. Each morning Gertie walked to the park, sat beside the lake feeding crusts to the ducks and watching mothers and nursemaids wheel perambulators past her. No one ever spoke to Gertie but a few women had begun to exchange smiles, to nod, to acknowledge her existence.

By half past eleven she was usually walking to the shops to purchase a slice of cold meat or pie, which she took back to her room. There she peeled or scraped her potatoes, put them into her one saucepan and boiled them. Meanwhile she read or perhaps wrote one of her postcards. She ate her meal sitting at her window, reassured by the regular movements of local people – the old man who always walked his dog in the afternoons, 'Mrs. Redcoat' with a child holing each hand, one who skipped happily along at her side and one who always looked down at the roadway as if searching for something lost. Gertie knew the smart green equipage that trotted down the road at two o'clock and back again at three. She looked for the milk cart and its patient horse, which made its slow progress down the road, stopping at almost every house to ladle its wares from churn to jug. She listened for her own front door to signify that her landlord's wife had gone out with her flat basket loaded with her tenants' motley collection of containers, performing one of the many little services that she did for them so willingly.

Gertie had named the kind lady 'Mrs. Mouse' for, from her vantage post upstairs, she could see the top of the good lady's head – a smooth, warm brown like a shiny-coated field mouse – and beneath it her scurrying, pattering tiny feet. At the cart Mrs. Mouse twitched nervously, constantly looking round as if afraid to be out in wide-open spaces and longing to scuttle back into her wainscoting.

Milk collected, the neat little body would hurry back into Number 52 and put the jugs and jars outside the door of each tenant's room. Two doors she tapped at. One just swung open when touched and Gertie would hear a muffled exchange of conversation and then the creak of the door, once more pulled to. That was the signal Gertie awaited each day. Within seconds, she knew, there would be a tap on her own door. She would clear her throat nervously, preparing herself to speak after so many hours of silence. And then - tap, tap, tap, "Your milk, Mrs. Nightingale, ma'am". Gertie would be just inside, hand poised on the knob of the door ready to turn it.

"Just coming."

The door would open smoothly, quietly, to admit Mrs. Mouse with her last jug of milk - a large, round, white jug its top half dotted with multicoloured spots, the creamy milk slopping richly inside it. Gertie loved the feel of that cool, round jug. It was the first thing she had bought for her own little household, had chosen it so carefully for its practical handle and good pouring spout.

For days the milk had been left with a quick, bobbed curtsey and a, "thank you ma'am" and then one of them had ventured a comment on the weather and the other on the peace of the neighbourhood until eventually two very lonely women had rushed headlong into a conversation that allowed them to mention everything from the park ducks to the price of potatoes but never anything personal. No first names, no comments about health or family, no reference to the bruises on the inside of Mrs. Mouse's arms or the one on her cheek bone that shone and changed colour from red to black to blue and yellow. Despite the superficiality of their discourse both women took comfort from simply knowing that the other one was there, in the house, just in case.

Milk delivered and conversation done, Gertie made herself go out again in the afternoon. Her treat was her weekly visit to the library but some days it was just a walk to the post, back to the park or up to the shops to gaze into windows. Each afternoon Gertie bought one piece of fruit and in September there was plenty to choose from. She carried a little fruit knife, which Mrs. Peake had once given her. It had a mother-of- pearl handle and its own little velvet-lined box. She usually took her fruit to the edge of the park, to a seat near the bandstand and there she would carefully peel her luxury, trying to take off the rind in one complete piece so that it hung down like a semi-coiled spring. Sometimes children played in the bandstand, running up and down its steps or marching together whilst playing their imaginary instruments.

Gertie stayed out as long as she could and then back she would go to bread and tea and maybe a little jam. She took her eating seriously now - a duty to the unborn.

Whilst it was light she read, thankful that she could, and more appreciative now of the love and loss in her novels than ever before. When the light faded she rarely lit a precious candle but undressed in the soft light of the night and then, cocooned in her shawls, she would sit by her window to enjoy her 'company'.

Gertie had begun to save her socialising until darkness, a pleasure to be savoured when no other could be found, a treasure to be hoarded until only the twinkling eyes of Heaven could see.

In these long hours of darkness the passive reader turned author and Gertie composed narratives in her mind, peopled from her past.

On this particular September night, whilst the over-blown, ivory roses rustled their parchment petals like so many dry diary pages, Gertie sat at her open window anxious for the heat of the day to give way to an evening coolness. She clasped her cup of milk and allowed her mind free rein. It took her tumbling backwards into tentative moments in the library, strolls along streets and bridle paths; it took her into Mrs. Peake's dining room, sitting room, book room; to theatres, concerts and dinner parties. In every scene she found the shadowy presence of Richard – his features less distinct, his remembered form less tangible- but his aura no less loving. She relived conversations, shared glances, stolen caresses and dwelt upon the joyous unfolding of her first and only love.

By the time the soft lights of neighbouring houses had been extinguished and her own firelight glow was reduced to warm, grey cinders Gertie had finished her milk and her reveries. As the church clock struck its final chime before slipping into its nocturnal silence, Gertie allowed her muse to slip into the future - a future in which Richard shared her waiting, her miracle, their life. They explored a twilight world together furnishing houses, interviewing nannies and governesses, travelling to Europe. They laughed as their son took his first steps, shared delight in his first word and grew old together gracefully as he paraded before them in his university cap and gown.

By the time the stars began to recede and the first streaks of dawn were fingering the sky Gertie was ready to move to her bed - slowly, laboriously and strangely content, full of positive emotions and a lifetime of experiences that she would never have.

The child moved in her womb - a small shrug of a shoulder, a caress like a butterfly's wing or the soft brush of eyelash on a lover's cheek. Gertie laid her hands on her stomach and in the coolness of morning she slept.

Had Gertie's orderly existence continued then she would have coped, supported by her letters from her mother, Abel and Clara. She had maintained the charade of her promotion, writing about the library and characters from her imagination. She described her lodgings as rooms with a family, sent menus of celebratory meals and planned visits home that were destined to be postponed in the next post. To Mrs. Peake she simply sent her greetings, afraid to display too much of her make-believe life lest the good lady spot errors and - in any case - not relishing lies.

Then, quite suddenly, life became more complicated – letters from home stopped. For two weeks nothing came and then, just when Gertie was becoming frantic, one arrived: a garbled, disjointed, out pouring of horror from Clara detailing Abel's arrest and the summary justice that had put him into prison for eight long years. Clara believed Abel innocent of the charge of embezzlement. He would never have taken Detheridge money but she failed to understand why he had no defence. She believed he was protecting someone, behaving honourably towards a fellow worker, perhaps one with some terrible problem. Mr. Ben Nightingale had taken it all badly. Stormed out of the court after the guilty verdict and swore he had no son – even forbade Mrs. Nightingale to speak of Abel ever again. Of course, Clara had seen to him, taken his things, razor and such like. She'd gone every day with pies and bottles of clean water, because she didn't trust prison taps but he'd been moved on and now – well - she'd write again when she knew more.

Gertie's pent-up emotion overflowed. She wept and sobbed so loudly that she didn't hear Mrs. Mouse's knock or the doorknob turn. She failed to register the neat little body putting down the jug and turning to go and only became aware of her when, summoning her courage, the good lady dared to put her skinny arms around a crying, devastated young woman.

"There, there, my dear! Life will go on. Whatever's the matter isn't the end of the world – more's the pity!"

No more words were spoken. Mrs.Mouse held Gertie until her weeping quieted then she put the kettle on the fire and busied herself brewing tea.

Once Gertie sat holding the cup of hot sweetness, Mrs. Mouse simply ran the back of her fingers down Gertie's cheek in an affectionate, gentle gesture and quietly left. No questions. No platitudes. She just left an oasis of calm behind her - a feeling that what could not be altered must be endured.

And Gertie endured.

Exactly three weeks later the afternoon tap on the door gave entrée to Mrs. Mouse, the jug of milk and a stout lady of voluminous proportions wrapped in a travelling cloak and carrying a square, brown paper parcel which could only have been several volumes of books. Mrs. Peake had arrived.

"Gertie, my dear! I got your address from your mother and started to write. Then I thought, 'If my dear girl is in some kind of trouble what is the good of a letter?' So here I am."

The retreating Mrs. Mouse caught sight of her lodger's face on which a series of emotions were flashing in quick succession. Horror, fear, embarrassment and, at last, the crumpling of a mask, to be replaced by a face glowing with affection and relief.

As the door closed soundlessly Gertie stumbled to her feet and crossed the distance that separated the two friends, to be enveloped in strong arms and clasped to a firm, motherly bosom. Gertie's girth was immediately apparent.

"My little love. Why ever didn't you say? Why all these lies, this web of deceit and cunning? So unlike you! I know. I know you must have been so very afraid."

"Not of you. Not of my mother. Father. He w….would have," Gertie's voice trembled with emotion..

"Yes, I understand - really I do. He probably would have nearly killed you." Mrs. Peake led Gertie through the arch and to the bed, sitting her on the edge whilst she divested herself of her outdoor garments. Then she perched next to Gertie, clucking and tutting, hugging and tidying back wisps of stray hair. "And here you are in this dowdy room, the two of you managing on goodness knows what."

"Not exactly two yet", Gertie smiled through her haze of tears.

"But Abel is here with you, surely? He's not at home, Gertie. He's not at Detheridge's. Your family are angry with him, presumably for leaving a good job to follow you here."

"Oh Mrs. Peake, dear Mrs. Peake, that was the plan. Abel was to join me eventually, act as the father my child will never know. We had decided to make a sort of little family but no! – I didn't know where Abel got the money to set me up. I believed he'd borrowed it from Mr. Detheridge but it seems………"

Gertie poured out the story of Clara's letter and at last Mrs.

Peake began to understand, to appreciate the mixture of emotions she had stirred in Sarah Nightingale when all she had gone for was an address. Then she realised that she was perhaps the only one, other than Abel and Gertie who knew the full story, for the Nightingales must still believe that at least one of their children was a credit to them and an honest citizen.

But now what was to be done? It was obvious that Gertie could not stay here, alone. The child would run mad. She couldn't go home with Mrs. Peake. That would set the cat among the pigeons. If the deception was to continue then the postmark needed to remain the same on letters or more lies would be imperative. Little by little Alice Peake began to see daylight. Another lodging! Perhaps an apartment with a reliable concierge to make her friend feel secure! And regular medical attention! But for the moment……. a hotel!

Gertie was in a daze of relief. She was perfectly content for her bossy, organising friend to call Mrs. Mouse who scuttled around at Mrs. Peake's bidding, collecting, passing, folding and finally summoning two young lads to help load Gertie and her few possessions into a cab.

She heard her friend establish firmly with her landlord's wife that an advance payment must have been made and that it would serve instead of notice but she did not discern the lowered tones of the continued conversation which h floated down, however, to pricked ears in the basement.

"Mrs. Nightingale's affairs have been in somewhat of a disarray, my dear," Mrs. Peake had said encouraging a swift and effective intimacy by laying a friendly hand on Mrs. Mouse's sleeve in a disarming gesture. "Thankfully they are now in order and she will be in a rather different position, you understand."

Her so charming little accomplice had twitched her head to one side, looked intelligent and rubbed her small, neat nose with the back of her hand, its thumb tucked in so that even to Mrs. Peake it seemed to resemble a tiny paw.

"I'd appreciate sensitivity on your part, dear lady. Perhaps you

might even forget my friend was here. Should any…err…..
undesirables come looking for her, please be as unhelpful as possible."
With that request Mrs. Peake passed five coins into that anxious little paw, hoping that even if Abel were unwise or desperate enough to enlist the aid of any prison acquaintances then they would meet only a dead end so to speak. "Thank you so much for your trouble," accompanied the comfortable clink of the coins changing hands and then Mrs. Mouse was left alone on the kerbside watching the cab move away and one of her most favourite tenants depart.

When she re-entered the house it was to descend to the basement, where her husband awaited her.

Gertie had never seen Mrs. Mouse's husband, whom she thought of as 'Dirty Rat'. Had she stayed for ever it is quite probable that she would still never have set eyes on him for he was, as Abel had seen, crippled, paralysed from the waist down. Whilst his lower limbs had wasted and shrivelled, his torso and arms had built up their strength and, sitting down, he looked a powerful and evil man. He relied on his wife for almost every basic care and yet he valued her only as chattel. He abused her verbally and then sometimes took her into a loving embrace, only to sneer at close quarters and to cuff her ear or smash his fist into her face. He had heard the valise thumping down the stairs and, possessing his fair share of native wit, he soon established that they were losing a tenant. His sharp ears had heard the cultured tones of Mrs. Peake and surmised that his tenant had been 'rescued' from her plight and that the young gentleman's well-laid plans had been thwarted. No doubt the girl's family were hoping that she had seen the last of him and were prepared to spirit her away. Whatever the situation he had no intention of being the loser in this transaction.

"It's your bloody fault," he thundered at his submissive partner, "you've done something. I know you 'ave. Won't you get it when I find out the truth o' the matter. Oh ar – I'll gie you one an' it 'll be a good un." He picked up a policeman's truncheon that lay conveniently near his chair and ran his hand appreciatively over its smoothness. "I'll ram this down your wasin. I'll choke the livin' day lights out of yer!" he threatened.

Mrs. Mouse backed away, her fingers closing tightly around the five hidden coins and her heart thudding as her husband continued to stoke his temper to unprecedented heat.

"So. We've lost our little 'widda', ave we? Widda!" he spat. "No widdas live 'ere. They stay wich their famblies – cheaper! 'Arlot she was. I 'eard er – vomitin and walking slower and slower up them stairs. Woman o' the night she is. No matter wot 'er precious relatives think, she'll spawn and be back to 'er sin and corruption. Leopards never change their spots!. "

Mrs. Mouse almost ventured, "She was a nice lady," but thought better of it and closed her mouth again.

"Well – 'er so called brover-in-law left me a tidy little sum he did – twelve months rent in advance and enough for what he called 'medical attention if necessary'– if bloody necessary. He won't see a penny of that back, not a halfpenny, not a bleedin' farthin'. Let me think it out now – a strategy, yes a strategy is what we need."

Chapter Seventeen

Abel's cell was one of the worst or one of the best depending upon the season and the weather, for its barred window was unglazed. In winter or exceedingly inclement weather a thoughtful guard might supply a wooden shutter that could be bolted into place. This improved the temperature but excluded light. Overworked or lax guards simply failed to respond to snowflakes melting on the hard prison bed or rain beating onto the thin, damp mattress. In summer the window let in light, air and life.

The cell itself was furnished with a stone slab, reminiscent of a mortuary. This was beneath the window and was covered by a thin, straw mattress and its complementary blanket. Beneath the shelf was Abel's bucket and on the wall his handle. The handle simply turned. It turned nothing, did nothing. It was a relic of the former prison governor's regime of harsh punishment. Prisoners had been kept in line by a process that was brutal and degrading and which often involved them in monotonous, purposeless work. Sometimes the work went by the name of shot drill - an exercise that demanded the movement of piles of cannon balls from one side of a room to another. When completed the pile of exceedingly heavy harbingers of death was lifted back again. Crank Drill had focused on the previously mentioned wall handle. It had to be turned so many thousand times for absolutely no purpose other than the edification of a guard who strutted the corridor, beating the walls with his cudgel and ensuring the cell inmates turned their handles to his beat.

The new governor was enlightened. Punishment was still intended to be unpleasant but there was no reason why society should not reap some benefit from the jailbirds housed at Her Majesty's expense. His favourite saying was, "We're not a lodging house, you know." In consequence Able sewed or sawed, copied or wrote letters to dictation and kept a tally of the days on his cell wall, desperate to be free, to get back to his life and to his sister.

Abel was allowed to receive both letters and visitors. His first letter was from his mother, written to his father's dictation he had no doubt. He was informed that he had no name, no family and no home. The ink was smudged and he could imagine the tears shed as she had reluctantly penned his father's words. Yet written them she had and read them he must.

Abel's first visitor was Clara. He hadn't expected anyone. Certainly not Clara. And yet it could have been no one else. Her skirts had whispered her arrival and her gentle, capable hand had closed over his own, her voice urging him to look up and speak to her for time was short.

Abel's first reaction had been bewilderment that Clara should have made such an extravagant gesture in coming. At her touch he had looked up, his own white and callused hands closing around hers.

"Prisoners do not touch. Stand apart if you will, madam!" The gruff voice of the guard startled them both. They sprang apart. Clara settled herself on the stone bench opposite Abel, trying to hide her horror at his gaunt and haggard face. There was a silence between them, awkward, embarrassing. Both had so much to say and yet neither knew how to begin.

It was Abel who broke the silence.

"How? How did you manage to come, Clara? It's so far and what will you do tonight? You'll not get home again."

"The carter. You know, the one who brings round fresh fish and always brings our wandering Bob home on 'is cart."

Abel looked blank.

"Bob – you remember, our black and white mongrel Bob, the dog who adopted us. Oh!" Suddenly Clara recollected how long it really was since she had seen Abel. Months! Of course he wouldn't, couldn't, recall the stray that had walked in one night, wet and bedraggled, settled himself before the fire and remained. Bob knew when he'd found a good home but he still occasionally suffered from the wanderlust and disappeared for a few days. He might have found it hard to discover Clara's house in the maze of urban squalor but he could always find the fishmonger's cart. When he was ready for home he simply followed his nose, ate heartily of the heads and tails in the rubbish bucket and then sat amongst the piles of fish-waste, waiting patiently for the carter to call in Clara's street.

While the fishmonger's wares were being shouted, Bob would sit up to attention, one ear up and one flapping endearingly over his right eye. Clara would come bustling from the entry, see Bob, thank the carter and then drag Bob off by the scruff of his neck to be bathed and freed from the pungent fishy odour. Quite a friendship had been struck between the old fishmonger and the young woman. He was a kind-hearted fellow and he had time for a lass who gave a home to a stray.

Never did Clara imagine that one day she would be glad of being able to sit on that odorous cart.

"Well", Clara tried desperately to pick up the thread of the conversation, "the carter had just brought Bob back again and 'appened to mention that it was lucky 'e was at home when Bob arrived else he'd 'ave 'ad to wait another two days. Then he explained as e'd taken on a run cartin' coal one way and bringing back fish t'other. Keepin' the cart clean enough for one job, it being dirtied by the other, was a bit of a problem, but he'd sorted it, and his market is so close to 'ere as you wouldn't believe. On a 'ot day I bet you could smell it."

Abel thought that Clara was going to prattle on about dogs and carts for ever, but she brought the topic to a close with, "So I asked 'im if I could come with 'im and he said I could and what's more I'd be welcome to stay with 'is niece who's married and got an 'ouse. So 'e knew, see; 'ed guessed as how I'd want to get to you if I could. An 'e'd med it easy for me to ask im. He's charged me nuthin' and says e's glad of mi company."

Abel was glad of her company too, just to sit with her was the tonic he needed. She began to tell him about home.

"Yer mother's fine. At least health wise she is. Talks about you and Gertie a lot. Feels bad that she's lost you both and at the same time. Said most particular that I should say she never sent that letter. It was all 'im. 'E talks about Gertie but 'e don't let anyone mention you. Oh, Abel, what will you do? You can't go back 'ome, – not as long as your father's alive an 'e's that tough 'e'll go on for ever." She didn't stop for any answer but looked at the guard worriedly, afraid that, noticing a moment's silence, he might think that visiting time should be over.

Nervously she continued, "Gertie, Abel. Have you heard from 'er? I've 'ad two letters and your mother's 'ad two. Both are strange somehow, full of details about her lodgings and the quaint souls she's fell in with – oh, and summaries of books she's read but she doesn't mention the library much. Perhaps she isn't happy there. And that Mrs. Peake came round to pay 'er respects and to see if anyone minded her writing to Gertie. I thought it was funny she 'adn't Gertie's address but now she 'as and I bet she doesn't just write – she'll be off up there visitin' and pokin' her nose".

"She musn't do that!" Abel interrupted her, his voice suddenly so loud that it startled Clara, "She must leave Gertie alone. Gertie doesn't want to see anybody."

"But why, Abel? There is something wrong, isn't there? I knew there was. She's writing all serious – no life in 'er letters at all."

Abel was afraid that this visit was going wrong. He suddenly longed to take Clara in his arms and tell her the whole dreadful truth, explain his own part in the turmoil of Gertie's life. Instead he just held Clara's gaze and said, "I am innocent, Clara. I took that money for an honourable purpose and I took it, not like a thief but like a businessman would. It was to finance a venture that Mr. Detheridge would have agreed with .And I'd have paid him back, Clara. They all know that."

" I know, Abel, I know." Clara leaned forward as if to touch Abel again, to reassure him. Anticipating her gesture Abel's hand moved into the space between them and was ready to take Clara's fingers into his own. This time the warder turned away.

"Look, Clara, I can't say much but I'm not in here for ever. I'll get a job, somehow, somewhere. There is still a future. Say that you......." Abel's voice was urgent. Then, suddenly, his eyes ceased to hold Clara's gaze and his head drooped as he remembered his sister's plight along with his promise to stand by her, "Say that.... er. Saying that's easy, isn't it?" he finished lamely.

Clara was confused. She felt that Abel had been on the verge of telling her something momentous, earth- shattering and then he'd suddenly withdrawn again into himself. Yet he hadn't loosed her hand and their fingers had interlaced like branches grafted together on a single tree. Abel raised his head, their eyes met and he leaned further forward so that their fingers steepled and their palms touched, fused together in a shared symbol of prayer. For a long, lovely moment their flesh was one and in this dark and dingy place, with its walls like running sores, and its terrible, echoing corridors leading to unspeakable scenes, two young people confirmed their love in silence and in pain.

A bell clanged somewhere in the prison depths, an incongruous bell which sounded like a school hand bell - too normal and out of place to be used as a signal for separation, but that was what it was.

Clara, unable to move herself away, remained on the cold stone and watched as Abel's warder hustled him away, guarding him so closely that not even a backward glance bridged the widening gulf between them.

Chapter Eighteen

Horace Kendrick was not what he appeared to be. He was a big man, tall, upright, of impressive military bearing, but his well-developed exterior disguised a small mind and an even smaller heart.

To be fair to the man, life had not been kind to him. Born into an impoverished gentleman's family he had quickly learned his place as a second son who would have to make his own way in the world. There had been sufficient funds to buy him a commission in the Army but Horace, despite his physique, was no fighting man. His younger brother was, however, and he quickly stepped into what might have been Horace's shoes. Parental respect and affection went in two directions. Neither was his. By the age of twenty-one Horace knew that he had never been loved either by his mother or his father, that he was merely tolerated by his elder brother and ignored almost completely by his younger one. He looked on at his, otherwise, close-knit family and wondered why he was the odd one out. What was the flaw that left him so alone and so lonely?

Horace had also never been attractive to the fairer sex. It was odd that someone with such imposing physical attributes and such fashionably regular features could apparently appear invisible in company but that was what he was. He had become accustomed to being ignored by his family but to be passed over by young ladies who managed to look through him, around him, behind him but never at him, was unnerving. The fact that their mothers might have mentioned his lack of funds did not make Horace feel any better and so his bitterness boiled within him just awaiting its chance to erupt.

Desperate to discover a niche in life that would offer some social standing and boost his self-confidence, Horace accepted the first post which responded to strings being pulled for him – that of prison governor. It actually suited him perfectly, for he was able to indulge his latent desire to strut importantly and bombastically in front of his inferiors, and he had ample opportunity to inflict pain and cruelty on both subordinates and inmates.

Becoming prison governor changed the marriageable situation somewhat. He was solvent, enjoyed the perks of extensive rooms within the great castle fortress itself and had the entrée of both business society and officialdom. Perhaps the prospect of living in proximity to dangerous criminals did not seem too attractive to many young ladies but there was at least one doting papa who steered his plain and rather mature daughter in Horace's direction. Emma Davies knew her place in the great scheme of things. She lowered her eyelashes demurely, blushed like a green girl and pretended to be moved by Horace.

After they were married she set up home in the prison's staff quarters, produced six daughters at regular intervals and never raised her eyes once to look her husband in the face. She allowed him to assume a dignity and a role that pleased him and never, by word or deed, did she betray her knowledge that he was anything other than the gentleman he seemed to be outside the prison walls.

Once he walked out of their suit of rooms and into the prison proper, Horace allowed his benign and honourable mask to slip. His eyes narrowed, his lips compressed beneath his flourishing moustache, whilst his hands clenched and bunched into fists.

From behind his desk the governor maintained a regime that his younger brother would have found impressive. Horace's institution was clean, orderly and, according to the prison board, a credit to him. There were rarely any 'incidents', never any escapes, and hardly ever any complaints. Warders jumped to attention if they so much as wandered into his periphery vision. Prisoners quaked at the very idea of being called before him.

Horace enjoyed his position and he became adept at discovering new ways of exploiting it. With his power, of course, also came responsibility. Horace was in charge of budgeting and purchasing for his prison. A little skimping in the prisoners' meagre diet put more food on his own table. An order for uniforms placed in the right direction produced a tailor eager to provide Horace's wardrobe. Similarly wise purchasing dressed his daughters, fed his horses and gained him numerous invitations to dine with the up-and-coming business industrialists of the city. Financially, Horace was sound.

Power over his employees was similarly linked to finance. If the men wanted to work they jumped at his command – and they did.

With the prisoners it wasn't so easy. Punishment, of course, equalled power but Horace needed something more subtle than beatings and starvation to enjoy. He found his pleasure in the mailbags, not in watching men hunched over the coarse material in cold workshops, backs stiff, fingers numb and bleeding – no, in the contents of the mailbags.

A good governor needed to check mail, know what was passing in and out of his institution. Plots could be hatched in writing, complaints forwarded to goodness knows whom, prisoners' equilibrium upset by the wrong kind of news! Horace made sure that only the right kind of letters reached their destinations.

It was amazing how important news became to men starved of familiar embrace. It was incredible how far men would go to discover if a sick child was still alive, a woman brought safely through a birthing. Grown men would cry when taunted with details of wives unable to wait longer for a postponed release, descriptions of daughters abused, sons dying in inform for a Queen who detained their fathers at her pleasure. Horace knew how to put the news. He was a master when it came to manipulating the English language and an artist in leaving certain things unsaid. He not only censored mail but he also offered a personal literacy service; he, caring man that he was, would write letters for certain of his inmates and read their replies to them – after all so many poor souls were illiterate. It amused him to alter messages, misread replies, play God a little with people's lives.

Sometimes Horace was frustrated by a prisoner who received and sent no mail or appeared immune to punishment. He enjoyed the subsequent challenge, the fascination of searching out the weakness, the breaking point and invariably he found it. Abel Nightingale was such a challenge.

Prisoner 24133201 was clearly an educated man, another upright individual whom Fate had surely treated unfairly. Horace could almost have felt some brotherly compassion for the man except for his aloofness, his apparent self-sufficiency. Such a man was dangerous. Leave him alone and he might display leadership qualities, be a source of power to the underdog, a spokesman. Better to destroy the dragon in its egg than let it hatch to breath fire and create destruction.

Horace watched Abel and waited his chance.

One letter had arrived for this silent, aloof young man from his mother – only one. It was a stilted, painful missive, which stated almost formally that his father would no longer recognise him as a son, and that he had no home to return to nor any family. She regretted that she was forbidden to communicate with him.

The Governor expected some reaction. Abel appeared unmoved. Perhaps there was no mileage in pursuing any family contact.

The woman, Clara, wrote boring details of a family and community left behind. Unimportant letters filled with trivia.

Then cards began to arrive – plain, white cards with a simple, repeated message. 'Am well.' This did begin to intrigue Horace – their regularity, their lack of news. Who was 'G'? What was she to Nightingale?

His painful curiosity was salved one day when an envelope arrived, brown and coarse, addressed in a heavy masculine scrawl and forwarded from the Detheridge establishment by a sympathetic Howard Huggins to Mr. Nightingale Esq. The Governor's fingers trembled in anticipation as he inserted his paper knife and made an incision along the edge of the envelope. He unfolded the cheap notepaper and gloated over the contents. Here, indeed, was what he had been waiting for. Not only did it answer his question about 'G' but gave him the precise location of 24133201's Achilles heel.

Dear Mr. Nightingale, Sir,
I regret to trouble you with family business at your place of work but not aving your ome address leaves me in a difficult position.
I am sad to 'ave to write the news that your poor widowed sister-in-law Gertrude Nightingale, as passed away.
As you anticipated she did need expensive medical attention. In fact we ad to ave the services of a night nurse as well as a midwife. My dear wife did what she could, runnin up them stairs wiv boiling water but in the end, the labour being early and too long, she ad to fetch a churgon. This good man was greatly distressed to see the sufferin of your poor, dear relative and determined to put it to an end. He performed a Caesar – a clever hoperation but I am sad to say it failed.
We ave made all the arrangements for the burial, a costly two coffin arrangement. (I was sure you would not want to stint on coffins) All is in hand and dealt with.
I regret that the money you left is all used up, gone on medical bills and funeral. Of course the room ad to be cleaned special and new linen purchased, being as all else was bloody and unusable.
As I said there is no change from your payment and if you should want eadstones that will be extra.
I am sorry to bear bad tidings.

    Your most faithful servant in all,

    Mister Littlejohn, Esquire..

Governor Kendrick immediately knew where his duty lay. Clearly 24133201 was dealing with some clandestine family business. A young, pregnant 'widow' was a situation more usually left to parents to discretely handle. The parents had a right to know of their daughter-in-law's demise or that of their son's mistress! Yes, they should know. He lost no time in pursuing an official letter informing Mr. Nightingale that, in the process of his pastoral care, he had discovered the sad death of a relative of which he felt he should inform him. He included a detailed account of the tragic end of 'G'.

Then he called 24133201 in and allowed him to read the newly arrived letter. The governor even offered a chair to the slowly blanching young convict. He had to admit that the fellow covered his feelings well. It was tempting to tell him of the other letter, the one that lay on the desk addressed to the father but Horace wanted to play this one out – watch what would happen. He sympathetically allowed his charge to return to his cell for a few moments of privacy while his own communication joined others in his 'out' tray.

The next scene in the drama followed hard on the heels of the first. A second letter arrived. The governor recognised the writing at once, the regular, sloping copperplate – 'G'. It must have been written before her death, delayed somehow by the post. Once more he inserted his surgeon's knife into the belly of the envelope and spewed its contents onto his desk. The letter was long and the white paper tainted with death. Almost reverently the governor unfolded the pages.

As he scanned the neat paragraphs found himself sinking into a story of intense fascination. He read of Gertie's initial distress at Mrs. Peake's arrival, her reluctance to alter what Abel had so generously established and then her dawning delight in being 'found' by her friend who was so willing to take care of her from now on. Gertie described how Mrs. Peake had gathered her up and insisted on going straight to The Metropole where she had organised hot tubs, soft beds, healthy meals of just the right balance for a young mother-to-be. Instead of being judgmental Mrs. Peake had actually been excited about the baby. They had already been shopping for a layette and were now looking for a suitable little out- of- town house, with a small garden. Mrs. Peake had agreed that Gertie must somehow maintain her widowed status and was talking of a post natal trip to France or Italy – perhaps as a respectable married lady with a husband overseas – one destined to die young.

Gertie's letter was bubbling with excitement and pleasure until in her last paragraph she let her distress and sympathy for her brother's plight spill onto her page. She concluded with the hope that eventually they would be together, free to be a little family as planned.

The governor smiled. He folded the letter, slipped it neatly back into its envelope and, leaning towards his fireplace, consigned Gertie's happiness to the flames. He leaned back and contemplated how intricate this particular web was, how well things were developing and he marvelled at how many people he was touching without even leaving his desk. The deceitful content and pecuniary motivation of the landlord's letter was quite easy to understand. In fact Governor Kendrick was rather taken by the idea of a partnership with another manipulator, even though his one was patently an amateur.

Somewhere out there in the darkness of the governor's kingdom a man wept for the death of a live sister, wept unnecessarily. "Ah!" light dawned in the governor's little mind – the man was incarcerated for embezzlement and now he knew why.

The spider had trapped his fly and could devour his victim before wrapping a shroud around its remains and leaving it to gather dust in some forgotten corner. He had set father against son irrevocably, possibly destroyed a daughter's reputation and definitely severed that very close bond which used to bind brother and sister so tightly. Horace was content with his machinations. But where did that neat little body which had visited fit in? Why didn't she write to Nightingale any longer?

Chapter Nineteen

Ben Nightingale's earliest memories were of standing in the Williams's draper's shop doorway whilst his mother was doing business in the pawnshop across the hall. He had stood, his little hand caressing a bolt of brown velvet that leaned against the wall waiting to be shelved. He had stroked the soft, silky pile, breathed in the smells of lavender wax and known that he belonged to cleanliness, order and the good things in life.

He never forgave Fate for having played the cruel trick of his humble birth upon him, a trick that ensured he was cocooned in roughness. His blanket was rough, his mother's hands were rough and his father's voice was rough. He hated growing up amidst quarrels and harsh words, guttural single syllable responses to practical questions. He despised the bed that he shared with his siblings and the appalling feeling of warm urine spreading under him from his younger sister. She dreamed and always, when her limbs thrashed or struggled to do so in the confines of the overcrowded mattress, she relieved herself. In consequence the room always stank of dried urine and often, so did Ben.

Ben's father was a carter, a man whose livelihood depended upon his horses. He should have treated them with respect but he bought winded old nags and drove them hard until they welcomed stumbling into an early grave. He topped up his family's income by exploiting his pugilistic skills, hammering his opponents above the belt in sight of the referee and kneeing them below it if a discreet opportunity arose. He often arrived home in a fighting mood and if he wasn't booked to meet a man in the ring then the woman on his hearth was the recipient of his fists.

None of the Nightingale family was slow-witted or lazy. They simply had no high standards to which to aspire, no awareness of the finer things in life, no experience of any but the most basic of emotions. Their only ambition, and it was a daily one, was to have a full belly, or in the case of Mrs. Nightingale – an empty one. Ben was different. He had the capacity to feel elation and the trigger, the stimulus, could be almost anything. It could be a mote of dust dancing in a sunbeam, the spine tingling peal of the church organ or the blood gushing from the cut throat of a stuck pig. He was hungry for experience and for answers. If others saw him pulling the wings off a fly and they labelled it cruelty then that was their mistake. Ben simply wanted to see how wings were fixed on, what made them work.

Mrs. Williams was Ben's Sunday school teacher and she was an experience in herself. She appealed to Ben's senses. He sat next to her and found opportunities to touch the soft material of her skirts. He wallowed in the gentle tones of her voice, inhaled the clean smell of a washed woman's body, fed his hungry soul on her Bible stories and followed her home whenever he could.

Like the other children, Ben gained access on Friday nights to that home and there he sat, in his shadowy corner, drinking in more than just Shakespeare's stories. He fed on the textures of the materials, the velvet curtains, the soft plush of the chaise longue. He luxuriated in the colours of the Indian carpet, the gilt of the heavily framed oils. He lost himself amongst the big horned, highland cattle that grazed in their dour scenes. He loved the burnished little Dutch boy who stood to attention on the hearth, his back hooks home to fire-grate utensils. This room with its lady and gentleman was meant to be his. He felt at home here.

Ben rarely spoke and so people thought he had nothing to say but how wrong they were. His mind was active. Like a hive it accumulated the honey of years, the appreciated nectar of the finer things of life. His thoughts and machinations buzzed in his brain like busy worker bees and his dissatisfactions were stored like a million stings.

Sarah's father had probably been the first person to feel that the world might have underestimated Ben Nightingale. He could never quite put his finger on what it was about the quiet lad that did not seem genuine. Mr. Williams only knew that the silent presence in his shadowy corner emanated power, an aura that disturbed him. He didn't like the eyes that followed his wife so hungrily and he was wary of the day when they might turn upon his daughter.

Ben's friendship with old Sydney was another thing that some people questioned. The relationship had been a surprise to anyone who knew him and even to the old fellow himself. Sydney was so used to being alone that he had almost forgotten how to be lonely – and then this young bugger had turned up. He'd just been there one day, sitting at the lock, legs dangling over the edge of the canal and waiting to do the heavy work. No words spoken between them, he'd jumped up and manhandled the gates and then just watched the barge move off again. The next night he was there again and so it went on until Sydney looked for the stocky figure and his old dog's tail thumped at the sight of the lad.

It hadn't been long before Ben was travelling on the barge as far as he could go and still walk home, except for Friday nights of course when he had other fish to fry. He became familiar with the old bargee, his ways and his business. Perhaps people wondered what Ben was getting out of the situation but the honest truth was nothing – until one night old Syd went to sleep and didn't wake up again.

Ben had walked up the towpath that night looking for *The Queen of Diamonds*. The old dog knew he was coming long before he was in sight and stretched her rope far enough so that she was on the very edge of the boat. When they saw each other she jumped up and down and barked. She went to leap onto the towpath at the same moment that Ben jumped onto the boat. It moved. She didn't reach dry land but fell into the canal, her rope just tight enough to hold her neck above the water.

Ben had left her there and moved into the cabin. When he came out he was smiling. He fetched the boat hook, reached over the edge of the barge, aimed the long pole and pushed the dog's head under the water. When the struggling stopped, he just cut the rope and let the body float.

Ben did everything properly then – doctor, burial. Nobody thought about a will and nobody thought about the barge – except Ben and maybe that wasn't such a new idea either.

The story of Ben's phenomenal hard work and the way he turned *The Queen of Diamonds* into a very lucrative business was well know in Duddington Port, although there were always those who wondered quite how it had all happened so quickly. There were a few who muttered about muffled shapes moving about when decent people were asleep, coal-sacks that clinked like metal when moved but they were jealous voices, of course.

It was those same voices that questioned his visits to the Williams' household and watched with narrowed eyes his progress from the shadows to the great double bed. Words like 'mercenary' were used to describe his courtship and 'jumped up bugger' his successful married state. The anxiety felt at Nightingale's progress up the ladder was ameliorated by the satisfaction felt when he was swallowed by the snake. A ' For Sale` sign went up outside his Eden and his attitude to Sarah matched Adam's to Eve. She had become the temptress whose guile had lost him his world. He was never going to forgive her but he had too much pride to wash his dirty linen in public. Nightingale's relationship with his wife would be a private war.

A lot of people were secretly satisfied to see Ben Nightingale back where he started and expected his lady wife to be another well-deserved millstone around his neck. They had never felt very much sympathy for the 'Miss Williams as was' because for her to have married the 'avaricious young bastard' denoted some flaw in her character. Their grudging admiration was an emotion which wormed its way unexpectedly into their hearts as a consequence of Sarah being such a surprise, a young woman who accepted her lot and got on with what had to be done, learning and copying and applying a lot more common sense than they'd given her credit for. And Nightingale - well, people had to admit that his behaviour left them in a considerable dilemma for he had become a pillar of the Church, a God fearing teetotaller; taciturn and morose but always observing the codes of respectable behaviour expected of a Christian. So, what a pickle for the congregation and the less religious residents of Twenty-Four Court! A young man, so long detested for his good fortune, falls on ill luck and apparently undergoes a character change for the better. A man who prays and digs pauper graves, a man who works all day and night to mend the vicar's roof after a storm and takes his turn at watching beside the newly dead cannot be ignored, cut, isolated. Ben had found another ladder – ecclesiastical acceptability was to put his feet back on to the rungs of respectability.

No one saw what went on behind his closed house door. People could only surmise that things went ill with his wife, despite the fact that he refused to let her go out to work and that she was never seen bruised. This supposition was based entirely on the alteration in Mrs. Nightingale's demeanour and the transparent reluctance of her friend, Em, to indulge in any enlightening gossip.

That Ben Nightingale had slowly suffocated his wife by the sheer weight of his character and that his children failed to develop any love for their father, however, did not go unrecognised but it was not spoken of. One did not, could not, criticise an apparent pillar of the community...... until it was noticed that he had begun to wander in the wilderness, from which he returned with unsteady steps.

Of course, Horace Kendrick, governor of Her Majesty's Prison, knew nothing of Ben Nightingale's character and so was not in any position to recognise the fellow feeling that he might other wise have done; the self interest, the desire for power over other people's lives, the readiness to play at being God. Perhaps it was a kind of divine retribution that Ben actually became the victim of a man so similar to himself, a man ready to manipulate others for his own satisfaction without concern for their feelings.

The victimisation came in the form of an easily recognisable letter from the governor, an officious communication that arrived one morning and sat behind the spill jar all day until Mr. Nightingale came home from work and allowed his wife to read it to him. Her hands had shaken as Sarah opened the envelope and held what she feared was a notification that some ill had befallen Abel in that terrible place. She read automatically of the over zealous governor's perception that it was his duty to impart information which had been revealed during his routine scrutiny of prisoners' mail. He had actually quoted lines from a letter sent to Abel Nightingale, 24133201, which referred to the death of his 'widowed sister-in –law', their daughter by marriage, if the governor was not mistaken. He regretted having to pass on what would undoubtedly be distressing information, especially as it involved such a prolonged and horrific death ending any hope that they may have harboured of an expected grandchild. Horace Kendrick, had reiterated his assumption that Mr. Nightingale would respect his professional diligence and not judge the messenger by the dreadful content of the message.

The full impact of what she had read did not strike Sarah immediately. She was lost in the quagmire of error, believing that there was some mistake, identity confused, letters wrongly addressed, misread.

There was no such confusion in Nightingale's mind. Immediately he saw the truth, the so-called improved library position, Abel's anxiety to see Gertie settled, Abel's silence in court. His anger burst upon his wife, a stifled staccato of terrible oaths. He blamed her for Gertie's plight, laid Gertie's lonely death at her mother's door. He shouted that he had no son, that Abel was hers, a replica of her treachery, spawned by the Devil. Nightingale ranted against womankind's responsibility for man's fall from grace and turned on Sarah, his eyes wide and wild like those of a cornered boar. It was her fault, her fatal flaw. The guilt of all women had conspired to plunge his family into disrepute; and then he had really begun to lose control, moving towards her menacingly, raising his white-boned knuckles, narrowing his eyes. His boots were ready for her, as they had always been, but this time he meant to use them.

Suddenly Nightingale's rage had changed to fear, a choking, rasping, gulping for air. His bunched fists had opened into great bird's claws – frightened, frightening claws that pulled at his collar as if it were a noose and then at the door curtain as he fell, heavily, onto the red quarries already frothed with his bloody spittle. His vision had narrowed while he lay paralysed and in panic on the cold floor. All he could see was the vortex of a whirlpool. He felt as though something pressed him down into cold water. He could not breathe. He was choking, drowning in his own blood.

When his body was quite still, she lifted the tea things from the table, pulled off the linen cloth and shook it. It billowed and then sank to rest hiding the hated body from her sight.

Outside, somewhere in the darkening court, a dog whined, howled and then barked with satisfaction.

Chapter Twenty

Had Gertie been able to escape she would not have tried but in the eventuality there was no opportunity. From the moment Mrs. Peake had swept into that rented room Gertie had been pressed to the good woman's practical bosom and, metaphorically, imprisoned in her silken but determined embrace.

Mrs. Peake had been shocked to find Gertie 'enceinte' but her natural inclination was to blame menfolk for taking advantage of the weaker sex and she immediately saw her young friend as a victim rather than 'a fallen woman'. To discover her in such a condition, and alone, inspired her protective instincts. It also had to be admitted that the good lady was not totally surprised, for she had known that something was amiss even before her uncomfortable visit to Twenty-Four Court.

It had been such a relief to actually discover Gertie relatively safe and unharmed, and so very satisfying to be in a position to be of practical assistance. She had had to admit, however, that her young friend's brother had not done a poor job in establishing a new identity for his sister. Even so, she had been glad to shake off the dust of that lodging house and to escape from the inquisitive, beady eyes of that strange little body. Mrs. Peake knew that she would never be able to refrain from smiling when she recalled the swiftness with which Gertie's Mrs. Mouse had secreted those coins away.

As that transaction was being accomplished Mrs. Peake was unaware that, although the landlord could not see his wife's secret acquisition, his sharp hearing could discern their quiet words. Exhortation to secrecy was music to his ears. If he was reading all the signs aright then a certain gentleman was going to be quite relieved to have no further responsibilities for his fruitful one-time mistress.

In the basement two grasping hands closed on the air and punched it viciously, whilst already narrowed eyes disappeared into slits of determination. Mr. Littlejohn had absolutely no intention of losing money in this predicament, nor was he averse to making a little trouble for the toffee-nosed bugger who had paid the bills for that young flibbertigibbet. Even before his wife reported the situation he had heard sufficient to put two and two together. If he could manage to keep hold of the generous payment and relet the room then he was in clover.

★ ★ ★ ★ ★ ★ ★ ★ ★ ★ ★ ★

Gertie had been so very grateful to Abel for finding her this bolt-hole with its cloak of respectability that she had never thought of her room as anything but a haven. She had been blind to its threadbare furnishings, chipped paintwork and the smell that permeated the whole lodging house – a smell of cabbage and the dankness associated with damp cellars. Now that she leant back against the padded, sprung seats of the carriage Gertie had to acknowledge that she felt relieved, and then immediately became alarmed that Abel might consider her disloyal to be leaving what he had provided and at such a cost.

Her face had always been a mirror to her thoughts and Mrs. Peake immediately appreciated the wistfulness that had crossed her young friend's face.

"We'll write, my dear," she said "just as soon as we have got you settled. Your brother only wants what's best for you. We'll write."

The carriage rolled then swayed and bumped its way over the cobbles of the Old Quarter towards the very heart of the city and there, beneath the comforting shadow of the great cathedral, Mrs. Peake requested the driver to halt. She asked Gertie to wait whilst she did 'a little organising'. The hotel had already put a small suite at her disposal that morning but she was anxious to improve conditions if she could. In consequence by the time Gertie was helped from the carriage and into the reception hall, a porter stood with the keys waiting to lead them to a much larger and quite imposing set of rooms. He had sent an underling rushing to Mrs. Peake's former suite and, since no unpacking had been done, it was a small matter to unite the baggage in the one accommodation.

By seven o'clock Gertie sat in front of a crackling fire thanking her friend profusely with as much warmth in her heart as was emanating from the leaping flames before her.

"I would have managed, dear Mrs. Peake - you know that I would. Abel had left me quite comfortable. But I have to admit that at times I did feel terribly alone and not a little afraid."

"Of course, my dear. And I'm not criticising your brother. He did his best for you, but how I do wish that he'd come to me instead of getting mixed up with that Detheridge business."

" Mrs. P, so do I - so do I. Never a day or night goes by without my wishing all this had never happened. And the idea of Abel in a prison! Why, he's so upright, so good, so very good."

"Now, my dear. Don't upset yourself. In your condition it is not right for you. And, in any case, Abel was fortunate to get prison. Most healthy young men in his position would have been in the colonies by now. As it is he's still here and we must see what can be done. Samuel will take care of that side of things, if, indeed, anything is possible".

"If only. If only it were possible, Mrs. Peake, but I am already in your debt."

" Don't talk of debt between friends, my dear."

"I am though. You have already done so very much for me and then I repay you by becoming a disgrace. I dare not let my own parents know my predicament and yet you, who are no blood relation, come like a good Samaritan and sweep me into ...." It was too much for Gertie. Her shoulders shook as she tried to control her sobs, but as she failed her friend left her seat and balanced herself on the wide arm of Gertie's chair.

The two women held each other and for a while it would have been hard to be certain which one sobbed the most.

Eventually it was the elder who collected herself. "Gertie, dear. To me you have become a daughter. This is not what I would have wished for you, nor is it the way I would have wanted to become a grandmother, but that is what I intend to be. Abel wanted..... wants.....your child to have a family, and so it shall, my dear. We shall be a family. In fact, I feel we already are."

Gertie's bed was turned down and warmed for her that night and as she lay amongst the softness of down pillows and flock mattress she allowed herself to think of Richard. This is how things would have been, she mused. Richard would have cared for both of us and I must not deny his child the chance to be brought up in Richard's world. Again the tears flowed but this time for the two young men in her life – one dead and one who might as well have been.

Two letters were composed next day, both destined for the prison. The first reached Abel via Horace Kendrick and was the deceitful indication that all his efforts on his relative's behalf had been useless and that she was dead. The second took longer to write but followed hard upon the heels of the first. It was Gertie's account of her removal from the lodgings. The last part of the letter held such grateful words, such burning anguish for her brother's plight that had he ever received it he would have been moved to tears. As it was the paper burned as well as any other in the governor's fireplace.

In the false security that at least her brother had been reassured about her position, Gertie became almost serene. She took to talking to Mrs. Peake about Richard, their shared hopes and intentions and even once declared herself prepared to let his family know of the birth of his child and her own family the truth of her situation. "At least then they would have the opportunity of contact, Mrs. Peake."

But that lady, with her greater experience of life, was cautious, "We can't afford for tales to spread, my dear. What is the point of us making such careful plans to give the child some 'background' then for you to give people the chance to recognise the child as a b

…..Well, you know what I mean."

"Yes, of course, Mrs. P; but, although I can see that you're right in a way, it does seem hard that they should lose their son and grandchild."

"Did they try to find you after Richard's death? I can't believe that, at least towards the end, he didn't mention you. Surely they could have made some effort to discover you. After all enough people saw you together. My advice is to leave it, dear. Leave things alone – at least for now."

★ ★ ★ ★ ★ ★ ★ ★ ★ ★ ★ ★

The next weeks passed for Gertie in an almost contented haze of security. It seemed as though for her the sun perpetually shone. After the loneliness of life in her room Mrs. Peake's motherly presence was wonderful, her wealth an unlooked- for boon. There were moments when she blocked out her distressing concern for Abel and felt truly at peace.

Mrs. Peake, on one of her trips out of the hotel, discovered a delightful house in a little close on the other side of the cathedral. It had a drawing room, a dining room, a small sitting room and kitchen as well as three bedrooms, one of which could easily be designated as a nursery, as well as maids' rooms on the top floor. Trees overhung the secluded garden and yet the sun shone all the day in one of its various nooks and crannies, bowers and terraces. The house was a veritable paradise of exposed beams and crooked floors, all polished and waxed and echoing the industry of generations. It was furnished already and so the addition of only a very little soon made it an ideal place in which to have Richard's child.

The two ladies moved into their new home with genuine excitement and were swiftly at ease with their cook and maids of all work. Such a small establishment had need of few staff.

A midwife and doctor were organised and so, having done all

that was possible to make Gertie secure and comfortable, Mrs. Peake settled down with her to knit and stitch and wait. Their peace was interrupted only by the occasional visit from Mr. Samuel and their growing anxiety that Abel appeared to be unable or unwilling to respond to any of their letters. Gertie's erstwhile employer, having displayed nothing but pleasure at being reunited with her, resolved to see what he could do.

Had the prison governor been gifted with magical long sight he would undoubtedly have gained considerable pleasure from the similarity between the description of Abel's sister-in-law's imagined death and the actual experiences that Gertie actually went through.

The midwife had done her best to ready Gertie for what was to come but the good lady had failed to prepare herself to witness the dreadful agony of Mrs. Gertie Nightingale. For two long days and nights the young 'widow' lay alternately calling for her mother and for Richard until poor Mrs. Peake was almost demented with worry. At last, totally worn out, Gertie's exhausted body was prepared for an operation. She was not expected to survive. It was just as the implements were being washed ready for use that Gertie's body relaxed from one of its now weak contractions and the midwife yelled that she had a little arm and could manoeuvre a shoulder. Gertie's daughter was born, bruised and blue but whole and destined to be perfect. The new mother was a very poorly young woman for several weeks, but she slept on feathers, her sheets were clean linen and what little food she ate was nutritious and appetising. In her lodging house Gertie would have almost certainly died and so would her child. In the shadows of the cathedral, lulled by the comforting sound of its tolling bell and the sonorous psalms of the faithful, she lived.

Fate, having been cheated, turned its back on Gertie and went into a sulk, leaving her free to improve her health enough to enjoy attending to her baby. Mrs. Peake was utterly delighted, totally relieved and ready to forget that it had not been her name that Gertie had called in her agony. Both women now were able to indulge themselves in their new roles as mother and grandmother and this they did with pleasure, Mrs. Peake punctuating their domesticity with counselling Gertie to be patient in the matter of contact with home.

Meanwhile, Horace Kendrick sat in the centre of his malicious web, appreciating the taut black thread at the end of which dangled Abel. He savoured the trouble that he hoped he had caused in the Nightingale house, and toyed with the idea of some mischievous response to Gertie on her brother's behalf.

Chapter Twenty One

For over a quarter of a century Sarah Nightingale had lived for the day when she would be free of the weight of her husband. She had married him through a misguided sense of obligation and, once she had become his possession, she had simply done her best in whatever situation she had found herself. Bereft of immediate family, she had allowed her feet to follow the path on which Fate had placed them.

This was not the attitude of a woman without spirit. A person of lesser character would have dissolved into tears, uttered words like, "I can't", "I won't", but Sarah had faced her lot with an acceptance and a determination that would have been more profitably directed elsewhere.

A novelist might have allowed Sarah's spirit to dominate her circumstance. She might have discovered some lucrative business such as her mother's draper's shop or exploited her social advantage and so maintained the subservience of Ben Nightingale. But this was not the case. In fairy stories characters are extremes of good and evil. If Ben Nightingale was evil (and he was), Sarah should have been the epitome of goodness and inner strength. Final success should have come her way. But this was reality. Sarah's character was not ideal.

Years of being in Nightingale's shadow had taken their toll and by the time she sat, with his dead body ignobly stiffening beneath its tablecloth, she was too worn out to enjoy the freedom that Death offered her. Those final curses and the reason for them had left Sarah as battered as if Nightingale had actually struck her.

When Clara found her, Mrs. Nightingale was sitting beside a dying fire, her husband stiff and cold on the hearth. She had one foot on the fender and the other on his covered corpse. Her own expression was totally blank. She was as if she had been carved out of stone.

Clara had run to fetch her father, her sisters – anyone who could help. Neighbours had crowded in and suddenly Clara had been ashamed for them to see Mrs. Nightingale so still and without tears. It was somehow indecent not to weep, and her foot still pressing on the body. That had to be moved. People had noticed, been shocked. Everyone had stood as if posing for a snap shot. Clara had broken the stillness, moved towards Mrs. Nightingale and gently raised her to her feet. Then in silence she had walked her to the stair door and helped her away from the gaze of the onlookers.

Between them the neighbours had done what was needed and Clara had ministered to the bereaved widow – or tried to do so.

It was not easy to manipulate a life- sized puppet, for that was what she seemed to be. Sarah did as she was told. She ate, she washed, she even did simple household tasks when asked to do so. She behaved like a good child who had been told to be seen and not heard. Her voice, once so vivacious, was quite stilled. Only occasionally did her lips move in inaudible whispers or bend themselves around unidentifiable verses.

Clara had no experience of a grief like this, if indeed, that was what it was. There were no tears. She found it impossible to believe that Gertie's mother was not relieved to some extent to be free of her hated husband and – if so – why the depression?

Clara appreciated that she had to let Abel know what had happened, and Gertie too, but her spirit quailed before a letter that had to contain the distressing plight of their mother as well as the news of the death of their father. Each day Clara put off writing, hoping for some change in Sarah's behaviour. Eventually she could avoid the task no longer. She wrote to Abel first. Her second letter was to be to Gertie. It was not easy to write of a father both dead and buried.

Horace Kendrick was delighted to receive Clara's communication. He was in no doubt that it was the stress of his own missive that had prompted the demise of its recipient and he relished the passing on of such dramatic contents. On this occasion he would wield his power personally.

Abel was ushered into the Governor's presence at eleven on the night after the letter had arrived. To tell a prisoner old news, information that had been withheld, was power in itself, to do so at an unexpected moment was clever. The rest of the prison slept.

"Ah! 24133201"

"Sir."

"You had a letter yesterday."

"No, sir."

" I repeat – you had a letter yesterday. I have been too busy to read it to you until now."

"I can read, sir. I can read it myself. I would prefer ….."

"No, indeed. It contains sad news. I could not allow you to distress yourself. It is my duty to ….."

"I would prefer, sir, to distress myself, whatever the news. I am a private person, sir. Please, give me my letter."

" I must remind you that you have no letter. You are my prisoner, 24133201. Anything you have – your clothes, your food, your letter, I give you; by Her Gracious Majesty's permission, of course."

Abel looked down at his boots. He knew now that this was a game of cat and mouse and that he had no hole in which to hide.

"Would you like to know the news from home, lad?" The hardness had gone out of the governor's voice. Abel was almost deceived by the velvet paws - almost. He did not answer. "Well if it's too much for you …." Claws were unsheathed. The governor raised his voice, "Brittlestone!" The door opened and a warder leered into the room expectantly. "Take 24133201 back to his cell."

Governor Kendrick expected his prisoner to turn, to beg, to ask for the letter to be read. He was disappointed. Abel allowed himself to be led away.

For three days Abel lived in torment. There was only his mother or Clara whom he cared about. What could have happened to one or the other of them? He could not sleep. He paced his cell.

His work was less than perfect. Common sense told him that whatever had gone wrong he was powerless, helpless. Knowing could make no difference. He held out.

Horace Kendrick, deprived of his initial sport, devised another plan. Prisoner 24133201 was sent for.

"I am impressed by your strength of character. You may read your letter and I shall be pleased to write your reply."

"Thank you, sir." Abel's hand trembled only very slightly as he took the single page of paper. His face betrayed no emotion as he read of his father's death. Only the movement of his eyes revealed the fact that he reread the lines describing his mother's state.

"Now settle yourself, my man," the Governor indicated a straight chair beside his desk, "You can dictate your reply. I'll take it down most faithfully, I assure you." He had half expected Abel to insist on writing his own letter but he was taken by surprise with the words,

"There is no reply to write, sir."

Damnation! The Governor's face hardened. He rarely lost but, he sighed, it simply sharpened the game.

Clara wrote her second letter, as planned, to Gertie. Until recently she had passed notes to Mrs. Nightingale to be included in any letters sent. On this occasion she needed to address the letter herself and asked for Gertie's postal designation. Only by the movement of her head did her friend's mother indicate the papers behind the spill jar. Clara reached them and began to sift through them, looking for the address she sought. Her eyes caught the prison mail, the formality of its arrangement on the official notepaper. Ever hungry for news of Abel, she allowed herself to scan its contents.

"My God!" Clara's intake of breath became a wail. Now she understood what had affected Mrs. Nightingale so badly. It wasn't the death of her hated husband that had turned her mind but Gertie, dear, clever, adventurous Gertie – and to have died in such a terrible way.

Clara looked up at Sarah Nightingale. She was sitting at the scrubbed table sorting her dried herbs. It was a task she did repeatedly, mixing thyme and mint together and then re-dividing them into their appropriate bunches. Whilst she did this she often whispered about rue and pansies, making reference to another's madness which was lost on Clara. This time she had ceased to whisper and was gazing at Clara, her eyes great and sorrowful in her increasingly old and haggard face. Clara gestured to the letter, displaying its contents.

"I've read it," she said. "Now I know too."

Nightingale held out her arms to her young neighbour who, in utter desperation, sank to the floor and buried her head in her dead friend's mother's lap.

Now three deaths bound them together, and, at last, the women wept.

From that night Sarah's state improved a little. She tried to pull herself back into reality, to show an interest in Clara's home life. She helped with washing, ironing and even baking. She welcomed Clara's sisters into her kitchen but she never ventured further than those two homes. Nor would she talk about Abel, Gertie or Nightingale's funeral. The latter had been conducted from the Watkins' house. She did, however, listen to Clara and from her learned about the young man with the flowers and the possibility that Gertie had been in love with him. She allowed Clara to explore the likelihood of Abel having resorted to temptation on Gertie's behalf but she expressed no opinions, no castigation of anyone involved.

Nightingale had cursed her for having been responsible for her children's downfall and, inside her head, Sarah repeatedly acknowledged her fault. She had educated them above their station. All that reading and writing! Without it Gertie would never have fallen in with Mrs. Peake, not gone to work in the library, not lost her innocence and her life. Without it Abel wouldn't have been in charge of the office and had access to a safe full of money.

Sarah Nightingale blamed herself, saw only herself as the cause of her children's misery. If she had been sufficiently brave to end her life she would have done so. She talked of suicide often. But that thread of weakness in her character left Sarah incapable of initiating action. She could only follow a direction dictated to her. In consequence she spent hours before her kitchen range, neither sleeping nor speaking, just gazing into the fire when Clara had lit one and into the empty grate when she had not.

When weeks had gone by without any word from Abel, Clara began to consider a second visit to the prison. It was a big undertaking, especially as it meant leaving his mother to do so. She was torn between visiting the man who she now knew to be the pivot of her life and leaving his mother in a condition that could deteriorate.

It was during the days of deliberation that another of Gertie's white cards, somehow delayed, arrived with its usual message. The card served to increase the distress of the two women and to delay Clara's leaving still longer. Mrs. Nightingale had slumped into her darker mood again and could not be left.

Gertie's letter arrived two weeks later, the fullest and most animated that she had ever written and dated only a few days previously. It clearly described her busy life, her meeting with a gentleman whose family lived in France and her delight in his company. It seemed she half expected 'a development' but was anxious not to seem forward, especially since he was the son of a friend of dear Mrs. Peake, who was visiting and acting as chaperone. There had been talk of a holiday in France.

Clara had read the letter first, incredulous and confused, until very slowly she realised that whatever the governor had written must be wrong, that somehow he had jumped to a mistaken conclusion and that Gertie was alive. Clara's initial emotion was one of relief and joy. She knelt at Sarah's feet and looked up into those blank eyes.

"Mrs. Nightingale, look at me. We've a letter from Gertie. That is, you've a letter. It's true. She's not dead at all. It's all a mistake.

Listen." She had read and reread the letter until at last her friend's mother had wrinkled her brows and snatched the paper to read the words herself, as if unable to believe her own ears.

Then, laughing and crying, she hugged Clara but the young woman's original joy had slowly gone cold. A thought had crystallised amongst the relief and the laughter, a tiny, hard piece of glass that had twisted and turned and cut itself into a many-faceted weapon, sharp and hurtful. It had moved from her head and now lay amidst the beating, heavy pulse in her throat. An agony of jealousy tore at Clara, for, if the identity of Abel's ' sister-in-law' was not Gertie, who was the woman who had died? Who had Abel stolen for and why?

Gertie had always been the more imaginative of the two girls but now the seeds of intrigue and passion sowed by her friend's storytelling grew to horrible proportions in Clara's mind. She actually saw Abel embracing a faceless, graceful creature, heard their murmurings, witnessed the intensity of their desire. She felt heavy, unattractive, dreadfully embarrassed. Her face flamed with shame when she recalled her visit to the prison, her obvious misinterpretation of Abel's feelings. Why, he had only ever been like a brother to her! His hands brushing hers, shared glances, intimate conversations had been nothing more than normality shaped by her own desires into far more meaningful experiences than they were ever meant to be.

There was now no possibility of visiting the prison. It was totally out of the question. Abel would know the identity of the young widow and this was one piece of heartbreaking news that he would have to bear alone. She had done her duty by informing him of Mr. Nightingale's death and, if his mother's reported state concerned him, then he would need to write to her. No doubt he was in direct contact with his sister. Clara could not bring herself, cheapen herself, to be available any more. She must make herself content with her joy in rekindling her friendship with her dear Gertie, who would undoubtedly make time to visit home soon.

Meanwhile, Abel, in the depths of despair in his own particular hell, remained painfully concerned for his mother's state of mind. He awaited another letter from Clara. He knew that he should write but some sixth sense warned him that the Governor was intent on meddling and that his intervention was to be feared.

Abel, had a staunch belief in Clara's reliability, however. He had long recognised that he loved this plain, stalwart girl. That hidden behind her practicality, there was a generosity of spirit and an enormous capacity for affection that he admired. He had passed through the stage of being drawn to pretty faces and tiny wasp waists. Abel had learned the value of a woman, not a fainting counterfeit. In consequence, Abel was convinced that Clara would eventually contact him and so he waited, mourning his sister, worrying about his mother and increasingly concerned by the silence of the one person in the world whom he had left to depend upon.

Wickedness is like a heavy stone dropped into still waters. It spoils the calm surface and sends its ripples out in far-reaching circles. The governor's malicious interference had spread its influence. Abel was quite isolated. Letters from Gertie were being regularly destroyed and no communication issued from a distressed and hurt Clara.

Horace Kendrick watched his prisoner's now obvious agony with satisfaction. Abel's shoulders drooped, his already pale face grew increasingly haggard, and he exhibited the lack lustre expression of a dangerously depressed young man. Able had begun to feel that he had little left to live for and death was looking more and more like the easy option.

Chapter Twenty Two

Gertie had lain for three weeks, a torn and exhausted scrap of humanity. The baby had been brought to her breast and she had fed the mewling infant lying on her bed. Sometimes the satiated child had lain face down upon Gertie's stomach sleeping, and in those moments Gertie savoured motherhood. But when she tried to move or see to her toilet she felt so sore, so sad and so very light-headed.

At last the horror of the actual birth began to recede but the awareness that she had needed her mother remained. The bond of motherhood, the appreciation of what it meant to bring another life into this world, was now something that she understood.

Mrs. Peake was wonderful, attentive, affectionate, taking on the role of adoptive grandmother and surrogate mother. But she had been unreasonably hurt when Gertie had called for her mother at the height of her pains. Alice had had to acknowledge that she had wanted to be the one who was needed and her possessiveness reared up before her, an unmistakable and unattractive trait that her younger brother had recognised and warned her against.

When Gertie broached the subject of her parents, Alice heard herself conniving at avoidance. She felt her manipulative streak grow strong and managing. She wanted to be the one to give – a very selfish benevolence.

"Of course, Gertie, you feel that you need your mother right now – a natural, instinctive reaction. And, my dear, it's only right that she should see her grandchild. We must arrange it – but not yet. If Isabelle is to have a respectable background we need to create it for her. That can't include letting anybody – and I mean anybody - in on our secret. You have to play this one out, Gertie. Marriage; widowhood; and then – home. Write, my dear. Write to your mother and sow the seeds of a romance."

And so Gertie had written that letter, so different from the regular, secretive little cards she used to send – a lively letter full of excitement coloured by her memories of those first weeks she'd shared with Richard.

Meanwhile, she grew in strength and enjoyed her daughter. It was a bitter-sweet experience loving her baby, knowing it to be part of Richard and having to live with the emptiness of his place beside her.

Mr. Samuel was marvellous. This rather precise man, who abhorred untidiness and noise, who had never married and never held a child in his arms, doted on the baby. He was not perturbed by smells or cries, by flailing arms or kicking legs. He would take off his coat, hitch up his sleeves into his sleeve-bands, remove his fob watch in case the metal was cold for the child, and then take Isabelle into his arms. He would coo and croon, walk up and down the room, wonder at the baby's growth, awareness, articulation of most definitely recognisable sounds and generally exaggerate the child's development in the manner of any new grandfather. Sometimes Alice Peake felt that her brother was behaving more like the child's father – she had even felt a little out of place, 'de trop', unnecessary, when the four of them were together – a stupid, imagined sensation which she tried to overcome.

Samuel had taken to visiting the little house every weekend. Always he brought a gift, at first for the baby, but on this last occasion, for the new mother – a delightful locket, a silver replica of an open book with space sufficient for a tiny lock of the baby's hair to be rolled inside. Alice caught the delight in Gertie's face and the satisfaction in her brother's. Samuel seemed to have taken on a new lease of life. Why, he was approaching fifty and behaving like a young man. It was unseemly. Alice had to admit that she was irritated by her brother.

For several reasons Alice needed to get Gertie away to a different environment. She developed her suggestion of a trip abroad but her young friend had become increasingly worried about Abel. Whilst she had been pregnant there had been no possibility of her going to the prison. It would have been unthinkable, but now that she had resumed her slim prettiness and felt able to go into society once more Gertie was desperately anxious to see her brother. He had replied to none of her letters and she feared that either he was angry with her for altering the situation which had cost him so dear or that some other ill had befallen him.

When Gertie broached the subject of a visit, Mrs. Peake was once again anxious to avoid family contact, "Gertie, don't even consider such a visit. Why, my dear, think of the baby. You are feeding the child. She would need to go with you. How could you consider exposing her to such a miasma of contagion?"

Alice was for once glad that her brother was there as he joined in her argument with, "Nasty places -prisons. Damp. Could have diphtheria or anything there. And remember, the child's father had a weak chest. No, my dear," and Alice noted that his voice shook, ever so slightly, as he expressed that unusual term of endearment, "you leave visiting to me. I'll go for you — try to sort things out."(In truth he had already begun to make tentative enquiries as to the wellbeing of the young man amongst those of his associates who had useful connections.)

"Would you really, Mr. Samuel? Oh, Mrs. Peake, I'd be so grateful if ….."

"Well, that's settled then. We ladies, Gertie, will be off to the seaside. We have to organise your 'husband' and Samuel will do his best to get to the bottom of what has gone wrong with Abel."

"Yes, I'll see what I can do for that brother of yours — make him more comfortable at least, if I can, that is." Mr. Samuel had taken off his glasses and was cleaning the lenses vigorously. Without them Gertie noticed that he looked younger, vulnerable somehow.

The next weeks were busy with buying and packing, planning and booking. Letters went to Dover. Replies were received. The shipping line made reservations in Bordeaux. France was to be their destination.

Gertie panicked about taking so tiny a baby abroad but was eventually persuaded that the sea air and mild climate was just what was needed and finally the new mother relaxed into letting Mrs P. do what she was good at, and organise.

Two more letters had been sent to her mother, one detailing her growing relationship with 'Richard' and a second, her intention of accompanying Mrs. Peake to Bordeaux.

In the meantime, she wrote again to Abel and entrusted Mr. Samuel with a second letter in case he managed to see her brother in person.

If you have wealth then there are many difficult situations that arise which it can ease. Gertie's life with Mrs. Peake was so very much more comfortable than it otherwise would have been. Even so there are fixed points around which we all revolve regardless of pecuniary advantage.

And so it was with the child, Isabelle. She had been born and it was now imperative that she should be baptised and her existence recorded for posterity in some church register. That she should be named Isabelle was a delight to Mrs. Peake. Gertie now had to consider how to cope with the registration. What family name should she give and what name for the father?

One Saturday, as the little artificial family was at lunch, Gertie raised the issue of whether she should be Churched before going out into society again and where the child's baptism should take place. It was Mrs. Peake who broached the, until now, avoided, subject of the names to be entered on the official documents.

"It's all very well, Gertie, to be talking about the when's and where's but what about a name, dear?"

"Why Mrs. P. we all call the baby Isabelle but …. " and here Gertie's eyes filled with tears and her words were bitten back as she tightened her lips upon a sob. She had spent hours worrying about how to get round this name predicament and still hadn't done so.

"Now, my dear, don't distress yourself," Samuel half rose in his chair to come to her but his sister was quicker. Her arms were around her friend and she was comforting her and speaking with her usual practical firmness at the same time.

"I know dear. It is a difficulty. I had thought of offering my name. Isabelle Peake does not sound so ill but that would mean you taking it too, for I am too old to be accepted as the mother."

"But not I for the father." Mr Samuel's voice was quiet, coming from the far end of the table where he sat in a pool of sunlight.

Gertie heard Mrs. Peake's intake of breath, "Samuel. Are you thinking straight?"

"I am, sister. It's not only you with the capacity to give, you know!" His voice had taken on a sharpness, the recognisable authority of the library. "Besides I'm fond of ……. the child."

"But if you gave your name, brother, and I grant Isabelle Lees sounds a respectable beginning for the child, what would Gertie sign herself as?"

"Lees, of course. We must assume a union – a marriage of …… of convenience."

"Mr. Samuel I ….." Gertie was breathless, confused. The conversation was happening too fast.

"Yes, my dear. I appreciate that we would look like a spring and winter union but all this nonsense of inventing French fathers who die. Think how all this will affect the child. She'll expect a band of French relatives, holidays in the sunshine, an inheritance – to be 'frank'," and he laughed, Gertie joining him, the quickness of his wit lightening their mood. He rose and came to their side of the table.

Mrs. Peake sat, serious and grim. Her face had taken on a closed and almost secretive look.

"This way young Isabelle would have a father. In fact, now that I'm thinking properly why shouldn't we wed? Name only, of course. It would solve so much, so very much." His eyes had caught Gertie's, a boyish glance, a hopeful, fleeting look, trusting and trustworthy. "You would have nothing to fear my dear."

"Why, Mr. Samuel, I ….."

"And I'd be the aunt, I suppose – not grandmother but aunt!" – Mrs. Peake's voice was sharp, selfish, a spoilt and pouting child.

Suddenly it all felt wrong. Gertie was the adult with two children falling out about her, both waiting for a decision that could please only one. Her sensitivity to tones of voice and the expressions on her friends' faces scared her. Here was a solution for her child but what would it do to her life? And what would be the effect on dear Mr. Samuel?

Gertie's natural affection for people came to her aid. She wanted to accept Mr. Samuel's offer. He was a good man. They had much in common but she didn't want to loose Mrs. P's friendship. She knew that, as possessive as Mrs. P.'s affection had become of late, it was genuine and she had to trust her.

"Mrs P. you have been as a mother to me," the carefully chosen words softened the older woman. The stiffness went out of her. She relaxed. "Please, advise me. What is best for all of us? For I am concerned that no one should suffer further for my fault."

Mrs. Peake looked at her young friend, the appealing softness of her face now rounded with motherhood and framed by that wonderful, gleaming golden hair. No wonder her brother was prepared to offer his very life to help her. She tucked her jealousy away, looked down and adjusted the exquisite froth of lace on her much-admired bosom and found herself again.

"Why, Samuel, you are a kind and generous man. Why not? Indeed it's time you had a daughter and I a niece. A marriage would tie us together properly. We would have family bonds not just a friendship."

"Could we face the gossips, Alice? Could you at your tea parties? People would wonder why we married at a distance and in secret. They would try to pin an age on the child." Her brother was suddenly aware that Alice was, indeed, a part of all this too.

"Let them, Samuel. If we say nothing but assume a dignity, it will act like a shield."

"Indeed, sister, and there would be nothing to prevent you both from taking your planned holiday whilst I let a little news sneak out at home .Let them assume the marriage took place months ago, shortly after Gertie left."

"And Isabelle your honeymoon child. Why, Samuel, I do believe you are better at deceit than I could ever be," and Gertie was rewarded by seeing her two friends' glances joined conspiratorially as they smiled.

Gertie never actually replied to Mr. Samuel's offer of marriage- Mrs. Peake had done that for her – but she married her knight in shining armour at the local church where her conditions of residence had been met. It was a quiet affair, of necessity, with only the flowers she carried making any change from her normal dress and her champion's smile hiding his age quite well.

Samuel Lees was in a cheerful mood and produced an admirable sense of humour for the occasion. He adopted a dramatic pose and behaved with such exaggerated courtly gestures that he was almost clowning and soon had the small wedding party laughing.

Mrs. P. was the one witness, their cook the other, and so, unavoidably, the wedding party returned to a cold luncheon and a sweet-tempered baby admirably cared for by the midwife, who had returned to the house for the occasion and joined them for lunch. It seemed that all social boundaries were simply there to be crossed and the result was a very relaxed, good-natured atmosphere.

After lunch, Mr. Samuel offered his apologies for leaving early but explained, with a smile, that he had some rumours to start as well as a train to catch. Gertie was certain that his benevolent intention was to lessen the awkwardness of their new relationship.

Mrs P. set about the arrangements for a Dover baptism – a second church register far enough away from the first. The trip to France could continue.

Gertie Lees heaved a sigh of relief, held the child to her breast and prayed silently that Richard would understand why she was no longer a Nightingale.

Chapter Twenty Three

Miss Agnes Detheridge knew that she was no beauty. Her father had too often reminded her of her plainness for it to escape her notice. She had loved her father and knew that his references to her shortcomings were not intended to hurt her, but to protect her from any fanciful notions of romance – an experience that was unlikely to occur. He had balanced his criticisms of her looks with very many compliments to her good sense, of which she was appreciative. His generosity had been extreme so that she was the best dressed, if the plainest, young lady in their circle, possessed of the finest horse, the most sporty little chaise and the largest personal library of any of her acquaintances.

Agnes had officially taken her mother's place as her father's confidante and hostess when she was twenty, her mother having finally succumbed to the gradual decline that had kept her cheerfully bedridden for some years previously.

By thirty Agnes was used to running the house and taking more than a passing interest in her father's businesses. She had learned to turn a blind eye to her elder brother's capricious and querulous behaviour, knowing full well that it would serve no useful purpose to open their father's mind still further to his son's fallibility. Arthur Detheridge was the son and heir, whatever else he was – that was an unalterable fact. It meant that, one day, Agnes might expect to receive her annuity from her brother's hand and that, in her own best interests, she should keep her mouth shut about his shortcomings.

Agnes might have been plain but she was by no means dull. She enjoyed society, especially that of men, who seemed able to forget the niceties due to her sex and continue with their talk of finance and business in her company. In fact, on numerous occasions she was the only female present at her father's dinners and remained at table when the port was brought. She enjoyed conversation. She loved to listen to interesting talk and thrived on heated debate.

Agnes was fortunate in her friendships. Women who might have been wary of an attractive friend enjoyed her sensible company and were happy to introduce their beaux and their young husbands to her. What with her father's affection, her successful social life and her love of literature and music, Agnes considered herself fortunate.

Indulgent though Mr. Detheridge was with his daughter, there were things of which he did not approve. He disliked her membership of the new Free Library, saying over and over again that touching second-hand books was a dirty habit and he didn't like them in the house. The library, he said, was for the poor, who couldn't afford to buy. Agnes took no notice. She loved the atmosphere of the library, not only its books, and she had no intention of giving it up.

Another thing of which Mr. Detheridge heartily disapproved was ladies in a place of business. He was happy to discuss his affairs at home with his daughter but he did not expect her to follow him to work. She occasionally did visit him and took tea with him in the inner office but she was expected to sweep past the employees graciously and she did, nose in the air, appearing a trifle disdainful and actually hiding her shyness. Amongst strangers Agnes was shy because she was painfully aware of how very plain she was. Nevertheless, no matter how preoccupied Agnes was with fulfilling her father's expectations and coping with her own embarrassment, she found the opportunity to appreciate the smoothly run office and sought appropriate moments in which to open Mr. Detheridge's mind to her willingness to be more actively involved.

The death- no, the dying - of her father was the worst part of Agnes's life. She had mourned her mother but that passing had been a slow, almost easy process of gently wilting - not the battle fought by a father who had not been ready to die. Old Mr. Detheridge had had several bouts of illness, each one longer and more debilitating than the previous but he had refused to give in, stumbling and bumbling into his clothes as soon as he was able, taking meals in the dining room again and his coach to the offices.

That final illness had been awful. He had borne the pain with such bravado, trying to maintain his bluff camaraderie with his serving man and doctor.

Towards the end her father had had no sleep, no rest. The sounds of the whole house had been muffled. Servants went on soundless feet, plates were placed against each other gently. The coachman even cuffed the air above his lad's head rather than an ear, which might have provoked the customary yell. Even so, peaceful rest eluded the patient.

Arthur seemed to be the only one in the household unperturbed and even he managed to put on a mask of concern when he visited his father's bedroom.

On that last night, Agnes recalled that she was sitting beside her father's bed reading to him - nothing heavy, just a newssheet. He wasn't listening but he found the regular rise and fall of her voice comforting. The door had swung open quietly and Arthur had entered, dressed, obviously, for the theatre or a smart dinner, white silk evening scarf, silver headed cane.

"How is he, Agnes?"

"I'm not dead yet, me boy. Talk to me, not about me."

"I'm sorry Father. How are you?"

"Getting better. Ha! That startled you, didn't it? Upset your apple cart if I did."

"No, Father. Don't talk like that. Ridiculous thing to say."

"Off out again, no doubt. Couldn't stay in and ….." a spasm of pain took his breath momentarily, "and read to me could you? No, thought not."

"I'll be off then, Father. I'll call in later, if you're awake."

"Don't bother. With a bit of luck I'll not be – here I mean."

Agnes stood. She could see her father getting agitated. She plumped his pillows, straightened the sheet. When she looked up Arthur had gone, his soft- soled dancing pumps soundless on the stairs. She ran her fingers down her father's cheek. It was hollowed now and the whiskers of evening made it rough to touch. She longed to put her cheek against his but he turned away his head, self-conscious of his tartared tongue and unpleasant breath.

"No, love. Don't be sad. I didn't mean anything by it – just gone to the office- that's all." He managed a smile. "Office. Office. Why hasn't young Abel been to see me? He should have come. I'd have staked my life on him coming. Perhaps he will – tomorrow."

"I'm sure he'd want to, Father, but perhaps he's reluctant to intrude."

"Yes, yes. Very likely."

"In any case – all must be well. You always say how capable he is."

"Agnes – he is a good lad. When you've charge of the business keep 'im on. Don't lose 'im. He'll see you right. Give him one of the best houses. Trust him in all things. Raise his salary annually. Marry'im if you must."

"Father!"

"Don't 'Father' me. I know what I'm saying."

"You need to rest now, Father. You're talking rubbish." She was genuinely concerned for his state of mind.

"No I'm not. Listen, Agnes. I've not talked wills to you before – not wanted to - but now! Arthur's not getting everything – just the legal side. He's the lawman. Plenty of money in the bank too. Got his own pad – I know and who lives in it. Thought I didn't but ….." the old man managed a weak smile. "House is for you, my dear. You've run it long enough. As long as you don't marry it'll stay yours. Leave it where you like when it's your turn to go. Trust you, Agnes."

She was shocked, surprised. She hadn't ever expected this and she knew now that her father was perfectly lucid. Arthur wouldn't forgive him, though, for not getting the family home– or her. But what was that about the business? She held water to her father's lips. He needed to rest but she needed to know.

"The business, Father. What about the property business?"

"All the property and the office. All yours. You'll be decent to the tenants. Can trust you to carry on. Abel – he'll be your right hand man. Good lad, Abel. I owe him so much. These last months. You'll see him right, Agnes. See the lad right."

He'd slept then, better than for days. Agnes had left him peaceful, not tossing, not cringing in pain. She'd gone to her room just to lie down in her clothes on top of the bed, just for an hour. It was six hours later when she opened her eyes and heard the clock on the landing strike. It was dawn and her father lay dead – stiff, cold and gone from her.

Agnes had stemmed her grief long enough to organise the mourning, the funeral, the cemetery. Arthur did nothing at all.

"Got to 'and it to you, sister mine. You run the old place as well as any business. Pity you weren't born a lad. Could have helped me out in the practice or the business."

Agnes had been tempted then to turn on him, to stop his self-satisfied gloating, for that was what he was doing. He'd never cared for their father, only for what he could get out of him. She would take a delight in seeing the back of her brother but she had to maintain her outward affability until the will had been read and that would not be until after the funeral. Mr. Merridew, her father's own solicitor would see to all that. Agnes half feared that her father had spoken of what might have been and not of reality. She dreaded disappointment.

The days leading up to her father's funeral were unbelievably busy. Announcement cards to be sent, the house to be draped in black, mirrors covered, servants properly attired, her own dress to be seen to, service, cemetery, the funeral board to be organised; cold meats, pies, pastries, tarts and puddings. She resented that part the most – the almost festive food and drink to be consumed by long-faced mourners some of whom hadn't seen her father for years and whom she hardly recognised.

The bereaved young woman did her very best to be the epitome of good sense that her father would have wanted. Some strength beyond her imagining helped Agnes towards an outward serenity that impressed her brother and resulted in the servants scurrying to do her bidding with more alacrity than usual. Yet there were moments when she nearly lost her self-control. The slightest, silliest thing could almost break her spirit – a candle guttering before its flame finally died, the last stroke of the hour that held and echoed and then drifted away, her father's bed sheets billowing on the line as if being prepared for use again.

But at last, the day of reckoning did arrive. Agnes was glad of the family custom that sent the men off in the carriages to see her father to his last resting- place and left the few women present to remain in the darkness of the whispering house awaiting their return. At least Agnes did not have to bear the service and the internment – her private grief would wait until her lonely visit to her parents' grave. To think of her father there, in the damp darkness beside her mother at last, made the tears prick behind her eyelids and she felt the corners of her mouth turn down and tremble. She busied herself repositioning the already perfectly laid table until she had herself under control once more and prepared for the mourners' return.

It was two and a half hours before the drama reached its final scene. By then the blur of white countenances had either left or relaxed into one of the small groups hiding their conviviality behind their refilled glasses and long faces. Agnes' particular friends had done their best to support her, being at her elbow if she seemed to falter, hiding their concern behind matter-of-fact statements, knowing full well that she would break if signs of their sympathy reached her.

Mr. Merridew, the elder, had left his particular group of acquaintances and walked purposefully over to where Mr. Merridew the younger, forty if he was a day, sat on a straight backed chair, looking into thin air and trying hard to appear as if he were involved in some secret business which maintained his full attention. The already balding gentleman had remained quite alone during the whole of the proceedings, taking no part in the polite small-talk Several times Agnes had done her best to drift towards him, a sympathetic effort to ease his obvious awkwardness. Each time she had failed, for as she had approached he had looked at her with such apparent sorrow in his warm brown eyes that she had felt unable to speak to him. Somehow she felt that he was sharing her agonies, appreciating the effort that kept her back stiff and her mouth under control. When their eyes met she felt as though her hands might clutch onto him and her mouth would open in discordant, terrible anguish. She could not afford to indulge herself in such grief yet and so they kept apart, both occupying themselves in their own way and yet feeling a tight rein of unspoken emotion linking them together.

At his father's approach young Mr. Merridew reached down and picked up a thin leather case, more like a music satchel than a lawyer's brief box. This he clutched, as he followed his father in Arthur's direction.

At their advance Arthur coughed and caught the eye of several people whose attention had been surreptitiously focused upon the late Mr. Detheridge's lawyer. At his signal the previously notified few rose and followed Mr. Detheridge into what had been his father's study.

Agnes had prepared the room carefully. The exact number of chairs needed had been placed around the edges of the small room, all nine angled towards her father's desk, which had been cleared – painfully cleared – of his clutter: his last cigar end, his used glass, his magnifying lens. That had been a hard task, shared sadly and silently with Bills, his faithful manservant, himself old and not in the best of health.

Now the beneficiaries of the will filed into their places, Bills standing behind Agnes's chair in his accustomed pose until she smiled gently at him and signalled the empty seat beside her. He half turned his face as if resisting and then, at her insistent nod, slowly moved to take his place beside his mistress. He sat, awkward amongst his betters, his hands splayed self-consciously on his knees, their veins knotted and their paper-thin skin flecked with the brown freckles of age. Agnes felt ashamed that she had not noticed his frailty before. It was too easy to take servants so much for granted.

Arthur lounged at his father's desk, the vacant space that had been prepared for the lawyer before him. The two Merridews sat, papers balanced precariously on their knees, and Arthur remaining impervious to their discomfort.

The study door had remained open. Arthur coughed and looked pointedly at Bills. Out of a lifetime's habit of servitude the old man stood and, walking stiffly, closed the door gently.

Arthur coughed again and looked towards Mr. Merridew. It was a hard look – impatient, almost angry. It was not lost on the older man who returned the glance with one equally as meaningful – penetrating and cold. There was clearly no bond of affection between these long-acquainted men of the same profession.

Arthur was condescending, "I think you may begin Mr. Merridew."

"Thank you, Arthur," the sharp voice of the lawyer who had know his deceased client's son since he was a child indicated his unwillingness to be anything other than the conveyor of this proceedings. Agnes noted the use of her brother's first name and felt satisfied by Mr. Merridew's clever use of familiarity to prick her brother's puffed-up self esteem. She glanced towards the younger Merridew partner and found him already looking at her, his eyes lighter and happier, almost reassuring in their steadiness.

"It is my sad duty to make known to you the last wishes of ...."

"My dear, sir," Arthur interrupted in his best legal voice. "We all know whose will it is, why we are here, etc. etc. I think we all agree that what we need is just the facts and figures. Can't we cut the red tape and the blather for once?" He looked around the room for support. He found none. Eyes looked down at boots, at carpet, at hands; not at him.

"Irregular", said the voice of Mr. Merridew, senior.

"The procedure needs to be carried out with due respect for the deceased," Mr. Merridew junior's voice was low but firm, "and," he added, looking kindly and directly at Agnes, "with deference for those with affection involved."

"I can't agree." Arthur was prepared to argue.

Agnes had never corrected any male member of her family either in public or in private. On this occasion she simply said, "Arthur!"

It was enough. Her tone surprised her brother into a shocked silence. He sat back in his chair and stared rudely at his sister.

Mr. Merridew resumed his opening speech and was not interrupted.

Agnes listened with pleasure to the kind words and bequests made by her father to old friends. He had managed to leave each one some meaningful momento of their association: a bottle of old tawny port for one, his collection of small snuff boxes to another friend, a small prayer book and fan which had been his wife's to her sister. With each one went a gift of money, which he decreed was intended for pleasure.

For Bills there had been his master's clothes, his own room and board for the rest of his life. He was to be a fixture in the house, no matter who owned it, along with the sum of £125 per year. The old man listened with his head bent and then held a handkerchief to his mouth whilst his bowed old shoulders shook with emotion.

Eventually all bequests had been read except for those pertaining to Agnes and Arthur – left until last as was to be expected.

What came as a surprise, however, was Mr. Merridew's pause; a shuffling of papers and then a long look at each individual whose business was now completed. He then addressed them most seriously, "Well, now ladies and gentlemen, it seems that I have to ask you to do something a little out of the ordinary. The late Mr. Detheridge expressly required that the final part of his will be read in private, that being the section appertaining to his natural children –'natural', you understand being used as a legal description; not that there are any unnatural." He was trying to be light-hearted, to help people to feel free to smile and to stand and exit from what had been serious and moving proceedings. It was not easy to feel close to a dead man and then walk away. "And so if you would be so good ....."

Mr. Merridew the younger had moved towards the door, was holding it open, was bowing slightly – for all the world like a butler trying to usher people out of the room.

They left in silence, the recipients of that encouraging smile, that almost imperceptible nod, which reassured the leavers that they were doing the right thing, that their exit was as free as if it had been their own choice.

As the door closed once more Mr. Merridew senior, deposited his papers on his son's vacated chair and pulled it around so that its seat became a work table. His younger partner chose to seat himself beside Agnes, between her and the desk – a buttress against attack. She felt the security of his intervening presence.

"An unusual bit of activity there, Merridew." Arthur maintained his superior attitude – rudely, Agnes thought.

"Indeed, but absolutely in accordance with your late father's specified wishes."

"Why would he signify this pantomime? Oh, don't answer me, just get it all over with."

"Just so – all over with. That's exactly what your father...... late father.... Wrote; I quote, 'So that you get the will reading all over with, without too much public fuss, see that my wishes are read to Agnes and Arthur in private. Any disapproval or trepidation can be registered behind closed doors.' In fact Mr. Detheridge's very words to me were, though he didn't write them, you understand – 'don't want any dirty linen washed in public'."

"Dirty linen? What are you talking of, man? Why, I do believe there is some nonsense afoot. To the will – let's get the damned business done."

And so Mr. Merridew, his voice ringing like a great church bell - suddenly resonant, vibrant and full of strength - began to read. Gone was any gentleness, almost obsequiousness with which he had attended to the other beneficiaries. Now he enjoyed his power knowing none could gainsay him.

"To my daughter, Agnes, beloved of her mother and very much the child of my heart – the house in which she has lived and of which she has grown to be mistress, plus sufficient funds - £5,000 - with which to maintain its fabric. The interest from building society moneys, already established in an account bearing her name, should cover wages and regular bills.

As to my daughter's personal needs, I do not wish her to be beholden to anyone and therefor I leave her the means to independence. Into Agnes's care I pass my properties and the business office along with its profits and obligations, trusting her to act wisely and favourably towards tenants and employees. Agnes knows my mind in all things. I trust that my spirit will support her in her continued good sense and kindness."

Tears filled Agnes's eyes. She swallowed hard. For a moment her composure slipped. She felt the light reassurance of a comforting pressure against her arm and sensed the younger lawyer there, beside her, supporting her just by his very presence.

Agnes didn't listen to the list of sums and benefits left to Arthur. She had no need and did not care for his situation. She did, however, notice his compressed lips, his tight, cold face and expected his anger when the last notes of the will reading echoed around the still study. He was now a wealthy man but had expected to be even wealthier.

Arthur surprised them all. His only words were, "Thank you, Merridew. Congratulations, sister. I've done a little business at the property office these weeks, tidied up a bit of nastiness. Didn't realise it was on your behalf but never mind. Good afternoon to you all," and with that the bereaved son, now in possession of a law firm and a considerable fortune, left the room and the house.

Agnes was to see Arthur infrequently in the future and then only by accident.

The rest of that day passed – not in an agony of grief, nor in a fever of anticipation. It just passed. The mourners became steadily less mournful as their numbers diminished until only those who had been Agnes' father's closest friends, and who felt his house as comfortable as their own, remained.

Agnes didn't even long for them to leave. She just sat quietly listening to their reminiscing, with their laughter echoing the good times of that house. She almost felt that her father was there with them, his generous spirit comforting her, giving her something to replace his passing – the business. Why, she could hardly wait to look at the properties, discover who her tenants were, check that their houses, her houses, were in good repair. She had so much to learn – yet Abel Nightingale would be there to help her.

At last the old men around the fireside seemed to become aware of Agnes sitting quietly in the enclave of the bay window. A sort of general shuffling of embarrassment began amongst them as they suddenly felt concerned that they might have overstayed their welcome and that perhaps their joviality was unseemly, out of place. As they stood to collect coats and take their leave Agnes saw Mr. Merridew also stand. He had been sitting, long after his father had left, in the chimney corner as quietly as she had been. He hung back, ensuring that he would be the last to leave and the manner in which he stood, almost protectively beside her, nodding to his acquaintances as they left, made her feel less alone than she might have done.

When at last this rather quaint, middle aged man bent over Agnes' hand to take his leave, the gentle pressure from his warm fingers and the kind, reassuring look from his so very honest straightforward eyes, made her certain that he had remained on purpose just to support her. Was this meant as a personal kindness or did he just like to do his duty to a client exceptionally well?

"Goodnight, Miss Agnes. I do hope that you can get a little rest now. You have done very well, very well indeed, today."

"Thank you, Mr. Merridew. I have appreciated your company." Agnes flushed a little as she made what might have been a professional interest sound personal.

"And I yours, ma'am. I shall hope to meet you again soon in .... ah! .... less difficult circumstances. Goodnight to you – a very good night indeed."

★ ★ ★ ★ ★ ★ ★ ★ ★

Agnes surprised herself by sleeping soundly and only woke when Bills drew her curtains and referred to the hot water on the marble washstand and the tray of tea beside her.. She had woken with a start, for a moment alarmed by an unusual presence in her room. She was accustomed to a cold-water morning wash and never indulged herself in the luxury of a hot drink in bed unless she was ill. Agnes almost commented on these unusual luxuries and then stopped short, realising that the old man was simply doing for her what he had done every day for her father.

"Thank you, Bills. I appreciate the hot water and the tea is a wonderful start to the day."

"I'm glad, Miss Agnes. Shall I light your fire?"

"No, thank you. I'll be up and about shortly."

But Agnes did not go out shortly, or even eventually. For, as she was fastening the small gold brooch that she normally wore at the neck of her black stuff walking dress, a vivid memory of a particular occasion flooded her mind. She had been breakfasting with both her mother and father so many years ago and had cracked her boiled egg – to find it hollow. On upturning the shell she had discovered the little brooch nestling amongst fine shreds of tissue in her eggcup. How her mother had laughed at her protestations that it was not her birthday, nor even Christmas. Her father had smiled and explained that it was to reward her for her good temper during the weeks of preparing Arthur for university, when he had received so much attention and she so little.

The memory was bitter sweet and unlocked the floodgates holding back her grief. Agnes had wondered when she would cry, and now she wondered when she would ever stop.

It was to be three days before she eventually emerged from her room. During that time she had repeatedly wept and pulled herself together and then wept again. She had let Bills mother her with minding her fire and delivering trays of titbits and then spent hours reminiscing with her father's old servant, the two of them laughing and crying together – a catharsis for both of them.

At the beginning of the third of what Agnes was to think of as her self-indulgent time, she splashed her eyes with cold water and emerged from her room determined to be self controlled and optimistic.

Of course, the house was still in mourning and expected to remain so for a respectable period but Agnes had decided enough was enough. She was sufficiently brave to disregard convention and her spirit told her not to regret her father's passing any longer but to celebrate his life. She ordered a flurry of activity. Curtains opened halfway, black drapes, bows and black edged sympathy cards removed from pictures, mirrors and mantelpieces. "The house," Agnes, told Bills, "is to smell of flowers and polish. I want new candles in the holders, lamp wicks trimmed, gas lights lit. If we have callers let our optimistic attitude be obvious. I don't want visitors to push us back into our sad moods."

Bills had nodded his assent and gone to communicate matters to the household.

When the bell rang and Mr. Merridew the younger was admitted a few evenings later, he found himself in a very different atmosphere to the one which he had left only a week before. He stood in the hall, declining the offer to step into the lounge to await Miss Agnes.

"No, no, indeed." His voice betrayed his awkwardness, "I'm not here to stay, only to enquire how your mistress does. I'm on my way home, expected for dinner. ……. And - as I was passing - I felt… err…. obligated to call." These last three words were issued in a flush of embarrassment.

Agnes drifted into the hallway in time to hear the word 'obligated'; it rankled. She did not feel that she wanted to be an obligation, not to anyone. In consequence Agnes's voice was sharp, chill – a polite response that assured him of her steadiness and gave no indication that any further enquiries were necessary.

Mr. Merridew shifted his weight from foot to foot repeatedly, turning his hat in his hands as if he were shaping its brim at that very moment. His lawyer's fluency had deserted him totally the moment that he had uttered that badly chosen word. Obligation was not what he felt for Agnes; just sympathy for her loss and a very warm - yes exceedingly warm - appreciation of her considerable qualities.

He had hoped that she would be pleased to see him but here she was, cold and polite, her chin up, determined not to let him see any chink in her armour.

But there was a vulnerability that Agnes failed to defend and Mr. Merridew, deserted by his powers of speech, was nevertheless able to penetrate her steely exterior. Agnes wore no visor and her eyes suddenly found themselves locked into the depths of her visitor's gaze. Gone was the gentle sympathy she had formerly appreciated and in its place a raw need, the look of the unchosen puppy, solitary behind its pet shop bars. With a start Agnes realised that this man who came to offer himself as support was indeed doing just that.

She had long given up any notion of romance. She remembered how her father's reference to Abel Nightingale and his words 'marry him if you must' had gone between her ribs like a knife blade. She had never been attractive and was long past conventional marriageable age, and yet here was a man, a mature and successful gentleman, obviously taken with her

Agnes had had no practice. She did not know how to respond. She took refuge in polite behaviour and offered Mr. Matthew Merridew some warm refreshment before he left. The good gentleman, his equilibrium restored and his waiting dinner forgotten, followed Agnes into her parlour, the twinkle returning to his eye and a mood of optimism settling lightly on his shoulders.

Chapter Twenty Four

Mr. Samuel Lees, erstwhile bachelor and now married family man, unlocked his library and entered its hallowed halls in an unusual mood. His steps, generally quiet, fell with uncharacteristic sharpness on the parquet floors, his breath came out on what was surely a hum and the fingers of his right hand definitely tapped out a little rhythm on the issue desk top. He was a very happy man. He had discovered that for most of his adult life he had been mistaking contentment for that elusive emotion which had suddenly arrived, unbidden and unexpected, in his heart. After almost half a century of existence he had begun to live.

Samuel was under no misapprehension that the protective adoration that he had developed for Gertie was returned. He knew that what she felt for him was respect and, he hoped, a growing affection. However, this new emotion that had wrapped its coils around his organs was such a delightful and incredible sense of elation that for now, at least, he was content. He felt himself most fortunate to be in such a wonderful position – one that offered him so much opportunity to give whatever he had to this delightful young lady. He was sure that given time, their shared interests in literature and her, he corrected himself, their daughter would blossom into a more normal nuptial relationship. But for the present he was content to be patient, and even secretive, about the intensity of his feelings for his new wife.

It was really rather a shock to have discovered this kaleidoscope of emotion. He had quite genuinely offered himself as father and husband in a logical, altruistic gesture. He had been aware of his concern for Gertie and his admiration of her, but it had been his sister's almost catty comments about the reality of his feelings for Gertie that had actually alerted him to the truth. After his offer he had panicked; the discrepancy in their ages would be a subject for gossip – the possibility of Gertie's distaste for the idea alarmed him.

When she had seemed in favour Samuel had become embarrassed, but, having made the offer, as a gentleman, he could not withdraw and - indeed - did not really wish to.

In fact, everything had gone marvellously. Alice had adapted remarkably swiftly and arranged such smooth, civilised proceedings that, far from being awkward, there had been a degree of joviality and a distinct feeling of relief at the marriage ceremony.

Samuel perched his half glasses on his nose, settled himself at his desk and tried very hard to become Mr. Lees, librarian – at least, for a while.

As members of the public began to arrive it became easier for the librarian to assume his usual bearing, but it was well into the afternoon before routine tasks were completed and he had the opportunity to begin to review some new deliveries. The library was quiet, just a couple of newspaper readers rustling their pages officiously.

Samuel was soon deeply involved in his work, only half an ear supervising the almost deserted library. In consequence he was not immediately aware of a lady, whose polite cough indicated that she had been awaiting his attention for some time.

"I am so sorry," the discomforted librarian apologised, "New books. Just in. Wanted to post the reviews as soon as possible. Can I help you?"

"Yes, please." The lady was familiar, one of his original borrowers, but he was aware that he had not seen her recently. "I have some very overdue books. You have written asking me to return them but I have been so dreadfully engaged that I omitted to respond."

"Your name?" Samuel was momentarily aggravated. He disliked people disturbing his systems. Overdue books were a nuisance. "Other borrowers may have been inconvenienced," he muttered.

"Detheridge. Agnes Detheridge. I do apologise but my father - he passed away you see and for a while I couldn't ….." she faltered.

"Detheridge – Detheridge! Samuel was so familiar with that name. Surely there could be no other family and in such a situation. It must be Abel's employer. His promise to Gertie to do what he could was fresh in his mind – but what was he to say, what was he to do? He couldn't just begin a conversation about a court case here at the issue desk. Events had overtaken him. He felt unprepared.

Agnes was aware of a change in the librarian's manner. He seemed to hesitate and then was softer towards her. She assumed that he felt sorry for her loss, perhaps had even known her father. She pushed her books towards him along the polished desktop. He turned away to find her ticket, a soldier on parade in one of the array of little trays over which he loomed. He busied himself slipping cards into the returned books and passed the empty ticket back to Agnes.

"The fine would have been considerable but under the circumstances ….." he waved his hand as if to dismiss the amount. Miss Detheridge was touched by the librarian's sensitivity. "I hope that you will feel able to choose something else to read, Miss Detheridge."

"Thank you, and yes, indeed. I shall try. I have become more settled. I feel able to read now. It's quite some time since I lost my father but ….. his death, I have had so much to do. I have taken over part of his business you see and I have had little time to myself. Things are more organised now. I feel able to concentrate on my hobbies again."

Clutching her ticket, Agnes turned to the book stacks and began to move along them. She felt a little shy to be searching for the area that interested her but slowly, she moved towards the shelf labelled 'Housewifery' and reached up to 'Advice for Young Wives'. Taking it down, she smiled, contemplating Mr. Merridew's reaction. Their friendship had blossomed quickly during the last few weeks. Last night he had proposed to her and, true to form, had refused to let her answer, insisting that an offer from an older man like himself deserved contemplation. No rushed responses. He would return for her answer - of which neither was in any real doubt.

Agnes had decided to plague her lover a little, appear cold and uninterested, be deep into some book. At an appropriate moment she would let him see the title and how they would laugh — an ageing bachelor and a plain spinster — laughing together, delighting in each other's company.

"Miss Detheridge!"

Agnes was startled.

"I wonder.......could I speak to you a moment?" The Librarian had left his desk and was looking at her most anxiously. He cleared his throat nervously. "Miss Detheridge. Could I ask you? This is most irregular but — could I call on you?" Samuel was all angles and stiffness. His usual confidence had deserted him as he trod unknown waters.

Agnes stepped back. Her mind had been on romantic matters — a realm that she had never expected to enter. Nevertheless, her involvement predisposed her to misinterpret the librarian. Briefly she entertained the rather shocking thought that this man — a comparative stranger, was taken with her — wished to approach her personally. Her soul, as plain as her homely face, momentarily soared.

"It's about Abel Nightingale. I would very much appreciate a word."

Agnes didn't know whether to smile with relief or die of shameful disappointment. She smiled. "Of course, Mr. Nightingale was an employee of my father's. Sadly, he had left the firm before I took over."

"You took over the property business?" Samuel confirmed, surprise raising his eyebrows momentarily.

"Yes. My late father entrusted it to my care. I ….."

Their conversation ceased abruptly as both became aware of the silence. Papers no longer rustled. Ears were straining to listen to their stage whispers, which were carrying clearly across the library.

"Would you be so good as to allow me to call on you this evening, after the library has closed, Miss Detheridge? I would not impose but young Nightingale is now my brother- in-law and I owe him a debt of honour. I would like to ……."

"There is no need to explain," Agnes raised her hand to signify that there was no more to be said, "Abel Nightingale is a mystery to me – my father's right hand man, who suddenly disappeared. I should be glad to talk to you."

They had meandered slowly towards the issue desk, where Agnes confirmed her address and then left the library with just one volume of advice clutched to her breast and a degree of curiosity in her mind.

* * * * * * * * *

Mr. Merridew junior had enjoyed working in his father's shadow. It had never been a problem to him to take advice or even orders from the senior partner whose experience he respected and of whom he was inordinately fond. The only aspect of his position that he found at all irksome was his title. He had, for some years now, felt that his appearance belied the youthful aura expected to surround one referred to as 'junior'. His thinning, greying hair could not be described as premature for it framed a Toby -jug face of smiles and wrinkles, which sagged alarmingly in repose. Ageing itself had really not troubled Mr. Merridew junior. It was the mismatch between his title and the actuality that annoyed him and yet he dreaded the inevitability of its alteration, for he loved his father.

That young Mr. Merridew had not married had been a topic of conversation in drawing rooms for years. Anxious mothers had steered daughters in his direction at balls and invited him to numerous dinners and musical evenings, ever hopeful of catching his interest in one of their progeny. None of their machinations had been successful, and the consensus of opinion was that Mr. Merridew had not committed himself simply because he and his father had failed to see the necessity of any change in their comfortable situation. Widower and bachelor son shared a smoothly run home life and an equally well- oiled business machine.

Time had crept up surreptitiously and left its mark upon the curving spine of Mr. Merridew senior as well as on the changing features of his son, but even so they had cherished their partnership and failed to contemplate any change. Failed, that is, until Mr. Merridew junior had discovered the secret of rejuvenation – an interesting chemistry which provoked a sluggish heartbeat into a particular rhythm, restored a twinkle to the eye and lifted sags and wrinkles into becoming smiles and affability. What had been a professional responsibility had quite quickly become a personal interest and then a delight.

For the fist time in his life Mr. Merridew junior acted independently of his father and fell in love. The object of his affection was a daughter whose relationship with her father had mirrored his own. He had felt her loss keenly and had wanted to support her against her plainly cold and acquisitive brother. Sympathy had turned to admiration as he noted her capacity to cope alone. Soon he had discovered so many attractive qualities behind her composed and rather plain countenance that he ceased to look at the outside and became totally enamoured by the very same qualities which old Mr Detheridge had valued. Agnes was sensible, level headed and hid her generous, affectionate spirit behind her firm no-nonsense attitude. She loved her home to run smoothly and very quickly she had learnt to facilitate an equally well-run business. Mr. Merridew junior was impressed.

In the space of what Agnes and Mr. Merridew counted as months and the rest of their shocked circle as 'only weeks', they had become a couple, sharing a humour and fireside intimacy which astonished their friends by its speed and its happiness. Marriage was inevitable and the proposal, gentle, hesitant and totally expected.

On this particular evening Mr. Merridew had arrived at Agnes's house to receive his answer. He anticipated a reply in the affirmative but his solicitor's training alerted him to every eventuality and he rang the bell with a certain mixture of optimism and just a little trepidation. He was shown into the small parlour by a smiling Tweeny, who had long since been directed to give Mr. Merridew junior free access to her mistress without the need for prior reference.

The little sitting room was a golden cavern of fire and lamp glow, the object of his visit sitting on her lady's chair, skirts spread comfortably around her and her concentration apparently totally absorbed by her reading. Young Mr. Merridew felt very slightly perturbed. He had hoped that Agnes might have been waiting for him, come to meet him in the hallway, shown her pleasure at his arrival. Instead she was cool, absorbed in a book. A vague feeling of alarm insinuated itself into the solicitor's heart.

"Good evening, Agnes."

"Matthew," she raised her eyes to his, affecting a slightly startled demeanour, "I'm sorry …. I …… er …… wasn't aware of your arrival. It's this book. It is so fascinating."

Mr. Merridew was nonplussed. Surely the first item on the agenda deserved to be her reply, and yet she was determined to focus on this damned book. "It's full of facts which are so interesting. For example, Mathew, did you know that brisket should be boiled for two and a half hours before adding the vegetables? And that to remove stains from bed linen two teaspoons of salt should be added to water for overnight steeping. And ……"

"Agnes, my dear – I'm sure all this is quite, quite fascinating but haven't we something else to discuss? I asked you a question yesterday I ……" Mr. Merridew's face was serious, his smile creases sagging so that his countenance had assumed the jowled and sad expression of a boxer dog. His brown eyes, serious and questioning, held Agnes's sparkling blue ones.

"But Matthew……you have your answer, my dear. Not that my reply was really ever in any doubt. I've been showing you my response quite clearly ever since you walked in."

Mr. Merridew's puzzlement increased.

"Look!" Agnes raised her open book and shook its cover in his direction. "Surely those old eyes of yours have not become so decrepit behind their bits of glass that you can no longer read."

Mr. Merridew junior allowed his glance to focus on the title 'A Young Wives' Compendium of Housewifery.'

Bustling down the passageway to announce dinner, Tweeny heard two peals of laughter coming from the small sitting room. The laughs began separately, one slightly after the other, lower pitched and hearty, whilst the feminine notes of her mistress's entwined itself about those base ones belonging to what must surely be her new master.

Tweeny hesitated at the door whilst a rustle of silks composed itself inside and a silence ensued. She paused a moment longer and then knocked politely. For once the little maid did not open the door to announce dinner but judged it prudent to do so loudly from the passageway.

The family dining table had been set very carefully for dinner, with the candelabra and best cutlery usually brought out for only very festive occasions. The extra leaf had not been added and so it was a relatively small table this evening, attractively decorated with posies of flowers. Agnes usually maintained respectable formalities, placing herself at one end of the oval and her guest at the other. This evening Mr. Merridew's place was set at the head, hers close to him, on his right.

With fingers interlaced at intervals between courses, the two friends enjoyed their companionable meal, exchanging details of their day and making plans to share their happiness with Mr. Merridew senior on the next evening. It was very much a convivial scene at that table, a meeting of minds and a combining of interests, much deeper than any transient short-lived flowering of youthful attraction.

By the time Matthew was accepting his Stilton and biscuit,

Agnes had reached the details of her morning hours, which she confessed to have 'stolen' from the office in an attempt to put her teasing plan of the book into action. She mentioned the librarian's request to call and, glancing at the mantle clock, expressed her expectation of his imminent arrival. "And Matthew, I am so glad you are here. For I confess that the librarian's manner was so intense, so obviously worried, that I feel sure something quite awful is about to emerge. Abel Nightingale was my father's right hand man. I had met him, liked his clean- cut looks, his direct glance. My father often spoke of Abel's honesty and abilities. He used to smile and say, 'Abel by name and able by nature!' In fact, Matthew, he even once suggested I could do worse than marry the young man."

"Really!" a pair of eyebrows raised in mock jealously.

"Really! And you know my father would not have made that suggestion lightly. Then, when eventually I discovered that I had control of the business and emerged from my distress in any condition to visit the office, I found my right-hand man gone and an associate of my brother's in 'temporary' situ as manager, clearly expecting to stay there. I just accepted Abel's absence as a consequence of my father's demise. I tentatively asked what had happened but no one seemed to be in a position to answer me. Grass being greener elsewhere I supposed."

"No, my dear. Not exactly."

"Matthew! You know about Abel Nightingale? Why? How? What happened to him? Where did he go?"

"Prison, m'dear. Embezzlement. Your brother caught him. Fingers in the cash box, I believe. I always assumed you knew."

"No. I didn't. How is it that you do?"

"Well, I keep abreast of all local court matters and your family was known to me. Father and I weren't involved. Your brother used Detheridge solicitors to organise prosecution though another firm actually took responsibility for the court proceedings, to avoid indelicacy – you know!"

"I don't, Matthew. I don't. Why wasn't I told about this? Why was it all hushed up?"

"Perhaps your brother was sparing you worry."

"Or perhaps he didn't think I would approve! There's something not right, Matthew. I feel it."

The sound of the doorbell alerted them to a caller and Agnes rose, reaching the dining-room door as Tweeny announced – "A visitor ma'am, a gentleman, a Mr. Lees – says you and he are acquainted through the library. He has been speaking to Bills, miss, outside on the steps. I hope that it's alright".

"Matthew. Please – you will join me?" Agnes turned towards her fiancé.

Matthew laid down his napkin, pushed back his chair and felt his legal mantle fall about him. He, too, had a growing certainty that something was wrong with Abel Nightingale being behind bars.

Agnes met Samuel Lees standing in the hallway, holding his gloves and hat in his hands and wondering where to begin. He was aware that he knew so little of the young man whom he had become determined to defend and even less of the circumstances of his accusation. He felt that he was badly prepared for this interview, only having read the transcription of the court proceedings.

"Please, Mr. Lees, follow me, but do divest yourself of your outdoor things."

Agnes led her visitor into the parlour and, after introducing him to Mr. Merridew and seating both in chairs, took her place on the chaise longue and looked at her visitor expectantly.

Samuel cleared his throat nervously and began, "Miss Detheridge. I don't find supplication easy but that is why I am here. Although you appear to have been the victim of embezzlement, I believe that a miscarriage of justice has occurred. I am here to repay the sum involved and attempt to put matters on an even keel".

Agnes felt an enormous relief. Why this was an interview designed to improve matters, not to make them worse.

"Mr Lees. You have an advantage over me. The alleged misdemeanour occurred whilst I was in mourning for my father. Somehow I have failed to appreciate the situation completely. I only know that your ….. er ….. relative was highly esteemed by my father who would have trusted him with his life – or mine, for that matter." She shot a glance at Matthew.

"Yes, indeed," Matthew supported his newly affianced. "Perhaps, Mr. Lees, you would be good enough to tell us what you know of the situation which the court chose to recognise as embezzlement. We must not forget that such an offence is serious."

"It is embarrassing," said Samuel, "but I don't deal in half-truths and so I shall be direct."

"Please do, Mr. Lees. We shall appreciate that", encouraged Agnes.

Samuel felt suddenly comfortable with these two people. They seemed genuinely concerned to share his knowledge and he felt already an unspoken sympathy emanating from Agnes. "My brother-in-law, Abel Nightingale, I believe he worked for your father ……. in ah …… a trusted position. He kept keys to the premises and the safe. My wife has taken pains to impress upon me the very good relationship between employer and employee. A family matter of very serious importance necessitated Abel obtaining some £150 fund swiftly – not for himself you understand, but to ah……………. establish the security of a vulnerable relative. We believe that he tried to see the late Mr. Detheridge to arrange a loan, being quite sure that his employer would be as anxious as he was to attend to the welfare of one in need. Unfortunately, though he came to the house, this house, on more than one occasion he was not admitted to Mr. Detheridge's presence. I have taken the liberty of speaking to your Mr. Bills on this point, at your tradesman's entrance, tonight before I rang your bell."

"I'm so sorry. My father was very ill but why did he not ask to see another member of the family?"

"He saw your brother ma'am and was told to go away – to sort out matters to do with the office independently. Your Mr Bills overheard that quite clearly. Abel had the keys and money was in the safe. He took what was needed in the full knowledge that, though it was not right – it did not appear to be wrong. It was not underhand and, knowing your late father's inclination to be a ...."

"Benefactor. I quite understand - and agree. So what went wrong?"

"Your father, Miss Detheridge, was inconsiderate enough to die. He allowed Nature to take its course and ..... he ..... died."

"But prosecution ......I don't see."

"Mr. Detheridge, junior, ma'am, checked the safe. Had young Abel wished, he could have removed that letter and covered up the missing money in a hundred ways, but no – he left it there to be read; and it was, by your brother. The result was peelers called in, cells, court and finally prison. It was a black and white case. He had no defence. He admitted to taking the money, clarified the circumstances but refused to acknowledge the reason for having done so. To explain would have been to risk the reputation of the one whom he had helped. He couldn't do that."

"And the one who he'd helped. Was the reason blameful? Was it to pay debts unadvisedly accrued?" Matthew's morality was stirred.

"No indeed, sir. Not at all. I can say to you the relative was his sister – a victim of cruel circumstance."

"Your wife, Mr. Lees?" Agnes's curiosity was stirred.

"Yes ma'am – my wife, a generous, innocent, beautiful creature and a victim of her own affectionate nature."

"Ah! I see – and you subsequently married her." Matthew had been leaning forward, hands clasped. He relaxed, leaned back, his gesture reflecting the sudden realisation of the exact nature of the young sister's predicament. "And you, Mr. Lees, if I may say so, appear to have been blessed with the same honourable disposition as our young Mr. Abel Nightingale. You, discovering the situation, did the right thing – eventually."

Samuel cast a puzzled look at the solicitor and then, catching his drift of thought, allowed his expression to reflect his angry disapproval.

"No indeed, sir. I did not do the 'right thing'. It was not I at whose door the blame lay."

"Then my apologies, sir. I rephrase my words. You have acted in a righteous, Christian manner – I am proud to make your acquaintance – though I believe you and I may be in a minority where society's values are concerned."

Agnes had lost the thread of the conversation. She had not been able to read the innuendo only the exchange and alteration in the men's moods. "My only observation, Mr. Lees, is one of horror. Had my father lived I am absolutely positive that this charge would never have been brought. I am ashamed that it was."

"Miss Detheridge, I am relieved to discover that we are of one mind. Would you allow me to repay that money and clear the debt?"

"No indeed, Mr. Lees. I feel that Mr. Nightingale has already done that and, if anything, I owe him a debt for my brother's over hasty actions."

Mr. Merridew, all affability now and practicality, shifted purposely in his chair, "Well, we need to see what can be done to execute a release. Not as straightforward as it seems – a court judgement was made. We need to lodge an appeal; we may be able to argue that only the last owner or the present one could say that money was taken dishonestly."

"And the present one will act in line with her father's heart. There is no charge and should never have been one!" Agnes spoke with determined authority whilst her memory focused on a remark made by her brother after the will- reading. What was it he had said about sorting out some nasty business at the office for her? She should have requested an explanation there and then.

Samuel let out a relieved sigh. He was already envisaging the delight on Gertie's face and anticipating the feel of her slight arms around him when he took her the news of his accomplishment.

"Leave the matter with me," Mr. Merridew junior spoke in his most professional tone. "I'll see what can be done, dear sir. Let me see what can be done."

Chapter Twenty Five

How Samuel contained himself when he arrived at his 'weekend retreat" he never knew.

The hall of the little house was piled high with trunks and boxes and the atmosphere was one of excited anticipation. The journey was about to commence on the following morning. An adventure was in the offing. Samuel acknowledged a tinge of regret that he was not to accompany them but his sister was obviously enjoying the opportunity to indulge her domineering, possessive nature. Gertie would be hers for three months. By the time they returned she felt that she would be secure in their relationship once more. She would have been so generous. They would have shared so much – the baby, the travelling, the foreign experiences.

In the face of such a hive of activity, Samuel practised restraint and kept his good news to himself until the evening repast should be over.

Dinner was a sparkling affair with Mrs. Peake at her best and wittiest. Gertie was clearly a little on edge, anxious to please both her benefactress and husband, though that title sat awkwardly as yet on Samuel. He preferred to think of himself as the father of the family, the mature head of his little household.

When the port decanter was ensconced at his elbow and the servants had retreated to their steamy stronghold, Samuel looked at his unbelievably pretty wife and then at his chattering sister. The severity of his glance stilled the conversation and both ladies looked towards him expectantly.

"Abel?" Gertie enquired, her brother's welfare being uppermost in her mind. "Samuel – you've made contact."

"Not exactly! In a way, better than that. I've seen a member of the Detheridge family. It seems that the son who brought the prosecution did not inherit the business. The late Mr. Detheridge left it to his daughter. She believes that her father would have lent, and maybe even given, Abel that money. It seems he was a bit of a social philanthropist, approved of cheap, decent houses for the working class and set about supplying them. Totally in tune with your brother's politics, he was, and generous to a fault. She is like her father. She refused repayment of the money and has set her tame solicitor on to see what can be done to reduce your brother's sentence – or even scrap it completely."

Gertie's eyes shone with unshed tears. "Abel free! I can't believe it! Abel in the position to return to Mother!"

Samuel, despite his anticipations, was quite unprepared for the bundle of soft material and perfume that pushed back its chair and launched itself directly at his person. A pair of bare arms encircled his neck and a soft cheek pressed his own. "You dearest, best of men," murmured Gertie. "How blessed my child is to have you for a father and I to have such a husband."

Only the ticking of the clock disturbed the long hush that fell upon the room. The thin wail of a tiny baby issued from the nursery above, "Excuse me," Mrs. Peake said, a trifle huffily, "the child." She rose busily and bustled from the room, leaving her brother to enjoy the lingering embrace of a young wife who appeared to be taking their marriage vows very seriously.

Gertie was almost ready to cancel their trip to France in order to be near to Abel. It was not to be thought of that she should actually go into the prison but she very much wanted to be on its outside when her beloved brother walked to freedom. She was also increasingly concerned by the lack of any letters from her mother, who by now would surely have received her new address.

Unselfishly, her husband urged her to go to France, assuring her that legal wheels turned slowly and that she would most likely be returned before anything was finalised. By that time he would have made the acquaintance of her mother, found a way to impress her father and laid the foundations for her to visit home without any embarrassment.

Gertie found it hard to believe that her father would be able to forgive her transgression or her mother understand her hasty marriage, but she trusted Samuel as she had done Abel and began to see an end to her most fortunate misfortune. Besides, Mrs. P. would have been so disappointed to cancel arrangements and so Gertie, always eager to please, eventually said a chaste, "Au revoir" to her husband but pressed his hand so meaningfully that she left him with hope of a very real marriage on her return.

The carriage was piled high with luggage, carrying Mrs. P., Gertie and an excited Tweenie, who was to act a s both nurse and lady's maid. A very peaceful, good - tempered Isabelle lay wrapped in her shawls, quite content to be passed from lap to lap.

The uneventful journey was at times tedious and uncomfortable, at others an exciting adventure. Gertie loved the wayside inns with their bustling yards and bright, chintzy bedrooms. She enjoyed passing through the villages and towns and hated the ruts and jolts of the endless country miles.

They crossed the channel in a flurry of travelling rugs, and almost drowned in hot beef tea, brought to them with amazing regularity as their grand ship ploughed through the gentle swell of an unremarkable crossing.

French country roads were not dissimilar to English ones though they seemed longer and straighter. The villages were just as attractive, the farmsteads, if different in shape, just as prosperous. Only the language in the inns was remarkably different and the food served in an odd order with the extremes of simplicity and extravagance conflicting between each course. Gertie was enchanted, increasingly so as the further south they journeyed the more apparent the differences between countries became.

Gertie often had time to think of Richard and of how it might have been to share this journey with him. When she wrote her long, descriptive letters to Samuel it was really to Richard that her mind spoke and she felt guilty as the two men's identities merged so frequently. Gertie also wrote to Abel and spilled out her longing to be with him and for them both to be with their mother.

Gertie wrote of the baby, now growing into a rounded little body full of sunny smiles and gurgles. She described the land, the people, the villages, and the food, some of her letters astonishing Samuel in their style. He really did believe himself to be a remarkably fortunate man.

One of Gertie's letters described their arrival in the little village that was to be their home for the next two months. The house in which the English ladies were to stay belonged to a Monsieur Lescouriez - a gentleman involved in the wine trade, a business acquaintance of the late Mr. Peake.

Monsieur Lescouriez's life had involved regular trips between Bordeaux and London, with the occasional venture into the Midlands. On several occasions he had stayed with the Peakes and, anxious not to be considered a sponger, had offered French hospitality whenever they should enjoy a sojourn abroad. Of course, Mr. Peake had never even considered such an idea but Alice had buried the seed until such time as it might germinate. When at last, years after the original invitation, Mrs. P. had written to Monsieur Lescouriez, he had been delighted to suggest that the ladies stay at his estate, now in the hands of his son, where there was plenty of room. The alternative that he had offered was his small village house near to the coast. Not wanting to impose upon a family whom she had never met, Mrs. Peake had chosen the latter, a most successful decision. Both ladies were totally enamoured of their delightful accommodation and Gertie took pleasure in committing her impressions to paper.

My dear Samuel,
Yesterday evening we arrived! After three whole weeks of travelling, our lumbering conveyance drew to a halt in Heaven – for that is what this place must be – saving the absence of some of those I love best in the whole world. Terracotta roofs huddle like conspiratorial families bonded together by colour and proximity. Long, sloping, overhanging eaves jealously protect man – whitened walls whilst geraniums, hot and scarlet, spill from balconies and

windows. Whiteness dazzles. Tiles flame a welcome. All doors are open. My senses seem alert, more responsive than ever before – I swear my eyesight is keener. As I write now there is a hen on the far side of the yard. I can see it fluff its feathers and settle into the grey dust. Another struts, head jerking, comb quivering and makes for the attractions of the long grass. A swift skims the dusty surface of the square beyond the yard and curves into the darkness of the dilapidated barn.

This place is so casual. Wooden props lean idly against the walls, their roots stuck into might-be-useful pots and broken cartwheels. Yet it all looks so fine – as if an artist has placed everything just so, ready for his still life sketch.

The haystacks, Samuel, are so wonderful – small, squat little things, speared through with sapling poles of pine and the women too are short and square but dark. They are so strong and capable. They herd the cows and milk them just like the men .No silly drawing room stuff and nonsense here!

Our house is marvellous. Its thick stone walls make it cool even at midday and its wooden shuttered windows make me feel so safe and so - oh, I can't say – romantic.   Great tree beams decorate the eaves and lie like Herculean guardsmen across the lintels of the doors.

The dark red floor tiles are so cool. They are worn in places into paths trodden, I imagine, by the cares of men whose names I can never know, whose women groaned in deep despair on the eve of battle or, perhaps, of loveless match. These tiles seem grouted in with cries of birth and woe, their cracks worn smooth by faltering steps of babes and aged crones.

This house is so much more than wood and stone. It is a home – a real and marvellous home. I wish that you could see it, Samuel. I truly do.

It is not always easy for me to speak to you, Samuel, but writing and perhaps being here and writing, I feel free to use words honestly and without constraint.

I owe you a debt of gratitude. You have given me a life and my child a name. For this alone I honour you, but more than that, I grow in affection for you, Samuel, a very deep affection.

 miss you. Our child misses you.

Gertrude.

Samuel's reply was equally illuminating.

My very dear wife,
I received your last letter with much happiness. I revel in your descriptions that are vivid enough to transport my spirit if not my body to your side.
Pray — do not talk or write of debts of gratitude for as we get to know each other more I feel as if I am the fortunate one, for your company delights me as does your writing. Moreover, I now share with you the care of little Isabelle, a joy I never thought to have.
You do not mention my sister in your letter. How is she? Not wilting in the heat I trust. She has not written.
Mr. Merridew has assured me that he has lodged his petition to be heard regarding Abel and I have written to the prison for permission to visit.
Now comes the difficult part of my letter, dear Gertrude. Yesterday I visited your mother. What a sparkling, tidy little home it is and how nice to see such a worthy collection of books on her wall shelves.
When I called a young woman, Clara Watkins, admitted me and stayed whilst I spoke to your mother, who is not well and has become somewhat depressed . As Mrs. Nightingale seemed rather reluctant to converse, the young lady spoke on her behalf, reading her signals as you or I would read a newspaper. And this, my dear, is the difficult part of my letter, news that I would have preferred to have delivered in person, but, as things are, I cannot deprive you of the right to know.
You have told me of the hardness of your mother's life at the hands of your father — his coldness, his dour pessimism. That is at an end for he passed away some little time ago. It would be about the date of the birth of Isabelle.
Miss Watkins was most emphatic that I should say that she has written to you several times to inform you of your family news. Clearly letters have not kept pace with your junketing about. During your months without contact so much has happened and it seems quite likely that correspondence has gone astray or been misdirected. It was clear that you had not been appraised of the circumstances at home, as your letters did not refer to your father's passing.

It seems your father received news that agitated him somewhat and caused some kind of fatal fit. Your mother has not mourned your father and in fact, Clara told me, is glad to be freed from him. It is not the loss of Mr. Nightingale that has caused your poor mother to retreat into herself.

It seems that the nature of the news which so angered your father was passed on by the prison governor, who culled it from some communication to your brother. He led them to believe that you were dead in childbirth. The shock to your mother was very great indeed.

Your subsequent letters showed your mother that you were, in truth, alive, but the shock left her uneasy, locked out of your life. Poor lady has missed you dreadfully it seems; living, existing rather – only until you and Abel should return.

Money has been a trouble but your friend, Clara, has been resourceful, using the pawn shop and her own supplies in order to maintain your mother's standards where she could. This is, thank goodness, a difficulty that it is my pleasure to resolve.

I did not want to make any of your letters appear less than the truth and so I have simply embroidered on top of your fabric a little. I explained that my affection for you has always been strong and that faced with your budding French friendship, I declared myself quite hopelessly. My surprise and joy in your acceptance was great and our marriage hasty so that you could avoid upsetting my sister's plans for her excursion. You are now in a position to write with the news of our wedding – if you are of a mind to do so.

Both Clara and your mother seemed to take the news quite easily and were polite enough not to berate me for my selfishness.

Their joy at learning my news of Abel's situation was – well, quite an experience. Briefly, I explained how I had met with the new owner of the Detheridge property business - Abel's former employer's daughter. I told them how she had been unaware of your brother's predicament and now, being informed, is anxious to undo the intolerable situation. Miss Detheridge, incidentally, remains quite convinced that her father would have supported Abel in any altruistic action that he felt it right to perform, not that the details need worry your poor mother.

I left her quite a changed lady with a new brightness in her eye and some *hope in her heart. She has lost all appreciation of time and so you may safely bring Isabelle home with no questions asked.*

Your friend, Clara, is most anxious that I should pass on her affectionate good wishes. She begs you to write and rekindle your old friendship.

Clara has visited Abel, but I sensed that she was reluctant to speak of him. Something seems not right there but perhaps I am expecting too much candidness of an unmarried young lady and, as yet, I must be quite a stranger. Give my love to our child — for I think of her as mine now. There seems to me no reason why she should not have three parents, though she can only ever know of two. Believe me, my dear, I would not wish to thrust Richard from your memories. Trust me. All will be well. When you return who will ever question that Isabelle, as a child of ours could be anything but forward? Give my blessings to my dear sister.

I remember you all in my prayers and look forward to your next letter.
    Your husband,

    Samuel.

Such letters passed between husband and wife for almost a quarter of a year. The form of communication suited them well, both being adept with the written language. Innermost feelings were described and referred to with a lucidity that would have been unlikely in any spoken exchange. Gertie, however, never wrote of Richard, Samuel only twice, the second being an admission.

"I know what Richard meant to you and that I can never take his place. I have not the attraction or the vigour of youth. I can only be the caretaker of what he left behind. But, my dear, you will find me a most efficient caretaker and I remain so thankful to have been trusted with a wife and child, and such a wife!"

Gertie had been very touched with Samuel's admission of affection, though her lips had curled wryly at the misconception of poor Richard's youthful vigour.

The sojourn in France continued, a peaceful time marred only by Gertie's guilt that she was so far away from her responsibilities. She had no tears to shed for her father and had the wisdom to appreciate that her mother was in good hands. Even so, Gertie's thoughts frequently fled to England and to those she loved.

Chapter Twenty Six

Horace Kendrick was the master puppeteer. He was the string puller but Abel Nightingale had turned into a Pinnochio, a marionette with a will of its own. This was a situation that Horace did not like at all.

Governor Kendrick particularly enjoyed exercising his power over his departing inmates. The governor would find an opportunity to make some reference to the approaching end of a sentence and the imminent freedom, but he was also adept at suggesting, very subtly, that a specific date could have adjustments, minor adjustments – a week, a month perhaps – to respond to good behaviour.

To a man incarcerated in a tomb for years an extra week could be unbearable. As freedom approached men crawled along the tunnel towards the light. Any spark of spirit that had flickered at the beginning of a sentence was extinguished by the necessary cloak of servility: "Yes, governor. No, governor. Three Bags full, governor."

The governor's shoes shone like mirrors, not a speck lay on his cuffs or his floors, his horses' coats had a sheen envied by many of his acquaintances, and even his coal supplies were sorted according to the size of their lumps. Men walked free but not tall, weighted down with promises to their erstwhile governor – promises of labour, promises of maintaining contact, of doing whatever, whenever, wherever. Men left the portals of the prison slowly, turned the corner and then ran!

Horace did, however, have one human trait. He didn't like other people telling him what to do. He certainly didn't like official letters granting appeals and freedom without him being even consulted. And when the prisoner involved was one whom he had failed to master, then he was distinctly irritated.

The governor had known of the Nightingale appeal first from Gertrude's letters – all filed of course in his flames.

He had not burned the official communications from

Merridew and Merridew, but had passed them on to Nightingale with the veiled suggestions that he had been instrumental in questioning the sentence. Untrue, unlikely, but enough innuendo to confuse the prisoner ever so slightly, enough to unnerve that spirit just a little. Then, eventually, the letter that gave 24133201 his freedom arrived.

The letter was brief and to the point. It appeared that there had been a miscarriage of justice and in consequence 24133201 had been wrongfully detained. It was Her Majesty's pleasure that he be released as soon as was practically possible

Kendrick was annoyed. He could see no leeway to pull any strings, to make the little Nightingale jailbird sing for his supper. He had never known such a how-do-you-do. What made matters worse was that the official letter had been delivered in the same post as one from Merridew and Merridew. This latter missive confirmed the expectation of an almost immediate release and the intention of the junior partner to meet with his client on 16th November to support him directly prior to and upon release. Everything was too neat. He hadn't got this one under control. He didn't like a prisoner leaving without his mark upon him.

Nor did the Governor fancy the idea of Nightingale being within the prison walls with a solicitor in tow – no, he didn't at all.

Prisoner 24133201 was in his cell, pacing, stretching, trying in the small space to maintain some mobility and strength. The summons to the Governor had made his heart beat and his mouth go dry. He had so many questions unanswered. He knew of the appeal but not its full circumstances and, moreover, he thought it odd that he had not been questioned or recalled to court at all. Furthermore, Abel had not received a letter from Clara for weeks - not since the news of his father's death.

A rumour had reached him, however, that a man had called to see him on the very day that the Governor had noted his pallor and had him admitted to the hospital wing. According to one particularly sharp-eared convict engaged in mopping floors that day, the visitor suggested that he return the following morning, only to be advised that Abel was in the fever ward and likely to stay there. This Mr. Mease, Pease, Lees – or whoever he was – did not appear to have been too experienced at getting inside goals.

No communication with home had left Abel adrift and terribly depressed. Even the prospect of release left him with the unanswered question of, release to what?

If only Samuel had been able to reach Abel that day when he had been spirited away to the hospital wing, he might have answered all of Abel's questions. If only the spirit of Gertie's smouldering letters could have coiled itself around Abel's heart and kept hope alive. If only Mr. Merridew had met Abel as planned then he would have had the pleasure of informing him that a family awaited his homecoming and that his old job was ready and waiting for him. As it was Governor Kendrick forestalled what might have been. It was so easy for a busy man to misread a letter – make an error.

"Ah 24133201."

"Sir."

"It appears that your appeal has been granted and that, given completion of the necessary paperwork, you should be able to walk out of here a free man on 15th November."

"Eight days' time, sir!"

"Exactly. Time enough to make your arrangements, I believe."

"Plenty, sir, though I really have none to make."

"You'll need to let your family know."

"Will I, sir?"

"Of course. Want to meet you at the station, surely. Natural enough."

"I don't know, sir." Abel's mind was in turmoil.

"Here, lad. Pen. Paper. Write what you like. Seal it in that envelope. There's sealing wax." He pointed to a tray on which a small candle burned and a stick of red wax lay ready on a plate beside his own official seal.

"Thank you, sir."

"I'll leave you awhile." Governor Kendrick, uncharacteristically, retreated from his study leaving Abel at the great desk to write the hardest letter of his life.

The governor gave him time, pacing the corridor, annoyed that this little game seemed to have ended prematurely. This was one prisoner he'd be glad to see the back of. He'd apologise to the solicitor. Say he'd mistaken the date. Suggest he followed him to his forwarding address. If he missed him, then so much the better.

The governor's study was large but warm and well lit. Just to be in this room was a welcome charge from a cold cell with oozing walls and sagging, straw-stuffed mattress.

Abel stretched his hands to the candle flame; warmed some life back into his fingers and began a letter to the house that he had been told was no longer his home.

Chapter Twenty Seven

A jolt and a screeching of metal on metal woke Abel with a start. Metal on metal. Metal in metal. Keys in locks!

He glanced anxiously out of the railway carriage window at the rapidly slowing scene. A station boarding wreathed in steam drifted past. A hurrying porter overtook the train, which eventually sighed to a halt with a petulant hiss.

Abel closed his eyes again and leaned back against the padded seat. Another four stations before home but even so he might not get off. He had bought his ticket straight through to Birmingham. Getting off early was a possibility, a remote possibility. His chest tightened and a pulse fluttered in the base of his throat as he contemplated the future, anxiety beginning to rise.

The carriage door was jerked open. A lady, white haired and very obviously plump, heaved and pushed parcels, basket and body into the compartment. Abel leaned forward, steadied the basket with one hand and reached for the door with the other. An officious porter slammed it as the whistle blew. Simultaneously the train shuddered, then puffed and clanked its way over the points and past the signal box, leaving the little town behind.

She was perhaps sixty, soft white hair drawn off her face into a bun, skin puffed up – soft like a cushion, clean and glowing. She smelt of lavender, newly washed linen and freshly baked bread.

Abel couldn't resist taking a deep indrawn breath. The lady, settled now opposite Abel, smiled in recognition of his awareness, reached into the basket and took out a bundle wrapped in a spotless blue and white checked cloth. She set it on her knees, unknotted the cloth, unfolded it and looked apologetically at Abel.

"I'm sorry. No knife," she said, "but we can break off a piece. You look ready for some sustenance – or do my eyes deceive me?"

Abel nodded, his eyes meeting hers and making firm contact. An unaccustomed smile tried itself out, settling lopsided and awkward onto his pathetically thin face.

Somehow it was only a small step from the breaking of bread together to a sharing of his life. She listened. He talked. It was so out of character for the increasingly introspective young man to suddenly feel so at ease with a stranger. During all those long months in prison Abel had never talked of himself. In fact, he had hardly spoken at all. Now it was as if the dam had burst open, letting free a torrent of pent-up thoughts and emotions.

Release from prison had not been accompanied by the burst of joy that all prisoners anticipate. In fact the sheer enormity of space outside that gate had been fearsome. Abel had stood whilst the great wooden door shut behind him, listening to the key turn and the bolts drawn across. The world had suddenly seemed large and terrifying. To be alone, without a job, without a home was nearly unbearable.

Yet, in the almost cosy railway carriage, with its comfortably upholstered seats and seemingly huge windows that let in so much bright, white light, facing this reassuringly understanding lady, Abel felt both free and oddly secure. He found himself talking of his sister's predicament and the events that had lead to his imprisonment whilst kind eyes met his sympathetically and white hair nodded encouragement.

"I wrote to my mother just as soon as I knew that my release papers had arrived. I've been so anxious about her, you see. I've wondered at her long silence, especially since my father's death. I'd felt sure that she would write then but no word ….. nor from Clara, either."

The old lady tutted her distress at his lonely confusion and busied herself with folding her cloth and repackaging her basket, casting an occasional glance at Abel as if to reassure him of her attention.

"I wrote. I wrote as soon as I could – said that I'd be on the mid-morning train, that I'd bought a straight-through ticket but I'd get off if they wanted me to. I'd look out you see!"

"Look out?"

"Yes. The line runs at the bottom of our yard. The train slows down at the signal – always slows to enter the station. You can see into the court – I'd look for the signal. If they want me to get off they have to have washing on the line – all white, no coloureds. It's Friday. The lines are always empty on a Friday. If they are empty today I'm not welcome."

"Your mother'll want you home, lad."

"Are you sure? She might want her son but will she welcome a jailbird?"

"But you've been freed – pardoned, let out, declared innocent."

"It doesn't alter the fact that I've been inside."

The old lady retreated into silence, looked grave and concerned whilst Abel's jaw worked, all his pent-up emotion threatening to surface as he contemplated the emptiness that his future held.

"I can't look," he said, "Supposing I'm not ...... there isn't."

"Sit you still lad," the old lady's hand rested momentarily on Abel's knee "Be still. On a Friday if there's washin' on the line it'll be yourn. As the train slows down, I'll look for you."

Abel clenched his fists and stared down into his lap, physically unable to raise his eyes.

The train slowed. The screech of breaks began.

"It's a line full of shirts, all white, the old lady cried, "and tablecloths and sheets and – oh, my goodness. God is in his heaven after all. Come along, young man – you'll miss your stop. No! Don't go looking through windows. Gather your bits and pieces. Don't want to miss your ...."

Abel leapt to his feet, planted a kiss on the old lady's brow and, clutching his parcel, pulled on the strap, let down the window, leaned out and opened the carriage door. As his feet touched the platform and the steam hissed the train's exhaustion, Abel felt that he was truly coming home.

★ ★ ★ ★ ★ ★ ★ ★ ★ ★

Inside the little house in Twenty-Four Court Abel's mother sat by the empty range humped in her shawl of regrets, staring at its cold, black bars. No fire burned in her hearth and there was no warmth in her body. Even her heart felt cold and as heavy as lead.

Sarah's life hung about her like the dank folds of a wet cloak. Some days she felt unable to move she was so weighted down with woe. So much distress had worn her very soul away – a daughter dead, a son in prison. Even the welcomed death of her husband had become a disaster, relief being coupled with pecuniary concerns and the inescapable guilt. Her body had swathed itself in a fog of pessimism and, no matter what good news came her way, it failed to find its way through.

The news that Gertie was truly alive had pulled Sarah from the very brink of madness but it was only Clara's daily ministrations that had kept her from slipping back down into the abyss. Then, Mr. Lees, the librarian, had come with his almost unbelievable statement of having married Gertie and having been instrumental in lodging an appeal for Abel's release. Too much, too soon, too quickly. It was easier to slip back into the darkness. Her body was in tune with morose depression. It pulled her mind down into oblivion.

A letter from the prison lay unopened on the table. The envelope reminded her of another one – one whose news was unbearable. She would not read this one. Leave it! Let it lie there.

Sarah didn't hear Clara's footfalls in the entry, or when she rattled the latch on the door. She only became aware of the warm, bustling presence when sticks flamed momentarily before coal lumps were placed gingerly upon their temporary ferocity and water poured steadily from the jug into the kettle.

"Come on now, Mrs. Nightingale! Let me rub some life back into your fingers. Cold as ice you are. No breakfast I'll be bound. Let's get some bread on the fork and you hold it by the bars for me while the kettle boils." Clara moved familiarly around the kitchen trying to make it homely once more.

"Look there. Coal's caught. No need for the draw tin or the bellows. Wind must be right. Now keep that toasting fork close – bread will never cook so far away."

Clara talked to Sarah as if she were the elder, coaxing her friend's mother along like she would a child. "Fancy that Mr. Lees coming again, Mrs. Nightingale; proper gentleman he is. Did you like him? Left a parcel this time – look – tea, butter, a seed cake. Why, he is a thoughtful man."

Clara's eyes fell on the letter, recognising the prison stationery at once, "Oh, Mrs N. Here's a letter unopened. It could be important." She held it closer, recognised Abel's neat script and turned excitedly towards Sarah. "It's from Abel, Mrs. N. Open it, please, open it."

Sarah gave no sign of responding to the request, but gazed at her hands holding the thin wire of the toasting fork as if that action needed her total concentration.

In sheer frustration Clara tore into the envelope and gasped at its contents. "Mrs Nightingale! Oh, my goodness! Abel is coming home. Friday the.... Today! He expects a signal. Washing on the line!"

As she read the hopeful words of the young man who had meant so much to her for so very long, the steady sound of an approaching train came to her plainly.

With a cry of determination Clara tossed the contents of the table onto the chairs, pulled at the white tablecloth, grabbed the linen crockery cloths, a white blouse hanging drunkenly on the back of a chair and ran out into the yard as if her very life depended upon it. She had thrown only the table cloth over the line when the mid-morning train, slowing but still moving fast, thundered along the line at of the end of the yard.

To Clara the line was as good as empty!

"Too late," she sobbed, "we're too late. He's gone. He won't get off. Oh, Mrs. Nightingale. I don't think I can ever forgive you."

Her arms hugging the cloths to her breast, Clara walked

dejectedly back into the Nightingale house to find Sarah sitting before a blaze – "The toast's done, Clara," she said brightly.

Clara could have shaken Sarah Nightingale, but she didn't. She just took a piece of old towelling, poured a little water from the already singing kettle onto it and proceeded to wipe Sarah's face and hands quite gently.

Footfalls in the entry, heavy like a man's, hesitant like stranger's. A soft, knock at the door. A lifted latch. A tall shadow slipping into the half- light of the November kitchen.

"Abel! You're here!"

"Of course. The signal. Lucky you got it in again so quickly. It's beginning to rain." Abel's smile was wide, a Christmas-morning smile that reached his eyes and pulled Clara's very heart into her throat. Abel's arms were about his mother, cradling her head against his waist, kissing the top of her grey hair and reaching backwards with his free hand to search for Clara. She moved towards him and clasped his hand in both of hers, her eyes alight with love and all of her jealous doubt dispelled in that one trusting gesture.

Abel did not give a thought to the old lady of the train, who sat in her carriage thundering towards her destination and praying quietly that God would forgive her one little white lie. His mind was full of his mother, who sobbed quietly now in his arms, and the capable young woman who moved about the room making tea, buttering toast and cutting cake into hearty slices. For Abel the joy of coming home was immense, but spoilt by his dreadful awareness that there was no Gertie to share his return.

As the emotions of the two women subsided a little he took his father's wooden armchair beside the fire and faced his mother. "Mother. I'm so sorry about Gertie. So sorry that we didn't tell you the truth – the web of deceit that we wove to protect her and then – no, Clara, don't try to excuse me; I did what I did for…"

"Excuse me, Abel, but I must stop you. You obviously believe as we did that Gertie died. She didn't! She's alive! In France."

Abel was incredulous. "But….. she didn't write. I had a letter which said she had….."

"Yes, Abel, I know. Whoever wrote that letter – it was not Gertie who died. Perhaps someone else." The memory of jealous thoughts brought a flush to her face. She quickly thrust it aside. "Believe me, Abel. She is fine. Married – to Mr. Lees, the librarian."

Abel could hardly believe what he was hearing. It was a dream. He had shed so many tears in the prison darkness. It was incredible and impossible to comprehend.

Clara scrabbled on the mantelpiece – a bundle of cards and letters were thrust into Abel's lap. " Read them. It's true! Gertie's letters! And her husband has been! Twice!"

Mr. Samuel Lees chose that Friday evening to call again in Twenty- Four Court. His original discomfort at finding himself in this quarter of town had lessened and he admitted to a certain degree of satisfaction at the opportunity to do a service for the really very respectable, Mrs. Nightingale.

He knew, of course, of Abel's imminent release and of Mr. Merridew's intention of meeting the young man to ease his return home. He only wished that his own earlier attempt to gain access to the prison had not been thwarted by circumstance.

To enter the cheery little kitchen that night to find Mrs. Nightingale quite herself again and playing hostess with the politeness and dignity of a real lady was delightful. To make the acquaintance, unexpectedly, of his brother- in -law was rather a surprise. So too was the ardour and intensity of the young man's genuine pleasure at meeting him - as Abel jumped to his feet and clasped him about the shoulders for all the world like a real brother.

"My good sir. I am so very pleased to meet you." Abel's voice was firm and his honest eyes looked directly into Mr. Samuel's.

"And I you, Mr. Nightingale. At last! I have heard much of you and of your goodness to your sister - my wife."

"No more than any man would do, sir. But, please, I am your

relative now – Abel, at your service, sir. And if we are bestowing honours I believe you should have your share."

"I'm not sure of your…. er…. meaning. Abel, I…… er," Mr.Lees prevaricated.

"I think you are, sir. I believe you understand me very well. I honour you, sir. Indeed I do."

What remained unsaid between the two men was, even so, thoroughly understood. For whilst a few gaps remained in the women's knowledge of Gertie's life the two men were fully appreciative of the facts and of how each had so unselfishly helped a young woman to avoid ruining her life.

It fell to Samuel's lot to enlighten Abel as to Miss Detheridge's part in his freedom and her determination to reinstate him in the business at his earliest convenience.

The more Samuel spoke the more Abel liked him and the difference in their ages and stations slipped away with the hours. By midnight Abel was walking with Samuel to the cab rank some streets away, as relaxed and comfortable as if they were old friends.

Samuel waved his goodbye as his cab trotted away into the night and he managed a wry smile as he contemplated his enjoyment of an evening spent in Twenty- Four Court with an ex-convict. There was some excitement in the unusual, a sense of adventure in slumming it a little. Then Gertie's husband cast such unworthy thoughts away and considered his wife's home coming and the wording of the note to be dropped through Merridew's door in order to save him a wasted journey to the prison on the morrow.

Chapter Twenty Eight

The gentle downward slope of the meadow made walking easy for Gertie as she strolled away from the village and down towards the sea. It had become a habit for her to take this morning exercise as soon as Isabelle had fallen asleep after her first feed of the day. With Tweeny and Mrs. P. to look after the now chubby, healthy, little girl, Gertie had no concern in leaving her for a couple of hours.

The end of 'les vacances' was now in sight. In only two weeks time the trunks would once more be on the roof of their swaying carriage and their faces pointing northwards to home. Their host, Monsieur Lescouriez, had tried to persuade Mrs. Peake to allow him to arrange passage from Bordeaux to Bristol, assuring her of the brevity and relative comfort of the journey, but she was determined to travel as little by sea as possible.

As Gertie walked through the dewy dampness of the morning she contemplated the approaching departure with some sadness, even though so very much called her home. During her weeks in the village Gertie had felt an increasing sense of belonging. She had loved their ancient house and the simplicity of the uncomplicated rural life that surrounded it. Reassured by letters from Samuel that he was doing his very best for both Abel and her mother, Gertie had felt more and more relaxed. A recent affectionate communication from Clara had further set her mind at rest and she no longer experienced her earlier guilt at being in such comfort and so far away from those who might have needed her.

The local people were simple, fishing and farming folk who kept body and soul together at a basic subsistence level, only raising their standard of living by their seasonal employment in the vineyards. They were naturally a friendly community but had been shy of these ' foreign ladies' who had taken up residence in their monsieur's village house. It had taken the priest's visit to open the proverbial door. He had brought his black-clad coolness into their house, blessed them and left them with his invitation, delivered in his stilted text-book English, to attend Mass and to send for him in the event of any emergency. He had chosen to assume their membership of his Church, though he had felt their prickly Anglican attitude through his cloth. Nevertheless, his visit had given his tacit approval to the new arrivals and as a result his flock had befriended the little family.

The villagers had perceived it to be an unusual thing for ladies, alone, without the support of any male member of their family, to be venturing abroad and their presence evoked intense curiosity. In consequence, when welcoming gifts arrived at the back door they were carried by one person and escorted by a little troupe of locals, most of whom had joined the procession for no other reason than the chance to look at these corseted, upright ladies, who had such white complexions and spoke no French at all. Presents of creamy goats' milk, frothing in enormous brown pitchers, warm speckled eggs, wonderful fresh, crusty bread, fish in woven baskets—all appeared with amazing regularity. No payment was expected and if Mrs. Peake tried to push money into rough working hands it was vehemently refused. All was conviviality, a nodding of heads, a pumping of hands and a display of mutual appreciation.

When Monsieur Lescouriez had arrived with his wine and fruit, soft cheeses and candles, he had laughed off Mrs. Peake's talk of embarrassment. He had said that generosity was the custom of his region and commented that she had been benevolence itself to him in England. "Now it is the turn of La France," he had insisted, his brown eyes twinkling under the shady overhang of his brows and his chubby childlike hands staying a fraction too long on Mrs. Peake's shapely shoulders. He had impressed upon her the need to adopt the continental attitude to life, to relax and to enjoy God's good bounty in a land of wine and honey.

Despite Monsieur's reassurance, Mrs. Peake had become quite agitated by her inability to return any favours to these warm-hearted country people who were, in reality, so poor. So, true to character, the resourceful lady had developed and put into operation a little plan.

Gertie recollected her friend's disappearance down the dusty street, swathed in black lace veils, her upright carriage and determined bearing reminding anyone who saw her of a schooner in full sail – a dignified and doubty vessel.

An ancient church presided over the village, its solidarity lending a permanence and security to the houses that nestled in its shadows. Mrs. Peake had directed her stride towards this building, mounted its wide stone steps and pushed firmly against the heavy, black timbers which seemed designed to bar her entrance rather than to facilitate it. The door had swung open surprisingly easily and Mrs. Peake had later recounted how she had stepped from the glare and brightness of the day into the cool dimness of what surely had to be Aladdin's cave. Used to the sobriety of her own church, Mrs. Peake had been amazed by the breathtaking beauty of the vaulted edifice. For once in her life she had truly felt the power of Heaven and the insignificance of man, the smallness of the individual in the whole universal scheme of things. This was surely no ordinary village church.

All was cool. All was peaceful. There had been no sound save the whisper of her skirts as Mrs. Peake had drifted down the aisle towards the altar. Nothing moved except herself and the flames of the candles in the Lady Chapel flickering in the wake of her passage.

As her eyes became accustomed to the dimness Mrs. Peake's appreciation of the building mounted: the vastness of its arches, the magnificence of its carvings, the glory of the gilt framed oils of Biblical scenes and characters. Everything was an individual masterpiece, a craftsman's tribute to God.

A statue of the Virgin Mary stood on a plinth, adorned in heavily embossed, gilded materials, painted and decorated in such elaborate detail that she looked like some treasured doll.

Mrs. Peake approached the intricately carved rood screen and there she spied what she sought – a wooden plate, placed ready to accept the congregation's hard-earned offerings.

As she quickened her movements Mrs. Peake had felt the back of her neck prickling with awareness. She had known that eyes were watching her from the bell gallery high above the nave. Nevertheless, she had reached her goal and, opening her reticule, had extracted a plump bag of coins, which she placed reverently upon the plate. She had crossed herself – without, she hoped, any ostentation – and retraced her steps, once more returning to the startlingly bright sunlight.

★ ★ ★ ★ ★ ★ ★ ★ ★ ★

It had taken only a matter of hours for the English lady's generosity to reach the villagers and for days the ripples of her action had continued to have their effect on the inhabitants of the more isolated dwellings. The gifts to the visitors continued – nuts, flowers, live chickens, dead rabbits – and the warmth of the accompanying smiles increased. The community had taken the ladies to its heart and Gertie recognised that neither of them was going to find it easy to pull free.

The weather had been kind during the weeks of their visit, the sun beating down from cloudless skies, its heat moderated by the cooling, gentle sea breeze. Gertie had thrived in the warm climate, her skin taking on a healthy, golden glow. She had read and written and walked and on this particular morning was heading towards a small hamlet, a straggle of fishermen's cottages clinging to the margin of the bay.

It was a usual morning stroll for Gertie, now accustomed to the vagaries of the pathway, which ran down the meadow into a deep, steep-sided little valley. At the bottom of this a swift stream ran down to the sea. It was the same water that tumbled and swirled under the village bridge. As she left the wide, open meadowland, Gertie felt the change in the air around her. Down amongst the trees vying for position along the cool water's edge, the early morning was already a foetid heat. Gertie felt the perspiration prickle her skin. She quickened her steps along the narrow path that twisted and looped to keep pace with the widening ribbon of slowing water. Quite suddenly the woodland ceased and Gertie felt the earth change beneath her soft-soled shoes, the warm leafy ground giving way to colder sand.

The stream moved on, its clear water spreading and dividing in its haste to reach the sea. Gertie hesitated on the edge of the bay, breathing in the coolness of the open air and looking at the activity on the sand.

It was early yet – early enough for the few fishermen to be still busy with their crafts in the shallows, hauling in nets and tackle, re-stowing ropes and furling sails. The smaller boats were pulled up on the beach itself and, in amongst these, people were strolling and stopping to chat in the midst of their bartering. Gertie could see produce changing hands-a rabbit for a fish, eggs for a crab. The village women could choose from amongst an infinite variety of fish of all shapes and sizes, displayed in all their sad glory upon the wet sand.

A man holding a horse's head was gentling its nervousness, reassuring it as its hooves sank repeatedly into the soft, wetness. The animal shifted restlessly between the shafts of a small, wooden cart onto which two boys were loading fish picked out from amongst those laid out on the giant shop counter of the beach. The man choosing the cart's load wore seaman's boots and carried a stick, which he used to flip over certain fish and to point to those he wished to purchase.

Picking up her skirts, Gertie moved into the little knots of villagers, smiling in all directions, her old awareness of her eyesight problem making her wary of seeming rude. Conversation drifted around her, totally unintelligible, making her truly feel she had slipped into another world. Here and there groups of women leaned against the edge of boats chatting, children played tag around the grounded lobster cages, and a bent old woman tried to engage Gertie in a , hopelessly one-sided discussion.

So entranced by the activity of the fisherfolk and village people was Gertie that she failed to notice that the fresh breeze had changed direction. Suddenly she became aware of the snapping of billowing sailcloth, buffeted by a sharp, new wind. The women, too, had realised the imminent change in the weather and the beach began to empty as they scurried away with their baskets of fish and the anxious horse, rolling its eyes, plodded its way towards firmer ground. Several women beckoned to Gertie to follow them, pointing towards the rapidly darkening sky where black, billowing clouds loomed up from the horizon, approaching land at an alarming rate.

Gertie had no shelter. She knew that the storm would overtake her before she reached the house. Already the mild ocean had changed its smooth countenance to one of ever deepening troughs and waves that were quickly becoming mountainous, its blueness altered to an inky black. The anchored boats were dipping and rising with the quick tempered swell, their deserting crews wading to shore and dragging the smaller rowing boats higher up the beach towards the woodland.

As Gertie hesitated, wondering whether to take the path back into the woods or the track to the village, she felt a tug on her skirt. On looking down she recognised the black, tousled head of the little boy who often sought her out on the beach. He frequently dogged her footsteps and had taken to approaching her if she sat for a while. Usually he brought her a gift – a pretty shell, an unusually shaped piece of driftwood, a piece of attractively grained rock or a bloom of sea thrift. Today his little hands were full only of her skirt, which he was shaking anxiously. Having obtained her attention, he reached up and took her hand, towing her along the beach, his eyes full of concern. Gertie had little choice but to follow.

It was soon clear that she was being pulled towards a tiny dwelling, one of those fishermen's cottages which squatted determinedly close to the shore, surrounded by some small acreage of scrubland on which a few goats scavenged. As they neared the dilapidated cottage the first spots of rain fell, isolated, enormous drops that stung the skin, cold and menacing.

The boy hustled Gertie towards the door, stood on tiptoe and managed to touch the latch with the tip of his fingers. As it rattled Gertie could hear the sound of movement within the cottage, then the door opened just as a gust of wind caught her skirts and propelled her through the open space into the confines of the tiny dwelling.

At first Gertie could see little, for the one-roomed cottage was ill-lit by a single, small window rendered almost useless by the overcast gloom outside. As her eyes adjusted somewhat to the dimness Gertie could make out that the room was floored with worn blocks of uneven stone, bordered with cold, stone walls and covered by a wooden roof hung with strings of onions, garlic bulbs and drying fish.

There was a hearth, cold and uninviting, stocked ready for lighting with twisted, white driftwood and twigs, no doubt collected by the tiny hands of the little boy. Stacked to one side of the fireplace were a few heavy cooking utensils: pot, skillet, kettle – all mat black and dented with age. On the other side of the fire was a high-backed settle, an earthenware jug standing on the floor beside it. The only other furniture was a square, scrubbed, wooden table with its three straight-backed chairs and a cupboard on which a tin basin stood beside an enamel ewer of water. On the wall opposite the window was a bed, set into the wall, boxed in and curtained like a gypsy caravan.

The little boy led Gertie to the settle, then ran back towards the door where a very old lady was still heaving it to, having to push against the strength of the wind which now howled around the bay.

"Grand-mère!" the child shouted. When the old lady's eyes

focused on him he began to pantomime the storm and the need for shelter, pointing at his mouth and stomach. Then he combined his strength with hers and pushed the door to, its latch jumping automatically into place.

The old lady kissed her hand, placed it on the boy's tousled head and shuffled over to the cupboard. From inside Grandmere reached a glass and a bottle. She poured out a little of the clear liquid, which she passed to Gertie. It was a fiery brandy that made her cough and thereafter sip slowly but it warmed her.

The old lady sat herself at the table and in the dimness located some white twine and a bobbin. Soon her gnarled old fingers were twisting and working rapidly, lace flowering at her fingertips.

Gertie was clear now about two things. Grandmere was deaf and kept body and soul together with her lace making.

There was no attempt at conversation while the wind and rain lashed the little cottage and, as midday approached, the world was literally like midnight.

The little boy did his best to dispel the awkwardness, diving into a dark corner to emerge with his treasures, which he loaded into Gertie's lap. Mostly they were pretty stones and seeds of varying shapes and sizes, cones and odd shaped fish bones but amongst them was a crumpled piece of linen that might once have been a lady's handkerchief. This last was the child's greatest treasure —he clutched it close before laying it almost reverently on Gertie's lap. "C'est le mouchoir de ma mere," he said, raising his eyes to Gertie's. She was alarmed to see tears clinging to this rough little urchin's eyelashes.

At last the storm abated, and as the little room lightened somewhat the old lady ceased her silent labours and opened the door to let in a beam of sunlight. Outside the world steamed and Gertie felt that she must leave at once or be the cause of concern to her friends and distress to her daughter.

As she rose the old lady caught her hands. Startled, Gertie drew back, but quickly realised that the purpose of the unexpected assault was only to solicit her attention. Using a repertoire of signs and odd words, the woman was trying her very best to communicate.

She pointed to the child and back to herself, "Grandmere. Non!" she said, shaking her head sadly. "Non! Non!" she repeated. "Il s'appelle Danton – Danton de la Mere".

The child moved towards Gertie, held the softness of her skirts and repeated, " Je m'appelle Danton".

"Danton," repeated Gertie, "Bonjour, Danton". They smiled at each other, now formally introduced.

"Et tu?," said the child, "Tu es ma mere?"

Gertie's French was impossible. She had learned the odd expression and just enough to be puzzled by the little boy's words.

Before she could attempt to refute his statement the old lady began gesticulating again. Pointing out to sea, she motioned waves as high as houses, a ship tossed and broken upon the rocks. Her fingers became the villagers rushing to the beach carrying lanterns, bodies washed upon the shore, all dead, dead, dead. Then one young girl – like Gertie, English, long hair, but her stomach big with child and alive, both of them alive.

Gertie's mind was seeing the violence of that night – the tumultuous, turbulent sea, frothing and bubbling around the breaking wreck, the white bloated bodies being pulled upon the beach and then the old lady herself, opening her door to receive the young gentlewoman, almost unconscious, her birth pangs just beginning.

The old woman's tragic expression reflected the terrible happenings of that night, her hands bringing forth a child and then digging a grave to bury the body of the new mother.

She crooned over the newborn in her arms and very gently carried it over to Danton. Then opening her hands she let the ghost-child slip away into the shadows whilst her hands raised to show her boy growing.

She pressed Danton to her, miming her affection and care, then thrust her gnarled old hands, their knuckles swollen and twisted with rheumatism, beneath Gertie's gaze. She dramatised the uselessness of her body, her hunger, her poverty and then she pushed Danton towards her visitor very gently and Gertie caught that word again: 'maman'.

Gertie's heart was pounding. Even without language she was in no doubt that she was being given a child, that the old woman, who had taken responsibility for the little boy, was now desperate to relinquish it.

She was already too old and too poor to care for herself let alone another – but English ladies simply do not walk off with other people's children and Gertie's small voice was already uttering, "Non!"

She moved towards the door, looking down at the little boy still clutching her skirts, his hair like a tousled sweep's brush, his ragged clothes too small and his little feet shoeless. His eyes were large in his thin, upturned face and Gertie, who was no stranger to poverty, understood in that moment how poor this child's life had been. He must often have gone cold and hungry, despite Grandmere's efforts. Instinctively Gertie appreciated the increasing distress of the aged woman's plight, so dire that it must often have caused her affection to be tested by the immediate concerns of poverty and pain.

Emotions pulled Gertie apart, her common sense at war with her maternal instincts. The dampness of the old lady's cottage seemed to wrap itself around her like a shroud whilst outside the warmth of her alternative world called. It seemed in that split second as if she held that little child's fate in her hands and she was simply unable to run into the sunlight, leaving Danton in the darkness. Despite her better judgement, Gertie reached for the old lady and, taking the lined, old face between her hands, she placed her kisses gently on the wrinkled apples of two wizened cheeks. Then, taking Danton's hand in hers, she left the cottage and strode out for home.

When Gertie arrived back at the house it was to much relief and expressions of gratefulness that God had spared her during that terrible storm. Isabelle was awake and demanding her feed and so it was a while before Gertie was free to explain to Mrs P. that Danton was an orphan for whom she felt an obligation as well - she admitted - as some budding affection.

Mrs Peake, generous as always, emphasised that she was certainly not averse to taking in the child temporarily but she was extremely anxious about the legality of any permanent situation. " If only the language or lack of it was not such a barrier and if only we had more time to check our position properly," she had mused. "Really, Gertie, I do believe that you have taken leave of your senses to even consider it."

Gertie could see that Mrs. Peake was far from delighted at the idea of adding Danton to their little patchwork family but she totally failed to recognise the intensity of her friend's dismay at the whole idea or her determination to protect Gertie from what she judged to be such a rash act of total foolhardiness. . .

With experience of a life that had exposed her to a string of difficult situations for which often totally unexpected solutions had arisen, Alice was not one bit surprised when the answer to her predicament arrived in the guise of her old friend, Monsieur Lescouriez.

Danton had been with them for three days, long enough for Tweeny to have run up breeches from a black stuff skirt and a shirt from a white, cambric nightgown. His shoeless state had not yet been remedied but there was hope of this at the Saturday market. Danton's hair had been tidied and his naturally inquisitive ebullience was carrying him through a variety of new experiences, such as total emersion in hot, soapy water.

The elderly Monsieur Lescouriez, whose fondness for the English had been cemented by his forays into their country in search of a market for his wines and a glass that didn't shatter when under pressure from fermentation was quite a character.

Now retired, with his son having taken control of his

considerable acreage, and being a widower with few responsibilities, Monsieur was able to indulge his fancy – which today had been to search out the English ladies. He intended to share with them some of his fine wine and to stay the night in his own house after enjoying what he trusted would be a splendid dinner. His arrival, unannounced, caught them, as he had intended, dressed only in their wrappers and totally relaxed.

"I'm sorry, mesdames, I regret my unlooked for arrival. Do please forgive me."

"Monsieur", Mrs. Peake spoke sincerely: "This is your house. Of course you must feel free to come and go as you wish. I hope that, with us here, your freedom to do so feels more like a welcome than a "droit de seigneur". They laughed at the slightly suggestive skill of her repartee.

Within minutes the day was planned to take advantage of the fine weather, which had returned, culminating in dinner to be taken on the terrace in the coolness of evening. That proved to be the best time for Mrs. Peake to approach Monsieur Lescouriez about her dilemma.

"An orphan, Mesdames – a French orphan! And you propose taking him to England. You are so fine! But, I must protest. This child is a French responsibility. I will take heem. I should 'ave thought of it before. I feel very ashamed at …how do you say… my tardiness. I can apprentice him in the vineyard. He will have a good life, a better one than subsisting on the beach amongst the fisher folk".

"You go too fast, Monsieur Lescouriez. We need your language, sir, to first establish the wishes of the grandmere and of Danton himself. We need to be sure that what we surmise is correct, that the old lady does indeed mean for the child to be taken from her and that Danton himself appreciates the finality of that situation. He may view this separation merely as a holiday. In fact he loves the old lady – visits her daily since he joined us here." Mrs. Peake clarified the situation, taking care to place emphasis upon that bond of affection that she hesitated to break

"There you are", Monsieur Lescouriez nodded his head sagely, "another good reason for the boy to stay in France – he can see the old lady – she can see him. Let the boy come to me."

Mrs. Peake did not try to hide her relief that such an offer was being made. " It is such an uncomplicated solution! The boy will have his good fortune without loosing his family. Nobody will have his nose put out of joint. You are absolutely correct, of course. No language problems. No explaining to be done. Nobody having to take on a responsibility without being consulted, if you see what I mean, Gertie, dear."

Gertie had not been mistaken in her assumption of her friend's negative attitude to Danton but until now she had not fully comprehended the reason for it. She had been aware that the child had not taken to Mrs. Peake; he had been totally fixated on the younger woman, who had responded so warmly to him. Gertie had, quite innocently, allowed the child to come between them, and that was why Monsieur's suggestion was a good one as far as Mrs. Peake was concerned. She did not share Gertie with anyone easily and was unable or unwilling to view this child as anything other than competition, a cuckoo in the nest.

Gertie had listened until now, concerned by the direction their request for help was taking. Her maternal instincts were strong, perhaps doubly so being such a new mother herself.

"Monsieur, Mrs P. dear, please don't forget that the old lady is very old. She cannot live for ever and Danton is an affectionate child. He needs a mother, love – not just, forgive me, a position in life, an apprenticeship."

Monsieur Lescouriez shifted a little in his seat, " I appreciate what you are saying, my dear. I have sons, grandsons – Danton could never be their equal. You propose – do you not – adopting him? I regret that I cannot."

"Just so," agreed Gertie.

"Is that possible?" queried Mrs Peake, her eyebrows arching.

" That remains to be seen. Tomorrow morning I shall visit the grandmere. Now, let us try a bottle of my champagne."

★ ★ ★ ★ ★ ★ ★ ★ ★

The seasons were indeed changing, for the next morning's dawn was a glittering, golden affair, the lightening sky streaked with purple cloud weighted with glorious aureate underbellies. But by the time Monsieur had completed his 'toilette' and drunk his chocolate, a sharp wind was heralding another storm and already bending the trees to its will. The gold had gone and sky was dark.

Gertie watched Monsieur leave the house and cross the little bridge over the white, racing waters. The surrounding houses looked less inviting now, their shutters closed against the inclement weather, the nodding geraniums mere stalks deprived of petals by the bad-tempered wind.

Gertie held Isabelle, rocking her, crooning; Danton sat at her feet, gazing up at her. He snuggled into the material of her skirts and listened to the lullaby. How Gertie wished she could talk to him, tell him a story, play a game.

Monsieur Lescouriez was back by lunch, dishevelled by the wind and soaked through by the downpour that caught him only minutes from their doorstep.

Mrs. Peake refused to hear a word until her friend sat before a blazing fire in dry clothes, clutching a brandy and considering whether he would prefer a rabbit stew or fish. Gertie sat near to him, close enough to see his expression clearly, Isabelle sleeping on her lap and Danton cuddled, as always, amongst the folds of her skirt, rubbing his cheek against the soft material. He loved to touch softness. She had found him rolling and luxuriating in the billows of the feather bed, seen him sitting amongst the clothes newly washed and awaiting ironing, stroking satin ribbons, following the intricate lines of warp and weft in her woollen shawl.

"Well, Monsieur Lescouriez – have we a child or have we not? Do we need to return him?" queried Alice, hopefully.

"Non, mesdames. If the leetle boy is content with you, he is yours. Danton's guardian gave me an account of his birth that tallied totally with your own. She took care of the baby simply because, as a good Christian, he became her responsibility. She loves the child but knows she is too old and ill to continue to care for him. Your arrival in her home seemed to her simple faith like an act of God." He shrugged, "And…er….per'aps it was.

Danton's mother had long hair like yours, Madame Gertrude, though it was dark, not like the summer wheat. She spoke English. Danton has been fed descriptions of her and that is why he has been dogging your footsteps for weeks, why he asked you if you were his maman and, partly, why he is devoted to you so completely".

Gertie's hand strayed to the little boy's curls. She caressed the dark head nestling against her. A little hand stole up to catch her fingers.

"The child has no papers, only a baptismal certificate which confirms 'Mother – an Englishwoman. Father unknown.' Under those circumstances no one is likely to make a fuss if you take him out of the country. I can satisfy my gentlemanly sense of responsibility by adopting Danton's 'grandmere. She has done her duty and deserves some recompense."

"We shall take Danton to England," said Gertie quietly.

"And I shall take grandmere clothes, food and some creature comforts", the old gentleman waved his arms expansively. "I shall enjoy becoming her protector. Generosity suits me." Monsieur Lescouriez smiled and as his old eyes met Gertie's young ones a wave of understanding flowed between them and the warmth of shared complicity was almost tangible.

Mrs. Peake, meanwhile, drumming her fingers on the windowsill, effected to be suddenly preoccupied by the sky and felt herself totally excluded.

No one bothered to enquire of the little boy what he wanted, for his contentment was quite plain to see.

"Danton shall be the child of my heart – if not of my body", whispered Gertie and the kind old man patted her hand in understanding.

"And how do you expect Samuel to take this?" asked Mrs. Peake, her head poised questioningly on a stiffening neck. She had not expected this outcome.

"I think he will be delighted to be presented with a son," answered Gertie rather more confidently than she actually felt, her heart beating rapidly as she assumed insight into her husband's reactions and, for the first time in their friendship, she overruled the stronger will.

"I certainly hope that you are right, my dear," came the slightly acid retort. " If not, then Danton may need to live with me. Swap one grandmother for another – eh, Danton?" Mrs. Peake reached down to touch Danton's shoulder – apparently a mere gesture of affection but the little boy retreated from her touch, glowering at her from beneath his drawn brows.

★ ★ ★ ★ ★ ★ ★ ★ ★

A cold wind flowed down the valley, bestirring the grasses and sending yet more leaves tumbling from the trees bent jealously over the turbulent water. All summer they had shaded this stream, protecting it from the violence of the sun, husbanding its nourishment for their thirsty roots. Now they tossed their tresses like self conscious girls, scattered their leaves generously onto the water and trailed bare, twig fingers through swift white shallows.

Beside the stream Gertie sat, an unaccustomed chill seeping into her bones. She had wrapped her travelling cloak about her and was hunched on a rock beside the busy water.

Behind her, the house was quiet, its shutters closed as if hiding from the sight of their departure. A pile of trunks and portmanteaux was assembled beside the door, where Mrs. Peake held court with Isabelle in her arms and Monsieur Lescouriez at her side. A small knot of villagers had assembled to wave their goodbyes and were making much of Danton who stood beside Tweeny, his eyes alternately resting for politeness on the smiles of his neighbours and then flicking nervously towards where Gertie sat alone.

She glanced up, recognised Danton's discomposure and struggled to her feet. It was time that she too said her farewells.

Change was inevitable. Gertie could see it around her. The wild, white water that had beckoned her with its coolness in the heat of the summer now appeared cold and uninviting. The seasons would not go backwards, only forwards, through winter to another spring. The sun would return. The earth would be green and fruitful again.

Gertie walked quickly towards Danton and the smiling, nodding group of people. As she approached the little boy ran to meet her, wrapped his fingers in her skirts and kept pace with her, standing in her shelter whilst she reached to take Isabelle into her arms.

The rattle of the approaching coach was clear now, its clinking and creaking rising above the rush of the water and the murmur of the little group of friends.

It was time to go home.